For Stan and His Best Girl

AND THEN IT HAPPENED . . .

"Get down, he's armed," a woman shouted over the gathering crowd.

But Gardner had a large handgun pointed directly at Josie's back and had succeeded in clearing a path to his van, easily discouraging any would-be pursuers along the way. He forced Josie inside and slid into the driver's seat next to her. He brought the handle of the gun down viciously on her left temple as Harrigan watched helplessly from his own car.

Then, in a flash, the van veered sharply into Harrigan's lane from the switchback above the turnoff, coming at him full bore, leaving him with no time to think. Acting on pure adrenaline, he crushed the accelerator to the floor, sending the Audi spinning against the rocks on the opposite side of the highway. The van continued toward him, missing the swerving Audi by a mere six inches.

Harrigan could hear, but did not see, the van skidding into the turnoff. . . .

THE LAST APPEAL

THE
LAST APPEAL

BILL BLUM

AN ONYX BOOK

ONYX
Published by the Penguin Group
Penguin Books USA Inc., 375 Hudson Street,
New York, New York 10014, U.S.A.
Penguin Books Ltd, 27 Wrights Lane,
London W8 5TZ, England
Penguin Books Australia Ltd, Ringwood,
Victoria, Australia
Penguin Books Canada Ltd, 10 Alcorn Avenue,
Toronto, Ontario, Canada M4V 3B2
Penguin Books (N.Z.) Ltd, 182–190 Wairau Road,
Auckland 10, New Zealand

Penguin Books Ltd, Registered Offices:
Harmondsworth, Middlesex, England

First published by Onyx, an imprint of Dutton Signet,
a division of Penguin Books USA Inc.

First Printing, May, 1997
10 9 8 7 6 5 4

 REGISTERED TRADEMARK—MARCA REGISTRADA

Printed in Canada

PUBLISHER'S NOTE
This is a work of fiction. Names, characters, places, and incidents either are
the product of the author's imagination or are used fictitiously, and any
resemblance to actual persons, living or dead, events, or locales is entirely
coincidental.

ACKNOWLEDGMENTS

Thanks to all the usual and unusual suspects who helped make this book possible: To my editor of first resort, my wife and chief collaborator, Gina Lobaco; my editor of last resort, Ed Stackler; my agent, Mike Hamilburg, and his associate, Joanie Socola; and to readers Verna Wefald, Mark Rosenbaum, and Eric Blum. Thanks also to Bob Stafford for his knowledge of things automotive, and to David Ulansey, my guide to contemporary Berkeley.

In his eleventh thesis on Feuerbach, Marx wrote, "The philosophers have only *interpreted* the world, in various ways; the point, however, is to *change* it." While Marx's observation was pathbreaking for its time, it was only half right. Before the world can be changed, it must first be saved.

—Henri Debray,
Manifesto of the
Saviors of the Earth,
1977

Though justice be thy plea, consider this,
That in the course of justice none of us
Should see salvation.

—William Shakespeare,
The Merchant of Venice

ONE

On a scale of one to ten, the sex was a six point five. A seven at best.

It was far more his fault than hers that it wasn't better. From the moment they began knocking back rounds of J&B at the Dodsworth Grill to the moment they hit the sack back at his place, Harrigan knew that Sheri Landis was everything his friend Mark Clemons had said and more. A self-made and highly successful real estate entrepreneur in her mid-thirties, she was poised, confident, and sufficiently attractive to cause every other adult male in the bar to spring an instant hard-on. And just as Mark told him, "the lady loves to bonk."

Yet here he was, naked as a newborn, lucky enough to have scored—not once but twice on the first date—lying next to a woman with a body to die for but thinking of his deceased wife. It always seemed to go this way. He'd build up a great head of steam, show his lady friends a good time, and then at the moment of climax, or shortly thereafter, he'd wind up wishing he was with Stephanie and searching his mind for the quickest way to say good-bye to his current partner.

This time it was his visitor who made the first move. Rising abruptly from bed, Sheri stood before him, affording him one last full-frontal view of her undersized but well-formed tits, flat, muscular stomach, and perfectly triangular brown muff. "I have an important meeting at eight and it's past midnight," she said, slipping into her silky black French-cut panties and bra. She let her gaze drift from Harrigan's eyes down his torso, pausing to notice not only his deflated member but even more so the amputation that had left a smooth, rounded stump in place of his left calf and foot.

"Mark told me you were different," she said idly, continuing to dress. "And I don't mean that in a bad way. I had a good time." She leaned over and gave him a soft kiss on the lips. "I'll give you a call."

And then she was gone.

Harrigan hopped into the bathroom to wash up, hoping that when he got back under the covers, the nightmare that had been disrupting his sleep with increasing regularity would not return. It was a futile wish.

The dream came back, as it always did, in images mirroring the events of his life with only the slightest distortion. A picture-perfect Saturday in the middle of May 1988. The sky a cloudless azure, the air without a trace of smog, a pair of red-tailed hawks circling lazily overhead.

Stephanie and the boys had suggested a drive to the beach. David, their eleven-year-old, couldn't wait to test his new wet suit in the surf; Johnny, five years younger, just wanted to squish his toes in the sand. It was Harrigan—always Harrigan—who insisted that they drive up into the mountains instead. "The view from Mount Wilson will make you forget all about the beach," he told them. "We'll take the camera. It'll be lots of fun."

Just thirty-eight years old, Peter Harrigan was leading the kind of idyllic life that other people only glimpse on TV or the movies. A man of rugged good looks, standing just over six feet tall with thick sandy brown hair, pale blue eyes, and a cleft chin that looked like it was set in granite, Harrigan had a loving family, a new ranch-style home nestled in the foothills of Altadena, and a burgeoning career as one of the top criminal defense lawyers in Los Angeles County. In another week he was scheduled to pass yet another professional milestone, arguing a death-penalty appeal before the California Supreme Court. The case of *People* v. *Ashbourne* represented the greatest challenge in Harrigan's career, one he embraced almost to the point of an obsession.

In the dream, the vision of Harrigan's home as he backed his Honda Accord down the driveway was always one of peace and invulnerability. The neatly mowed green lawn, the well-tended flower beds on either side of the winding redbrick path that led to the front door, the clean, straight angles of the roofline and the picture window in the living room—all spoke of domestic solidity.

The images of Angeles Crest Highway, the main route into the San Gabriel Mountains east of the 210 freeway, were equally fixed, but were filled with inescapable terror. After a steep climb to four thousand feet, the highway became a maze of sudden switch-

back turns as it plunged sharply before resuming its
upward grade. Harrigan maneuvered the Honda
around the turns, accelerating into the curves as he
and his family took in the breathtaking vistas of the
canyons and the valley below.

Unlike the warning sound of a blowout, there was
no advance signal of the brake failure that sent the
Honda spinning crazily off the highway and down a
boulder-strewn embankment. It all happened in an
instant. In the dream the images formed a mosaic of
futility, pain, and fear. Harrigan furiously pumping
the brake pedal that had fallen limply to the floor.
Harrigan reaching desperately for the emergency
brake. The boys screaming, their bodies colliding.
Stephanie, her long, dark hair dancing wildly across
her panic-stricken face, shouting, "Oh, my God,
Peter. Oh, my God." The blackness that followed.

Harrigan awoke in the dark, his heart racing, his
neck and face covered in sweat, the arch of his left
foot still cramped from a last-ditch effort to shift the
Honda into low gear. He looked desperately for the
paramedics, then sank back into the pillows as his
head cleared and his eyes focused on the digital display of the alarm clock on the nightstand next to his
bed. The bright green dial read 4:00.

Seven years had passed since the accident that took
the lives of Stephanie and the kids and left Harrigan
with a mid-calf amputation. His shrink had told him
that dreams like his were quite common in cases of
post traumatic stress disorder marked by survivor's
guilt. The dreams, the depression and the guilt, she
said, would eventually go away. His orthopedist, on

the other hand, had informed him that the phantom limb syndrome, which left him with sensations that seemed to originate in his lost foot, would stay with him forever.

Both doctors agreed that the best therapy was to resume what they vaguely referred to as a "normal life"—to eat right, exercise, begin dating again, to return to work but to pull away, at least emotionally, from the Ashbourne case. Harrigan took their advice on eating and exercise, holding the dreaded middle-age spread in check with a daily regimen of garden salads, morning jogs, and nighttime sit-ups. The dating, as his just concluded session with Ms. Landis attested, was fairly frequent. But it never amounted to more than a series of weekend stands, sufficient for sexual release but invariably ending with apologies for his inability to pursue a long-term relationship.

As he avoided any emotional entanglements, his attachment to the Ashbourne case only grew stronger. To a certain extent the attachment was unavoidable and might be seen, at least in a professional sense, as healthy. Death-penalty appeals were, after all, unique, not just in terms of the stakes involved but the time they took to litigate. Unlike even the most complex trials, which with preliminary procedures might run a year or two at the outside, the appeal process in capital cases was limited only by the creativity of the condemned prisoner's lawyer. Some appeals could last fifteen years or more. After losing in a lower court, a good lawyer would take his client's cause to the next level, raising new claims and relitigating old ones until he finally succeeded in finding a sympathetic judicial ear. The goal was to keep your client alive, even if you had to work around the clock to do it.

This was also a goal, Harrigan's shrink had told him in one of their early sessions, that was not unlike the responsibility a father has to his wife and kids. But it was one thing to work your butt off for a client, his shrink added, and quite another to use your client's case to work out your own psychological "issues."

At first Harrigan bristled at his therapist's insights. Although he was well schooled in using psychologists as expert witnesses to show that a defendant was legally insane or suffered from diminished capacity or some other mental impairment, he never saw much use for psychobabble in his personal life. "Shrinks are for sick people," he used to say, "and for litigants who need the services of a stuffed shirt with a Ph.D. and a ten-page résumé to impress a jury."

The accident on Angeles Crest changed that attitude forever, and in time Harrigan came to accept his shrink's observations. Still, he was unable to make the prescribed separation from the Ashbourne case. The case had been, he realized in his more desperate moments, the only constant in his life since the loss of his family, the only thing he retained from the time before his personal world collapsed. Losing the case and seeing Ashbourne executed would mean much more to him than the death of his oldest client. In an odd but very real sense, it would be like losing Stephanie and the kids all over again.

Maybe that was why the dream was returning, more frequently and more vividly than ever.

TWO

Harrigan sat up in bed and listened to the sounds of the night. In the distance, a pair of obnoxious bluejays squawked noisily, preparing for another predawn hunt for food. A neighbor's German shepherd began to bark, as if annoyed by the jays' lack of consideration. Soon the morning paper would be delivered, and another day would begin in earnest.

Realizing he was up for the duration, Harrigan reached for the three-ply woollen stump sock he always left on the nightstand for emergencies. In a routine that had become as second nature as tying shoelaces, he pulled the sock over the rounded remains of his left calf, making sure to smooth away even the smallest wrinkles, and slipped into the laminated below-the-knee prosthesis that allowed him to walk like an able-bodied man. In another five hours he would be in a downtown L.A. courtroom arguing a motion to suppress evidence in a cocaine bust. That left him more than enough time to scramble an egg, go over his notes for the motion and, most important of all, review the latest developments in the Ashbourne case.

As he flicked on the lights of his study, a cup of

strong black coffee in one hand, Harrigan gazed at the transcripts stacked on the credenza alongside his desk. Together, they made up twenty volumes of legal argument, voir dire, direct and cross-examinations, five thousand dog-eared pages in all, documenting every word spoken in open court during Ashbourne's long-ago trial.

Unlike ordinary criminal cases, in which the jury's sole function is to determine guilt or innocence, death-penalty trials like Ashbourne's are divided into two distinct segments, or "phases." In the guilt phase of his trial, Ashbourne had been convicted of two counts of first-degree murder with "special circumstances." In the penalty phase, his jury had received the standard instructions to balance and weigh the statutory factors in aggravation and mitigation, and promptly decided that he be sentenced to die for his crimes rather than serve the rest of his life behind bars.

Although Harrigan's law office in the Old Town section of Pasadena was a scant ten minutes away, he had removed the transcripts to his home when the California Supreme Court, following a lengthy delay caused by the accident, denied Ashbourne's appeal without a dissenting vote. Keeping the transcripts in his study and also maintaining a working file at the office ensured that even as an overburdened solo practitioner, he would be able to observe his devotions to Harold Ashbourne and his special legal needs any hour of the day or night.

Having lost in the state system and gotten nowhere on a *certiorari* application to the United States Supreme Court, Ashbourne's case was currently before the federal district court in San Francisco on a habeas corpus petition filed four years earlier. In addition to myriad lesser legal arguments, the petition claimed that Ashbourne had been denied his constitutional right to effective assistance of counsel during both the guilt and penalty phases of his trial because his alcoholic public defender—a paunchy, disheveled windbag known to the bar as J. Arnold Barnes—was so fond of Johnnie Walker and his single-malt cousins that he neglected to investigate or present Ashbourne's alibi at the guilt phase or his history of child neglect at the penalty portion. Barnes' substandard performance, Harrigan contended, had resulted in the conviction and death sentence of an innocent man.

Such claims of ineffective assistance of counsel, known in the trade by the simple abbreviation IAC, were commonplace in the appellate stages of death-penalty cases. When all other legal arguments failed, the condemned and their post-conviction attorneys routinely attempted to lay the blame on the defendant's trial lawyer. Harrigan knew that IAC claims were often trumped up by library-bound appellate lawyers who had never tried a case in front of twelve human beings with heartbeats and pulses, but he had no misgivings about raising the issue for Ashbourne. The important question, however, was whether the claim would succeed.

Although the "privilege of the writ of habeas corpus" was still enshrined in the Constitution, the "Great Writ" had undergone a judicial makeover during the 1980s and 1990s, particularly as it applied to capital cases. Pushed by the law-and-order frenzy

of the times, the United States Supreme Court had
issued one decision after another aimed at disman-
tling the legal obstacles to executions. Under the latest rulings, a defendant alleging IAC had to prove
that his trial lawyer's performance fell below contemporary professional standards. The defendant also
had to prove there was a "reasonable probability"
that but for his counsel's errors, the result of his trial
would have been different. This was what the high
court called showing "prejudice."

Few habeas corpus petitioners could be expected
to meet the exacting two-part standard. When all the
legal wrangling was said and done, the vast majority
of petitioners were so overwhelmingly guilty it
didn't matter whether they had Perry Mason defending them at their trials or Donald Duck, Esq.

Ashbourne's fate now lay in the hands of the Hon.
Stanley Blake, a seventy-five-year-old silver-haired
senior judge with a weak heart and a reputation as
one of the last flaming liberals. Blake was in no hurry
to endorse an execution and had placed the case on
the slow track, requiring only occasional briefing
from the parties and granting virtually all of the discovery and funding requests Harrigan made on Ashbourne's behalf. Now, forced by declining health to
trim the cases on his docket, Blake had set Ashbourne's habeas claims for an evidentiary hearing
that was slated to begin next month.

The hearing would be just like a trial, except that
its scope would be restricted to the IAC issues, and
Judge Blake rather than a jury would serve as the
trier of fact. If Ashbourne prevailed on the guilt-
phase IAC claim, Blake would issue an order grant-

ing the writ, requiring that Ashbourne either be released from custody or afforded a new trial in state court. If he won only on the penalty issue, he'd earn the right to a new sentencing hearing and a second chance to avoid execution. If he lost on both counts, Harrigan would pursue a routine final round of appeals until all legal challenges were exhausted. Ashbourne then would join the likes of Ted Bundy, Gary Gilmore, Robert Alton Harris, and the mushrooming ranks of child killers and serial murderers across the nation who had received the law's ultimate sanction.

Barring a legislative repeal of capital punishment, the evidentiary hearing would be Ashbourne's last viable chance to overturn his conviction. Even with a judge like Blake, Harrigan assessed the odds for victory as falling somewhere between slim and none.

More than twelve years had passed since a Bay Area jury returned its death verdict against Harold Ashbourne III before a packed courtroom. BANKER'S SON RECEIVES DATE WITH DEATH, the page one headline in the *San Francisco Chronicle* screamed the next morning. A sidebar to the main story described the long and improbable road Ashbourne had traveled as he made the transition from former prep student and hippie radical to the newest resident of California's death row for male inmates at San Quentin prison.

As Ashbourne's appellate lawyer, Harrigan was almost as familiar with the disastrous turn in his client's life as he was with his own personal misfortune. The common thread of an undeserved fall from grace was one of the things that drew Harrigan to Ashbourne. It permitted him to feel a degree of empathy seldom seen among death-row lawyers, some of whom would have considered his attachment to Ashbourne unproductive at best and unprofessional at worst.

Like thousands of other kids, Ashbourne had been swept up in the cultural whirlwind of the late sixties and early seventies. Drugs, free love, rock music, the clarion call of perpetual youth spent in communal harmony, the illusion of a world liberated from pain and adult responsibilities. Ashbourne had fallen for all the Day-Glo clichés. Dropping out of U.C. Berkeley in the middle of his sophomore year, he took off on an extended tour of Europe and India in search of spiritual discovery, financed by the trust fund his father, an influential Marin County investment banker, had established on his fifth birthday.

By the time he returned to Berkeley in 1974, he had quenched his thirst for metaphysics and mysticism but was no closer to deciding who Harold Ashbourne really was or what he should do with his life. With his trust practically depleted and his father determined to teach him a lesson in the hard knocks of survival, Ashbourne reenrolled in school as a polisci major and began to dabble in the "revolutionary" politics found at every street corner and coffeehouse along Telegraph Avenue.

It was in another moment of soul searching and personal drifting that he first encountered the charismatic instructor Henri Debray. A transplanted Brooklynite, born to trade-unionist parents as Henry Dershaw, Debray's claim to fame was that he had spent the spring of 1968 in Paris as part of a junior-year-abroad program and, as destiny would have it, had taken part in the May–June uprising that nearly toppled the Gaullist government. The experience opened Debray's eyes to the possibilities of what he considered a new style of revolutionary politics, combining the egalitarianism of traditional socialism and the environmentalist movement's concerns for planetary integrity. He took on a suitably Left Bank nom de guerre and returned to the citadel of imperialism to spread the gospel.

From Harrigan's perspective, Ashbourne made his first big mistake when he signed up for one of Debray's exclusive seminars. Ever in search of authority figures to fill the void left by his disinterested father, Ashbourne found in his new mentor a man who had a vision he could easily embrace as his own. Not only did Debray talk like a revolutionary, he also looked like the genuine article, with an explosion of thick, unruly red hair scattered like a field of tumbleweeds atop a permanently furrowed brow, gold wire-rim glasses that evoked comparisons to the political firebrands of a bygone era, and a full beard flecked with streaks of gray.

"I guess I'd always been seeking answers to life's big questions," Ashbourne once wrote Harrigan from San Quentin. "Debray seemed to have them all."

The two became fast friends, first as student and teacher, then as roommates, and finally as political collaborators. Ashbourne managed to earn his B.A. and was accepted into the doctoral program in the political science department while Debray landed an assistant professor's position. Guided by Debray's messianic sense of purpose, they joined forces with a small group of like-minded leftists to found an organization they hoped would someday serve as the vanguard of the new revolution, transforming Berkeley and the world at large into one big hippie commune fueled by the sun, the wind, and the honorable intentions of an empowered citizenry. In an abject display of immodesty, they named their group Saviors of the Earth.

For a time the Saviors contented themselves with peaceful proselytizing. Although the group never amounted to much in terms of numbers—at its height, the collective that ran the organization numbered no more than seven dedicated souls—they published a small newsletter and grew to be something of an intellectual lightning rod in the Bay Area political movement.

Then came the transformation. After a protracted battle with the head of the poli-sci department, Debray was denied tenure and summarily dismissed from the university for conduct unbecoming a scholar. It was never clear exactly what the unbecoming conduct was, but Debray attributed his firing to a political vendetta waged by the department chair, Professor Gilbert Denton. Denton held impressive environmentalist credentials of his own, but Debray branded him a turncoat for joining forces with California's industrial elite in the looming fight over the proposed Peripheral Canal project. To those inhabiting the insular world of ultra-left politics, the accusation was the moral equivalent of Stalin fingering an unsuspecting commissar as a Trotskyite.

The Peripheral Canal and the controversy that once surrounded it were well known, even to single-minded criminal defense attorneys like Harrigan. The canal was the last great California water venture, and it was opposed by virtually every environmental organization, all of whom saw it as the harbinger of catastrophe. As envisioned by the state's powerful water lobby, the canal was to be a forty-three-mile, four-hundred-feet wide channel that would divert water from the north around the Sacramento Delta into the multibillion-dollar aqueduct systems that moved millions of acre-feet of the wet stuff each year to hydrate the farms of the Central Valley and the thirsty cities to the south. Denton's endorsement would have given a much needed boost to the waterway's supporters, who faced (and would go on to lose) a voter referendum on the project in the state's June 1982 election.

In truth, Denton never announced his position on the canal. He never got the opportunity. In May 1982, his one-story wood-frame home in the Berkeley Hills was firebombed. The professor and his teenage son, both asleep with the flu, died of smoke inhalation and third-degree burns. Had the professor's wife not been out of town, the crime no doubt would have been a triple homicide. Based on the statements of neighbors and their own crime scene investigation, the local arson squad determined the time of the bombing as eleven p.m. They also determined the fire had been ignited by two Molotov cocktails, wine bottles packed with oil and gasoline, hurled through the windows of the home.

Except for a thumbprint on the shattered remains of a third bottle found on the sidewalk in front of the professor's home, Harold Ashbourne III might have gone on to complete his Ph.D. But the print, together with an elderly neighbor who saw two men running from the scene and calmly identified Ashbourne as one of them at a pretrial lineup, was more than enough to charge Ashbourne with the murders. The ensuing publicity so scandalized his father that the old man refused to fund his son's defense. Like a common indigent, Ashbourne was left in the hands of the public defender's office, which assigned the case to J. Arnold Barnes.

Harrigan opened the middle drawer of his desk and fished out the manila envelope with a Bakersfield postmark that had arrived in his mailbox a week ago. He unfastened the clasp, recalling the stormy conflict that had erupted between Ashbourne and Barnes during the trial.

"We had a series of really acrimonious conferences," Ashbourne had repeatedly explained to Harrigan. "Barnes was always stewed. He told me to exercise my Fifth Amendment privilege and keep my mouth shut."

Ashbourne, however, told Barnes that he had nothing to do with the bombing and demanded to testify. Adamantly he claimed to have spent the evening with Debray, discussing the future of Saviors. He was able to retrace his exact movements on the night of the crime, from the time he met Debray at Sproul Plaza around nine to their parting a couple of hours later at People's Park. He even remembered that Debray had one of his cherished May '68 buttons from the Sorbonne pinned to his denim jacket.

As is the fate of so many alibis, however, Ashbourne's suffered from a single overriding flaw—the absence of corroboration. After he and Debray separated that night, Debray vanished.

In the end, Barnes prevailed in the test of wills, and the jury never got to hear Ashbourne's alibi. But the strategy of keeping Ashbourne off the stand and winning the case on reasonable doubt backfired like a badly jammed handgun. In the absence of an affirmative defense case, the prosecution succeeded in characterizing Ashbourne as a remorseless killer who had taken to murder despite growing up in the lap of luxury. "If anyone deserved the death penalty," the jury foreman later told the press, "it was Harold Ashbourne."

Over the years a small coterie of left-wing fellow travelers, conspiracy buffs, and freelance journalists had logged hundreds of hours debating and exchanging their views on the life and times of Henri Debray and why he left Berkeley in such a rush. Debray was wanted for questioning, but no warrant had ever been issued for his arrest. Why, then, had he fled?

Like Elvis sightings, the rumors that swirled around Debray were plentiful and persistent. At first he was said to have been a stowaway on an East German freighter bound for Libya. Later he was reported teaching English at a secondary school in Cuba's Granma Province, and working as a Green Party activist in West Germany. There had also been occasional letters, some sent to Bay Area newspapers and a few directly to Harrigan, from people attempting to pass themselves off as Debray. But none of the letters ever proved genuine, and none of the many sightings led to anything but false hopes.

Slowly the rumors, and the prospects of gaining a new trial for Ashbourne, began to dry up until Ashbourne was left rotting with his crazed cronies on "the row" and little more to hope for than a painless execution by lethal injection. The last choice Ashbourne would get to make in his life would be the selection of his last meal.

Until the arrival of the manila envelope, Harrigan too had nearly given up. From inside the envelope he removed a photocopy of a handwritten note. Harrigan had sent the original to an independent lab for analysis and was still waiting for the results. Holding the copy to the light, he studied the handwriting for what must have been the hundredth time.

"The period of exile is over," the brief note began. "If the truth is what you want, I will see you at noon by the fountain in Sproul Plaza on Wednesday, the 20th of September. Don't look for me. I'll recognize you." Below the message was the signature "Debray."

It was probably just another hoax, Harrigan thought to himself as he glanced out the study window at his front lawn, now awash with color in the morning sun. But unlike all the other Debray letters he had either heard of or seen, this one contained a memento from the past that set it apart.

Harrigan reached inside the envelope again and pulled out the rusty old button that had been mailed with it. There was little doubt about its authenticity. Overlaid against the background of a red rose now faded to pink with age was one of the visionary slogans that had been scrawled on buildings and walls throughout the Left Bank during the May–June uprising. It was a slogan that Debray had written often in his antiestablishment broadsides and shouted in impassioned speeches on the streets and the corridors of academe. *L'imagination a pouvoir*, it read in French. "Power to the Imagination."

THREE

Harrigan stepped off the elevator on the ninth floor of the Criminal Courts Building and walked past the crowds of jurors, witnesses, and spectators waiting for the trial courts on the floor to open for business. Arriving at the end of the corridor, he stopped to check the list of cases posted on the marble wall outside of Department 316. Harrigan's matter—a suppression motion in the case of *People* v. *Garcia*—was the only item on the morning's calendar. He knew from past experience that the motion hearing would be brief, and that in a few hours he'd be free to return his thoughts to Harold Ashbourne.

Harrigan pushed open the walnut-stained courtroom doors and directed his eyes toward the bench and the stone-faced countenance of Superior Court Judge Thomas Taneda, the man criminal defense attorneys had nicknamed "Yojimbo" after the calculating samurai hero from the Kurosawa movie. Although disrespectful and on the politically correct crowd's censored list, the comical moniker fit the stiff and imperious Taneda to a T.

While Harrigan shared the general consensus of his colleagues in the defense bar, he knew that

Taneda was far too resourceful and complex to be dismissed so easily. He had tried three criminal cases in front of Taneda in his career, and he understood that what the judge lacked in legal scholarship, he more than made up for in dogged persistence and an affinity for the kind of dull, factual details that often determine the outcome of criminal trials. Taneda was, by any yardstick, a jurist to be reckoned with.

Taneda, for his part, respected Harrigan's skills as a trial lawyer but regarded him, like all defense attorneys, as an adversary to be parried and foiled in the greater crusade for justice. A former prosecutor with the Los Angeles district attorney's "central trials" unit, Taneda was the son of poor Japanese immigrants who had carved out a middle-class lifestyle for themselves and their children through hard work and adherence to the old-fashioned American virtues of individual responsibility, respect for property, and obedience to the law.

A bachelor, a social loner and a renowned workaholic, Taneda had earned a well-deserved reputation as a no-nonsense judge who relished throwing the book at the unfortunate souls in his courtroom who found themselves convicted of felonies. Nothing got Taneda's blood pumping like bleeding-heart attorneys who tried to win cases by invoking legal technicalities or high-priced psychobabbling shrinks who sought to excuse violent behavior by portraying worthless defendants as victims of social deprivation. Ambitious politicians, like the governor who had initially appointed him to the court, loved to tout Taneda as a minority success story who had pulled himself up by the bootstraps and brooked no excuses from anyone unwilling to do the same.

Now, after a decade of standing tall on the superior court, Taneda had been rewarded with the honor of a lifetime: the United States Senate, on a unanimous voice vote, had confirmed his appointment as a federal district court judge. Hearing Harrigan's motion this morning was to be Taneda's last act as a sitting state court jurist before being officially sworn in as the newest member of the federal bench in California. By agreement of the parties, the remainder of the case was slated to be transferred to another judge for trial and sentencing at the conclusion of the suppression hearing, permitting Taneda to report for federal court duty by the beginning of next week. Anticipating a rapid climb up the judicial ladder, Taneda had already moved his personal belongings from his superior court chambers and announced his intention to assume his new post without the luxury of taking even a single day of vacation. First, however, there was the matter of Harrigan's motion.

As felony defendants go, Harrigan's client, Eddie "El Gato" Garcia, was enough to raise the hackles of any judge, let alone a law-and-order taskmaster like Taneda. A fast-talking *cholo* from the mean streets of East Los Angeles, the thirty-five-year-old Gato had a rap sheet three pages long, consisting of a series of drug, theft, and joy-riding offenses committed as a juvenile and multiple residential burglaries and a dealing conviction as an adult, for which he had served a short stint in state prison. Although he had managed to stay out of trouble since taking over his father's "tuck-n-roll" auto upholstery shop on César

Chavez Avenue, Eddie had gotten himself popped for possession of a gram of cocaine.

Ordinarily a conviction for simple possession of such a small quantity would have carried a maximum three-year term. With a good attorney and a soft judge, the offender might even get off with a probationary sentence, a fine, and a hundred hours of community service. But the era of leniency in criminal sentencing was dead and buried, especially for punks like Eddie, who had spent a lifetime caught in the revolving door between the slammer and the streets. Under California's then-existing three-strikes statute for habitual felons, Eddie was looking at a potential sentence of life in prison if Harrigan failed to find a way to suppress the tiny plastic bag seized from Eddie's El Sereno home.

Harrigan walked slowly to the counsel table and turned to shake hands with his counterpart, deputy district attorney Barbara Sterling. A four-year veteran with the prosecutor's office, Sterling was a thin, high-strung young woman with neatly groomed brown hair cut just below the ears in a businesslike bob and a face made unnaturally pale from too little fresh air and too many nights researching briefs in the DA's law library. Professionally, she was known as an outspoken feminist and, when it came to macho men like Eddie Garcia, a turbocharged bitch on wheels.

"Nice to see you again, Barbara," Harrigan said courteously, his sharp blue eyes meeting Sterling's in a momentary assessment of wills before the verbal combat ensued. Sterling returned a perfunctory tight-lipped greeting, and Harrigan directed his attention to Eddie, who slipped into the seat at the counsel table beside him.

Eddie had come to court, as Harrigan had requested, suitably attired in a pair of crisply pressed mushroom-colored chinos and a blue pinstripe oxford, with the sleeves snugly buttoned at the wrists to conceal the jaguar tattoos that adorned each of his forearms. In his conventional attire, Eddie could almost have passed for a graduate student or the "independent businessman" he liked to call himself. Thin and wiry, with his jet black hair slicked back off his forehead, he weighed a trim hundred forty-five pounds and stood no more than five feet eight inches tall in his Italian loafers.

"I hope you done your homework, *Ese*," Eddie whispered to Harrigan, a nervous smile creasing his lips and causing his dark eyes to narrow. "I had to put up my house as collateral for bail." If there was anything Eddie hated in this world, it was confinement. The thought of spending the rest of his days in the joint, locked in an eight-by-ten-feet cell with a bunch of burned-out *vato locos* and or emissaries from *La Eme*, the Mexican Mafia, was almost enough to make him wish he'd followed his grandmother's advice and become a priest.

Noticing the fear on his client's face, Harrigan laid a reassuring hand on Eddie's shoulder. "Relax, this shouldn't take long," he said. Outwardly, Harrigan was a picture of calm in his smartly tailored double-breasted gray suit. Clean-shaven and alert, Harrigan had set his thoughts of Harold Ashbourne aside and prepared himself for what promised to be a morning of fireworks. Inwardly, Harrigan was only slightly

less anxious than his client. Although he was capable
of litigating a suppression motion in his sleep, he
knew that if he lost this one, Sterling would never
agree to a plea bargain. If the case went to trial,
Eddie would in all probability call the Department
of Corrections home until they carried him out of
prison in a cheap pine box.

Taneda cleared his throat to call the morning calendar to order and nodded in the direction of the court
reporter. "*People* versus *Garcia*," he intoned deeply.
"The record shall reflect that both counsel for the
People and the defense are present, along with Mr.
Garcia." He paused just long enough to look contemptuously at Eddie and Harrigan before continuing. "I note that the matter is on calendar for a
pretrial defense motion to suppress evidence pursu-
ant to section 1538.5 of the penal code. Are the parties ready to proceed?"

"We are, Your Honor," Harrigan and Sterling answered in unison.

"Your Honor," Sterling added, rising to her feet,
"the People stipulate that the arrest of the defendant
and the search of his home were conducted without
a warrant."

"Then it's the People's burden to show that the
search and seizure fall within an exception to the
warrant rule," Taneda interjected, slowly stroking the
contours of his neatly trimmed black goatee. Although everyone in the courtroom, including Eddie,
understood that the law permitted warrantless
searches only under certain narrowly defined circumstances, Taneda had a fetish for seeing that the transcripts of his hearings were as free from ambiguity

as possible. The clearer the record, the less chance of having his rulings overturned on appeal. Satisfied that he had clarified the scope of the proceeding, he gestured toward Sterling. "How many witnesses do you plan to call, Counsel?"

"Just one, Your Honor," the prosecutor answered. "The People call Officer Frank Hernandez." The hard-nosed, olive-skinned police officer seated next to Sterling rose and walked to the witness stand.

"Please raise your right hand," Taneda's court clerk, a fortysomething black woman, said in a monotone that betrayed both familiarity and boredom with a ritual performed all too frequently. "Do you swear that the testimony you give in this proceeding shall be the truth, the whole truth, and nothing but the truth?"

Hernandez answered in the affirmative, settled into the upholstered, low-back swivel chair on the witness stand, and looked directly at Sterling. Outfitted in his navy blue uniform, Hernandez was an imposing specimen, with a police-issue crewcut, closely trimmed black mustache, square jaw, and a set of biceps and shoulders pumped up to Schwarzenegger proportions from long hours of training in the weight room. If his investigative skills were only half as impressive as his anatomy, he would have made detective grade long ago. But Hernandez was what the Latino brothers on the force called a *baboso*, a fumbler prone to ignoring established procedures and, on more than one occasion, making false arrests.

Sterling was well aware of Hernandez's less than superlative record, and even with Taneda peering down on her from the bench like some grim guardian

angel, she was visibly concerned. If the defense succeeded in suppressing the cocaine, she knew the People would have no alternative but to dismiss the
charges. She stood and walked to the lectern behind
the counsel table. "Officer Hernandez, what is your
current assignment?" she asked, folding her arms together in a defensive posture.

"I'm assigned to neighborhood patrol."

"How long have you been with the police force?"

"Ten years."

An entire decade, Sterling thought to herself as she
paged through her file, and he hadn't learned to prepare a decent crime report. Replete with spelling and
grammar errors that would have shamed a self-re-
specting third-grader, the write-up on Eddie's arrest
was the most embarrassing piece of police work Sterling had seen since graduating from law school.
Carefully avoiding any unnecessary references to the
report, Sterling launched into a series of background
questions usually employed to impress juries. Responding to the inquiries, Hernandez dutifully recounted his recruitment by the department from the
same East L.A. neighborhood where Eddie Garcia
grew up, his graduation from the police academy
and his training in the identification of controlled
substances. So far, so good, Sterling thought to
herself.

"During your tenure with the LAPD," Sterling
continued, "approximately how many arrests have
you made?"

"Hundreds, maybe thousands," Hernandez barked
like an army sergeant.

"And of those thousands, how many were for controlled substances?"

"About a third," Hernandez answered proudly.

"In drug cases, Officer, is it important to make arrests quickly?"

"It's of the utmost importance."

Sterling paused for an instant and looked at Hernandez, as if reminding him of how they had rehearsed his examination in her office. "Why is that, Officer?"

"Because of the added risk of suspects destroying evidence," he responded, looking pleased that he had not forgotten his lines.

Sterling, also looking relieved, moved on to establish that Hernandez was familiar with Eddie Garcia, having once arrested him outside of the tuck-and-roll shop for possession of two joints of marijuana. The charge was subsequently dismissed after Eddie paid a small fine.

"Officer," Sterling said, closing in on the present cocaine bust, "did you have occasion to arrest the defendant at his home on July 20th of this year?"

"Yes, I did."

"And was that arrest made without a warrant?"

"It was," Hernandez acknowledged.

Sterling's body tensed as she delivered the next, all-important question. "And what caused you to enter the defendant's home without a warrant?" During the prehearing rehearsal in her office, Sterling had warned Hernandez that if he blew the answer, she'd file a formal complaint with his supervisors and have him sent back to the academy for retraining. She waited breathlessly for the officer's reply.

"I received information from a confidential informant," Hernandez said with a surprising degree of self-confidence, "that the defendant was getting ready to move a 'brick'—a kilogram—of cocaine from his house."

"Had this individual given you reliable information in the past?"

"Several times," Hernandez answered sharply.

So far, so good, Sterling thought again. She was heading for the home stretch and doing better than she had any right to expect. "And what did you do with this information?"

"I drove to the defendant's home, commenced a search of his house, and placed him under arrest," Hernandez replied, choosing his words carefully.

"And what did you find?"

"I found a plastic bag containing white powder in the dresser of the master bedroom. The powder appeared to be cocaine. I called for backup to transport the defendant to the station for booking."

Taneda, who had been observing the proceedings with rapt attention, interjected with a slight smile, "Will Counsel stipulate that the bag contained cocaine?"

"Yes, Your Honor," Harrigan assured Yojimbo.

"Officer," Sterling asked, resuming the attack, "why didn't you apply for a warrant?"

Hernandez took a hard swallow and composed himself. "I was afraid the suspect would either have destroyed or sold the evidence by the time I got a warrant." He smiled broadly, like a Hispanic John Wayne as Sterling yielded the floor to Harrigan.

Opting to remain next to Eddie at the counsel

table, Harrigan rose to his feet, a copy of the arrest report in his right hand. "Officer," he began, flipping through the pages of the report, "how much cocaine was in the plastic bag that you found?"

Hernandez squirmed uncomfortably for an instant, then settled in his seat, his large hands folded on his lap. "A little more than one gram," he answered.

"Your Honor," Sterling interjected before Harrigan could fire off another question. "Whether Officer Hernandez found one gram or a kilogram is immaterial to this hearing. For all we know, the defendant had but one gram of the contraband left because he had already sold the rest."

"You're quite right, Counsel," Taneda quipped cheerfully, signifying to Harrigan with a nod of his head to continue.

"What day of the week was it when you arrested my client?" Harrigan asked.

Hernandez looked puzzled at the question and appeared to search his memory. "Thursday, if I'm not mistaken."

"And what shift were you working?"

"Graveyard. My partner and I returned the squad car to the station around eight a.m., and I left alone about fifteen minutes later in my own car."

"And yet you arrested my client, according to your report, at a quarter past twelve?"

"I think that's right," Hernandez answered thoughtfully. "Technically, I was off duty."

"And without your partner?"

"That's also right."

"You know, Officer," Harrigan said in a conversational tone that might have passed for friendly banter, "your report states that you encountered this confidential informant inside a local drugstore. But it doesn't say when that encounter occurred."

"Objection, Your Honor," Sterling shouted from the counsel table. "No motion has been filed to disclose the informant's identity."

"I'm not asking for his name, Judge," Harrigan assured the court, "only for the time when the alleged encounter between Officer Hernandez and the informant occurred."

Taneda stroked the edges of his goatee. His face began to flush, and a small vein above his right temple started to swell with the mounting friction between Sterling and Harrigan. Defense attorneys who appeared regularly in Taneda's courtroom had long ago learned to gauge the strength of their cases by the diameter of that vein. The bigger and bluer it got, the closer the defense was to victory. Taneda shook his head at Sterling's objection. "The witness shall answer," he instructed.

Hernandez cast a contrite look at Sterling and turned his eyes to the floor. "About eight-thirty," he said in a near whisper.

"Why, then," Harrigan continued, "did you wait until twelve-fifteen to arrest my client and search his home without first obtaining a warrant?"

Hernandez was like a man struck dumb, unable to find the words to explain, much less excuse, his conduct.

"We're waiting for a reply, Officer," Taneda prompted from on high, the blue vein turning darker by the millisecond.

"I had an important personal errand to run," Hernandez answered after another long hiatus.

"And what was so important that it took precedence over applying for a warrant?" Harrigan prodded, arms upraised, eyes shifting from the witness to the judge's vein. "Where were you between eight-thirty and twelve o'clock?"

Hernandez rubbed the fingers of his meaty right hand across his forehead. "I'm sorry, Ms. Sterling," he stammered like a schoolboy in the principal's office. "I was at a gym in North Hollywood."

"A gym, as in a place where one pumps iron, does sit-ups and leg-lifts?" Harrigan suppressed the urge to laugh.

"I went there to meet a couple of buddies," Hernandez confessed, slightly more at ease now that he had told all. "If I signed them up, I would be eligible for a free year's membership. They were late and I stayed around to work out."

In one contained admission Hernandez had sounded the death knell for the prosecution. Harrigan signaled that he had no further questions, and the courtroom fell into a deadly silence as Hernandez slunk back in his seat beside the seething Sterling. Taneda, who appeared on the edge of a coronary, trained his gaze on the prosecutor. "I don't know what you can say, Counsel, but I'll give you the opportunity to argue your position," he said with barely concealed disgust.

Sterling rose respectfully from her seat, distancing herself from Hernandez with her body language. "Your Honor, despite Officer Hernandez's revelations about visiting the gym—and I want to emphasize that I knew nothing about that until just now—the warrantless arrest of Mr. Garcia and the search of his home were justified by exigent circumstances, as the law permits."

Sterling's face reddened, and the sinewy cords in her neck strained with tension as she groped for the words that might salvage the People's case. "Whether Officer Hernandez searched the home at eight-thirty or at twelve," she continued in a quavering voice, "the seriousness of the offense, possession of cocaine, and the likelihood that evidence would be destroyed persisted, particularly in light of this defendant's long criminal history. Under such circumstances a warrant should not have been required." She took a deep breath and waited for the judge to respond.

"I quite agree, Counsel," Taneda reasoned, "that no warrant would have been required at eight-thirty, but how can you justify a delay of nearly four hours? This was, after all, a Thursday. The courts and the DA's office were open."

"Your Honor," Sterling implored, appealing to the career prosecutor in Taneda, "by twelve o'clock it was even more imperative for decisive action to be taken against this defendant." She pointed contemptuously at Eddie, who sat nervously next to Harrigan, his chin propped on his right hand, his eyes avoiding any contact with Sterling. "The People should not be penalized simply because Officer Hernandez allowed his hormones to get in the way of his duty."

Taneda shifted his gaze to the defense. Harrigan rose to his feet, his voice confident and strong. "Your Honor, in 1976 the supreme court of this state declared that warrantless arrests within the home are per se unreasonable in the absence of exigent circumstances. Even allowing for the high court's current conservative leanings, there was no exigency here that excused officer Hernandez's failure to obtain a warrant. A four-hour delay for the sole purpose of allowing the officer in charge to set a new personal best in the bench press will never pass muster on appeal should you overrule our motion."

The blue vein, now a deep indigo conduit of truly imposing dimensions, made it almost unnecessary for Taneda to announce his decision. "In view of the evidence," he hissed, nearly choking on his words, "and in light of established precedent—with which this court does not necessarily agree but is nonetheless bound by—the defendant's motion is granted. I assume the People will make a motion to dismiss."

Sterling answered in the affirmative, and Taneda uttered the ruling he hated most, suppressing the cocaine and releasing the defendant from all further proceedings. "This is the kind of case," he hissed as he brought his gavel down to conclude the proceedings, "that causes our social fabric to unravel."

Eddie reached for Harrigan's hand and shook it with a sense of relief known only by those whose asses have been singed by the flames. "Whatever it takes, homes," he said, grinning from ear to ear. "If you ever need a favor, you know where to find me."

"I'll keep it in mind," Harrigan said with a chuckle. "Just make good on the rest of my retainer, and I'll be a happy man."

From out of the corner of his eye, Harrigan could see the sneer on Taneda's face as he descended from the bench and headed for the refuge of his chambers. He watched the judge disappear behind closed doors and could hear Eddie laughing with a few of his homies as they left the courtroom in high spirits. Packing up his briefcase, Harrigan lingered a moment to say good-bye to the bailiff and court reporter. As a trial attorney he knew the value of remaining on the best possible terms with the functionaries who made the courthouse work.

Outside the courtroom the ninth-floor corridor had emptied out for the lunchtime recess. The frenzy of the justice system had paused for an hour of calm. Harrigan could hear his footsteps echo off the marble-tiled walls as he followed the last of the noontime stragglers onto the elevator. The social fabric was no less intact than it had been this morning, he thought to himself as he pushed the button for the lobby. No more and certainly no less.

FOUR

It was the ultimate irony, Harrigan mused as the elevator doors opened on the ground floor, how some people caught up in the jaws of the court system get ground up like cheap hamburger while others waltz back to their families and friends. Eddie Garcia clearly was one of the blessed, an inveterate scofflaw whose crime-prone years were largely behind him and who had escaped the gulag only because of sloppy police work. Harold Ashbourne had no such luck. The police work in his case had been swift, decisive and effective, as was the performance of the senior deputy DA who had prosecuted the case and had no trouble convincing a jury of the defendant's morally affronted peers to return twelve votes for execution. Was the law essentially a crap shoot, dependent upon whose lawyer could be a bigger prick, or was our adversarial system, with all its warts and imperfections, still the best device on the planet for finding the truth and doling out punishment?

Harrigan could have remained in the lobby contemplating the vicissitudes of justice for another hour, but the economic realities of running an office allowed for no such dallying. Recalling that his secretary was scheduled to take off early for an afternoon of bargain hunting at the South Lake shopping district, he hurried over to the bank of pay phones in the courthouse lobby to call in for his messages. If there was anything that irritated Harrigan about managing a one-attorney practice, it was how dependent he had become on the timely receipt of phone messages. A missed call could result in anything from the loss of new business to a screw-up in the scheduling of a deposition or a mixup in the service of a subpoena. He had often thought of clipping a cellular phone to his belt or buying a car phone, but the idea of looking like a Hollywood agent led him to develop instead an unerring instinct for the nearest Pacific Bell hookup.

The phone rang three times before the polished voice of Dennis Witter answered. "Law offices of Peter Harrigan," Dennis nearly sang into the receiver. A deeply tanned, blond-haired Pasadena native, Dennis was, in addition to being a slave to fashion, a physical fitness addict. About two inches shorter than Harrigan but without a trace of the "love handles" that advancing middle age had begun to deposit around Harrigan's midriff, Dennis had recently celebrated his thirtieth birthday with a "white-water" rafting trek on the Kern River. Dennis had been with Harrigan since he reopened his practice after the car accident and was not only Harrigan's secretary but his office manager and paralegal as well. He was also the first and only gay male with whom Harrigan had developed a personal friendship.

"El Gato flies with the eagles," Harrigan announced cheerfully, knowing that Dennis would be pleased with the news of the morning's triumph. "Any needy new clients beating down the doors?"

"No, except for a social call from Mark Clemons," Dennis said, a touch of sarcasm at the word *social*. "You're all clear on this end, and I'm out of here in twenty minutes." As he spoke, Dennis cradled the phone between his left shoulder and ear, freeing his hands to operate a two-hole punch as he busied himself logging documents into one of the office's closed files. "I'm taking my mom out for a makeover. Poor thing, she hasn't had her hair done properly in years. She looks like Barbara Bush after a long winter at Kennebunkport."

"You're a good son, Dennis," Harrigan said, amused as always by his secretary's glib one-liners. "What did Mark want?"

"He said that if Sheri didn't work out, he had a new secretary, with hair like Julia Roberts, eyes like Michelle Pfeiffer, and tits that could provide shade for a small boy. He wanted you to meet her, at least for starters. His words, not mine."

Harrigan and Dennis shared a knowing chuckle at Clemons' gutter humor. Clemons was one of Harrigan's old law school buddies and had handled his personal-injury and wrongful-death claims after the Angeles Crest crash. An unreconstructed skirt chaser and a hard-nosed litigator, whose offices were also in Pasadena, Clemons had urged Harrigan to hold out for a seven-figure settlement and nearly resigned from the case when Harrigan insisted on resolving the matter quickly for half of what Clemons thought a jury would award. With his family gone, all Harrigan wanted was enough money to cover his medical bills, pay off the mortgage on his home, and make a few donations to local charities like the Little League his kids had played in. He wasn't being a saint, a masochist, or a fool, he told Clemons, just trying to get on with his life in his own way.

Clemons reluctantly acceded to Harrigan's wishes and, after what he considered an appropriate period of mourning, took it upon himself to see that his friend resumed the life of a healthy heterosexual. Although Harrigan appreciated Mark's efforts, and had in fact met Sheri Landis on his intro, he preferred to rely on his own abilities to attract female talent. "What did you tell Mark?" Harrigan asked.

"I said that you were a big boy and could make those hard decisions on your own." Dennis laughed again, warming to the opportunity to trade juicy tidbits with the boss.

"Smart thinking, Dennis. I knew there was a reason I hired you." Harrigan glanced at his watch and noticed the time slipping away. "Any news from the lab?" he asked, suddenly sounding all business as his concerns shifted back to Ashbourne and the tests being run on the latest letter from Debray.

"No, not a thing," Dennis replied. His tone was equally as worried as Harrigan's, if not more so. "I'll call over before I take off and leave a note if I hear anything."

"Okay, Dennis, take care, and say hello to your mother," Harrigan said, his disappointment evident. There were only two days left before the promised meeting with Debray in Berkeley, and Harrigan had no intention of making the trip without receiving confirmation of the letter's authenticity. He had stopped believing in Santa Claus and the Easter Bunny as a small boy, and he thought his chances of catching up with the elusive Debray were just about as good as meeting either childhood idol.

Repair work along what passed as the fast lane on the Pasadena Freeway made the drive back to Old Town even longer than usual. Bumper to bumper all the way past Chinatown, Dodger Stadium, and the Arroyo Seco, and rush hour was still three hours away. By the time Harrigan had stopped for lunch and pulled his Audi sedan into the parking lot behind his office, it was already two-thirty.

Occupying half the third floor of a renovated turn-of-the-century brick building, the law offices of Peter Harrigan were located on Fair Oaks Avenue just two blocks north of Colorado Boulevard, in the heart of Old Town. The original business center of the city known for its annual New Year's Day parade, the Rose Bowl, and a unique blend of stately old mansions and Green and Green–style California craftsman bungalows, Old Town was a rare urban success story, with a checkered history as melodramatic as a soap opera starlet.

From its days of early prominence in the early part of the century, Old Town had entered a long era of seedy decline as Pasadena's commercial activity expanded eastward into the San Gabriel Valley after World War II. By the late 1970s, the eight-block area had degenerated into a skid row of peep shows, flophouses, and pawnshops. It was saved from the wrecking ball at the eleventh hour by an unusual combination of smart public planning, preservationist sentiment, and shrewd private investment, and had since blossomed into one of the tonier districts in California. The Art Deco and Spanish colonial revival styles of the community's low-rise storefronts had been lovingly preserved, and the flophouses and peep shows squeezed out of business, replaced by a dizzying array of open-air cafés, gourmet restaurants, cappuccino bars, first-run movie theaters, and up-scale clothing outlets. Every weekend hordes of well-heeled middle-aged professionals and gaunt-looking teenagers with gold nose rings and Doc Martens competed for room on the crowded sidewalks, two generations separated by appearance, attitude, and taste, yet united by the common purpose of sampling the area's wares, mixing in with the scene and, above all, spending money.

It was Stephanie, not Harrigan, who first had been attracted to Old Town. A volunteer with the Pasa-dena Heritage Society, she had believed in the revival and had urged Harrigan to buy the building on Fair Oaks when it had gone on the market a decade ago. Harrigan, however, still had his doubts about the place and misgivings about the way the city planners had made no provision for low-cost housing in the redevelopment project. In the end, he and Stephanie compromised on a long-term lease that the new own-ers, a pair of investors from nearby Glendale, had managed to renegotiate as the surrounding property values began to soar in the early nineties.

The only thing that Harrigan disliked about the office was its proximity to the Allen Carter Karate Academy, which had opened up two years ago directly across the street, in full view of Harrigan's reception and conference rooms. The academy was one of several in Pasadena that specialized in teaching self-defense techniques to children, yet another trend, along with the unending search for the perfect cup of *café latte,* that the Old Town renaissance had sparked. Every afternoon, beginning at four-thirty, and all day Saturday, kids of all ages would line up for large group sessions in their white uniforms with colored belts, signifying the degree of proficiency they had achieved, to practice and perfect their kicks, punches, and *katas.*

Harrigan knew his own two boys would be right in there with them if only he had listened to Stephanie and driven to the beach instead of the mountains that fateful afternoon. Sometimes the thought of what might have been was so unnerving that he took to rearranging his schedule to hold late afternoon meetings away from the office in order to avoid seeing the kids as they arrived for classes.

Harrigan's office had a look of orderly desertion as he pushed open the front door and kneeled down to retrieve the dozen or so letters that the postal carrier had slipped through the mail slot and which now lay scattered on the interior hardwood floor. He had begun to leaf through the letters when he noticed a note taped to the back of the chair behind Dennis' desk. Written in bold block lettering with a black marker on a single sheet of legal paper were the words: "LAB RESULTS NEGATIVE!! SEE YOU TOMORROW. D."

Harrigan set the mail down on the desk and stared at the paper, feeling a mix of anger and resignation.

It wasn't just the content of the note that bothered him. He had, after all, fully expected the Debray letter to turn out to be another phony. Dennis' flip tone, however, was another matter. The way the message was punctuated with two exclamation marks made it seem as if Dennis was pleased, or somehow amused, that they had arrived at yet another dead end in the search for Debray. Maybe he had made a mistake in permitting too much informality in his relationship with Dennis. A real secretary never would have left an important memo taped to the back of a chair. He and Dennis were due for a long discussion.

As he contemplated Dennis' flippancy, Harrigan slowly paced the reception area, gazing out the window at the scene below. One of the area's many street musicians—a black man with a full gray beard, a tightly woven African hat, and a flowery knit-cloth shirt—was setting up a pair of steel drums, getting an early start on what promised to be a profitable evening of musical requests in return for spare change. A young couple, the guy outfitted in jeans and running shoes, the woman in a tight-fitting red baby-doll sundress and matching suede pumps, was window shopping at an art gallery, pointing at a display of lithographs that must have been way beyond their budget.

As Harrigan stared at the young couple, a harried but prosperous-looking man in his late thirties, dressed in a business suit and tie, rounded the corner, leading his son into the karate studio for a private lesson. The kid, awkwardly clutching a pricy nylon gym bag under one arm, couldn't have been more than six, exactly Johnny's age, as his youngest would remain forever in Harrigan's memory.

Harrigan took a long, slow breath and twisted the window blinds closed. He gathered the mail from Dennis' desk and walked down the hall, past the conference room to the refuge of his interior office.

As he opened the door, his eyes met the assortment of diplomas, bar association certificates, and awards that hung on the wall behind the clear-stained beachwood desk that dominated the room and was tastefully complemented by a set of matching client chairs and an L-shaped corner sofa and coffee table. Intended to impress potential clients, the wall arrangement was like a road map of Harrigan's career, marking his transition from a new admittee to the California Bar to his election several years later as the county's defense attorney of the year.

At the center of the display was a framed black-and-white blow-up of an *L.A. Times* photo of Harrigan taken about a month before the Angeles Crest disaster and just two days after he had received another promising communiqué from Debray. The photo was published on page three of a Monday morning edition as part of an in-depth series the paper had run on death-penalty lawyers. The story gave prominent play to the Ashbourne case, emphasizing Ashbourne's claims of innocence and Harrigan's commitment to clearing his client's name. Although he had yet to receive the lab's work-up on the letter, Harrigan told the *Times* he was on the verge of an important, though unspecified, breakthrough that would confirm Ashbourne's alibi.

Stephanie had copied the article and had it framed.

" 'I have the support of my entire family,' says Peter Harrigan, attorney for death-row inmate Harold Ashbourne III," the caption below the picture read.

Although the caption seemed little more than a cliché that portrayed Harrigan as a white knight, it was, in truth, an understatement. Stephanie had not only supported his work on the Ashbourne case, she had also been part of it, helping to summarize the lengthy trial transcripts and logging countless hours proofreading the legal briefs Harrigan filed with the state supreme court. There had been times, he thought, when Stephanie was almost as anxious to see Ashbourne's conviction overturned as he was. But all that was part of the past and the painful memories that refused to die. Unlike Old Town, no form of urban renewal could revive the life Harrigan knew before the disaster on Angeles Crest.

Harrigan loosened the knot of his tie and sank into the high-back armchair behind his desk, still clutching the afternoon's bundle of mail in his left hand. He looked around the office, taking in the shelves of law books that lined the north wall, the two upright five-drawer filing cabinets containing his open case files, the new personal computer on his desk, the spiral notebook calendar on which he and Dennis scheduled the office's business for the coming weeks. This was his life, and as pathetic as it seemed at this moment, he was grateful for it. He made a conscious effort to shake the thoughts of Stephanie and the kids from his mind and began once more to shuffle through the mailman's offerings.

The letter from Forensics Laboratory Associates was the third item he opened, right after the monthly statement from the Westlaw computer data service and the alumni newsletter from the University of San Diego Law School. Inside the envelope from the lab were two pages. The first was a bill for the work-up on the Debray letter by Nathan Daniels, the institute's top questioned-documents examiner. The second was Daniels' report on the tests he had performed and the findings he had reached. "While we are not able to say with one hundred percent certainty," Daniels wrote in the report's conclusion, "it is our professional opinion that the author of the known exemplar was also the author of the questioned letter. Should you require the services of FLA to authenticate the match in court, we will be available for the usual retainer."

A good ten minutes passed before the full import of the report registered and Harrigan was able to reach for the phone to make plane and hotel reservations for the Bay Area. He would have the better part of tomorrow to rearrange his appointments, prevail upon Mark Clemons to make a minor Thursday morning court appearance for him, and to make amends with Dennis.

Only now did Harrigan realize that Dennis had meant to share the results of his quarterly HIV checkup in the note taped to his chair. He and Dennis were indeed due to have a discussion, about the self-absorbed schmuck Harrigan had become.

FIVE

The rest of California and the nation had long ago consigned the counterculture and the New Left to the status of museum pieces, but the People's Republic of Berkeley somehow managed to keep the zany spirit of the 1960s visible, if not fully functional. The college town nestled on the eastern shore of San Francisco Bay still teemed with street-corner orators bent on revealing the conspiracies behind the Kennedy assassinations and the AIDS epidemic, curbside vendors hawking tie-dyed T-shirts, strung-out panhandlers who fancied themselves Jim Morrison look-alikes, and dingy bookstores carrying all the political and bohemian classics. The older forms of protest and free expression mingled easily with newer forms, like the nude strolling and bicycling craze that had drawn national media attention in the early nineties and had been subsequently outlawed by the usually civil-libertarian city council.

It was eleven when Harrigan wheeled his white Chevy Corsica rental car into a bilevel parking structure on College Avenue south of the University of California campus. The morning fog had given way to one of those crisp and clear September days when the Bay Area shimmered with color. With such perfect weather and an hour to kill before the meeting with Debray, Harrigan decided to walk to Sproul Plaza. He adjusted the knee strap on his prosthesis and set out on a path to the university that took him down Dwight Way and through the main artery of the Berkeley scene on Telegraph Avenue. Although he had been to Berkeley twice since being appointed to the Ashbourne case, his visits had been confined to a few uneventful witness interviews and an inspection of the site of the bombing in the hills above the town. He hadn't taken a walking tour of the city since he was a college student immersed in the anti–Vietnam War movement more than two decades ago.

The experience was akin to time traveling, and Harrigan was flooded with memories from the summer after his graduation from the University of Colorado, when he and a couple of shaggy-haired buddies rented an apartment a few blocks away from People's Park. Except for a set of relatively new volleyball and basketball courts, the park, which he now passed on Dwight Way just east of Telegraph, was the same scrubby plot of dirt, sand, and crabgrass it had been since the student riots of 1969 turned it into a hangout for the homeless and stopped the regents from building a dormitory on the land. Rasputin Records, though housed in a new glass-and-steel building, still did a land-office business selling vinyl as well as CDs and tapes at the intersection of Durant and Telegraph. The Caffe Mediterraneum was still the reigning dowager of the area's coffee houses, and the shelves of the Annapurna, Berkeley's last "head" shop, remained stocked with incense, black-light posters, pipes, bongs, and rolling paper. All had endured the test of time, catering to the changing consumer habits of succeeding generations without sacrificing their tawdry Berkeley charm.

Harrigan hurried past the familiar sights, feeling slightly nostalgic for his own lost youth and more than a little self-conscious at the easy mark he presented for the legion of spare-change artists and itinerant fortune-tellers who descended on him, looking at his gray sports coat, creased charcoal slacks, and leather valise as though they were monogrammed with dollar signs. After handing his last three quarters to a weathered-looking red-haired woman in her early forties who had tailed him for a block, offering to preview his destiny with the aid of a deck of Tarot cards, Harrigan finally crossed Bancroft Way onto the grounds of the university and the outskirts of Sproul Plaza.

The plaza, too, was exactly as Harrigan remembered it. Even the most hardened cynic would have to concede that this was historic ground. It was here, on the steps of Sproul Hall, where the Free Speech Movement held its rallies in the early sixties and where, later in the decade, students protesting the war were teargassed like Vietcong by national guard helicopters called in by Governor Ronald Reagan. Even now, with "the movement" dead and buried, it was easy to see how an impressionable young kid like Harold Ashbourne could have gotten swept up in the illusion that a social revolution was in progress.

Harrigan made his way to the fountain in the plaza just as the carillon bells of the Campanile, the 307-

foot clock spire modeled after the Italian original
from the Piazza San Marcos in Venice, began to
chime. It was noon, and the square was filled with
roving minstrels strumming guitars, beaming Hare
Krishnas searching for converts, students lugging
laptop computers and backpacks filled with text-
books, and a few pipe-smoking professors looking
for a soothing cup of mocha java or a quickie between classes with a willing coed. But there was no
sign of Debray.

Harrigan took a seat at the edge of the fountain
and pulled out a copy of the morning edition of the
San Francisco Chronicle. He skimmed the front-page
headlines on the situation in Northern Ireland and
the continuing debate in Congress over welfare re-
form before turning his attention to a short wire-ser-
vice story on an inside page. An eleven-year-old kid
wanted by the St. Louis police for killing a teenage
girl had been found in a Dumpster, his body riddled
with bullet holes. The cops surmised that the kid, a
gang-banger who had been arrested no less than
eight times himself, had been eliminated by members
of a rival gang. According to the paper, the kid had
been neglected and abused since he climbed out of
the womb.

Harrigan was so engrossed in the eleven-year-old's
shocking story that he took no notice of the little man
with thinning red hair and pockmarked skin who
had taken a seat next to him until the man was halfway through a less than virtuoso harmonica solo of
Dylan's "The Times They are a Changin'." Harrigan
was ready to write the man off as yet another hapless
throwback when the man stuffed the harmonica into

the breast pocket of his denim jacket, turned to face him, and began to rave in a slightly discernible Southern drawl about the Central Intelligence Agency. "We kicked the CIA off campus years ago, man," he said in an accusatory tone, his dark eyes darting from side to side. "What the hell are you doing back here?"

Harrigan folded the newspaper under his arm and regarded his unwanted companion warily. He had learned from his long tenure as a criminal lawyer to keep his cool in the presence of loony tunes asking crazy questions. The best approach was to answer their inquiries quickly and directly and return as respectfully as possible to your own business. "I'm an attorney," he said in the measured voice of a hospital orderly. "I'm here for a meeting, and I have no connection to the CIA."

"CIA, KGB, FBI, DEA, EPA, ABA," the man muttered angrily, as though reciting some sort of demented incantation. "You're all the same." He stood up, shouted again, "You're all the same," then gathered up the army surplus duffel bag at his feet and scurried away with an observable limp through Sather Gate at the other end of the plaza, disappearing into the heart of the campus.

Harrigan tried to return to his paper, but the wind began to pick up, sending sprays of water over the cement perimeter of the fountain. Seeking to stay dry and maintain a lookout for Debray, Harrigan retreated to the steps of Sproul Hall, parking himself on a spot not far from where Mario Savio had once addressed throngs of fellow travelers. The plaza began to fill again with students hurrying to make their afternoon lectures, and the minutes wore on. By the time Harrigan completed his second perusal of the sports page, he knew everything he ever wanted to know about the 49ers' game plan for their upcoming meeting with the Lions. It was one-thirty and Harrigan felt like a dorky high school student stood up by his date on prom night. Maybe the Debray letter really was a fake, he thought to himself. It wouldn't be the first time the lab techs had been fooled.

He stuffed the newspaper into his briefcase and started to walk down the steps when a deep voice behind him called out. "You were supposed to stay at the fountain." Harrigan quickly turned around. The voice belonged to a man with curly brown hair, a full beard, and gold wire-rims. It was the voice of Henri Debray.

Harrigan didn't know whether to aim a right cross at Debray's nose for making him wait or embrace him like a long-lost brother. "I know a place where we can talk," Debray said before Harrigan could make up his mind. "Follow me."

Without uttering another word, Debray unfastened the waist button of his tan sports coat and with a large red gym bag slung over one shoulder led Harrigan across the plaza and into the afternoon foot traffic on Telegraph Avenue.

The Awakening was a small coffeehouse on Haste Street at the edge of the Telegraph fun zone. Its interior decor was a mix of beat, funk, rock, and political pop art. Noir photos of Berkeley icons like Kerouac, Ginsberg, Garcia, and Dylan adorned the walls, alongside 1960s psychedelic posters announcing concerts at the Avalon Ballroom across the Bay and framed news photos of memorable skirmishes from Berkeley's anti-war protests.

Harrigan and Debray settled behind a table at the back, where it was quiet and dark. A raven-haired waitress in her early twenties, wearing a Buddhist prayer medallion around her neck and matching gold nose and eyebrow rings, delivered their orders of biscotti and *café latte* and left them alone to talk.

"I've been looking for you since the day I was appointed to represent Harold Ashbourne," Harrigan said, breaking the ice. "Why did you abandon him?"

Debray smiled and shook his head, as if he'd been confronted by a naive freshman in a lecture hall. "History," he replied pompously.

"History?" Harrigan raised his eyebrows quizzically, his consternation beginning to show. "Whose history?"

"I see you're not familiar with the canons," Debray answered, sounding even more didactic. "The history of all hitherto existing society is the history of class struggles," he continued, invoking the famous passage from the *Communist Manifesto* and to all appearances dodging Harrigan's attempts to elicit a straightforward response. "Freeman and slave, patrician and plebian, lord and serf, guildmaster and journeyman, in a word, oppressor and oppressed."

"Look, I didn't come here for a lesson in Marxism 101, and I don't give a rat's ass about your socialist drivel," Harrigan snapped back, uncertain whether Debray was playacting for his own amusement or if he was truly lost in the maze of political theory he spouted so fluently. "Your old friend Harold Ashbourne is going to die if I don't get some answers."

"I *am* answering you, Counsel," Debray said, looking Harrigan in the eye. "I can't help it if I see my situation in political terms. That's one of the problems with Americans. So few of us see the big picture. I *abandoned* Harold, as you put it, because my life was in danger."

"And why was that?"

"Because I created an organization that *saw* the big picture and dared to change it." He paused dramatically to allow the profundity of his remarks to register. "Do you know what it means to be radical—I mean, really radical, as the Greeks understood the term?"

"Somehow I sense that I'm going to find out," Harrigan responded, hoping the latest detour from the Ashbourne case would be brief.

"It means to get to the root of society, to see the complex connections that reveal the essence of the system. *We* understood those connections—the connections between the cancer clusters at Love Canal and the fact that one percent of the population controls over a third of our net wealth. The connections between the fact that our prisons are overflowing with young black men who can't read or write and the atrocities we've committed in redirecting the course of our wild northern rivers to transform Southern California from a desert into a Disneyland of death and suburbia. The connections between politics as usual and the degradation of nature that threatens to annihilate us all."

"And what the hell does that have to do with Harold Ashbourne?" Harrigan asked, growing more exasperated by the syllable.

Debray took a time-out from his tirade to take a sip of his coffee and then suddenly lost his voice as he was overcome by a paroxysm of deep, chesty coughing. His face reddened and his eyes watered as he struggled for breath. If only for a moment, he seemed frail and perhaps seriously ill, as if the accumulated adversities of more than a decade on the run had finally caught up with him. Then, just as suddenly, the spasm abated.

"The same people who killed Gilbert Denton and his son wanted me and my organization dead." Debray resumed his discourse in a calmer tone. "They still do, if I'm not mistaken."

"So Harold Ashbourne really was with you on the night of the bombing?"

Debray nodded. "Harold. He was a spoiled child of the bourgeoisie when I first met him—so much so that I took to calling him 'Prince Hal' after Shakespeare's *Henry the Fifth*. But like Henry, he proved to be a man of uncommon courage. He's paid a heavy price for that courage."

"And where have you been while he's been paying that price?"

"Here and there," Debray answered. "I've been a cab driver in Portland, a bartender in the French Quarter of New Orleans, a deliveryman in Duluth, even a law clerk in Boston. All under different names, of course."

"You must have had some help. I mean with IDs and things."

"The underground is not without its resources," Debray said. "And no, I'm not prepared to tell you who killed the professor or why I've decided to come forward after all these years," he added, anticipating Harrigan's next question. "At least not yet. I'll need a week, two at the outside, to conclude some unfinished business. After that, you'll have all the answers to your questions and more than enough evidence to set Harold free. But I intend to act alone—*strictly alone*—and I want assurances that you won't interfere."

"But I can help," Harrigan protested. "We can work together." No trial lawyer worth his annual bar dues would willingly let his star witness wander off into the urban wilderness to conduct his own private investigation, especially when the witness fancied himself as the second coming of Karl Marx. There was no telling what Debray might do if left to his own devices. Short of wrestling him to the ground, however, Harrigan was powerless to stop him.

Debray slowly shook his head again, seemingly confident that he had the upper hand. "You'll just have to trust me." He lifted his gym bag onto his lap and pulled out a small pamphlet and a two-page document typed on lined legal paper. "Take them as a sign of my good faith," he said, handing the material to Harrigan. "You can review them while I answer nature's call." He nodded toward the men's room, and excused himself from the table.

The two-page document was a sworn declaration in which Debray affirmed that Ashbourne had been with him at Sproul Plaza and People's Park until eleven o'clock on the night of the firebombings. The declaration also listed the places Debray had lived during his self-imposed exile, beginning with a six-month stay in a cabin owned by his elderly mother in the Adirondack Mountains, followed by a cross-country odyssey that had taken him to a mind-boggling series of far-flung venues in over twenty states, Canada, and Mexico. Debray proclaimed his willingness to testify at the upcoming federal court hearing and signed the declaration under penalty of perjury. All things considered, it was a lucid, if incomplete, statement that would be useful in establishing Ashbourne's alibi and innocence, provided that Debray made good on his promise to attend the hearing and backed up the declaration with convincing live testimony. Judging from the professional quality of the document, it indeed seemed that Debray had received some training in the law.

Although Harrigan was relieved to have the declaration in hand, he felt a burning sensation in the pit of his stomach as he took in the account of Debray's transcontinental wanderings, particularly the part about the initial layover in New York. "My mother was old and frail," Debray wrote, "and after six months she refused to help me hide any longer. So began my more than decade-long odyssey."

In the winter of 1985, about a year after his appointment on the Ashbourne case, Harrigan had succeeded in contacting Debray's mother. Although ill and in her seventies, Esther Dershaw was still living in the family's apartment in the Crown Heights section of Brooklyn. Following an exchange of letters and a few brief phone calls, the old woman agreed to speak with him. By the time Harrigan's plane

touched down at LaGuardia Airport, however, Esther
was dead, the victim of a massive stroke. She was
found in her living room easy chair, a fading photograph of her husband, Morris, a former union orga-
nizer, cradled in her arms.

Harrigan never knew, of course, if Debray had contacted his mother, but he was Esther's only child, and
it only seemed logical that he would have wanted
to see her before she passed away. The declaration
confirmed his suspicions. If only he had tried to
reach Debray's mother sooner, he might have been
able to pick up Henri's trail before it became so im-
possibly convoluted. The thought was extremely
vexing.

Struggling to keep his mind from dwelling on
what might have been, Harrigan set the declaration
aside and picked up the pamphlet. A frayed copy of
the Manifesto of the Saviors of the Earth, penned by
Debray in 1977, the pamphlet was a study in megalo-
mania, filled with paranoid predictions of economic
and ecological collapse, messianic self-delusions, and
angry diatribes against the "eco-criminals" who were
bent on destroying the planet for their own selfish
ends. Despite the urgency of the moment, Harrigan
could not suppress his laughter at the self-important
tone of the manifesto's preamble: "In his eleventh
thesis on Feuerbach, Marx wrote, 'The philosophers
have only interpreted the world, in various ways;
the point, however, is to change it.' While Marx's
observation was path-breaking for its time, it was
only half right. Before the world can be changed, it
must first be saved."

So this was the real Henri Debray, a.k.a. Henry

Dershaw, the only child of Esther and Morris, who left home with a college scholarship only to become a self-appointed savior of the world and now, in his own sweet time and on his own arrogant terms, the savior of Harold Ashbourne.

"I see you find the manifesto amusing," the man with the thinning hair and pockmarked skin said with a trace of irritation as he took the seat across from Harrigan. It took a moment for Harrigan to recognize him—first as the CIA-cursing interloper from the Sproul Plaza fountain and then, as he stared closely at the man's corduroy sports jacket and intense dark eyes, Debray.

"As I said, the underground is not without its resources," Debray remarked, rising to leave and extending his hand. "My mother was a makeup artist for the old Yiddish theater. She used to take me along for weekend performances."

"That sounds really fascinating; I'd like to hear more," Harrigan said, hoping that an appeal to Debray's colossal ego might persuade him to stay.

"Some other time." Debray shook his head.

"But the hearing's only weeks away. How will I contact you?"

"You won't. I'll contact you."

Debray took a few steps toward the exit, then turned around, his tone and demeanor deadly serious. "I'll be in touch well before the hearing."

"You'd better," Harrigan said angrily, "or you'll wish I never laid eyes on you when I find you."

Debray locked his gaze on Harrigan as he reached across the left side of his face with his right hand and peeled a set of pockmarks from his cheek. "I admire your dedication," he said. "Harold is in good hands."

Turning away again, Debray hurried through the front door, leaving Harrigan to ponder how he would ever be able to find a man whose true face, he now realized, he had yet to see.

SIX

The state prison at San Quentin was California's oldest penitentiary and the site of the state's death row for male prisoners. As of the fall of 1995, over four hundred inmates—all convicted of first-degree murder and many of whom were also guilty of the most heinous acts of rape, sodomy, and mutilation this side of Vlad the Impaler—were jammed together in the institution's aging East Block building, a massive redbrick structure that called to mind images of medieval dungeons. Drawn from every ethnic group and geographic section of the state and ranging in intellect from the mentally impaired to the near genius level, the residents of the Row were united in one respect only—the hope that their court-appointed lawyers would discover a legal ground for reversing their convictions and save them from their engagements with "the little green room," as they referred to the execution chamber.

Ironically, the prison could not have been situated in a more tranquil spot on the north shore of San Francisco Bay in eastern Marin County. On clear days, visitors, inmates, correctional personnel and those who lived in the tiny Victorian village that bore the prison's name were treated to breathtaking views of the bay and the nearby Richmond-San Rafael bridge. It wasn't just the picturesque setting that made San Quentin such a visual oddity. Apart from the geography, the prison itself offered a truly strange mix of repressive architecture and the kind of public amenities normally associated with tourist attractions. In addition to its archaic dormitories, fortress-like gun towers, and exercise yards enclosed with chain-link fencing and razor wire, the prison ran an arts and crafts shop featuring high-quality inmate-made novelties, belt buckles, and paintings, together with San Quentin T-shirts and caps. The California State Prison Museum was also located just inside the institution's gates.

It took Harrigan less than an hour to make the drive from his hotel through downtown San Francisco to the prison. Although he had waited to phone the institution until after his encounter with Debray, the warden's office accommodated his last-minute request for an eleven o'clock visit with Harold Ashbourne without putting him through any of the bureaucratic hassles he might have encountered at other state prisons. Death-row inmates were treated differently, and in some respects much better, than other prisoners, especially when it came to attorney-client relations. The last thing the warden's office wanted was some federal court judge staying an execution because a death-row inmate hadn't been allowed to confer with his lawyer. As long as you behaved yourself and avoided wearing blue shirts or slacks that might be confused with prisoner garb, the prison staff seemed only too happy to arrange day-long chinwags, even on a few hours' notice.

It was ten-thirty and the morning fog was just beginning to lift when Harrigan pulled his rented Chevy Corsica into the visitors parking lot. The lot was set on a bluff overlooking the bay down a steep embankment from the diner-shaped one-story building known as "the Tube," which served as the visitors processing unit. In observance of the prison's security rules, Harrigan left his wallet and briefcase in the car and with a single accordion file stuffed with a legal pad and documents from the case file under one arm, he climbed the concrete steps that led to the Tube's entrance.

The Tube's reception area was an elongated corridor that looked like the interior of a poorly maintained railroad car. Inside, a group of a dozen or so women and young children, the wives, girlfriends, and kids of prison inmates, sat on a row of graffiti-scarred old wooden benches flanking the bay side of the room, waiting for the guards on the other side of the steel door with the one-way mirror mounted at its center to buzz them through for processing. From the tired looks on the women's faces and the way the older kids galloped up and down the narrow corridor, it seemed that many had been there since early morning. Unlike lawyers, the families of inmates received little solicitude from the prison staff. It was a depressing but altogether routine scene, and Harrigan had grown accustomed to it from the many visits he had paid Ashbourne over the years.

Harrigan maneuvered his way past a group of kids improvising a game of hopscotch and smiled meekly at an attractive young black woman who sat on the bench, breastfeeding a toddler, next to the intercom mounted to the side of the steel door. "Peter Harrigan," he announced, depressing the intercom button, "I'm here for an attorney visit with a death-row inmate." He held up his bar card and driver's license in front of the one-way mirror, and a few seconds later the buzzer sounded, releasing the lock on the door.

As Harrigan grabbed the door and twisted it open, he could hear some of the women mumble complaints about how long they had been sitting and the unfair privileges accorded lawyers. Their protests were entirely understandable, he thought as he crossed the threshold and the heavy door snapped shut behind him.

On the other side, a beefy prison guard with short, dark hair and a matching mustache greeted Harrigan from across a long wooden counter. The guard ordered him to empty his pockets, remove his shoes, and hand over his accordion file for inspection before walking through an upright metal-detection unit that would screen him for knives and other concealed weapons. Harrigan called the guard's attention to his artificial leg, and the setting on the unit was adjusted, allowing him to walk through without tripping the alarm. Satisfied that Harrigan was another harmless member of the legal profession, the guard returned his footwear and file. He handed Harrigan a visitor's slip indicating the date and time of his conference with Ashbourne and directed him through a set of double doors which led to the outdoor walkway that would take him to the visiting center. The initial processing plus a secondary metal screening outside of the center took approximately twenty minutes.

By eleven Harrigan was seated in one of the four Plexiglass booths in the main visiting room reserved for attorney-client conferences. It had been only a few months since Harrigan had last laid his eyes on the dimly lit visiting center, but the place never failed to send nervous shock waves through his stomach and down the backs of his thighs. Anyone who thought that prisons were country clubs where inmates wiled away the hours recreating in the sun had only to spend a few hours "on the inside" to feel the fear and despair that permeated the place like sewer gas.

Two of the other Plexiglas booths were already occupied by appellate attorneys conducting interviews with their death-row clients. One of the inmates, a sinewy Chicano in his late twenties with gang tattoos on either forearm, was engaged in animated conversation, loudly proclaiming his innocence and blaming his conviction on the "son of a bitch" public defender who had refused to call his girlfriend to the stand to establish his alibi at trial.

The other inmate, a muscular black man who looked to be in his mid-thirties, sat with his hands folded in his lap, eyes nearly expressionless, listening quietly to his lawyer and responding only in muted monosyllables to the questions that were put to him. It was impossible to tell whether the inmate was trying to concentrate on his lawyer's remarks or was suffering from severe depression. The two inmates were a study in contrast, the one inappropriately hyper, the other inappropriately withdrawn, yet each sharing a common fate that would in all likelihood end in their state-sanctioned executions.

Harrigan sat behind the small gun-metal gray steel table in his booth, contemplating the bleak surroundings, when he heard the doors open on the elevator that led to the cells on death row. Two guards armed with holstered handguns and black nightsticks emerged on either side of Harold Ashbourne, clad in a blue prison work shirt with hands cuffed behind his back and legs manacled loosely at the ankles. The guards slowly escorted Ashbourne into Harrigan's booth, eased him into the chair on the other side of the small table, and locked the door behind them. As an extra security precaution, they waited to release Ashbourne's cuffs until they were safely outside the booth and Ashbourne had backed his hands through an open slot in the Plexiglas. For the duration of their conference, Harrigan and Ashbourne would be shut inside the small booth while the guards looked on from the safety of their bulletproof observation station by the entrance to the visiting center.

It was always a risky proposition to speculate about how a prison inmate ought to look. In the public's mind, however, the typical con had a definite and enduring profile—he was young and poorly educated, wild-eyed and aggressive, buffed out from pumping iron and, more often than not, black or Hispanic, like the rough-hewn inmates in the adjacent interview booths.

There was no question that Harold Ashbourne did not fit the mold. It wasn't just because he was white or in his forties that made him stand out. Some of the most infamous killers on the Row were white and well into middle age. It was Ashbourne's entire persona that set him apart. Tall and thin, he was slightly stooped-shouldered and wore a pair of heavy horn-rimmed spectacles that shielded a set of sensitive brown eyes. Soft spoken even after years of confinement, he bore the look of a mild-mannered social studies teacher who had woken up from a bad dream one morning only to find himself trapped in a claustrophobic cell with no windows and wall-to-wall sociopaths as neighbors.

Although Harrigan visited Ashbourne regularly, he was always struck by how much his client had changed from the long-haired, bearded radical he had been at the time of his arrest and trial. If only a jury could see him now, with his glasses, graying sandy-brown hair, and the worry lines creasing his forehead, they would no longer regard him as the spoiled and remorseless rich kid people of moderate means love to hate. The sympathy factor might well run in his favor.

"How are you, Harold?" Harrigan asked warmly after the guards had passed out of earshot.

"No worse than the last time you were here. Life in happy valley doesn't change much," Ashbourne answered, rubbing the red marks the handcuffs had left on his wrists. "Actually, things have been pretty quiet. No lockdowns, no fights, no suicides, at least none I've heard of. I've been getting my yard time, and I've even started again on that autobiography you keep pushing me for."

Despite the encouraging developments, Ashbourne's voice sounded even flatter than usual, and Harrigan couldn't help thinking the autobiography

had something to do with it. The autobiography—
what death-penalty lawyers often referred to as a
"social history"—was something Harrigan had suggested several years ago, both as a form of therapy
and a means of discovering mitigating evidence
about Ashbourne's past that his first lawyer, J. Arnold Barnes, had overlooked and failed to present to
Ashbourne's jury at the penalty phase of his state-
court trial. To prevent prison officials from confiscat-
ing the writings, Harrigan suggested that Ashbourne
compose chapters of the work as a series of letters
addressed to him, thereby cloaking the material
under the time-honored privilege that protects attorney-client communications from disclosure to the
government and other third parties.

At first Ashbourne resisted the project, protesting
that he had already told Harrigan his life's story and
insisting that there was nothing "abnormal," as he
put it, about his early years. He also condemned the
autobiography as a device directed only at securing
a new penalty phase trial that would at best commute his death sentence into a term of life imprisonment without the possibility of parole. Like so many
of the long-term residents of the Row, Ashbourne
seemed almost afraid to reexamine his childhood and
professed interest only in issues that would win him
a new guilt trial and a shot at freedom.

But whether out of boredom, fear of execution, or
in response to Harrigan's insistence, Ashbourne
eventually began to write, at one time mailing Harrigan a four- or five-page letter per month. Although
he never communicated easily about his youth, he
ultimately revealed a deep-seated distrust and hatred

of his wealthy father, whom he blamed for abandoning him to the supervision of professional caregivers and later sending him away to virtual exile at a pricy boarding school. While Ashbourne Sr. projected a public image of the beneficent professional, he lived the private life of a tyrant, regularly berating Harold whenever he failed to live up to the old man's expectations in school, church, and sports.

Harrigan was moved by Ashbourne's disclosures and with assistance of one of his expert witnesses raised the issue of child neglect in the federal habeas corpus petition before Judge Blake. But while the judge found the matter sufficiently compelling to include it in the upcoming evidentiary hearing, Harrigan knew the liberal Blake was only throwing him a bone. To make the issue work, he would need to show a lot more than the fact that Ashbourne had a self-absorbed father who found it difficult to express affection.

Believing that he had only begun to scratch the surface of his client's domestic pathology, Harrigan pressed Ashbourne for additional details, particularly about his relationship with his mother. But apart from a few grudging general comments about being close with his mom and looking to her for protection, Ashbourne was either unable or unwilling to bare his soul any further. He wrote a few more chapters of the autobiography, dealing mostly with the formation and politics of Saviors of the Earth, and then the installments ceased altogether.

"I'm glad you're writing again," Harrigan said, wary of opening an old wound, "but I didn't come here to discuss the autobiography."

"What, then?" Ashbourne asked, preparing himself for the worst.

"I came about Debray. He's returned."

Ashbourne closed his eyes like a religious penitent in ecstatic meditation. "I knew he'd come back," he whispered. When he looked at Harrigan again, his eyes had a new spark, and a faint and seldom seen smile creased his lips. "He's the key to the case, Peter," he exclaimed. "When can I see him?"

Harrigan waited a moment for Ashbourne's excitement to level off. "He's the key to the case, all right, and I'm almost as happy as you," he said. "But there's also a catch, I'm afraid."

"A catch?" The smile faded.

"Debray's been on the run for years, Harold, and I'm not sure he can be trusted."

"Of course he can. You just don't know the man." Ashbourne's face flushed as he spoke, his prison pallor turning a bright pink.

Ashbourne's unwavering loyalty to Debray both amazed and annoyed Harrigan. "After all the time you've rotted away in this place, aren't you the least bit angry, Harold?" he asked, hoping to shake that sense of loyalty. "Aren't you the least bit suspicious that you've been played for a chump?"

"He must have had his reason for running, and it doesn't matter. The point is that he's come back. That's all that counts now." Ashbourne stared at Harrigan, then slowly bowed his head and turned his eyes to the floor. When he spoke again, the excitement had disappeared, replaced by the same flat affect he had displayed when the interview began. "Look, maybe I am a chump, but what else can I do?

I'm just hanging on to the little hope I have. Is that so wrong?"

"Of course not," Harrigan replied, adopting a gentle tone. Slowly and carefully he related the details of his meeting with Debray, from the ingenious disguises to Debray's cryptic pronouncement about the "unfinished business" he insisted on conducting alone.

Ashbourne took in Harrigan's description of the Berkeley scene like a homesick kid and shared a deep belly laugh with his lawyer at the way Debray had toyed with Harrigan at the Sproul Plaza fountain. "Debray was always playful, even in his most political moments," Ashbourne said. "That was one of the things I liked most about him."

"But you don't have time to play now, and neither do I," Harrigan said. "I can't sit around and wait for him to call or drop me a postcard. You were Debray's closest comrade. If anyone would know what he means by this 'unfinished business,' it's you. I want you to tell me what really happened on the night of the bombing."

"It was just like I told you before," Ashbourne said, his body stiffening as he spoke. "Debray and I met at Sproul Plaza and talked about the dissolution of Saviors. He said the organization had outlived its usefulness and it was time to move on. The next thing I knew, Debray was gone and a SWAT team was beating down my front door."

"Then we really may have no option but to wait for Debray to make good on his promise. I was hoping there might be something we could do ourselves, just in case he decides to run away again." The disappointment in Harrigan's voice was palpable. He gathered up his papers and stood to signal the guards that the interview was over. "I'll be in touch before the hearing, and in the meantime, let me know if you remember anything."

Ashbourne hesitated as he watched Harrigan prepare to leave. "Wait, Peter, there *is* something," he said abruptly, motioning Harrigan back into his chair. "Debray did say something else. About two months before the bombing, he told me he had spoken with Professor Denton. Their conversation must have taken place sometime in late February or early March. Denton and Debray were sworn enemies, but the professor tried to warn him that Saviors had been infiltrated."

"By whom?"

"I don't know. All Debray said was that Denton told him there was a 'Judas in our midst,' someone with ties to rich and powerful forces who opposed everything the ecology movement stood for. Debray made it seem very dramatic and apocalyptic, the way he made everything seem. The professor was supposedly working on a book or article that was going to expose the whole thing. At the time I thought it was just part of their ongoing feud and that Denton had made it up to make Debray feel like a fool. Now I'm not so sure."

"Why the hell didn't you tell me this before?" Harrigan asked, his irritation mounting. "We're getting down to the wire here, Harold." Next to combating the attorney general's demands for a speedy execution, Harrigan thought to himself, the most difficult aspect of being a death-row lawyer was dragging the truth out of your own client. Whether it was getting him to open up about his childhood or come clean about the circumstances of the crime, you could never be sure you were getting the full story.

Ashbourne looked away again and sighed deeply. "The way Debray split, it was like he thought *I* was the Judas, right down to my rich banker's son pedigree," he said softly. "I was afraid you might think that, too. After you've spent a few years in a place like this, the only things you have left are your dignity and self-respect. I didn't want anyone to think I was a traitor. Please, try to understand."

Ashbourne's words had a certain ring of truth, and Harrigan's agitation slowly dissipated. "You a traitor? I wouldn't have believed it in a million years," he said, "and I'm sure Debray wouldn't, either. Debray may be a genius or a fraud, or maybe both. I don't know and I really don't care, but I think he genuinely feels guilty about deserting you."

"So where does that leave us?" Ashbourne asked anxiously as the guards began to make their way over to the interview booth. "Be straight with me, Peter, it's my ass that's on the line."

Harrigan thought for an instant about delivering the standard line lawyers in hopeless cases feed their clients about trying to do their best and stretching things out on appeal. But this was a death-penalty case, and Harold Ashbourne deserved an honest answer, even at the risk of sending him into an emotional tailspin. "We have approximately one month to pull our case together. Even if Debray shows up for your hearing and makes a good witness, it won't be easy. I'd be lying if I told you otherwise."

Ashbourne's shoulders sagged with the gravity of Harrigan's assessment. "I know you'll do whatever you can," he managed to say through his disappointment, sounding like a cancer patient discussing a high-risk surgical procedure with his doctor. "But whatever happens, I want the hearing to go forward. I can't take it here much longer." He took a moment to gaze across the interview room, inviting Harrigan to do the same with a nod of his head. The grim scene, from the harsh overhead fluorescent lighting to the cream-colored institutional paint on the walls and the haunted, adrenaline-pumped expressions on the faces of the prisoners and their keepers, was starkly overpowering. "No more delays. Okay?"

The two men shared a moment of silence. Although Ashbourne was reasonably stable for someone in his position, Harrigan knew his client was prone to spells of deep depression and had twice before been placed on suicide watch. If the case dragged on much longer, there was no telling what Ashbourne might do to end his pain.

"Okay," Harrigan answered finally. He placed a comforting hand on his client's shoulder as the guards arrived and ordered Ashbourne to back his hands through the slot in the Plexiglas to be cuffed. Then he watched as the guards opened the door to the interview booth and escorted Ashbourne back to the elevator that would return him to his cell on death row.

SEVEN

As Harrigan made his way south on the 101 Freeway across the Golden Gate Bridge and back into San Francisco, he felt the future closing in on him. Debray had returned, but only to scurry away again, perhaps to rendezvous and settle an old score with a person of unknown name and undetermined age and gender, whom Harrigan would for the time being refer to only as "Judas." Harrigan's plan, if the torrent of images, hopes, and anxieties racing through his mind could be given that label, was to find them both as quickly as possible.

But having a plan was one thing; knowing how to pull it off was something entirely different. As an attorney, Harrigan had years of experience drafting briefs, cross-examining slippery witnesses, and delivering closing arguments that charmed the pants off skeptical juries. But locating missing persons was the kind of work lawyers usually delegated to a private investigator—someone trained in running skip traces, working surveillance cameras, and spending late nights holed up in the front seat of a car, sipping coffee and studying the racing forms, waiting for the lights to go on in an apartment window across the street.

Harrigan now realized that one of the big mistakes he had made in his handling of the Ashbourne case was losing touch with Carlos Guzman, the gruff, chain-smoking retired cop turned private investigator whom Judge Blake had appointed to assist him in federal court. It had been over three months since he had spoken with Carlos, and then it was only to alert him that he might be needed to serve a few subpoenas for the upcoming hearing. In the early days of his tenure on the federal case, Harrigan had used Guzman extensively, not only to follow leads on Debray but to locate and interview other former Saviors. But as the months wore on and each of the old radicals asserted alibis of their own, Harrigan had less and less need to send a gumshoe into the field. Or so he had thought.

It was just past four-thirty when Harrigan found a parking space off Valencia Street, a block from Guzman's second-floor office in the Mission District. He had no idea if Guzman was in, but "the Mission," a low-budget, predominantly Hispanic area of two-story Victorians and modest storefronts south of Market Street, was close to his hotel and he had nothing to lose except brownie points for courtesy by dropping in unannounced.

The gold block lettering on Carlos' office door—Guzman & Associates—seemed newly stenciled and caught Harrigan somewhat by surprise. As far as he could remember, Carlos ran a one-person shop. Maybe business was picking up, or Carlos was subcontracting work to other investigation agencies, or he was just following in the tradition of small business owners everywhere, trying to make himself look bigger than he truly was.

Harrigan's speculations about Carlos' business fortunes came to an abrupt halt as he opened the door and his gaze fell on the shapely Latina standing behind the reception desk. Outfitted in an expensive double-breasted burgundy blazer with a tight-fitting matching skirt cut a revealing six inches above the knees, she was struggling with both hands to remove a large gold hoop earring from her right ear. To say that she was appealing would have been about as much of an understatement as saying that Harold Ashbourne had a small legal problem. Harrigan couldn't remember when he had ever seen such luxuriant jet black hair and wide, dark eyes. And judging from the contours of the stretchy cream-colored lace top she wore beneath the blazer, she had a body toned and endowed in all the right places.

"I'm sorry," the woman said before Harrigan could mouth an introduction, "but my hair seems to be tangled. Would you mind giving me a hand?"

Harrigan stood motionless in the doorway for an awkward moment, looking a little too obviously like a deer caught in the glare of oncoming headlights. "My name is Peter Harrigan," he stammered, "and I've come—"

"My name's Josie, but we can handle the introductions in a minute," she interrupted, craning her neck to reveal the knot of hair caught in the clasp of her earring. "I promise I won't bite."

Harrigan set his briefcase on the floor and crossed the room, taking up a position by the side of the beautiful stranger. He watched intently as she brushed back the hair from the right side of her head, exposing the wayward strands wound around the earring.

Slowly and gently Harrigan freed the clasp, all the while struggling to keep his eyes from wandering. It was a losing proposition, and he could only hope to contain the attraction he felt as he took in the classic angles of Josie's neck and shoulders, her full lips, high cheekbones, and flawless olive-brown skin. "There, I think that about does it," he said, pulling the gold hoop away like a surgeon performing an appendectomy. "That must have been rather painful."

Harrigan handed the earring to Josie, who inserted it into one of the side pockets of her blazer for safe-keeping with an appreciative smile. "Thank you," she said with a curious mixture of playfulness and just a trace of embarrassment. "I'm really not in the habit of asking our clients for this kind of help, but you looked like the capable type."

She straightened her blazer and retreated a half step toward the window overlooking Valencia. The waning rays of the afternoon sun sent shafts of light across her face and shoulders. Harrigan had encountered many a fetching secretary in his day, but there was an engaging quality about this woman that extended far beyond her obvious physical charms.

"You were about to introduce yourself, if I'm not mistaken," she continued, smiling warmly and extending her hand.

"The name's Peter, Peter Harrigan," he said, attempting to turn his attention back to Harold Ashbourne, "and I'm here to see Mr. Guzman. We have a case together."

"I'm sorry, but Carlos isn't here. I wasn't aware that you had an appointment."

"I'm afraid I didn't have time to call ahead." Harrigan reached for his wallet and pulled out a business card. "I'm staying at the Hotel Mayfair near Union Square," he said, handing over the card. "I wonder if you could phone Carlos and set up a meeting for this evening. There's some rather urgent field work I need done, and I'm scheduled to return to L.A. tomorrow."

"I don't think that would be possible," she replied, her demeanor suddenly becoming serious.

"What about tomorrow? I can get a later flight if necessary."

"I don't think that would be possible, either, Mr. Harrigan. Carlos was in a very serious car accident two weeks ago. He broke his right shoulder and his left leg in two places. He probably won't return to work for several months."

"You're kidding." Harrigan stared back at her in disbelief, feeling all the more foolish for allowing himself to lust after his investigator's office help.

"No, I'm afraid not."

Harrigan ran the fingers of his right hand through his hair like a junk bond trader who had just taken a beating on the market. "Jesus Christ, I've got a client on death row and less than a month before his case goes to federal court. Of all the fucking luck."

He looked at Josie and caught himself before his misgivings became more colorful. "I'm sorry," he said softly. "That was out of line. Carlos is a good man, and I hope he has a speedy recovery." He took a few steps toward the exit and picked up his brief-case. "You wouldn't know where I might find an investigator on short notice, would you?" he asked, turning back for what he feared would be his final look at Josie.

"We never did complete our introductions," she answered, breaking into a wide grin. "I'm Josie Guzman, Carlos' niece. I've been a licensed private investigator for five years, and, as of the last two months, I've been Carlos' partner."

She opened the top drawer of the old gun-metal gray filing cabinet behind the reception desk and pulled out a large accordion file stuffed with legal documents, police reports and assorted notepads. "Ashbourne," she said, tucking the file under one arm. "I'm familiar with all of my uncle's files, including this one. In fact, I was planning to write you to see if anything needed to be done before the hearing." She gave the impression of professional competence as she spoke.

"Well, it seems I've saved you some postage," Harrigan said with genuine relief, his composure returning. He glanced at his watch and saw that it was already past five. "I don't know about you, but I haven't eaten since breakfast. Maybe we could grab a bite and go over the case. My treat, of course."

She paused for a moment, as if considering her plans for the evening, then gave him another of those wonderfully playful smiles. "There's a quiet Middle Eastern place not far from here," she said, reaching for her purse.

*   *   *

The Café Tyre was located in a converted store-front on Sixteenth Street. Shabby and uninviting from the outside, the place was shoehorned between a Spanish-language video store and a cut-rate clothing outfit that advertised used men's suits starting for as little as twenty dollars, "satisfaction guaranteed," according to a hand-painted black and yellow sign. Inside, however, the Café Tyre was dark and sooth-ing, with an assortment of small candlelit tables, wall tapestries depicting scenes from the Mediterranean, antique Oriental carpets underfoot and Moroccan arches overhead. The muted sounds of string music mingled with the aroma of exotic cooking to create a relaxed and intimate atmosphere.

A slight middle-aged woman wearing a white blouse and a long, pleated dark skirt greeted Josie by name and escorted her and Harrigan to a table in the rear. Josie and the woman—her name was Irina, the owner's wife—exchanged pleasantries, and Josie placed their orders without bothering to examine the menu. A few minutes later, Irina returned with a couple of Anchor Steam beers and appetizer plates of dolmas, hummus, and warm pita bread. The lamb and chicken combination plates, she promised, would be along shortly.

Josie took a slow sip of beer, and as Harrigan wolfed down a pair of dolmas, she reached into her bag and pulled out a pen and steno pad. "Ready whenever you are," she said, her eyes directly engag-ing his.

Harrigan began with a general overview of the Ashbourne case and the issues to be litigated in the upcoming hearing. "We're claiming that Ashbourne's trial attorney, J. Arnold Barnes, screwed up both the guilt and penalty phases of his case," he explained. "Barnes botched the guilt phase by not investigating or presenting our client's alibi defense, and he blew the penalty phase by withholding mitigating evidence of Ashbourne's history of child neglect." Harrigan was prepared to elaborate but soon discovered that Josie had indeed reviewed her uncle's legal file and was well versed in the habeas-corpus claims pending before Judge Blake. Her familiarity with the case enabled him to skip ahead to the reasons for his impromptu visit.

"Until this trip to the Bay Area," he said, referring to his encounter with Debray and Ashbourne's "Judas" revelation, "I really didn't think I had a chance of proving that Ashbourne had an alibi defense. I thought all I'd need Carlos for would be to serve a few papers. Now I need a whole team of investigators, and I have no idea where to begin." He drained his beer and ordered another as Irina arrived with their entrees. "If I didn't believe Harold Ashbourne was an innocent man, none of this would really matter. I'd just collect my fee and go through the motions—"

"No, you wouldn't," she interrupted. They stared at each other for a long moment, each knowing that she had hit a nerve. "You don't strike me as a man who just goes through the motions. Am I right?" She turned her attention to her food, as if to indicate by her silence that she expected an answer.

Harrigan did not know how to respond. It wasn't the nature of Josie's question that threw him. Coming from any other person he would have written the inquiry off as the kind of innocuous banter people use to break the ice while attempting a new relationship. But there was something about her manner that made the question sound insightful and sincere. Then again, maybe he was just getting carried away by the easy way that she spoke and brushed the hair off her forehead, the way her lips turned upward when she smiled and she allowed her eyes to linger on his as though she already knew him. All of this, he abruptly realized, reminded him uncannily of Stephanie. It was a sensation he found exciting but also troubling and, to be honest, more than a little frightening.

"You're probably right," he admitted. "But I didn't come here to be psychoanalyzed." As if to rationalize the sharp shift in his demeanor, he reminded himself that a good lawyer never becomes personally involved with his investigator. He had never discussed his private life with Carlos, and he resolved to keep things that way with Josie.

"No, you came here for help to find Debray and the saboteur you call Judas," Josie replied. She was ready to get back to business, neither upset nor visibly disappointed by his unwillingness to talk about himself. "Before I joined my uncle I had a practice over by the courthouse. I've worked on a number of cases that had me literally flailing about in the dark—complex murders for hire, mail fraud, even a civil RICO. One of the things I've learned is that you can't get overwhelmed. You have to use the leads you have and take things a step at a time."

"But we have no leads, " Harrigan said. "We don't even know that there is a Judas."

She shook her head like an annoyed schoolteacher.

"For the time being, I think we have to assume that there is and that Debray's 'unfinished business' is somehow connected to him . . . or her."

Harrigan gave Josie an interested look, encouraging her to state her position more fully. "Our Judas may or may not have been a spy in the classic sense of the term, but what if he was an actual participant in the firebombing?" she asked. "And what if his purpose wasn't to advance the group's left-wing agenda but to destroy it and have its leaders, or at least some of them, arrested?"

"Sounds like a whole lot of speculation to me," Harrigan said skeptically.

"But the Saviors did split up right after the crime," she pressed on with her hypothesis. "So if destroying the group was the objective, Judas certainly did his job."

"That's true," Harrigan conceded.

"You also said that Professor Denton was working on a publication aimed at exposing the infiltration of Saviors of the Earth. Well, I was a graduate student in the Latin American Studies Program at Berkeley when the professor was killed, and I know his academic papers were deposited with the Bancroft Library on campus. I could pick you up in the morning, and we could drive out there together. We could look at the professor's papers and see exactly what he was writing."

She flashed a self-satisfied smile. "If there's any truth to this Judas business, we ought to be able to find something helpful in Denton's work. If not, you'll still have plenty of time to catch an afternoon flight to L.A."

Harrigan was duly impressed. "Sounds like a plan," he said as he laid a wad of bills on the table to cover the dinner tab and tip.

"We'll also have to reinterview the ex-Savior members," Josie added as they headed for the door, "but we can get to that later. And you'll have to add Debray to your witness list, of course."

"Of course, and the sooner, the better."

"Well," she said, still all business, "if you'll give me Debray's declaration, I'll prepare the necessary notice for the court and a service copy for the attorney general tonight. You can sign them tomorrow. There's a process server in our building who can take care of filing them."

"That doesn't leave a whole lot for me to do," Harrigan said, pausing to retrieve Debray's statement from his briefcase.

"All you have to do is walk me home. I have a spare room set up as a home office, and I'll prepare the notice there. It's only a few blocks away, and I could use the company—that is, if you don't mind."

Outside, the fog had begun rolling in over the hills, turning the air cool and damp. They set a brisk pace strolling down Sixteenth Street, turning left on Guerreo, maneuvering their way past fellow pedestrians hurrying to make dinner engagements or complete other last-minute errands before heading home. Like elsewhere in San Francisco, people in the Mission District liked to walk.

Above the houses and assorted storefronts the blue dome of the Basílica de San Francisco—the early twentieth-century addition to the venerable Mission Dolores—was clearly visible despite the onrushing fog. Commissioned in 1776 by the Spanish *padre* Junipero Serra in honor of Saint Francis of Assisi, the mission was the historic center of the district that bore its name. Its chapel was the city's oldest building and one of the original adobe outposts the Spanish constructed over the length of colonial California to convert the local savages and expand the empire. Over five thousand of the now extinct Costanoan Indians who toiled for the Franciscan fathers were buried in an unmarked grave, the "Grotto of Lourdes," inside the mission's walled cemetery. Although the days of conquest were long gone, the mission survived, performing double duty right up to the present as a local church run by the archdiocese of San Francisco and a regional landmark offering daily tours to the public for the suggested donation of a dollar a head.

"The Mission Dolores," Josie said as they turned down a side street, "was where I was baptized, confirmed, and married. It's hard to believe, all that in the little chapel."

"Oh, so you're married." Harrigan tried to disguise the disappointment in his voice, but it came through nonetheless.

"I *was* married, as in past tense, to a secular Jewish guy from Palo Alto who had no objection to my parents' insistence on a Catholic ceremony. Marvin and I have been history for five years now."

"I'm sorry."

"Don't be," she replied. "I left my graduate program to put him through law school. He was going to go into public interest, but he became a partner in one of those buttoned-down corporate firms in the financial district. After that we just grew apart. I'm well rid of my ex. And besides,"—she gestured at the brightly colored Queen Anne Victorian row house they had stopped in front of—"he left me the house and enough money to buy the BMW you'll be chauffeured around in tomorrow. What about you?" she asked as she fished her keys out of her handbag. "Have you ever been married?"

"No." He blurted out the lie almost instinctively, as if to shield himself from the pain that a truthful answer might have elicited.

"Just haven't met the right woman yet, is that it?" She sensed his reticence and decided to back off without insisting on an answer. He seemed like the straight-up heterosexual type, she thought to herself, but in this town, you never knew. "Well, I've got some work to do," she said politely. "I'll pick you up at eight." She smiled and began to walk up the wooden steps to her front door.

"We'll have breakfast," he called after her.

"I'll look forward to it," she called back.

Harrigan watched her disappear inside, regretting as she closed the door that he had lacked the courage to level with her.

EIGHT

The night did nothing to dull Josie's image in Harrigan's mind. No matter how hard he tried to direct his attention to other matters, his thoughts drifted back to her. He envisioned her again and again struggling with the gold hoop earring at her office, taking shorthand notes at the Café Tyre, strolling down Guerrero Street, the wind tousling her incredible black hair. The images lingered as he took in the ten o'clock news over a quiet scotch and soda at the Hotel Mayfair bar. They broke his concentration as he retired to his room and tried to draft a memo on his meetings with Debray and Ashbourne. They even prevented him from finding refuge in the pages of the latest John Grisham potboiler.

Harrigan tried to tell himself that the attraction was only physical and would abate as soon as he returned to L.A. and connected with Sheri Landis or any one of several other oversexed women he had dated in the past three years. He reminded himself that he hardly knew Josie and that in all likelihood she would be in and out of his life in a month or two. There was no point in getting close to her.

By the time he finally convinced himself that he

had no business fantasizing like a lovestruck teen-ager, it was nearly three o'clock in the morning. He fell into a dreamless slumber that under other cir-cumstances might have lasted past noon. But he had left strict instructions with the night clerk for a wake-up call at six-thirty, and with less than four hours of sleep, he woke up feeling every one of his forty-five years.

Getting out of bed was always difficult, particu-larly on cold, crisp mornings, and today was no ex-ception. Slowly stirring to life, Harrigan switched on the nightstand lamp and tuned in the clock radio to KZSF, the local FM station that specialized in in-depth news reports and public-affairs programming. He listened to the morning headlines as his head cleared, then strapped on the special waterproof prosthesis he used for swimming, and in what seemed a supreme act of will, dragged himself to the shower. It wasn't until he had finished his shower and had lathered up for a quick shave that he heard his name mentioned on the radio.

Senior deputy attorney general William Pickering, his opposing counsel on the Ashbourne case, was being interviewed by John Aragon, one of the sta-tion's investigative reporters, as part of a larger series on the future of capital punishment. The sound of Pickering's pompous, adenoidal voice was even more disagreeable over the airwaves than in person, but Harrigan was only mildly surprised by the interview. The death penalty was an endless source of fascina-tion for the media, and as one of the deputies special-izing in federal habeas litigation for the San Francisco branch of the California Department of Justice, Pickering had a well-documented penchant for getting his name in the news.

"The people of this state, and the country as a whole," Pickering pontificated to his imagined listeners in radioland, "want to see the death penalty implemented, and my office is committed to seeing that it is."

"And how do the state's prospects look in the case of Harold Ashbourne?" Aragon asked, trying to steer Pickering away from rhetorical pronouncements and back to the details of the upcoming hearing.

"Harold Ashbourne was convicted in 1983 of two counts of murder resulting from a politically motivated firebombing in the Berkeley Hills one year earlier. A university professor and his teenage son burned to death as a result of Ashbourne's inexcusable and highly calculated actions. I'd say our prospects are very strong. Very strong indeed."

"I understand that Ashbourne's present lawyer, Peter Harrigan, is arguing that his client was denied effective assistance of counsel at trial. Would you care to elaborate on that point?"

"You know, John," Pickering said, affecting a world-weary tone, "these claims are raised in virtually every death-penalty appeal. If you can't win on the law and if the facts are against you, you attack the trial lawyer's competence. It's a perverse little game appellate lawyers like to play to buy time when they have no real issues to raise. In our view, Art Barnes, Ashbourne's trial counsel, was one of the most distinguished members of the Alameda County Public Defender's Office."

"Thank you, Mr. Pickering," Aragon said, nearly

cutting off the loquacious deputy attorney general in mid-sentence. "This reporter attempted to contact Harold Ashbourne's present attorney, Peter Harrigan of Pasadena, late yesterday afternoon, but there was no answer at his law office. We will provide continuing coverage of the Ashbourne case, along with several others, as part of a series examining the future of the death penalty in California."

It was only after Aragon had signed off and Harrigan returned his attention to the lather still spread across his face that he noticed the tiny rivulet of blood streaming down his left cheek. Realizing he had nicked himself below the ear, he washed the soap from his face and applied a styptic pencil to close the small but stinging wound. As he gazed at himself in the mirror, the metaphor was all too obvious, even at this early hour: Pickering had drawn first blood even before the Ashbourne hearing had commenced.

Harrigan found Josie waiting in the hotel lobby at twenty minutes to eight. Dressed in a pair of tight-fitting jeans, black turtleneck, and a brown leather jacket cut attractively at the waist, she was seated in an overstuffed lounge chair, sipping a cup of black coffee, her head buried in the front section of the morning *Chronicle*. A stylish slim valise rested by her feet.

"Good morning," he said, sliding into the chair next to hers. "I didn't expect you for another ten minutes."

She pulled the newspaper away from her face and gave him a friendly handshake and a businesslike smile. "I believe in getting an early start. I've reserved us a table in the coffee shop if that offer of breakfast is still on."

"You bet," Harrigan assured her. "Why don't you go on in and get started? I'll join you after I check out."

"I think you'll find your hotel bill's already been prepared. I've also made arrangements with one of the garage attendants to return your rental car for you." She surveyed the quizzical expression on his face. "Don't worry, he's a homeboy from the Mission, and I've slipped him a twenty for his trouble. I can drop you off at the airport when we're through," she assured him. "I hope you don't mind."

"No, not at all," Harrigan mumbled, more surprised than bothered. He deposited his car key in Josie's outstretched palm. It had been more than half a lifetime, since his mother stopped running his life in high school, that anyone had planned out his day the way Josie seemed to be doing this morning. Back then, he couldn't wait to get out from under his mother's thumb. Somehow he didn't mind Josie's efforts. But then Mom never filled out a pair of Levi's the way his new investigator did. Contented to follow Josie's lead, he trailed after her into the restaurant.

Although the coffee shop was crammed with businessmen and tourists revving up with caffeine for the day, Josie managed to secure a large booth normally reserved for parties of four. "I thought we might need some room to spread out," she said as they each ordered a continental breakfast and coffee.

Opening her valise, she pulled out the notice she

had prepared for the federal court to add Debray to the list of Ashbourne's witnesses. "I hope it's okay," she said, handing the document to Harrigan.

He perused the notice carefully. It was a short, concise document prepared according to the specifications of the district court's filing rules. It consisted of a short advisement that Henri Debray, also known as Henry Dershaw, would be called as a witness on behalf of the petitioner Harold Ashbourne III. The notice also included a brief declaration from Harrigan explaining that he had made contact with Debray only two days ago and was acting diligently in adding him to the witness list. Also attached was a copy of the statement Debray had given Harrigan at the conclusion of their meeting in Berkeley. Impressed with the quality of Josie's draftsmanship, Harrigan signed the notice and his declaration and handed the pleading back to her.

"We can drop the notice off at my filing service on our way out of the city," she said, slipping the papers back into her valise. "They'll take care of the AG's copy.

"So," she added, cradling a cup of freshly brewed coffee in her hands, "I see you've cut yourself shaving. You must have heard Pickering on the radio."

"As a matter of fact, I did." Harrigan gazed at Josie, blushing at the way she so easily read him. The woman had brains, terrific writing skills, long legs, a butt he couldn't take his eyes off, and now an uncanny sense of intuition. What else did she have to offer?

"They probably taped the interview last night," she speculated.

"Probably. Pickering's fond of burning the midnight oil."

"Is he as much of a weenie as he sounded, or am I just prejudiced against prosecutors who enjoy public executions?"

"In some ways he's even worse in the flesh. He's a skinny little runt, about five foot six. He always wears these dorky bow ties that make him look like a Harvard professor." They shared a laugh at the unattractive portrait.

"The trouble is," Harrigan said, resuming an air of seriousness, "he's a darned good attorney, and unlike a lot of other prosecutors he doesn't play games with discovery. He's given me complete access to the People's files in the case, not that it's done me any good."

"And Arnold Barnes, Ashbourne's trial lawyer? Is he really the bumbler we make him out to be?"

"J. Arnold Barnes used to be a pretty fair trial lawyer, but right before the Ashbourne trial his wife ran off with one of his former clients—some young stud who rode a Harley, had wild animal tattoos on his biceps, and had just done a stretch at Soledad for armed robbery. Barnes started hitting the bottle hard. He even showed up in court one morning stewed to the gills to argue a change of venue motion. He's in his late fifties now, and from what I gather, he's just marking time until he can retire to settle down to some truly serious drinking."

"So you think he really screwed up Ashbourne's case?"

"What I think doesn't matter," Harrigan said grimly. "The supreme court's really tightened up on these kinds of cases in the past few years. In order to win, we're going to have to show that Barnes' mistakes cost Ashbourne a fair trial. That's not going to be easy."

Josie finished her croissant and wiped the flakes from her lips. "Then we better get to work," she said, reaching for her valise and jacket. "If you'll get the check, I'll meet you out front with my car, say, in about ten minutes."

Harrigan watched Josie as she strolled out of the coffee shop, taking in her every move. He paid the bill and in the time-honored tradition of solo practitioners everywhere, he headed for the public phones at the rear of the hotel lobby to check on the messages at his office.

Although it was already eight-thirty, Dennis had not yet arrived, and Harrigan's call was answered by his own voice on the office message machine. Dennis was probably lingering over a cup of cappuccino and a cheese Danish in some precious café where the radio was permanently tuned to a classical music station specializing in Bach concertos. Harrigan made a mental note to cross-examine Dennis about his choice of coffee bars and then punched in the three-digit playback code.

The messages began with a personal call from Mark Clemons, touting the attributes of yet another perfect woman—this time an aerobics instructor with surprise, surprise, outstanding upper body development—whom he had met just the night before in an Old Town bistro. Clemons was followed by none other than John Aragon, who, true to his word, had tried to contact Harrigan for a comment on the Ashbourne case, albeit after five, when he might have known the office would be closed.

After Clemons there were two hang-ups. Harrigan was prepared to hang up, too, when the tape beeped again and another message started to play. "I'm calling for Peter Harrigan," the speaker said. It was a female voice, weak-sounding, raspy and hesitant, either that of an older woman or someone middle-aged in poor health or suffering from an anxiety disorder. "You don't know me, but I've been following the case of Harold Ashbourne for some time. I just wanted you to know that I support everything you're doing to free this innocent man."

The caller paused to catch her breath, then struggled to continue. "But I'm afraid for you. The people you're seeking have killed before. Please be careful. God bless you, and your poor departed family."

In his long career as a lawyer Harrigan had received more crank phone calls than he could possibly remember. They were a hazard of the trade, and he usually brushed them aside as quickly as he heard them. But as much as he might have wanted to dismiss this call as the ravings of another loony tune he found it impossible to do so. The caller sounded too genuine, too sincere, and, above all, too knowledgeable.

Harrigan quickly placed another call to his office and left a message of his own, instructing Dennis to preserve the tape and request that the phone company put a trace on the call. In all likelihood, Pacific Bell would tell Dennis to fly a kite, but at least he'd have something to occupy his time until Harrigan returned to fill his life again with mundane administrative chores.

NINE

Josie was waiting for Harrigan at the hotel's front entrance behind the wheel of her red BMW 735i.L sedan. Appointed with a glove-leather interior, a sunroof, and all the luxury trimmings except a car phone, the vehicle was far beyond the normal price range of a private investigator. Putting Marvin through law school did indeed have its compensation.

Josie expected to see Harrigan's eyebrows raise as he slipped into the passenger seat and was genuinely surprised by the pensive, troubled expression on his face. "I'm sorry I took so long," she said, hoping it was the unexpected delay she had encountered retrieving the car from the hotel's valet parking lot that was bothering him.

"No, it's not that," he said, preoccupied with the phone message from the raspy-voiced woman.

"What, then?" she asked as she weaved her way through the downtown traffic toward the Bay Bridge. "The IRS seize your assets? Your ex-wife increase her alimony demand?" She looked at him, expecting to evoke a laugh or at least a trace of a smile. Finding neither, and slightly annoyed by his reticence, she decided to continue to tease until he broke out of his sudden funk. "Oh, I forgot, you're a confirmed bachelor, and the quiet type to boot."

Harrigan looked at her, cracking a small grin as their eyes met. "You don't miss a beat, do you?"

"Not if I can help it, and, more important, not if I can help. It's what I get paid for."

Reluctantly, Harrigan told her about the warning from the raspy-voiced caller, stopping short, however, of relating the caller's references to his deceased family. Although he had misgivings about telling another half truth, he still wasn't ready to talk about his wife and kids. At least not now, in a car heading back into Berkeley.

"If it will make you feel any better, I can start to carry my .38." She took in his startled look and chuckled quietly to herself. "I can assure you I know how to use it."

"So you don't think it was a crank call, either."

"I think you should look at it as some kind of wake-up call. These kinds of cases are dangerous."

Harrigan gave her another confused look. She was revealing yet another side of her many-faceted personality, a rough, streetwise dimension completely at odds with her fashion-plate appearance and gentle, social-worker manners.

"Look," she tried to explain, "the state wants to kill your client—I'm sorry, *our* client—for murdering two innocent people, right?"

She didn't wait for him to answer. "If our client really is innocent, as you maintain, someone out there—the real guilty party—can't be feeling too happy about you turning over rocks and digging up clues he thought were dead and buried a decade ago.

I'm not saying that someone's going to try to knock us off, just that we have to be careful."

"I don't know what to make of you, Josie," Harrigan said as they crossed the bridge and took the freeway into Berkeley. "First you sound like my mother, getting my hotel bill ready and all, now you sound like a better-looking, female version of Humphrey Bogart."

"I'm a multitalented girl," she replied, looking pleased as Harrigan began to laugh. She had finally succeeded in puncturing his dark mood.

Driving into Berkeley with Josie was an entirely different experience from arriving unescorted and alone. She was a frequent visitor and knew the place like a native from her student days. Traveling along a confusing network of surface streets, they entered the city limits by ten o'clock, with Josie playing the role of personal tour guide. Among the featured sights she pointed out the coffee bar where she had worked on weekends as a college senior, the food co-op she had belonged to, and the apartment she once lived in off Benevue Avenue, not far from the building where newspaper heiress Patty Hearst had been kidnapped in 1974 by the Symbionese Liberation Army.

Harrigan was concerned about the time her little excursion was adding to their day, but he sensed it was important for her to share something of her college experience with him. Unlike him, she spoke easily about her life, and he raised no objections to what would in any event be a pleasant digression from the day's business.

"Living here was a real eye-opener for a good Catholic girl like me," she said as they found a parking space off Dwight Way near campus. "It wasn't all that long ago, but sometimes it seems like another lifetime."

"I know exactly how you feel," Harrigan said sympathetically. "I got my undergraduate degree from the University of Colorado and hardly recognized the place the last time I was there."

"Look, there's something I want to show you," she said, taking him by the hand as they headed down the hill for Telegraph Avenue.

They walked on for another block and a half when she came to an abrupt halt. "Here," she said, pointing at the section of sidewalk at their feet. Carved in the cement were the words BOYCOTT GRAPES.

It was a perfectly unremarkable piece of political graffiti except for one thing: the word *boycott* had originally been misspelled with only one T. Someone had come along later, before the cement had dried, added the second T with a proofreader's carat and, in the fashion of a schoolteacher, placed the symbol for a spelling error—"Sp."—next to the correction.

"I suppose you did that," Harrigan said bemusedly.

"In the middle of a farmworkers' strike," she confessed. "I was on the student support committee. Every time I come here, I check the sidewalk for my handiwork," she confessed. "As long as it's here, I feel connected to my past. I know it's kind of silly, but to me it's important."

Harrigan passed up the opportunity to comment on her observations, and in another moment they left

Josie's sidewalk shrine behind and hurried off to the university.

The past was what the Bancroft Library was all about. Though only a stone's throw from the trendy hubbub of Sproul Plaza and the zaniness of Telegraph Avenue, the library was something of an intellectual tomb. It was not only the repository of the university archives but the home of an astonishing collection of rare books and documents, from the diaries of Father Junipero Serra to the letters of Gertrude Stein, papers from the Donner Party, and the journals of Mark Twain. The library was also the final resting place of the manuscripts and collected correspondence of lesser-known figures such as Professor Gilbert Denton.

To protect its valuable collection, the Bancroft observed a strict protocol prohibiting any containers from being carried into the main reading room. Ink was also forbidden. The library provided its own pencils for note taking and permitted tape recorders and portable computers to be used, but only in designated areas.

Josie was acquainted with the rules from prior visits and led Harrigan to the library locker room, where they deposited their pens and briefcases before presenting themselves for inspection in the wood-paneled reception area outside the main reading hall. A harried little man with a pair of bifocals and a wispy red beard greeted them from behind a high-gloss modern desk, where he was feverishly working on a personal computer. Framed against a display of rich oil paintings on the walls depicting heroic scenes of covered wagons crossing the Western frontier, the man looked urban, uncomfortable, and out of place.

"I'll need picture IDs from each of you, and you'll have to fill out this registration form," the man said impatiently. He handed them each a three-by-seven-inch form to complete, barely taking his eyes off the computer screen.

"Are you sure you don't want to conduct a strip search?" Harrigan asked, offended by the man's officious tone.

"The Bancroft Library must do everything it can to guard against the theft or destruction of its collection," the man replied, peering over his glasses with a supercilious sneer. "The card catalogue is located right inside the double glass doors. Just write down the call numbers of the material you want to review on the registration form and hand it to the librarian behind the counter." His brief lecture completed, the man returned to his computer as Harrigan and Josie made their way through the double doors to the interior.

It took Harrigan and Josie only about five minutes to find the call number for Professor Denton's collected papers and another fifteen minutes for the librarian to deliver the two cardboard file boxes that made up the collection.

The librarian was a plump, good-natured white woman in her mid-forties, whose name tag announced to readers and researchers that she was Mary Henderson. Like the harried little sentinel at the reception desk, Mary also seemed the nervous type but without any of her colleague's nastiness. "Normally, we don't allow members of the public to remove the cartons to the library tables, but if you take a seat right over there," she said, motioning to the heavy wooden table closest to the reception counter, "I'll let you take the cartons with you. If you want anything photocopied, just let me know."

Professor Denton might never have qualified as a household name, but his life's work gave ample testimony to the breadth of his interests and academic accomplishments. Each of the cartons contained several accordion file folders crammed with typed manuscripts, handwritten notes, and letters. The files, which had been donated by the professor's wife, were organized in roughly chronological fashion and numbered sequentially, although without any comprehensive index or annotations.

The first folder appeared to contain a typewritten draft of Denton's Ph.D. dissertation, submitted in the early sixties, when he was a graduate student at Stanford. The manuscript was entitled "The Southern Pacific Railroad: Its Influence on the California Statehouse in the Late 19th and Early 20th Centuries." Written in readable if uninspired prose, it told how the early railway barons gained control over governmental regulatory bodies, acquired vast landholdings in the Central Valley, and managed, with the aid of local authorities, to consolidate their vast real estate empires with ruthless evictions of farmers from disputed land. The evictions, according to Denton, culminated in a pitched battle known as the Shootout at Mussel Slough in 1880 near the town of Hanford in what is today Kings County. Six farmers lost their lives, and the incident became part of the legacy of the American West, serving as the backdrop for at least two turn-of-the-century novels.

Denton's interest in California history and politics was also evident in his later work. Folder number two contained the draft notes of a humorous article published in a prestigious academic quarterly shortly after he achieved the rank of full professor at Berkeley. The article examined the little-known but persistent secessionist movements in the state's past. "From the inception of statehood to World War II and beyond, there have been nearly twenty attempts to divide California into two or three independent political entities," Denton began the article. A detailed profile of the organizations and individuals behind the secessionist drives followed, culminating in Denton's own tongue-in-cheek proposal for cleaving California into three new polities, corresponding to the predominant natural and social characteristics of the state's northern, central, and southern regions. The new entities would be named Logland, Fogland, and Smogland.

Harrigan and Josie laughed aloud at the professor's surprisingly droll wit. "I had no idea Denton had a sense of humor like that," Harrigan commented. "If you were a prosecutor, you couldn't ask for a more appealing corpse." Spoken at a very unlibrary-like volume, Harrigan's unsavory observations provoked disturbed stares from several readers at nearby tables and a stern "shush" from Mary. The librarian pointed at a small sign mounted on the reference counter which reminded patrons that the rule of silence was to be observed at all times.

Chastened by the reprimand, Harrigan and Josie

returned to their cartons and began to page through the draft manuscripts of two ponderous tomes Denton had written in the late sixties and early seventies. The first was a biography of California's Depression-era governor, Frank Merriam, the right-wing Republican who defeated the Socialist writer Upton Sinclair with the help of money from the Hollywood studios in the 1934 election. The second was a scholarly study, replete with hundreds of footnotes, of the Okie immigration into the Central Valley during the 1930s. Each work had been published in hardback, and though Denton probably netted less than a thousand dollars per book, the Merriam biography garnered him an award from the California Historical Society.

The mid-seventies seemed to mark a turning point in Denton's interests as the professor produced an impressive series of articles and one highly regarded book—*The Greening of the Golden State*—on the pivotal role of water in the history of California. Sounding anything like the conservative turncoat Debray had portrayed, Denton crafted *Greening* with the thoroughness of an academic and the heart of a level-headed environmentalist. "The struggle to control and manipulate scarce water resources," Denton wrote for a book jacket proof that his wife had attached to the typewritten manuscript for his collected papers, "has been at the heart of California's history since the earliest times. It has also been at the heart of the state's most expensive public works projects and some of its most Byzantine political intrigues."

"I've seen this one in the stores," Josie whispered as they scanned the manuscript. "Sounds a lot like

Chinatown," she added, referring to the movie about the power politics and double-dealing surrounding the construction of the Owens Valley Aqueduct, the early twentieth-century project that brought water from the east slope of the Sierras to Los Angeles, enabling the city to grow into a modern smog-choked megalopolis.

Oddly, however, after the 1979 publication of *Greening,* Denton's productivity appeared to decline precipitously. Apart from annual updates to his lecture notes, the only documents in the files bearing dates from the 1980s were letters contained in a thin volume of correspondence. There were letters to various colleagues about academic conferences, letters to various mainstream environmental groups, such as the Sierra Club, and even a letter to a friend in Madrid about a European vacation the professor had planned for the summer of 1980 to study the ruins of the old Roman aqueducts.

To Harrigan's disappointment, there was no reference in the entire correspondence file to Henri Debray or Saviors of the Earth. Only a single letter, a scant three paragraphs, written to Denton's editor on *The Greening of the Golden State,* offered even the slightest hint about the professor's dealings with the Saviors. Written in September 1981, the letter was a proposal for a new book on water policy. Unlike *Greening,* which offered a broad statewide overview of water policy, the new work was to focus exclusively on the water issues of the farm-rich Central Valley. Denton explained that he had completed about fifty percent of the research for the book and that he intended to collaborate on the project with a young professor named Charles West. Harrigan and Josie recognized West as a former member of Saviors, and now a tenured professor of political science at Berkeley.

Harrigan removed the letter from the correspondence file and walked it back to Mary at the reference desk. "I'd like a copy of this," he said, handing her the single sheet of paper.

Mary held the letter to the light and regarded it carefully. "This must be a pretty important document," she commented. "Someone else had me copy it the day before yesterday."

"What did you say?" Harrigan asked, taken completely off guard.

"I said that someone came in here Wednesday morning, looked through the same boxes, and asked for a copy of the same letter."

"Who?"

"I'm sorry, but I'm not supposed to reveal the names of our readers." She looked more tense than ever, clearly regretting that she had volunteered any information at all.

"Look, this is very important," Harrigan pleaded. "A man's life is in jeopardy. I wouldn't be asking if I didn't need to know." Sensing that his efforts at persuasion were failing, he removed his bar card from his jacket and displayed it before the increasingly anxious librarian. "You can tell me now or receive a subpoena for the information later this afternoon. I don't think they'll take no for an answer in federal court."

Mary tapped her fingers nervously on the counter as her facial expression changed from a look of agitation to resignation. "Wait here," she said in a defeated tone. She retreated through a rear door marked STAFF ONLY. Ninety seconds later, she re-emerged with a photocopy of Denton's letter and a registration form like the one Harrigan had handed her earlier that morning.

"Robert Randall," she said, standing defensively behind the counter. She handed Harrigan the photocopy and allowed him to peek discreetly at the registration form. The form bore Wednesday's date and the call number of Denton's papers. "He was a thin little man, with curly brown hair and wire-rim glasses. He spoke with a slight Southern drawl and had a really terrible cough, if I remember correctly."

Mary took a hard swallow, looking as though she had just violated a state secret. "I trust that's all you need from me," she said indignantly.

"Yes, thank you, you've been a great help. I didn't mean to upset you," Harrigan replied gently. Under more relaxed circumstances he might have offered a few more words of apology or made an attempt at friendly small talk. But Mary's revelations had caused his thoughts to race, and he felt the time slipping away. It was Debray, he knew, who had reviewed Denton's papers. He was still in the area and at least two steps ahead of them.

TEN

Professor Charles West had an office on the eighth floor of Barrows Hall, a nondescript concrete and glass fortress east of Sproul Plaza that the regents had added to the campus during the building boom of the early sixties. Fortunately for Harrigan, the professor had his regularly scheduled office hours on Friday afternoon. This was the time when West paused from his research to hold court for students in need of academic inspiration, guidance on independent-study projects, or frank explanations of the mediocre grades they had received on midterm exams.

The professor's room, though far larger than the usual academic cubbyhole, was a picture of clutter and disorder. Bookshelves crammed with hardcovers and paperbacks dissecting every great moment in Western politics, from the storming of the Bastille to the Lincoln-Douglas debates and the latest retrospectives on the Reagan presidency lined the walls from floor to ceiling. Magazines, undergraduate term papers, and other works in progress lay in untidy piles on the professor's old wooden desk and visitors' chairs. Heavy plumes of blue smoke from the professor's pipe also hung heavily in the air.

To those not already acquainted with Charles West, the professor gave the impression of being the quintessential absentminded intellectual, replete with a not so neatly trimmed salt-and-pepper beard, thick black hair that hung shaggily over his ears and shirt collar, and the trademark corduroy sport jacket that looked like a Salvation Army thrift shop special. In reality, West was anything but absentminded. While he would never win awards for housekeeping or sartorial splendor, he was the author of three controversial books on the history of American socialism and a tenured member of the political science department known for his sharp tongue, penetrating wit, and steel-trap memory.

Although West had met Harrigan only once before, during a brief interview in this very office more than two years ago, he instantly recognized him as Harold Ashbourne's appellate lawyer. "Ah, Mr. Harrigan," he said, hurriedly completing a final thought on his laptop computer, "I've been wondering when you would be getting around to me again." He gave Harrigan and Josie a friendly smile and invited them to take seats on the old sofa by the office window. "I remember you, but if I'm not mistaken, you were accompanied by an older gentleman the last time," he added, alluding to Josie's Uncle Carlos.

Harrigan nodded and introduced Josie, referring to her only as his new investigator. "We're here about Harold," he said, wasting no time. "His federal court hearing is set to go in less than a month."

"I know," West replied. "There was a short article in the *Chronicle* the other day. But I think I made it quite clear before that I have no idea who killed Gilbert Denton."

As West spoke, Josie pulled a manila legal file from her briefcase and began to flip through the pages until she came to the notes her uncle had taken at West's previous interview. "You said that you were playing Scrabble with two old friends. Fred Wallace and Sylvia Peterson. They were activists with the Saviors group, too."

"I think I also said that I had severed my relationship with Saviors before the bombing." West sounded irritated by what he regarded as Josie's aggressive tone. "Debray and I had come to a parting of the ways."

"Over what?" Josie asked.

West hesitated as though searching for the right words. "I was always less enamored of the marriage of Marxism and ecology than Henry—excuse me, *Henri*."

"You and Debray were rivals, weren't you?" Josie continued.

"In a small circle of left-wing radicals," West answered. "Debray was more of the visionary and I was more of the traditionalist, you might say. You know, all power to the working class." He looked at Harrigan and Josie to see if they were following along. "I believed that if you really wanted to change this country, issues of race, income, and the distribution of wealth were more important than the environment. Debray felt just the opposite. In time, the uneasy compromise we had worked out simply fell apart."

"So you retreated to the safety of the university?" Harrigan asked.

For a moment West seemed to take offense at Harrigan's sarcasm. "I was serious about my role as a scholar. Besides, the country was changing. America had elected Ronald Reagan president. I just didn't think it made much sense to be shouting about revolution on Telegraph Avenue. It was time to grow up."

"And Professor Denton?" Harrigan served up another question. "How did he fit into the rivalry?"

West stroked his beard and pondered the question. "Denton was the archetypal liberal intellectual. He recognized the inequities of the world but wanted everyone to love him. Sooner or later he and Debray were bound to clash. But, then, I'm sure you know the story."

"Refresh my memory, if you don't mind," Harrigan said, taking a strong dislike to West's superior attitude.

"We were just assistant professors—young white males who were lucky to have landed jobs at a university like this. To get along, we had to go along—I think that's the proper cliché. We had to play the game, teach our classes, genuflect before the senior faculty, and stay out of trouble. That was something Debray just couldn't accept. He pushed the Saviors business until it interfered with his responsibilities in the department."

"And Denton had no choice but to crack down on him," Harrigan said.

"He refused to renew Debray's contract for the winter quarter of 1982. Henry reacted like a wild man and leafleted the campus with an open letter accusing Denton of selling out the ecology movement over the Peripheral Canal. He delivered speeches on and off campus, linking the canal, and Denton, to the center of some mass conspiracy to pollute and enslave the planet. If you ask me, the canal was just a convenient excuse to vent his rage."

"Was it enough of an excuse to blow up Denton's house?" Josie asked.

"Frankly, I don't think Henry had either the stomach or the technical know-how to pull that off. And as for Ashbourne, he was the closest thing the Saviors had to a pacifist." West looked at his wristwatch as if growing weary of the interrogation.

"That's a relief," Harrigan said, "because I may want you to testify about Ashbourne's nonviolent character."

"No problem. Just let my secretary know when you need me." West looked at his watch again, hoping that he had answered his last question of the afternoon. He glanced at his office door, silently hinting for Harrigan and Josie to politely excuse themselves. He was visibly annoyed to see that they remained riveted to the couch.

"I also think you should know that Debray is going to testify for us," Harrigan said matter-of-factly.

West's pale complexion suddenly colored. He straightened his back and took a series of deep drags on his pipe. For the time being he seemed unable to speak.

"When?" West practically coughed out the question.

"I met with him the day before yesterday, in Sproul Plaza," Harrigan answered archly. "He said he's prepared to corroborate Harold's alibi and that he's committed to bringing the true perpetrators to justice." Harrigan was enjoying himself. Seeing West squirm at the mention of Debray was the most fun he'd had since leaving L.A.

"That's fantastic news," West responded unconvincingly. "What did he say about the real killers?"

"I'm afraid we can't reveal that," Josie interjected quickly, receiving a nod of approval for her deft thinking from Harrigan. "We were wondering, however, if Debray has gotten in touch with you."

"I haven't seen him since well before the bombing."

Before West could say more, a young girl poked her head into the office. She must have been no more than twelve or thirteen years old, with long, dark hair, blue eyes, a high, intelligent forehead and an expression far too serious for her age. She and West shared a moment of uneasy recognition. "You said you'd be finished by three-thirty," the girl said.

"Just give me a few minutes," West replied, waving the girl back into the hallway. She disappeared without protest, leaving Josie and Harrigan with the fleeting impression that she bore a striking facial resemblance to West.

"There's just one other thing, and then we'll leave you in peace," Harrigan said. "How did *you* get along with Professor Denton?"

"He was the head of my department," West answered quickly, anxious to bring the interview to a close. "I showed him respect and made sure I taught my classes, but I kept my distance. We didn't have much to do with each other."

"That's odd," Harrigan said, passing the letter from the Bancroft Library across the desk to West. "I obtained this from Denton's collected papers earlier today."

West read the letter slowly and carefully, like a CPA scanning an audit notice from the IRS. "I've never seen this before," he said finally. "Either Denton changed his mind or the book proposal was rejected, but he never asked me to collaborate with him. Was there anything else in his papers about the new book?"

"No, there wasn't," Harrigan said, thoroughly unconvinced by West's explanation.

West handed the letter back to Harrigan and rose to his feet. "I'm sorry, but I have to end our discussion now. Just let me know when you'll need me in court." He opened the office door and escorted Harrigan and Josie into the hallway.

As they made their way to the elevator, they could hear the young girl's voice again as she caught up with West. Even from the other end of the corridor, they could hear her refer to him as "Daddy."

"I didn't know he had a daughter," Josie said as she pushed the elevator's down button.

Harrigan's lips curled into a shape somewhere between a half smile and a sneer. "I didn't know he was such a lying sack of shit, either," he said.

ELEVEN

"It will take at least an hour to get to San Francisco International," Josie said, her eyes on the lookout for merging southbound traffic on the freeway leading out of Berkeley. "Okay?"

It was nearly four-thirty, and the main artery to the Bay Bridge was already choked with trucks, cars, buses, and delivery vans. As she drove, she checked her makeup in the rearview mirror, smoothing away imagined imperfections on her cheeks and eyebrows.

"Sure. What's another hour?" Harrigan shrugged his shoulders and gazed at the gridlock in front of him. At this rate it would be ten o'clock at the earliest before he got home. He hadn't spoken directly with Dennis since Tuesday and his office was likely to be a mess, but he hated the thought of leaving the Bay Area with Debray on the loose and a head full of unanswered questions. "I assume you'll contact the rest of the old Saviors up here and follow up on any leads," he said, suddenly feeling fatigued from his sleepless night.

"I'm already planning my itinerary, beginning with a juicy subpoena for our friend Charles West."

She gave him a sidelong glance as she tuned in the FM radio to the late-afternoon jazz program on KZSF.

"That seems to be everyone's favorite station around here," Harrigan commented idly as he tilted the back rest of his seat to a reclining position. He tried closing his eyes, but he was too wired to sleep.

"It's actually a little hole in the wall that broadcasts out of an old building in the Panhandle area near the Haight Ashbury. It's listener-sponsored, absolutely no commercials, and I've been a subscriber for years. It's run by a bunch of old sixties types."

They crossed onto the Bay Bridge as a medley of old Charlie Parker numbers came over the air, enhanced by the BMW's superior quadraphonic sound system. The sunlight and shadows moving across the dappled blue waters of the bay formed the perfect backdrop to Parker's moody inspirations.

"Come on, don't look so glum," she chided, taking in the tension on Harrigan's face. "I've got a good feeling about this case." She tossed a loose strand of hair from her eyes and moved her head and shoulders ever so gently to the rhythms of the alto sax.

"You really are an optimist, aren't you?" Harrigan asked.

"It never hurts to be optimistic."

"Or to be beautiful."

Harrigan's words caused an awkward silence. He had uttered them without thinking, almost as if talking to himself, and he instantly regretted his lack of self-control. "I'm sorry," he quickly apologized.

"It's okay," she replied just as rapidly. For the first

time since they had met, however, she looked slightly unnerved.

Fearing that he had offended her, he apologized again, sounding more clumsy with each effort. "I don't know what got into me. I mean you're very attractive, don't get me wrong. But I always make it a point not to mix business and pleasure. No, that's not right. I mean I never mix business and . . ." He caught himself before he inadvertently let the S word slip out of his mouth. "I mean business and personal matters. Anyway, I hope you won't hold it against me."

"Not at all." She laughed and shook her head. "Actually, I'm kind of flattered. I was beginning to think you might be—"

"Who, me?" Harrigan interrupted before the issue of his sexual orientation was called into question.

"Well, not really," she assured him, although in truth she hadn't been certain until now. "It's only natural that two people working together would notice each other. I can't say I haven't looked at you, either."

"Then we're even." He flashed a wide grin that made his blue eyes twinkle and his strong face look boyish. "I promise it won't happen again."

"Apology accepted," she replied in a friendly way. "No need to say more."

There was, of course, a lot more that each of them could have said. The attraction was mutual and had been building from the moment Harrigan stuck his head into Carlos' second-floor office.

They drove on in silence, lost for the moment in their own thoughts, oblivious to both the traffic and the fact that the jazz show had ended. The five o'clock hour signaled the beginning of KZSF's Friday evening news magazine, the first segment of which was a public-affairs program hosted by a nasal-voiced junior-college history teacher named Allen Bernstein.

Bernstein waited for his intro music, Otis Redding's "Dock of the Bay," to fade and welcomed his listening audience to another edition of Bay Area Beat, the name he had chosen for his spirited but homespun program. After announcing a list of guests and topics scheduled for future programs, Bernstein introduced his in-studio guest and proclaimed today's topic as "Water: The Rise and Fall of the California Dream." The topic, he explained, was also the title of a new book written by his guest, Robert Jenkins of the Environmental Action Council.

It was not until they exited the Bay Bridge and inched their way into the rush-hour traffic on the 101 Freeway that Josie and Harrigan recognized Jenkins as another former member of Saviors of the Earth.

"These guys are all over the place," Harrigan said, reaching for the radio dial to turn up the volume.

"Have you met him?"

"He's one of the Saviors I interviewed up here a few years back. He's a senior researcher with the EAC. They're a non-profit think tank with offices in Oakland and L.A. Not a bad guy, as I recall. Kind of long-winded, but he has a pretty decent sense of humor for a public-interest type."

As Harrigan gave Josie the skinny on Jenkins, Jenkins and Bernstein were already hot and heavy into the afternoon's agenda. "There have been many scholarly studies on the history of water management in California," Bernstein commented. "One that immediately comes to mind is *The Greening of the Golden State*, written in 1979 by the late Gilbert Denton. But none that I know of is as exciting or controversial as your thought-provoking book."

"You mean you actually read the book, all five-hundred seventeen pages?" Jenkins asked with mock surprise. "I was afraid you might only recommend it as a paperweight."

"Well, it might be suitable for that purpose, too," Bernstein chortled, warming to Jenkins' banter. "But all joking aside, this is really serious stuff."

"Yes, and I'm glad you mentioned Professor Denton, because in many ways I feel indebted to him for his trailblazing research, although I arrive at more far-reaching conclusions. In California, and throughout much of the western United States, water—the stuff we take for granted each time we take a shower, wash dishes, or flush the toilet—is the most vital natural resource we have, more important than oil and more valuable than gold. We can't live without it, we've gone to extraordinary lengths to get it, and while our efforts have paid big dividends in the short run, in the long run they may result in catastrophe."

"I realize that's the thesis of your book," Bernstein said, "and you devote many pages to developing it, but could you summarize your views for us in a few sentences?"

"Maybe the best way to explain my outlook would be to ask your listeners to imagine California as it existed before the arrival of the Spanish. Back then, there were no more than three-hundred thousand native people who patterned their villages and lives around the deserts, marshes, and the numerous wild rivers that made up the natural waterscape."

"Sounds like Jenkins knows his stuff," Josie observed. The traffic crunch began to ease as they passed the downtown area and neared Candlestick Park. Finally she was able to accelerate over twenty miles an hour. "We should make the airport by quarter to six."

"Forget the airport," Harrigan said abruptly. "How long will it take you to drive out to the station?"

"You want me to turn around?"

"As soon as you can."

Responding to the urgency in Harrigan's voice, she flicked on her turn signal and cut over to the nearest off-ramp, drawing a upraised middle finger from an angry motorist behind her. "If I take the surface streets and hustle, we might be able to make it before they're off the air."

Jenkins and Bernstein continued their colloquy as Josie fought her way onto the northbound lanes of Third Street.

"Apart from some minor irrigation," Jenkins said, "the native peoples did little to alter the natural water system. Tulare Lake, for example, in the center of the Great Central Valley, remained as it had for millennia, the region's largest inland body of water. In wet years it had a surface area four times that of Lake Tahoe."

"And today?" Bernstein fed him the obvious one-liner to move the discussion along.

"Today, Tulare Lake no longer exists," Jenkins answered, sounding like Leonard Nimoy hosting an episode of *Unsolved Mysteries*. "The lake has been drained to clear the way for the cultivation of cotton, rice, and other crops that really have no business being cultivated in the Central Valley, given the area's climate and sparse rainfall. Today the course of virtually every major California river system, from the Sierras to the Sacramento Delta and below, has been fundamentally altered—twisted and bent out of shape like so many quadruple heart bypasses. These rivers have been integrated into an enormously expensive and elaborate matrix of dams, pumping stations, and aqueducts to transport enormous quantities of water from the northern section of the state to the arid south. Instead of three-hundred thousand inhabitants we now have over thirty-one million."

"But isn't that progress, as they say?" Bernstein asked, playing the role of an unconvincing devil's advocate.

"From an engineering standpoint that's definitely true," Jenkins conceded. "We've poured billions of dollars into those dams, aqueducts, and pumping stations, and, like the ancient pyramids or the Roman roads, they are a wonder of design and function."

"So what's the down side?" Bernstein asked.

"The down side is that we've gone too far and we're already seeing signs of disaster. We're seeing the destruction of natural water habitats, the contamination of underground aquifers, and the permanent loss of thousands of acres of valuable farmland in the Central Valley to selenium buildup as a result of over-irrigation. We're even seeing animal mutations, two-headed frogs and ducks that can't float, in ponds where agricultural toxins have been drained. It's time to wake up and listen to nature's warning signals. We've got to kick the habit of always seeing more aqueducts, more water, and reckless economic growth as the solution to our problems."

"So what *are* the solutions?"

"Among other things, Allen, I advocate restoring as many river systems as possible to their natural states, and moving away from the cultivation of water-intensive crops like cotton, rice, and alfalfa. I also advocate radical recycling for the cities, and a ban on construction of new aqueducts and dams."

By the time Jenkins completed his admonitions, Josie had taken a left turn and was heading west on Sixteenth Street. It was 5:45 and depending on the crosstown traffic, she was less than fifteen minutes away from the station.

As Josie bobbed and weaved between trolleys and taxi cabs, Bernstein announced that he was "opening up the phones" to the listening audience for the program's final quarter hour.

A series of listeners called in from the far corners of the Bay Area. Some were crackpots and others were serious students and professional types. Some criticized Jenkins for being too radical, others for being too pedestrian. Some wanted to talk about nuclear power, saving the whales, and environmentally safe sources of energy like wind and solar power. Others condemned the environmental movement for wanting to take jobs away from loggers and people in the cities.

Then came the raspy-voiced woman whose phone message Harrigan had received less than eight hours ago. "I think it's important for you to point out, Robert," she said, sounding very much as though she was personally acquainted with Jenkins, "that the so-called water lobby, the people who control the state's water resources, have been on the run since the Peripheral Canal Initiative went down to defeat in 1982." She began to cough and seemed barely able to continue.

"That's the woman!" Harrigan exclaimed as Josie turned down Fell Street and headed down the homestretch for the station. "We've got to make it before she hangs up."

"I couldn't agree more, Kathy," Jenkins replied. "The Department of Water Resources is still working on a few spurs and branches, but the defeat of the canal marked what I hope is the end of the era of the great water projects."

The raspy-voiced woman began to prattle on about the need for what she termed a "revolution of social values" when Bernstein reminded both the woman and Jenkins that they were running out of time.

By the time Josie pulled into the parking lot, Harrigan had his seat belt unbuckled and was ready to bolt. "He knows her name," he shouted, setting a new amputee record for the twenty-yard sprint across the parking lot to the station's front doors.

Inside the station, a volunteer staffer sat behind an old wooden reception desk, listening to the live broadcast coming from Studio A. She was a frumpy-looking woman in her mid-fifties, dressed comfortably in a denim skirt and white blouse. She was also entirely unprepared to deal with a wild man like Harrigan. "I'm sorry, but you can't go in there," she shrieked as Harrigan ran past her toward the illuminated ON AIR sign he saw at the end of a long corridor.

The receptionist's screams brought the station manager and his young female assistant out of an inner office. Together, they raised their hands like traffic cops in an effort to bring Harrigan to a halt.

Determined to reach the broadcast booth, Harrigan reached inside his sports coat. His rapid movements elicited a shrill cry from the receptionist, who had left her post in hot pursuit of the intruder. "He's got a gun!" she shouted.

Everyone—the manager, his assistant, the receptionist, and two more staffers who had bravely ventured into the hallway—hit the floor. A crop of Marine Corps recruits dropping to the turf to give their old sarge twenty push-ups couldn't have reacted more quickly.

Realizing the ruckus he was causing, Harrigan halted his advance. From behind he heard Josie's voice, calm and clear above the chaos. "It's only a bar card," she said. "Everybody relax."

"Oh, shit," the manager mumbled. "Another fucking lawyer."

It took a few minutes for Harrigan to explain himself and convince the manager that there was no need to call the cops. By then Bay Area Beat was over, and the best Harrigan and Josie could muster was a brief interview with Robert Jenkins in a vacant office across the hall from Studio A.

Jenkins, looking much fitter than his forty-five years in a gray T-shirt and stove-pipe jeans, took Harrigan's unannounced visit in stride. After reaffirming his alibi for the night of the Denton bombing—he had been in L.A., having dinner with his parents—he cheerfully agreed to answer any and all questions.

"You could start by telling us the name of your last caller and how we can get in touch with her," Harrigan began. "You referred to her as Kathy."

"Her name's Kathleen Simpson."

"Does she have any connection to Saviors?" Josie interrupted.

"She was Debray's girlfriend, but I haven't seen her in at least a year." Jenkins also denied any recent contact with Debray. He seemed truthful.

Disappointed by the lack of a lead on Simpson, Harrigan decided to test Jenkins' knowledge of Charles West. He gave Jenkins a capsule summary of his encounter with West and showed Jenkins the letter from the Bancroft Library. "Do you have any idea why West would lie about having worked with Denton?" Harrigan asked.

Jenkins considered the question carefully, as if weighing the moral dos and don'ts of snitching on a friend. "Look, I'm not saying that Charlie lied, but I remember him complaining about the way Denton planned on making him his research assistant."

"He found the professor's attitude toward him degrading?" Harrigan asked.

"Denton was a liberal, but he didn't like the really left-wing types. He had just terminated Debray's contract with the poli-sci department, and he warned

Charlie that he was next. The research job was Charlie's last chance to prove that he could hack it as an academic rather than an ideologue. Things got so bad at one point that Denton started to 'Watergate' Charlie's office to see if he was getting the research done."

"Do you know what kind of work Denton wanted Charlie to do?" Josie asked.

"Various things," Jenkins replied. "Mostly a lot of legwork, like researching land ownership in the Central Valley, determining who the contractors were that built the California Aqueduct and the Edmonston Pumping Plant and how much they were paid." He noticed the uncomprehending looks on their faces at the mention of the Edmonston facility and decided to elaborate. "That's the pumping station at the foot of the Tehachapi Mountains. It might just be the most important one in the whole system."

Like West, Jenkins offered to testify in support of Ashbourne's nonviolent character. "I hope I haven't gotten Charlie into any hot water," he added, walking Harrigan and Josie down the hallway and out to the parking lot. "He's probably just stressed out like everybody else. The way things are going in this country, you can never be too careful who you talk to. And by the way, if you do find Kathy, would you let me know where to reach her? There's something I want to tell her."

"About the case?" Harrigan asked as Jenkins slid into the front seat of his VW bug.

Jenkins tapped his fingers lightly against the VW's small black steering wheel. "Oh, you attorneys," he said softly. "No, it's not about the case. It's to say good-bye. The last I heard, she had full-blown AIDS.

She probably doesn't have a lot of time left." He
started his car and pulled out of the lot.

If Harrigan was left without a clue as to Simpson's
whereabouts, he at least had an explanation for her
raspy voice. In a sense that was progress.

TWELVE

"I don't know about you, but I'm getting mighty hungry," Josie said as they headed back toward downtown.

Harrigan glanced at his watch. It was nearly seven and he had his mind on all the backlogged work awaiting him in L.A. "I wouldn't mind a bite, if you know a place on the way to the airport."

"I was thinking of skipping the airport, actually."

"You were what?"

"Don't get excited." She took her eyes off the traffic for an instant and turned toward him. "I was just thinking about West and Professor Denton. It seems pretty clear now that West's hiding something about Denton's last project. Wouldn't you like to find out exactly what Denton was working on?"

"You want to go back and see West? I'm not sure that would be a good idea."

"I'm not suggesting we go back for West. I think we should let him stew in his juices until the hearing."

"What, then?" The absence of nourishment since breakfast had taken its toll, and Harrigan was beginning to sound irritated.

"I think we should look up Denton's wife."

"We've tried that before," Harrigan said bluntly. "She refused to speak with us."

"Well, she's changed her mind." She waited a few seconds for her words to register. "I phoned her last night, and while she's not thrilled about the idea, she's open to seeing us. I didn't set up anything definite, but she told me she has no travel plans and would be home this weekend." She looked at him and gave him that smile of hers. "I guess it just takes a woman's touch. I think we should drive down there tomorrow."

"But she lives outside Bakersfield. That's a good three hundred miles away."

"Two hundred ninety-eight, according to Rand McNally. We can find you a hotel room for the night and make it by afternoon. I'll drive you home afterward."

"Can you afford to take that much time?"

"My older sister lives in Highland Park, and I can stay with her. There's also some work I need to do in L.A. with an old P.I. colleague on some divorce cases. It's no problem, really."

As Harrigan began to warm to the idea of a long drive back to L.A. with Josie, she drove her BMW across Market Street and back into the Mission District. After a few quick turns, she found a parking space on a side street off Valencia lined with modest Victorians. "I thought you wanted to grab something to eat," Harrigan said as she set the emergency brake.

"My parents are expecting me for dinner," she said, getting out of the car. "I hope you don't mind. My mom's a terrific cook."

"No, not at all. I could use a home-cooked meal."

Looking very much like a couple arriving for a Friday evening social engagement, they strolled slowly up the block. For the first time Josie seemed to notice the slight limp in Harrigan's gait. It had been a long day and they were walking uphill. He was tired and the stump sock he wore underneath his prosthesis had begun to wrinkle, causing a twinging sensation when he transferred his weight onto his residual limb. But whether he was just imagining things or she had truly taken note of his disability, neither of them said anything.

Mr. and Mrs. Guzman lived in a brightly colored three-story red, white, and brown "Eastlake Stick-style" Victorian near the end of the block. Except for a little gingerbread millwork on the facade, the house lacked the ornate touches of Josie's more pricy Queen Anne model. There were no rounded turrets, no gabled roof or "witch's hat" tower, but the house was well maintained, with a garage and basement, and large bay windows on the upper floors overlooking the street.

"This is the house my sister and I grew up in," Josie said as they climbed the steep set of concrete steps that led to the front door. "My father was a plant manager for the state Department of Transportation."

"*Mi hija.*" Her father greeted Josie with a loving bear hug. He was a stocky little man, possibly an inch shorter than his daughter, with a receding gray hairline and sparkling black eyes that made him seem younger than a senior citizen living on a government pension. "You're late, and Mama's been worrying about you."

Josie started to explain the reasons for her tardiness when her mother bustled into the living room. Mrs. Guzman threw her arms around her daughter and planted a wet kiss on her cheek. "I've been so worried," the older woman sighed. "You should have been here an hour ago." With her hair tied back in a tight bun and a floral-print apron that made her look plumper than she actually was, Mrs. Guzman was the portrait of an overly protective Hispanic mother, ruling over her home and unable, even after so many years, to adjust the fact that her children were grown and emancipated.

"I'm sorry, Mama," Josie replied when finally released from her mother's embrace. "I should have called, but you really shouldn't get so worked up. I know how to take care of myself."

"The streets today aren't safe, and with this job of yours, *ay*," her mother scolded. "You should have called."

Harrigan stood in the entryway, all but ignored in the hugs, kisses, and gentle reprimands around him. Finally, Mrs. Guzman glanced in his direction. As if acting on cue, Josie cleared her throat and touched Harrigan lightly on the arm. "Mom and Dad, this is Peter Harrigan. Peter's a lawyer, and we're working together on one of Uncle Carlos' old cases. I never knew you to turn a hungry person away, so I invited him to have dinner with us, if that's okay."

"Of course, *mi hija*," Mr. Guzman said, extending his right arm to shake Harrigan's hand. "Please, call me Francisco."

"And you may call me Consuelo," Mrs. Guzman added, a broad grin stretching across her expressive face. She gave Josie a quick sidelong glance and raised her eyebrows ever so slightly in a form of silent communication between mother and daughter. Ever since the divorce, Mrs. Guzman had been urging Jose to settle down with a good family-oriented man. By showing up for dinner, Harrigan automatically became a candidate, subject to a degree of maternal scrutiny nearly as exacting as that meted out by the Senate Judiciary Committee for Supreme Court nominees. The possibility that Josie's relationship with the handsome visitor was nothing more than a business association had not yet dawned on Consuelo Guzman. In any event, the look on her mother's face told Josie that the cross-examination would begin in earnest once they adjourned to the kitchen and left the men to get acquainted in the living room.

"I hope you like enchiladas and *albondigas* soup, Mr. Harrigan," Consuelo said, adjusting the strings of her floral print apron. "Why don't you and Francisco relax while we finish fixing dinner? Come, Josie," she commanded as she turned away for the brief trip to her inner sanctum.

The Guzmans' living room was tastefully furnished with overstuffed armchairs and sofas covered in durable earth-tone browns and darker fabrics that blended perfectly with the large handwoven oriental Bokhara rug that covered all but the perimeter of the room's high-gloss hardwood floors. The walls boasted an eclectic collection of framed museum reprints, ranging from early abstract Picassos and

Diego Rivera murals to a Frida Kahlo self-portrait depicting the artist sitting in the garden of the house she had shared with Rivera in Coyoacan outside Mexico City.

Harrigan and Mr. Guzman took seats in easy chairs separated by a mahogany coffee table across from a full-size fireplace. Atop the white marble mantelpiece was an array of family photographs—college graduation portraits of Josie and her sister, enlarged snapshots of the family unwrapping gifts on a Christmas morning long ago, a group portrait of what must have been the extended family at Josie's wedding on the outer steps of the old chapel at the Mission Dolores, and a few snapshots of Mr. and Mrs. Guzman having the time of their hardworking lives on the beach at Waikiki.

"Would you care for a drink?" Mr. Guzman asked, gesturing toward a silver serving tray on the coffee table stacked with an ice bucket, glasses, and an assortment of hard liquor. "I was just about to help myself to a scotch and soda."

"I take mine on the rocks," Harrigan replied. Josie's dad seemed the easygoing type who was enjoying retirement. Definitely a type B personality, Harrigan thought to himself as he accepted the drink and settled into his armchair, enjoying the hearty aromas emanating from the kitchen. Outside of a few late-night postcoital suppers prepared by some of his domestically oriented dating partners, he hadn't tasted a good home-cooked meal in years.

"So, what kind of law do you practice. Mr. Harrigan?" Franciso asked amiably.

"A little bit of everything, but mostly criminal. I have a one-person office in Pasadena."

"And what brings you to San Francisco?"

As Harrigan filled Francisco in on the Ashbourne case, Consuelo Guzman was putting Josie through her paces back in the kitchen. "So, I thought you were finished with lawyers," she said, chopping a cucumber into bite-size pieces with the dexterity of a sushi chief. "Now you have another. I suppose you can't avoid it with that job of yours."

"Mama, we're just working on a case together," Donning a pair of heavy-duty oven gloves, Josie lifted a tray of chicken enchiladas from the stove and began to cut them into four equal portions.

"That worthless Marvin wasn't enough for you?" Consuelo's voice took on an accusatory tone, as if she, rather than Josie, had been the real victim of the worthless Marvin's marital shortcomings. As she spoke, she added the cucumber and a diced red onion to the salad bowl and put the finishing touches on her homemade ranch dressing.

"Please don't bring Marvin into this."

"A man who didn't want children, *dios mío*," Consuelo muttered, ignoring Josie's protests. "I don't know what you ever saw in him."

"I thought you used to like Marvin, Mama. You were against the divorce."

"You're nearly thirty-six years old, Josie. You should be thinking of settling down and having children, like your sister."

"You're not going to get into that again. I have my own life."

"At least this Mr. Harrigan is a good-looking man. *Muy guapo.* He's not Latino, but he is a Christian, no? Maybe this time you've made the right choice." Consuelo cocked her head to one side and pursed her lips as if considering the pros and cons of a union between Josie and Harrigan. "I think I may approve," she added, loading a large pot of *albondigas* soup onto a black serving tray.

"I told you, we're on a case together. It's strictly business, okay?" Totally exasperated, Josie followed her dynamo of a mother through the swinging saloon doors and into the dining room, where Consuelo ladled out four steaming bowls of soup and summoned the men to the evening meal.

After the psychodrama of the kitchen, dinner was a tranquil affair, filled with idle conversation about the weather, 49er football, and the declining quality of life in the nation's big cities. Harrigan heard the latest news about Josie's cousins: Ricardo had been admitted to U.C. Davis medical school, Claudia was getting engaged just before Christmas, and Uncle Carlos was slowly recovering from the auto accident. He also learned that Josie's older sister, Lisa, was happily married, had four children, and lived in a big house in Highland Park, not very far from Harrigan's home in Altadena.

The Guzmans were a charming and loving group, and while Consuelo brought a somewhat exaggerated dimension of anxiety and nervous energy to the mix, all families suffered from some kind of mild pathology. It was part of the great biological order, inherent in the stresses and strains of parenting, child rearing, adolescence, and emancipation. If only for a moment, Harrigan felt an acute longing for his own family. It was the first time the emptiness had resurfaced since he had met Josie.

It was nine o'clock by the time the small talk ended and dessert and coffee were served. Harrigan asked to use the phone and was directed to the living room to ring up the Hotel Mayfair. A quick call to the hotel and five others he found listed in the yellow pages met with the same substantive response, even if the accents of the various night clerks varied from Chinese to Pakistani: It was Friday night in the City by the Bay, and an out-of-towner without reservations would be lucky to land a stand-up sleeper at a cheap motel off the freeway.

Preparing for a long night of motel hopping, Harrigan returned to the dining room. Josie and her father were chatting away over their coffee while Consuelo bustled back into the kitchen. The clattering of pots and pans could be heard in the distance.

"I'm afraid I wasn't able to book a room," Harrigan said with a look of concern. "I'll either have to find a place in Oakland or fly back to L.A. tonight and reschedule our visit with Mrs. Denton."

Before Josie could answer, the kitchen doors swung open and Consuelo popped her head into the dining room. She was still garbed in her apron and wielded a blue dishtowel in her right hand like a catcher's mitt. "You have a spare room, *mi hija*," she said nonchalantly, as if delivering a traffic bulletin on the morning news.

There were raised eyebrows all around, followed by an awkward silence. For a moment Josie considered the propriety of telling her mother to mind her own business. In the end, however, she realized that any such protest would only sow the seeds of future interrogations that were best avoided. Consuelo was just being herself, and Josie knew there was nothing she could do to change her.

"Thank you for dinner, Mama," Josie said finally. "I'm sure we'll work something out."

"You have a lovely family," Harrigan said back in the BMW as they pulled away from the curb.

Josie laughed and shook her head. "You're kidding, of course."

"Not at all. Your father's quite an interesting guy, and your mom—"

"My mom would be headed for the *yenta* hall of fame if she were Jewish. Ever since the divorce she's been on a holy crusade to get me remarried. It's so embarrassing."

"She just wants you to be happy."

"She thinks that women were born to breed, not have careers."

They drove on for a few blocks, taking in the sights of the Mission District on a Friday night, knowing that when they reached Valencia they'd have to make a decision. Josie broke the ice as they came to a stoplight. "I do have a spare room on the third floor. It really does make more sense than finding a room at this time of night."

Her tone was all business, and Harrigan received the invitation in the same spirit.

Despite its more ornate exterior, Josie's Queen Anne house was furnished much like her mother's with plenty of soft chairs and couches and oriental rugs. The artwork on the walls, however, was more varied than Consuelo's and included some political posters from farmworker rallies and the Chicano student movement in addition to a few Chagalls and Monets. The shelves of the living room were also stocked with books, mostly hardbacks, both fiction and nonfiction, and a huge collection of compact disks that Harrigan might have taken more time to peruse if he hadn't been so tired.

Josie led Harrigan up the stairs to the guest quarters, which were set up in an unusual octagonal-shaped room on the third floor just below the "witch's hat" tower that gave Queen Anne homes their distinctive design. "The bed's already made up," she said, handing him a fresh towel and washcloth. "I'll get you up around six-thirty." She smiled and made her way downstairs. Her friendly abrupt manner left no doubt that she intended their relationship to remain strictly professional.

Resisting the temptation to rummage through the dresser drawers, Harrigan slipped on a pair of cotton gym shorts and a T-shirt and fished out the paperback he'd been working through the past week. He read a chapter and a half, then turned out the lights, finally overcome by the urge to sleep.

The dream returned in the predawn hours, terrifying as always. He was back in the old Honda, careening down the sharp and rocky embankment below Angeles Crest Highway. Stephanie and the boys were screaming in horror. There was a clash of heads, the sound of metal twisting grotesquely out of shape, the world turning horribly upside down, the feeling of abject helplessness that he loathed above all else.

And then there was the light. Searing and bright, as though he were staring directly into the sun. He reached out his hand for Stephanie's, trying to clear his head. This wasn't the way the crash or the dream ended, he told himself in the midst of his confusion.

"You must have had a bad dream," Josie said soothingly, holding his hand as she knelt beside him.

In the course of his struggles, Harrigan had kicked off the bed covers, and in the glare of the overhead light, the stump six inches below his left knee was plainly visible. Smooth and rounded seven years post surgery, the residual limb had atrophied to the point where it was the size of a man's forearm. It wasn't exactly a gruesome sight, but Harrigan was always self-conscious the first time anyone new laid eyes on it. He thought about pulling the sheet over his leg but realized that Josie had already taken note of the leg and did not appear bothered. "An old car accident," he said, offering a quick explanation. "I'm really sorry if I woke you."

"Don't be silly. We all have nightmares." She gave his hand a squeeze, deciding for the moment not to comment on the leg.

"I usually have mine at home," he replied dryly, trying to regain his sense of humor.

"I'll make a pot of coffee," she said, rising to her feet. "It's nearly six. If we hustle, we'll make it to Mrs. Denton's by early afternoon."

Harrigan propped himself up on his pillow and watched her leave the room. With her long black hair spilling over her white nightgown, she was the closest thing he had ever seen to an angel, he thought to himself. And now the angel was about to fix breakfast for him. Life certainly took some strange turns.

THIRTEEN

The Great Central Valley, which figured so prominently into Gilbert Denton's life and work, is a broad alluvial plain surrounded by mountains. Four hundred and fifty miles long and forty to seventy miles wide, it stretches from near Redding in the north to the Tehachapi Mountains just above Los Angeles. To the casual observer gazing at a relief map of California, the valley looks like God dragged a giant ice cream scoop through the midsection of the state. Seen from the ground, the region seems more like an agricultural Valhalla, accounting for more than one-quarter of all the table food produced in the United States.

But like that other great enterprise centered in Hollywood, the source of the valley's prosperity was in large part artificial. If not for the massive importation of water from the north, the Great Valley would be what it had been for millennia—a rolling, semi-arid prairie that blossomed with color after the brief winter rains and baked under a relentless sun the remainder of the year. The endless fields of wheat, rice, tomatoes, corn, and cotton that dot the landscape would disappear within a generation.

What makes the prosperity possible and keeps America well stocked in T-shirts and breakfast cereals are the two aqueduct systems that feed the area: the Central Valley Project initiated in the Great Depression by the federal government and the State Water Project built in the sixties and seventies by California's Department of Water Resources. Together, the two systems include dozens of dams and reservoirs, numerous hydroelectric power and pumping plants, and nearly thirteen hundred miles of aqueducts and canals. With a construction price tag approaching four billion dollars, the state project remains the largest water program ever undertaken in the country.

As Bob Jenkins and Professor Denton before him had written, the water projects made fortunes for the corporate farms, large landholders, engineering firms, oil companies, and industrial-supply houses that profited directly from them. They were also a breeding ground for political conspiracy theories, some of them grounded in reality, others steeped in paranoia, such as those Debray had circulated about the professor in the months before the Berkeley bombing.

After a morning meal of croissants, blueberry scones, and strong Colombian coffee, Harrigan and Josie made a beeline for Cynthia Denton's home at the southern end of the valley, traveling due east along Interstate 580. By ten o'clock, they reached the turnoff for Interstate 5 south, just below Tracy, a small market town and the home of one of the huge pumping facilities that sent the waters of the California Aqueduct cascading through the valley and into Los Angeles County. For the next two hundred and fifty miles the interstate paralleled the aqueduct as the engorged concrete waterway snaked past farms, small towns, and truck stops before veering into the Kettleman Hills above Bakersfield.

Harrigan had made the southward trek along Interstate 5 any number of times, usually on business and almost always alone. Having Josie as company for the normally monotonous drive made all the difference. She not only vastly improved the scenery but, as he had come to realize, his new investigator was one of the few people he felt comfortable with on a personal level. She was engaging and alive, filled with curiosity and optimism, yet not without an appreciation of life's inevitable disappointments and tragedies.

He thought again how much she reminded him of Stephanie, and the idea sent a shiver through his midsection. He wanted to tell her the real story about his leg, but at the last moment unaccountably found himself pulling back. After all the half-truths and evasions he had fed her over the past few days, he wasn't sure how or if he could bare the ugly reality behind his recurrent nightmares. Maybe he was mired in a state of lingering guilt, as his therapist once suggested, and unconsciously looked upon the possibility of emotional intimacy with another woman as a betrayal of his wife and kids. Maybe he was embarrassed at how weak and needy he might seem if he opened himself up. Maybe he just was afraid that after all was said and done, Josie wouldn't really be that interested in his inner demons, or she'd be angry that he hadn't told her the truth. Whatever the reason, he couldn't quite clear the final hurdle.

With the traffic heavier than normal and Harrigan reverting to the good-natured silent type, Josie concentrated on the interstate and they spent the time listening to country and western music and engaging in idle conversation. Between cry-in-your-beer tunes about cheatin' wives and angry ballads about ball-busting bosses, Harrigan learned the names of Josie's nieces and nephews and heard all about the old family hacienda outside of Guadalajara, where one of Francisco's brothers ran a thriving produce business and lived with his three sons and their children in a form of multigenerational domestic anarchy. "I try to visit them at least every other year," she said. "It's only a half-day's drive from Puerto Vallarta. If you're ever headed that way, I could give you their address. They're *muy amigable* toward gringos."

"I'll keep it in mind the next time I settle a big P.I. case and can afford a vacation." Harrigan had no real desire to visit Guadalajara—he'd been there once as a college student on a second-class bus en route to Mexico City. But Puerto Vallarta was another story. "P.V.," as the tour guides called it, had been one of his and Stephanie's favorite getaways. Some of the happiest moments of his marriage had been spent sitting poolside, sipping margaritas at a little oceanfront hotel they discovered south of town. The biggest worry he had on those trips was whether he'd be able to find a decent cigar to smoke while watching the sun fall into the Pacific.

"We're almost there," Josie said finally, snapping Harrigan out of his brief reverie. It was nearly three o'clock, and they were south of beautiful downtown Bakersfield. Josie flicked the turn signal on and they headed for the exit marked BUENA VISTA LAKE.

Like Lake Tulare, Buena Vista was a remnant of the valley's distant past. Once a thriving freshwater habitat that extended nearly four thousand acres in wet years, Buena Vista had long since been drained to pave the way for agribusiness. Today only the name survived as a reminder of the indigenous wetlands that once occupied the territory west of Bakersfield.

Cynthia Denton lived in a modest ranch-style home on a hill above the old lake bed. Although Josie had made no definite appointment when they spoke over the phone, Mrs. Denton had assured her that she rarely strayed very far from home these days. Apart from a weekly shopping run into Bakersfield, she could be found most days puttering around in her garden and evenings working on the quilts she stitched together in her sewing room as part of a little cottage industry that served to keep her occupied as much as it did to bring in a few extra dollars a month.

True to her word, Mrs. Denton was in the front yard digging crabgrass and dandelions out of the long, narrow flower bed below her living room window when Josie pulled her Beemer to the curb. Seeing the sleek automobile come to a stop, she dropped her trowel to the ground, wiped the dirt from her hands, and walked to the street. Dressed in a pair of old blue jeans and a plaid flannel shirt, Cynthia was an attractive woman in her late fifties, slim and fit-looking, with straight, shoulder-length gray hair tied back in a ponytail.

"You must be Ms. Guzman," Cynthia said before Josie could utter an introduction of her own. She seemed neither surprised nor alarmed to have her Saturday afternoon interrupted by a legal visit from the team defending her husband's killer.

"Yes, and this is Peter Harrigan, the attorney I told you about."

Cynthia extended her hand to offer a pair of courteous if unenthusiastic hand shakes. "Well, I'm sure you didn't come all this way to look at my roses and daylilies. We can talk out on the patio in the backyard."

The front door opened onto a Spanish-style entrance with freshly whitewashed plaster walls, a raised wood beam ceiling, and polished terra cotta floor tiles. Visible beyond, through an open French door, was a formal dining room, at the center of which stood a heavy walnut-stained table and six high-back dinner chairs. To the left was a large combination living and family room furnished with a colorful assortment of white and green sofas, loveseats, leather easy chairs with matching ottomans, and a late-model thirty-five-inch color TV housed in a dark mahogany combination wall unit that also contained a tape deck and CD player. Despite the electronic appointments, the room looked like precious little entertainment was conducted within its confines.

Mrs. Denton led Josie and Harrigan across the family room and through the sliding glass doors that opened onto a raised flagstone terrace. Paved with angular gray stones and sporting a variety of white wrought iron lawn furniture, the patio was about half as large as the family room. Built into the sloping hillside on a concrete foundation, it afforded a panoramic view of the adjacent dry, scrub-covered hills and the farmland below that once had been Buena Vista Lake.

"It's a lovely view, especially on clear days like this," Cynthia said, sounding a little more relaxed than she had seemed in the front yard. "Why don't you make yourselves comfortable and I'll fix up some coffee."

Harrigan and Josie walked to the edge of the patio for a better vantage point. In the distance, a section of the California Aqueduct could be seen as it twisted around the old lake bed en route to the Tehachapi Mountains. At the foot of the mountains, after passing through two smaller pumping plants, the waters would arrive at the A.D. Edmonston pumping station Bob Jenkins had described. It was there that the great engineering miracle of the state water project was performed as fourteen motor-pump units, each over sixty-five feet tall and weighing approximately four hundred twenty tons, lifted the waters of the aqueduct two thousand vertical feet across miles of rugged mountain terrain. The technocrats who built the Edmonston station called the effect "Niagara in reverse."

"Help yourself to milk and sugar," Cynthia said as she emerged from the kitchen and laid a silver serving tray laden with cups and saucers on the round glass-top table in the center of the patio. "There's a tin of butter cookies, too. Homemade."

Tired from the long drive, Harrigan and Josie eagerly accepted the invitation and poured themselves each a steaming cup. Returning to his seat with a cup in one hand and a couple of oval-shaped cookies in the other, Harrigan couldn't help but feel a little guilty at the hospitality being shown him by Gilbert Denton's widow. As cordial as he might succeed in keeping things, there was no way of avoiding the fact that the purpose of his visit was to help win the freedom of the man convicted of Gilbert's murder.

"You have a lovely home here," Harrigan said, trying to begin the interview in a neutral way.

"Yes," Josie seconded Harrigan's observation. "It must be nice living away from the city. How long have you been out here?"

"About five years. I sold my old place outside Bakersfield and used the proceeds for a down payment." Mrs. Denton poured herself a coffee and settled into a lawn chair facing her guests. She smiled and ran her right forefinger along the rim of her coffee cup as she spoke, waiting for the real questioning to begin.

Harrigan finished the last of the cookies he had been holding and took a final swallow of coffee. "I really appreciate you seeing us," he said. "I know you've declined to be interviewed in the past, and I just wanted to thank you for this opportunity."

"I haven't changed my mind about your client, Mr. Harrigan," Cynthia replied firmly but without rancor. "I realize that you have a job to do, and I thought that after all these years it was important to hear what you had to say, even if I didn't like it."

"That's very decent of you," Josie said, looking at Harrigan as if to urge him to tread softly.

"My job isn't just to get Harold Ashbourne off," Harrigan began. "It's to find out the truth."

"I thought the jury determined that twelve years ago when it convicted your client."

Harrigan leaned forward in Cynthia's direction, an intense but controlled expression on his face. "I know this might sound like something every defense lawyer says, but I have reason to believe that Harold Ashbourne is innocent and that someone else connected with the group Savoirs of the Earth may be responsible for the murders of your husband and son."

"Is this just conjecture or do you have some new evidence?" To Harrigan's relief, Mrs. Denton seemed neither surprised nor disturbed by his claim.

"Your husband was working on a new project at the time of his death," Josie said, joining in the discussion. "He had just terminated Henri Debray's contract with the political science department and was going to fire Charles West, too."

"So you think West and Debray murdered Gilbert and my son?"

"Frankly, we don't know who committed the murders, but we think the crime may have had something to do with your husband's new book," Josie explained. "We've examined his papers at the Bancroft Library, and we know he was working on a new study on the role of the water projects in the Central Valley. The trouble is, the research for the new book isn't among his papers. Either it went up in flames or . . ."

"It's been stolen," Harrigan finished Josie's sentence for her. "In any case, we thought you might be able to tell us exactly what the professor was working on."

Cynthia stood up and quietly returned her coffee cup to the glass-top table. Turning to face Harrigan and Josie, she seemed puzzled and almost disappointed. "I can't imagine how that could help you," she said.

"Why is that?" Josie asked.

"Gilbert had a lot of difficulty coming up with a sequel to *The Greening of the Golden State*. At first he thought of doing a standard update. You know, a general overview of how things in the water-procurement industry had changed since the earlier book. But his publisher wasn't too keen on that idea."

As she continued, she walked to the railing of the patio and gazed at the horizon. "Then Gilbert decided to do what political scientists call a 'vertical study.' He was going to write a history of landownership in the valley's southern end, focusing on the region's most prominent landholders and the roles they played in getting the water projects built and profiting from their operation."

Mrs. Denton took a step back from the railing and turned to face Harrigan and Josie again. Without warning, her outer calm began to crack. "Unfortunately . . ." she said in a quavering voice. "Well, you know what happened. I have no idea what became of the research." For a moment it seemed that Cynthia might not be able or willing to go on talking. But she was a resilient woman long accustomed to fending off the painful memories that haunted her. "I'm sorry," she said, clearing her throat and wiping away the tears that had formed in the corners of her eyes. "I get a little sad sometimes."

Watching Cynthia deal with her grief, Harrigan grew quiet. Her anguish reminded him of his own personal tragedy. Although he tried to maintain a professional aloofness, her pain stung him sharply.

Josie, too, paused while Cynthia regained her composure, then asked softly, "What landholders was your husband going to profile?"

"Most of the big ones, firms like Tenneco, J.G. Boswell and the Slayer Land Company, the Chandler family."

"From the *Los Angeles Times*?" Harrigan asked, sensing that Cynthia was back on track.

"They're major stockholders in the Tejon Ranch, south of here. Gilbert was also going to look at some of the big oil companies that have large fields out here. Kern County is oil country, and Chevron, Shell, and Getty had been around for years." Cynthia straightened her shirt and walked back to the table to stack the cups and saucers on the serving tray. "Does that help any?"

Harrigan ran the fingers of his right hand through his hair, fearing that they had wasted both Mrs. Denton's time and their own. "Did your husband have any investments in the companies he was studying?" he asked, hoping to find a connection.

"No," Cynthia answered matter-of-factly. "He was, however, personally acquainted with the Ames family. They were also going to be included in the book, if I remember correctly."

"Are they the same folks that run Ames Engineering in Los Angeles?" Harrigan asked.

"Benjamin Ames is the head of the company. Gilbert had a job on the Ames Ranch, outside of town, when he was a teenager, and he and Ben became friends, after a fashion." She smiled wanly. "Well, not close friends, they were from different sides of the interstate, as we say out here. They disagreed a lot on politics, but they respected each other and Ben showed up for Gilbert's memorial service."

"Did they disagree over the Peripheral Canal?" Harrigan asked.

"Among other things," Cynthia answered thoughtfully. "Ben and his family were big supporters of the water projects. Gilbert more or less kept an open mind."

"So the professor never became a supporter of the canal?" Harrigan asked.

"Gilbert went to meetings held by both sides of the canal issue, for research on his book. He wanted to hear what everyone, pro and con, had to say. But no, he never threw in his lot with the water lobby." A contemptuous frown crossed Cynthia Denton's face. "No matter what those lunatics from Berkeley said, my husband remained a dedicated conservationist all his life."

"How did Ben Ames feel about the professor's plans to write about his family?" Josie inquired, rejoining the conversation.

"I'm afraid you'll have to ask Ben that yourself. I've never discussed the subject with him."

Cynthia excused herself and carried the serving tray into the kitchen. She returned in less than a minute with a white letter-size envelope in her hand. "Is there anything else I can help you with?" she asked.

Both her tone and body language indicated that she wanted to bring their visit to a close.

"Just one last question," Harrigan said. "Did your husband ever say anything about the Saviors being infiltrated by some kind of saboteur?"

"Never," Cynthia answered, sounding firm and certain.

Josie and Harrigan shared a searching look and slowly rose from their seats. "I appreciate the opportunity to speak with you," Harrigan said, extending his hand for a good-bye shake.

To Harrigan's surprise, Mrs. Denton declined his hand shake and instead handed him the white envelope she had been holding. "I think you should have this," she said. "It arrived this morning. I was going to open it before you drove up."

As Harrigan studied the envelope, his mouth dropped with wonder. The envelope was postmarked from Hayward, California, a residential and industrial town south of Oakland, whose two claims to fame were that it was the home of a major state university campus and that it sat astride one of the biggest earthquake faults on the West Coast. The letter was addressed to Peter Harrigan, Esquire, in care of Cynthia Denton.

Inside was a sheet of white photocopy paper with a single sentence typed in neat italic script:

You're getting warm.

Below the message was the single initial, "D."

FOURTEEN

"The bastard knows every move we make," Harrigan said as Josie shifted the Beemer into overdrive. He didn't know whether to laugh at being made to look the fool or roll down the window and scream Debray's name like an obscenity at passing motorists. Lacking a more productive outlet for his agitation, he began to pound his right fist into his left palm until his knuckles hurt.

It was early evening, and the wind was picking up on the Grapevine, as the pass through the Tehachapis on Interstate 5 was known. The chaparral shrubs and spindly oak and pepper trees on either side of the freeway were bent in thirty-degree angles from the sharp gusts, which also sent showers of dirt and gravel across the Beemer's windshield. Harrigan's anger seemed to mirror the fierce turn in the winds. "We don't even know what name he's using, let alone where he might be."

"He was Robert Randall when he reviewed Denton's files at the Bancroft Library," Josie reminded him.

"And today? He could be masquerading as Salman Rushdie, for all we know."

"Well, at least the letter shows we're on the right path." She eased up on the accelerator as they made it over the Grapevine and began the descent into the L.A. basin.

"Whatever that means."

"I have to admit he's one of the stranger characters I've come across. Maybe he's really out there trying to put all the pieces together before he contacts you again, and the letter's just his bizarre way of letting you know he hasn't forgotten."

"Maybe he liked to torture small animals when he was a kid, too."

"Or he just likes torturing attorneys," Josie said. "It's a popular pastime." Her quip elicited only a wry smile from Harrigan, and they drove on in silence as the open expanse of the northern fringe of Los Angeles County gradually gave way to the outer reaches of urban sprawl.

Harrigan gazed out the window at the changing terrain and slowly calmed himself. There was too much work to be done to waste his energy on matters beyond his control. Drawing on his lawyer's sense of efficiency, he decided to make the most of the last half hour of daylight and reached into his briefcase for his copy of Carlos' old investigation file. With or without Debray, he had to plot his next moves. Carlos' notes seemed as good a place as any to begin the process.

Among other things, the file contained Carlos' memos on the interviews he had conducted with the Saviors, together with a list of the Saviors' last-known personal and business addresses. Although Harrigan had read through the material several times before, he knew from years of practicing law that the more he learned about a case, the more likely he was to discover new clues in evidence once thought inconsequential. "Keep digging," one of his old professors used to say. "You never know what you might have overlooked earlier."

The old prof was an anal-retentive prig with a fondness for expensive booze, but he had also been a top-flight litigator before finding refuge in academia, where he spent the rest of his days pontificating in lecture halls about dues process and equal protection and ogling female students in tight sweaters and short skirts.

As luck had it, it took Harrigan only until the middle of the file to confirm the old teacher's maxim. "Hayward," Harrigan said in a barely audible voice.

"What about it?" Josie asked, happy that the silence had lifted, even if Harrigan's comment seemed to come out of left field rather than the passenger seat to her immediate right.

"It's where Bob Jenkins lives."

"Along with a few thousand other middle-class stiffs."

"It's where Debray mailed this letter." Harrigan retrieved the envelope Cynthia Denton had given him from his jacket pocket and pointed at the postmark.

It was Josie's turn for quite rumination as they crossed into the city limits of Los Angeles. The setting rays of the sun bathed her face with a soft pastel orange light, making her look sexy, pensive, and mysterious all at the same time. If only the circumstances were different, Harrigan could have allowed himself to forget that he was a lawyer with a client on death row.

"So Jenkins was lying when he said he hadn't seen Debray," Josie said after a good five minutes had elapsed. "Is there anyone connected with this case who isn't lying?"

"You mean apart from you and me, of course," Harrigan said, another wry smile crossing his lips. "Actually, I'm not so sure about Jenkins. Debray could simply be tailing his old buddies without their knowledge, as part of that 'unfinished business' he was ranting about."

"Maybe he's out there looking for Ashbourne's Judas, just like us."

Harrigan shrugged his shoulders. "All we know for sure about Debray is that he's mobile. He could be anywhere."

"That's a comforting thought. It's too bad we can't call out the Mounties to bring him in." She glanced quickly at Harrigan before completing the obvious reference. "They always get their man."

"The Mounties wear red coats," Harrigan retorted. "I think this might be a job for the guys in white."

The descent into black humor and bad puns continued as Josie followed the signs for the turnoff to the 134 Freeway into Glendale. The shift away from serious discussion was a telltale sign that stress, fatigue, and hunger were beginning to take their toll. Along with their frequent abuse of alcohol and drugs, lawyers were renowned for using gallows humor to cope with the tensions of high-stakes cases.

At least he and Josie were still able to laugh at themselves, Harrigan thought as they hopped off the freeway and headed for a Japanese restaurant. The teriyaki and sushi they ordered would relieve the hunger, and a good night's rest would do the same for the fatigue Harrigan felt from his three-day sojourn to the Bay Area. The stress, however, was a different matter. All the black humor in the world wouldn't alter the fact that Harrigan's life would remain a pressure-cooker until Harold Ashbourne either met his maker or had his murder conviction overturned.

When Josie finally pulled into Harrigan's driveway in Altadena, it was nine o'clock but seemed much later. A thick bank of clouds had rolled in over the San Gabriels, obscuring the moon and the stars that normally lit up the sky in the smog-free nights of early autumn.

Adding to the darkness was the fact that both Harrigan's porch light and the floor lamp by the living room window were out. Both were on a timer that was set to turn them on every evening at six. "I could have sworn I left the lights on," Harrigan said, opening the passenger door.

"Don't you have an alarm service?" Josie asked.

"I let it lapse a couple of years ago. There hasn't been a break-in on this block since I moved in." Actually, he had let the service go soon after the accident on Angeles Crest, when the idea of protecting his worldly possessions seemed trivial and inconsequential. The part about the neighborhood's low crime rate, however, was true.

"Well maybe the bulbs just blew or you forgot to

turn them on," Josie offered, reacting to the concerned looked on his face.

Her conjecture proved to be dead wrong.

Harrigan's look of slight concern gave way to one of near panic as they walked across the front lawn and found the front door closed but unlocked. He pushed the door open, hurried through the darkened entry and into the living room, where he flipped on the switch for the overhead light.

Harrigan felt the sense of violation every homeowner experiences after a burglary. His eyes darted across the living room, searching for missing possessions. Whoever had decided to make the house call in his absence had broken a side window in the living room for his entrance and had managed to find and dismantle the timer for the night lights, either out of sheer perversity or to better conceal the fact that there had been an entry. The guy also must have been a seasoned pro. Instead of the disarray normally associated with such crimes, the living room looked barely disturbed. The perpetrator had very cleanly disconnected and removed his stereo system from the middle section of the room's large modular wall unit and had left the rest of the room's contents untouched.

The scene was virtually the same in the kitchen and the master bedroom. Some dresser drawers had been left open. But only a few articles of jewelry—a wristwatch, some cuff links, and an old high school ring that he didn't care about—were missing. All things considered, the losses seemed light. Best of all, there was no sign of the intruder.

Harrigan's home office, however, was another

story. The thief had not only made off with his new laptop but had dumped the entire contents of one of his four-drawer file cabinets on the floor. Files from the Ashbourne case lay mixed together with materials from at least a dozen others in a chaotic heap. Harrigan and Josie bent down almost simultaneously to sift through the mess.

"It could have been worse," Josie said, stuffing papers back into their designated folders. "You'd better phone the police.'''

In the distance, to the rear of the house, the neighbor's German shepherd began to bark, breaking Harrigan's concentration. "I think I'll have a look out back first," he said. "I won't be a moment."

He left Josie and quickly walked through the living room to the double French doors that led to the patio. Like the front door, they were unlocked. Thinking the thief might have used the rear exit for his getaway, he pushed the French doors open cautiously and took a few halting steps forward. Apart from the dog, who kept up a baleful chorus of howls and groans, the night was still. He let his eyes adjust to the darkness and was about to turn around when he discerned the faint outline of his stereo receiver and laptop at the far corner of the patio near the wooden fence that separated his yard from his neighbor's property and the barking dog.

Without bothering to turn on the outside lights, Harrigan rushed to retrieve his property. A blow to the side of his face was delivered swiftly, by someone wearing latex gloves, the kind that allow for maximum dexterity but leave no fingerprints. Although it was just a glancing punch, it was still enough to send

Harrigan sprawling to the ground, clutching his head with both hands as he fell. Harrigan remained conscious, but was too dazed to tell if he saw one or two bodies jump the fence and run off to the dirt alley behind his home. All that he knew for certain was that when the altercation was over, the barking had ceased and the quiet of the neighborhood was restored.

Down for a good ten count, Harrigan picked himself up, rubbing his mouth with his right hand. He thought for an instant about calling after his assailant or giving chase but realized the futility of either course and opted instead to return inside.

He found Josie still seated on the office floor, holding a single sheet of paper in her right hand. The paper was an old yellow and black flier that featured the head of Harrigan's older son superimposed on the body of an NBA basketball player as the hoopster drove to the basket. COME CELEBRATE DAVID HARRIGAN'S 11TH BIRTHDAY, the flier announced in bold capital letters. A paragraph in smaller print explained that the Harrigan family—Peter, Stephanie, David, and Johnny—had reserved the indoor court at a local recreation center for an afternoon of ice cream, cake, and roundball.

"Why didn't you tell me?" Josie asked, rising slowly to her feet with the flier still gripped tightly. She held the brittle sheet of paper in front of Harrigan and stared at him. She sounded confused, concerned, and angry all at the same time.

"Where did you get that?" Harrigan asked. "I've always kept it in my nightstand."

"On top of one of Harold's files," she said, diverting her eyes momentarily to the pile of documents still on the floor. "Why didn't you tell me?" she asked again.

As he gazed at the flier, the image of his deceased son hit him much harder than the blow on the patio. He halted his advance across the room and stood motionless, about three feet from Josie. "Because they're all dead," he said in a hollow voice.

Harrigan's grim revelation brought on a feeling of loss so acute that Josie forgot her anger at being lied to. "I'm so sorry, Peter," she whispered. "It was the car accident, wasn't it? That's how you lost your leg." Tears welled in her eyes and ran down her cheeks.

Even in her distressed state, to Harrigan she looked as beautiful as ever and perhaps more so. "My car skidded off a road in the San Gabriels," he told her.

Despite his feelings of renewed grief he felt drawn to her, especially now that his secret was revealed. In another instant, without thinking about whether it would be right and without weighing the consequences for the future, they were in each other's arms. She rested her head on his shoulder and held him tightly. He caressed her hair and gently stroked the back of her neck. He closed his eyes and allowed himself to feel her warmth. If only for a moment, the pain he had been carrying for so long seemed to slip away.

If only he could have gone on holding Josie, the pain might have disappeared forever. As it turned out, their embrace must have lasted no more than ten seconds. When they parted, reality and all its attendant complications came flooding back. Not only was the office still in a shambles, but Harrigan's lip had begun to swell.

"What happened to you?" she asked, suddenly noticing the bruise.

"We must have caught the scumbag in the act. He saw me on the patio and decked me in the dark."

"You look like you could use some ice on that," she said, brushing his face gently with her hand. "I'll get some from the kitchen. And you really should call the police."

Harrigan took a step toward his desk to let her pass and saw the red message light blinking on his answering machine. "I'd better see who it is," he said as she walked by him on her way out the door.

Judging from the time it took to rewind, the message was a long and important one. Finally, the tape came to a stop and the speaker phone clicked on, filling the office with the mellifluous voice of Dennis Witter. "It's my office manager," Harrigan called to Josie, who had reached the refrigerator.

"Peter, I tried to reach you at the hotel, but you had already checked out," Dennis began, sounding relaxed and competent as always. "Anyway, welcome back and all that, but I wouldn't unpack my bags yet if I were you. You must have updated your witness list for the Ashbourne hearing while you were away, because Bill Pickering called Friday afternoon. He's calendared an emergency motion in front of Judge Blake for ten o'clock Monday morning. He's going to try to block your efforts to have Debray testify at the hearing. Sounds like things are heating up."

"Goddamn Pickering," Harrigan grumbled as he received the latest bad news.

"That's about all," Dennis continued. "Otherwise, things have been quiet down here. Let me know if you need anything. *Ciao, bello.*"

Harrigan followed Dennis' message with some calls of his own, first to the local sheriff's station to report the burglary and then to the airlines to reserve a flight back to San Francisco for early Sunday evening, a rental car and a room at the Hotel Mayfair, with an open-ended stay, just to be on the safe side. Then he tried to reach Dennis. After a call to Dennis' home came up with his answering machine, he managed to locate him at his mother's place in Pasadena.

"You poor baby," Dennis said. "I hope your insurance premiums are current." Like a trusted friend, Dennis agreed to drive to Altadena tomorrow morning to help shore up Harrigan's home and to meet the new investigator on the Ashbourne case. He also offered to house-sit, "if I can bring a friend along and use the hot tub," until Harrigan returned from his next trip.

By the time Harrigan finished up with Dennis, Josie had returned with a fistful of ice cubes wrapped in a cloth kitchen towel. "Your office manager sounds like a solid guy," she said, gently daubing Harrigan's wound with the ice pack.

"He'll be here for breakfast tomorrow." Harrigan took the ice pack from her and began to think about the flier. Maybe he hadn't stuck it in his nightstand drawer as he remembered. It must have been at least two or three years since he'd actually seen it. He could easily have slipped it into his office file cabinet by mistake. Either that or the creep who broke into his house had some weird fascination with David's picture and carried it into the office himself. There was no way of knowing, and for the moment at least there were far more urgent matters to deal with.

"While I'm in San Francisco," he said, struggling to get back to business, "I think it would be a good idea for you and Dennis to drive over to Ames Engineering. I'd like you to try to interview Ames himself, even if you have wait a few hours to get an audience. It might also be a good idea to check out that other ex-Savior in Glendora, Bob . . ." As he looked at her, he seemed to lose his train of thought. "Bob . . . whatever the hell his name is."

"Gardner," she reminded him, "and he lives in Pomona."

"That's right." He leaned back against his desk, his thoughts shifting to what had happened between them and, even more important, to where Josie was going to spend the night. She was supposed to stay with her sister in Highland Park, but that was before the break-in and the tender moment they had just shared.

A few heavy seconds ticked by before Harrigan spoke again. "Why don't you make yourself at home while I fix us something to drink? There are three spare bedrooms, and you can have your pick of the lot." He wanted her to stay but was still afraid to come right out and say it.

Josie was sorely tempted to take up the offer and had to struggle to stop herself from saying yes. Hesitating, she glanced nervously at her watch and saw that it was nearly ten-thirty. "I don't think that would be a good idea," she said, sounding friendly but firm.

"Is it your sister?"

"No. My sister knows I'm a big girl." She gave him a forthright stare that told him she had made up her mind. "It's me. If I stayed there'd be too many temptations to break the rules. And besides, the sheriffs will be here soon to take a report. You have a lot of things to take care of before flying back to the Bay Area tomorrow."

Harrigan thought about arguing with her but ultimately reconsidered. They found each other extremely attractive, and there was no question that they had been flirting in the car. But now she was putting on the brakes, and he had to admit she was right. If there was anything more dangerous than mixing business and sex, it was mixing business with a serious relationship. There was no way he and Josie could share a casual one-night stand, and a serious relationship between them would be a professional taboo. It would be hard enough for them to continue working together without the additional baggage that emotional entanglement would bring.

Resigned to his fate as a principled but lonely guy, Harrigan escorted Josie to her car and said good night. He watched her BMW pull out of the drive and disappear down the hill outside his home. He told himself they had made the ethically correct decision even as his head swirled with thoughts of what might have been.

FIFTEEN

Even if he was no closer to the truth, it felt good to be back in court. The flight from L.A. had been smooth and uneventful, and the staff at the Hotel Mayfair welcomed him and his VISA gold card like longtime friends. With his lip healing and Dennis and Josie minding the southern front, Harrigan was free to devote his attentions to the attorney general's latest legal maneuvers. Still, he didn't know quite what to expect come Monday morning.

All that Harrigan knew as he opened the doors to Judge Blake's courtroom on the seventeenth floor of the Federal Building on Golden Gate Avenue was that Bill Pickering, the deputy AG assigned to represent the state, wanted to knock Henri Debray off Ashbourne's witness list. Pickering had calendared the court session on an emergency *ex parte* basis, and Harrigan had yet to receive his copy of the moving papers, a fact that placed him at an obvious though by no means insurmountable, tactical disadvantage.

Like most federal courtrooms, Judge Blake's was stately and spacious. About the size of a modest movie theater, it featured expensive wooden counsel

tables stained in somber dark walnut, modern upholstered chairs in the jury box, and a mahogany judge's
bench of truly magisterial proportions, flanked by the
flags of the United States and the state of California.
The dark marble wall behind the bench sported the
great seal of the United States in embossed bronze
relief. Even seasoned litigators like Harrigan felt like
they were entering the holy of holies when they
pushed open the swinging wooden gate that divided
the spectator section from the interior of the courtroom, where the lawyers plied their trade.

Although Harrigan arrived a full half hour before
the proceeding was scheduled to begin, he found
Pickering waiting for him at the government's counsel table. A seasoned litigator, Pickering was something of an oddity for a prosecutor. A short and
slight man in his mid-forties with closely cropped
brown hair and a determined little Ronald Coleman-
style mustache, he had begun his career in the early
1970s as a dedicated liberal with the Alameda
County Legal Aid Society. But after being mugged
and robbed one night in Berkeley by a group of black
teenagers, Pickering's world view did a radical one-
eighty. He applied for a position in the AG's criminal
law section and gradually worked his way up past
the deadwood to a supervisorial post. Along the way
he became an avid proponent of the death penalty.
In addition to devoting fifty hours a week to his duties as a deputy AG, Pickering worked as a volunteer
adviser for a variety of victims' rights groups.

On a personal level, Pickering could be charming
and accommodating when the spirit moved. Harri-

gan had as yet never exchanged a cross word with him. Today, however, promised to be different.

"Good morning, Mr. Harrigan," Pickering said as Harrigan approached the counsel table. The formality of his address was a clear sign that Pickering was agitated and had come prepared to fight. "Here's a copy of our motion," he added, handing over a ten-page document neatly typed on numbered legal paper. "I'd also like to introduce the investigator who will be working with me at the hearing, John Goodnow."

Pickering motioned to the large man dressed in a gray sports coat and plain navy blue tie seated next to him. "Pleased to meet you," Goodnow grumbled, shaking Harrigan's hand in a vice grip that must have been intended to inflict at least a small amount of pain. From the neck down, Goodnow looked like an NFL linebacker. From the neck up, with his deep-set eyes and heavy brow, he looked like Boris Karloff's ugly brother. He was definitely not the kind of guy you wanted to take home to meet the folks, unless you wanted to drag mom and dad off to an interrogation session in the middle of the night.

Harrigan retreated to the opposing counsel table to nurse his tingling hand and study Pickering's papers. Though there were no expletives, Pickering argued in support of his motion to exclude Debray from the hearing with unusual vigor. "Although habeas corpus proceedings provide for judicial review of criminal convictions," he wrote, "such proceedings are governed by the Federal Rules of Civil Procedure. Under the applicable rules, parties are required to list their witnesses prior to the hearing, according to the schedule ordered by the district court." Since the time for exchanging witness lists had expired without the inclusion of Henri Debray, Pickering was requesting the court to preclude Debray from testifying.

All things considered, Pickering's motion came as no surprise. Had Harrigan been in the AG's shoes, he probably would have taken the same position. In the cutthroat world of high-stakes litigation, Darwinian principles prevailed, with each party relentlessly pursuing his own interests. As long as you invoked high-minded phrases like "due process" and "fundamental fairness," you could ask the court for almost anything, and occasionally get away with it.

That was where Judge Blake came in, and he was the reason Pickering had elevated his normally low-key rhetoric. Unlike many of the newer appointees to the federal bench, who were drawn from the ranks of former prosecutors and still thought that their fundamental purpose in life was to increase the size of the prison population, Blake was an appointee of Lyndon Baines Johnson. A one-time Democratic party activist, he had earned a reputation during his long tenure as a square shooter dedicated to the unfashionable notion that a trial should be a search for truth rather than a contest to see who could squeeze the most out of legal technicalities. Pickering knew that Blake would have no hesitation to rule against the government if he thought the AG was overreaching.

The problem with Judge Blake was that he had suffered a mild stroke two years ago. At the ripe old age of seventy-five, when most men had long since

retired to clip coupons and interfere with their wives'
marketing, he was still plugging away at the law,
though at a noticeably reduced pace. Only he and
his doctor knew for sure if he still had the stamina
to preside over an evidentiary hearing in a case of
capital murder.

Harrigan had barely completed his second review
of Pickering's motion when the bailiff, a bespectacled
man in his early fifties whose ample midsection be-
spoke years of desk duty, called the session to order.
"All rise," he bellowed as though he were addressing
a full courtroom. Except for John Aragon, the KZSF
radio reporter who had made the Ashbourne case
the centerpiece of his continuing series on capital
punishment, the spectator section of the courtroom
was empty. Either the mainstream media had not
gotten wind of the emergency session or they were
busy chasing down other late-breaking stories of
mayhem and murder. Even before an empty house,
the bailiff completed the morning ritual in a booming
voice. "The United States District Court for the
Northern District of California is now in session, the
Honorable Stanley R. Blake presiding."

A few seconds passed before the door to the judge's
chambers opened. Stanley Blake, a frail, wizened
figure of a man, stoop-shouldered, and standing
barely a shade above five feet, emerged. Clutching
the arm of a white-haired female clerk, he shuffled
forward. A stiff draft from the overhead air condi-
tioner or a hearty sneeze from one of the lawyers
seemed capable of knocking him over in mid-stride.
With the clerk's assistance Blake struggled up the

steps to his seat and all but disappeared behind the great mahogany bench.

Blake opened the manila legal file the clerk had deposited in front of him and announced the Ashbourne case. He asked Pickering and Harrigan to state their appearances for the record and paused to clear his throat. "I have a motion on calendar brought by the State to exclude a witness for the petitioner," he said, commencing the proceedings in a surprisingly strong voice. "But before we get underway, gentlemen, I want to advise each of you that I will be stepping down from my position as soon as my current docket is cleared, and the evidentiary hearing scheduled in this matter concludes. I apprise you of my plans to give you the opportunity to have the hearing transferred to another sitting judge if you so desire. I'll give you a moment to consider."

The news of Blake's retirement, while not intrinsically startling given his condition, was unexpected. Pickering and Harrigan returned to their respective counsel tables, the deputy AG for a quick confab with the lumbering Goodnow and Harrigan for a huddle of one to contemplate the pros and cons of changing judges in midstream.

Replacing Judge Blake presented each lawyer with a different set of strategic concerns that, ironically, led each to elect to retain Blake on the case. From Pickering's perspective, while any other judge would likely be more conservative, transferring the hearing to another sitting jurist would delay the hearing by months if not years. The Ashbourne case had been pending in the state and federal courts for well over a decade, and any further delay, on orders from the attorney general himself, had to be resisted at all costs.

From Harrigan's perspective, delay was the next best thing to winning a victory for his client. As long as the case was delayed, Harold Ashbourne would stay clear of the executioner. However, Ashbourne had made it clear that he wanted the hearing to go forward. Death row was a living nightmare and he wanted no more of it. Harrigan also knew that with Blake gone, the case might be sent over to one of the hard-line judges in the newly opened Oakland branch of the district court. In that event, Ashbourne's chance of victory would be less than the villain's in a Stallone movie.

After a brief off-the-record conference, Pickering and Harrigan stood as Harrigan announced their joint decision. "We'd like Your Honor to remain on the case for the duration of the district court proceedings." It might be the last time the parties saw eye-to-eye on anything more significant than the timing of the lunchtime recesses.

"Then let's get down to the business at hand," Blake replied. "I'll hear from the State first."

"Your Honor," Pickering began in a humble tone, "we have been greatly prejudiced by the eleventh-hour addition of Mr. Debray to the petitioner's witness list. The hearing in this case is set to begin shortly, and we are involved in the last stages of preparation. To receive such a surprise at this late juncture just isn't fair."

"What you're saying, Mr. Pickering," Blake interjected, "is that Mr. Harrigan has sandbagged you. At least that's what we called it in my day." Blake mustered a mischievous grin that made his pale, deeply wrinkled face look more rubbery than usual.

"Exactly," Pickering agreed and turned to face Harrigan.

"Your Honor, we're not trying to sandbag anyone," Harrigan assured the court. "I supplemented our witness list the day after meeting with Mr. Debray."

"Nonetheless," Pickering loudly interrupted, "Your Honor ordered the parties to exchange witness lists more than a month ago. Counsel has either forgotten the court's order or is deliberately disregarding it."

"If I could just finish stating my position," Harrigan protested, requesting judicial intervention to silence his opponent.

Pickering, however, was scoring points and had no thought of yielding the floor, even if he had stolen it from Harrigan. "It's not just the petitioner who has a right to a fair hearing; we have rights, too." His voice grew louder and more demanding.

"Your Honor," Harrigan protested again. This time he succeeded in gaining Blake's attention.

"You've had your turn, Mr. Pickering," Blake said. Waving a mottled hand in front of his face, Blake silenced Pickering, sending the chastised prosecutor slumping back into his seat. In addition to his reputation for judicial independence, Blake was well known for demanding proper decorum from the attorneys who came before him. Whatever sympathy Pickering had built for his cause going into the hearing had been diminished by his violation of courtroom etiquette.

Harrigan folded his hands together, the perfect picture of respect, as he prepared to pick up his train of thought. "Both sides in this case have been searching for Henri Debray for many years. The petitioner cannot be faulted if the witness, acting solely on his own, waited until shortly before the hearing to come forward."

"Mr. Harrigan, how important is this witness to the petitioner's case?" Blake asked.

"In my view he's absolutely essential to the petitioner's claim that he received constitutionally ineffective assistance from his lawyer, J. Arnold Barnes, at the guilt phase of his state trial. As Your Honor well knows, the prevailing legal standards on the IAC issue require us to show not only that trial counsel's performance was substandard, but that his ineffectiveness prejudiced the petitioner's case."

Harrigan took a deep breath and paused to make sure that Blake was following his argument before continuing. "The application of these standards to the witness Debray is clear. In order to prevail, we have to show not only that counsel failed to conduct an adequate pretrial search for Debray, but that if Debray had been found and brought into testify, he would have corroborated Ashbourne's alibi and claim of innocence. The only way we can do that, Your Honor, is to put Debray on the witness stand and have him subjected to the rigors of direct and cross-examination."

"Mr. Harrigan's argument makes perfect sense to me, Mr. Pickering," the judge said, directing a critical gaze at the prosecutor. "This witness may well hold the truth to what really happened in this case."

"Or the witness may simply attempt to muddy the water with testimony that should have been disclosed prior to the hearing," Pickering responded in a more modulated voice.

"If the State is so concerned about being surprised by what the witness might say, I'll permit you to take his deposition prior to the evidentiary hearing," Blake said.

"But, Your Honor, we have no idea where the witness is," Pickering reminded the court.

"Is that true?" Blake inquired.

"Yes, Your Honor," Harrigan answered. "We have only Mr. Debray's word that he will appear for the hearing. He refused to give me his current whereabouts."

Blake stroked his whiskerless chin with the fingers of his right hand as he pondered the situation. "I'm not going to play games with either of the parties in this case. When I started practicing law, game playing wasn't tolerated. Now it seems to be all I see from the lawyers in this state." The judge was rambling, perhaps from fatigue, perhaps because the peculiar facts regarding Debray's sudden appearance and equally quick disappearance allowed for no easy solution. Harrigan and Pickering had no alternative but to wait for Blake to finish his lecture before he returned to the subject of Debray.

Finally, after several more discursive asides about the decline of legal standards in the 1990s, Blake announced his decision. "What I'm going to rule, gentlemen, is that the State may schedule the deposition of Mr. Debray on as little as eighteen hours' notice to the petitioner. If the witness cannot be located prior to the hearing, I will entertain a motion to limit his testimony to the parameters of his written declaration. Since a copy of that declaration was attached to Mr. Harrigan's supplemental witness list and served on the state, I can't see how the State will suffer any prejudice from that procedure."

"And if the witness doesn't appear for the hearing?" Pickering asked.

"If the witness fails to appear for the hearing, Mr. Pickering," Blake answered with another withered smile on his face, "your prayers will be answered. In that event the declaration will be considered hearsay and inadmissible."

The attorneys acknowledged their acceptance of the court's ruling, and Blake called the session to a close. Leaning again on the strong right arm of his clerk, the judge struggled from the bench and slowly walked into his chambers.

Pickering remained in the spectator section of the courtroom to give a brief interview to KZSF radio's John Aragon. With electronic media banned from the courtroom, Aragon conducted his Q and A with pen and paper just like a newspaper reporter, intending to broadcast the deputy AG's comments with the evening news.

In the meantime, Harrigan made a beeline for the elevator. With Debray still on the loose, the last thing he needed was to join the mini press conference and answer a lot of open-ended questions. At this point the less the media and Pickering knew of his plans for the hearing, the better.

Unfortunately, Pickering's parley with Aragon lasted no more than a good sound bite, and the prosecutor managed to catch up with Harrigan outside the seventeenth-floor elevator. Despite his announced acceptance of Blake's ruling, Pickering was smarting from the thought that he might yet be sandbagged. With his prosecutorial suspicions multiplying by the nanosecond, his baser instincts soon took over. "I expect you to cooperate fully with our efforts to depose Debray," he snapped, seeking to put the fear of God in Harrigan. "I won't tolerate any b.s. on this thing."

"We have no intentions of being uncooperative," Harrigan replied vaguely.

"If I discover that you've concealed the witness, I won't hesitate to prosecute."

"Are you threatening me?" Harrigan asked. Although he was a little surprised at Pickering's thuggish tone, he had years of experience fending off the bullying tactics of prosecutors who thought they had a license to throw their weight around. Rather than intimidate Harrigan, Pickering's remarks only served to piss him off. Had the two men been alone in a dark alley, Harrigan might even have acted on the impulse he felt to slap the silly mustache and scowl off his adversary's face.

"No one's making any threats," Pickering quickly corrected himself, fearing that his comments might be overheard by others in the corridor. "But when and if you locate Debray, I expect you to tell us without delay."

There they were again, the words "without delay"— the leitmotif of the attorney general's office. Did the AG really believe that bringing a speedy end to Harold Ashbourne's life would make the streets of California any safer?

As Pickering completed his ultimatum, the elevator doors opened and Harrigan stepped inside the crowded compartment. As the doors began to close, Harrigan's eyes locked on the granite face of John Goodnow, who had been standing next to Pickering and doing his best pantomime impression of a nononsense cop.

"I'll be in touch, Mr. Harrigan," Goodnow said without a trace of emotion.

It was always the quiet ones like Goodnow who caused the most trouble, Harrigan thought as he stepped off the elevator on the ground level. The idea of Goodnow stalking him the next two weeks was almost enough to make him wish he'd become a tax attorney.

SIXTEEN

After an early lunch of linguine *à la vongole* at a little Italian restaurant near the courthouse, Harrigan hailed a taxi for the short ride back to the Hotel Mayfair. Like any good lawyer, he spent the brief interlude in his schedule assessing his performance. Had he said everything in court he had intended to say? Had he successfully rebutted Pickering's arguments? Had he left the judge with the impression that he was the best lawyer in the courtroom?

Harrigan considered the questions one by one and was by no means disappointed with his answers. While his presentation had not been flawless, the hearing could not have gone better. He had managed to keep Debray on his witness list, and even if Debray failed to surface in time for his deposition to be taken, Judge Blake would at most order that his testimony be restricted to the subjects covered in his declaration. Since the declaration confirmed Ashbourne's alibi and listed the cities Debray had lived in during his years of self-imposed exile, Harrigan was hard pressed to see a downside in the judge's ruling. With a little creative advocacy, he'd have ample room to craft a solid direct examination.

Harrigan also knew he'd been fortunate to escape from Pickering without disclosing his knowledge about Debray's plans to conduct his own investigation into the Denton murders. All that Pickering—or Judge Blake, for that matter—had inquired was whether he knew how to find Debray. He had answered that question truthfully and remained at least a step ahead of the prosecution in what promised to be a spirited contest to see who could locate him first. There was, to be sure, the possibility that Debray would decide to go underground again and leave Ashbourne twisting in the wind, but Harrigan had long ago learned that nothing in life comes with a problem-free guarantee. With or without Debray, he would put on a decent case. He owed as much to Harold Ashbourne, and to himself.

The rest of the afternoon held out the promise of a rare break from the action. Harrigan hadn't had so much as an hour of waking time to devote to recreational purposes for at least two weeks. Arriving back at the Mayfair just after one o'clock, he planned on hanging out at the hotel until Josie phoned later in the afternoon. Until then a hot tub and swim in the Mayfair's enclosed rooftop spa seemed like a good way to renew his spirits before resuming the grind.

As usual, his plans went awry, and even sooner than he might otherwise have expected.

"There's a gentleman to see you," the desk clerk called out as Harrigan made his way across the hotel lobby.

Before Harrigan had time to react, a well-dressed man with receding brown hair and a neatly trimmed full beard advanced toward him. With his right arm extended for a hearty handshake and a black leather valise clutched in his left, the guy was either a well-to-do Jehovah's Witness looking for new converts, an insurance salesman, or a fellow member of the profession Americans most loved to hate.

"Peter Harrigan?" the well-dressed man asked.

"That's me," Harrigan answered warily. The thoughts of plunging into the Jacuzzi faded from his mind as he shook the man's hand.

"Fred Wallace. Pleased to meet you."

"Likewise," Harrigan answered, trying to conceal his surprise at being visited at his hotel by yet anther former Savior of the Earth.

"I heard that you were in the Bay Area conducting interviews with the members of my old political group. I spoke to your investigator a few years back, and I thought you might want to talk to me again."

"And you just happened to guess that I was staying at the Mayfair. I'm impressed."

"Actually, I phoned your office this morning. Your secretary told me you were here. If this is a bad time, we can make another appointment. I have an office nearby in the financial district."

"No, I don't have anything pressing this afternoon." Duty before pleasure always, Harrigan thought to himself. It was a lesson he learned as a youth in Catholic school and a creed he had lived by ever since. "Cup of coffee?" he asked, turning his head in the direction of the Mayfair's restaurant.

"I'll buy," Wallace offered. For an ex-radical he seemed extraordinarily accommodating and prosperous, but then, the Saviors were nothing if not an extraordinary lot.

With the lunch crowd thinning out, Harrigan and Wallace had their choice of tables. They selected a quiet one with a view of the rose gardens in the hotel's interior courtyard. "How did you find out that I was reinterviewing the old Saviors?" Harrigan began their conversation.

"Bob Jenkins called me Friday night."

"So you and Jenkins keep in touch?"

"On an occasional basis. He's about the only one from the old group I have anything to do with these days."

"Do you still regard him as a friend?"

"Our relationship is both personal and professional. By that I mean, I like Bob a great deal and I occasionally sign on as an outside attorney on the lawsuits brought by the Environmental Action Council. I have offices both here and in Los Angeles, and I like to keep my hand in a little public-interest work."

Harrigan took a few sips from his coffee and pulled the file with Carlos' old interview notes from his briefcase. So far Wallace seemed like a typical self-centered lawyer in a three-piece suit. "So you still consider yourself an activist?"

"To a certain extent, but nothing like the old days." Wallace took the quizzical look on Harrigan's face as an invitation to elaborate. "Back then we really thought we were going to rewrite history and change the world. We thought it was possible to lead lives filled with social purpose, love, and what we liked to call 'community,' which was our way of saying that the party never had to end. All that without joining the rat race."

"I remember sharing some of that sentiment," Harrigan said. "And now?"

"I've got a deposition in a wrongful-death case tomorrow morning, an old client I got a $250,000 personal-injury settlement for wants to sue me, and the IRS has scheduled me for an office audit. Come on, you're a lawyer. I don't have to tell you it's a cold, heartless planet out there."

Harrigan nodded in agreement. "What about your wife?" he asked, gazing at Carlos' memo on Wallace. "You had a child. She must be . . ."

"Thirteen years old," Wallace answered. "She lives in Eureka with her mother. I see her maybe two or three times a year."

"That must be tough." Harrigan was beginning to feel sorry for Wallace and the way he had been shut out of his daughter's life.

"You get used to it. Sylvia, my ex, has changed her name back to Peterson." Wallace reached into his coat pocket and pulled out a date book and a ballpoint pen. "If you're planning on looking her up, too, I'll give you her address, phone number, and directions," he said, putting the pen to a sheet of paper torn from the date book. "She lives in an old Victorian on a hill. I'm still paying for the house," he added sarcastically. "Tell her hello."

"Look, I don't want to take up any more of your time than I have to," Harrigan said, "so let me get down to the point. I have reason to believe that Harold Ashbourne is innocent."

"If you mean that story about him being with Debray, I'm afraid I can't help you."

"Where were you when Professor Denton's home was firebombed?"

Harrigan's question brought out the irritable lawyer from behind Wallace's affable veneer. "I already explained that to the police *and* your investigator. I was in Berkeley, in my apartment, playing Scrabble with Sylvia and Charlie West."

"All night?"

"Until well past midnight. The three of us were crossword and Scrabble fanatics. It's just something we share in common."

There was a certain edge to Wallace's voice. Harrigan couldn't quite put his finger on the source, but he knew it was more than the standard discomfort most witnesses felt during the interviews. "Tell me about West," he said after a moment's silence.

"What's to tell?" Wallace shrugged his shoulders.

"What's your opinion of him?"

Wallace paused as if searching for the right words. Gazing out the window, he pointed at the rose garden. "See that rock?" he asked. "If you lift it up, the chances are something long and slimy will crawl out."

"I take it you don't like him very much."

"There's no love lost between us."

"Did the two of you have a political falling out?"

"No, it wasn't anything like that." Wallace began fidgeting in his seat and glancing anxiously at his watch.

It didn't take a rocket scientist to deduce that if the reason for the bad blood between Wallace and West wasn't political, then it had to be personal. Harrigan might have phrased his next query more delicately but opted instead for the blunt approach. "Did West have anything to do with your divorce?"

The blush that suffused Wallace's face was as close as Harrigan received to a direct answer.

"Why don't you run that one by Sylvia?" Wallace said testily. He looked at his watch again. "It's past two, and I think I've given you enough information for one afternoon." He laid down a five-dollar bill and managed a good-bye smile. "Good luck with your case."

Harrigan finished the last of his coffee and watched Wallace leave the restaurant. In the ancient world, he reflected philosophically, all roads led to Rome. In the case of Harold Ashbourne and the murder of Gilbert Denton, they all seemed to lead to Professor Charles West. It was still too early to hang the Judas bell on West, but behind the calm academic facade the professor seemed to have all the hallmarks of a man with zero tolerance for anyone who got in his way.

SEVENTEEN

If they had been in a trendier part of town, Josie and Dennis might have been mistaken for a Hollywood couple on their way to a power lunch. Dennis, lithe and trim and decked out in a brown leather designer jacket with black T-shirt, looked like he had just stepped out of an *Esquire* fashion spread. Josie, with her silky black hair spilling over her shoulders and her drop-dead body accentuated by a tight turtleneck and hip-hugging jeans, was definitely *Vanity Fair* material.

To Ernestine Daniels, the crusty old receptionist who guarded the front desk at Ames Engineering like a Pentagon sentinel, Hollywood might as well have been on the other side of the moon. In the mid-Wilshire district, where Ames Engineering, Inc., occupied the top five floors of a thirty-six-floor smoke glass and steel high-rise, the closest anyone got to box-office stars was the afternoon soaps. For Ernestine, Dennis and Josie were just another workaday pain in the ass to manage and contain.

A former elementary schoolteacher who had been bored out of her mind with retirement, Ernestine had been with the company only for a year and a half, but she was extremely loyal and, when circumstances dictated, quite tenacious. Unlike the young but attractive airheads who often held receptionist positions in corporate L.A., she was also highly competent. From a management perspective, her strongest quality was her unerring ability to distinguish which visitors to butter up and fetch coffee for from those she could treat like curbside solicitors.

Arriving unannounced, Dennis and Josie normally would have fallen into the curbside camp and been told to shut the double oak-finished hardwood doors on their way out. Given Ernestine's initial reaction, Josie was forced to resort to her now well-polished routine of displaying her investigator's badge and uttering the solemn promise of a late-afternoon subpoena for Ernestine's supervisor and the corporation's custodian of records.

"I'm here on a murder case," Josie emphasized, sensing that Ernestine's surly demeanor was beginning to soften. "You can tell that to Mr. Ames. The name of the victim was Gilbert Denton. I think the name will ring a bell."

As usual, the routine worked wonders. "Mr. Ames is a very busy man, Ms. Guzman," Ernestine said resolutely but with a sprightly new inflection. She wrote Josie's name on a memo pad and reached for the phone. "But I'll see what I can do."

"He is in, isn't he?" Josie asked in a tone that, while not openly hostile, made it clear that she had no intention of taking a rain check.

"Yes, ma'am, he is. But he's probably in a meeting. I'll just call upstairs and let his secretary know you're here. In the meantime, if you'll have a seat." She

gestured toward the standard-issue waiting-room
sofas in the corner of the reception area. "Would you
like something to drink?"

Josie and Dennis declined Ernestine's offer and
prepared for what promised to be a long sit. The
dark blue two-seater where they alighted afforded a
good view of the action on the other side of the reception area. A set of floor-to-ceiling glass doors
opened onto a spacious floor plan designed to mini-
mize waste and maximize efficiency. The room was
filled with well-dressed women and men, some
leafing through filing cabinets, others walking purposefully with important-looking blueprints and construction documents in their hands. At least a dozen
others were seated behind modern slanted drawing
boards, with T-squares, compasses, and expensive
calculators in their hands. As important as the work
performed in the room no doubt was, it was clear
that the real seat of corporate power resided on the
upper floors. Nonetheless, judging from the level of
exertion among the grunts, Ames Engineering wasn't
hurting for business, even if the rest of California
was still in a recession.

Finally, after they had skimmed through every
back issue of the *Engineering News Record* and *Forbes*
stacked on the reception area's coffee tables, the
doors to the main elevator opened and a small middle-aged woman with a brown Nancy Reagan-style
hair bob stepped out.

"Ms. Guzman?" the woman asked, eliciting an affirmative response from Josie. "I'm Agnes Dillworth,
Mr. Ames' secretary. If you and your friend will
come with me, Mr. Ames will see you now."

Inside the elevator, Agnes inserted a security card into the control panel that enabled them to travel to the top floor of the building. Within seconds the doors opened onto a high-tech anteroom filled with sleek Swedish-style sectionals, high-gloss chrome and steel lamps and end tables, and a recessed lighting system that announced to all concerned that they were entering a place of influence and discernment. Instead of the usual institutional semigloss, the walls were covered with a soft Navajo white fabric. An assortment of expensively framed black-and-white photo enlargements on the walls depicted various engineering projects in progressive stages of construction: aerial views of the Oroville Dam and the California Aqueduct, a wide-lens shot of the Edmonston Pumping Plant, an exterior picture of a wastewater-treatment facility from an unidentified venue in Southern California. There was even a 1950s-vintage photograph of former Governor Pat Brown at a bill-signing ceremony, the chief executive surrounded by a group of middle-aged white men in the kind of nondescript dark suits favored by government bureaucrats of the era.

Agnes led Josie and Dennis across the anteroom's clear pine hardwood floor and past a modular secretarial station staffed by an intelligent-looking young woman whose job it was to see that the visitors to the top floor had their every need attended to while the company bigwigs finished up their phone calls and memos before inviting their guests inside. "It's okay, Barbara, they're with me," Agnes said to the young woman as she opened another set of double glass doors that led to the interior.

Ben Ames' office was located at the end of the corridor, past the main conference room, with its gigantic boardroom table and panoramic view of the city and a succession of medium-size offices marked with the names of the company's vice presidents and department heads. It was already lunchtime, and except for an attractive dark-haired man in a three-piece suit who smiled amiably at them, the floor seemed virtually empty.

Agnes paused and knocked at the big wooden door with the name Benjamin Ames, CEO, embossed in large gold block lettering.

"Come in," a commanding voice called out from inside.

Agnes opened the door, introduced Josie and Dennis, and retreated obediently to her own secretarial station down the hall.

"Make yourselves comfortable," Ames said, motioning toward the pair of leather wing-backed client chairs in front of his large crescent-shaped black lacquered desk. With his suit jacket off and his shirtsleeves rolled up, he had the appearance of a man who would be equally comfortable closing a multi-million-dollar deal or hammering a fence post into a remote plot of ranch land. Though entirely white, his hair was thick and full, making him look far younger than his sixty-five years.

"Agnes tells me you're here about Gilbert Denton's murder," Ames said when everyone had settled in.

"We represent the man who has been convicted of that crime," Josie responded. "Mr. Witter and I are conducting an investigation for the lawyer handling the case, Peter Harrigan."

"I can't imagine what you want with me, Ms. Guzman, but I'll be willing to give you twenty minutes of my time." Ames paused to flip through a date book on his desk. "Before we begin, I just want to tell you that I don't appreciate the strong-arm tactics you pulled with my girl downstairs."

"We meant no offense." Dennis assured him.

"I could have had you thrown out on your ears and I'd have been within my rights. But a man like me gets used to dealing with lawyers, and I figured you'd simply come back later." Ames stroked his chin and trained his intense dark eyes at Josie, whom he immediately concluded was the brains of the outfit. "The clock starts running now, Ms. Guzman."

Josie gave Ames a capsule summary of Ashbourne's legal claims, avoiding any direct reference to Debray. Her efforts consumed a good five minutes of her allotted time.

"So you think your client might be innocent," Ames mused, "but you have no idea who the real perpetrators are."

"We think there may be a connection between Denton's murder and the last book the professor was working on."

"And what does that have to do with me?"

"Professor Denton was going to profile several of the most influential landholders in the southern section of the Central Valley," Josie explained. "Your family was among them. The problem is that all of Denton's research for the book has disappeared."

"And you think I might have it," Ames laughed. "Is that what this is all about?"

"No," Josie replied, showing a trace of frustration.

"We just wanted to ask what, if anything, you knew about the book and how you felt about Denton. His wife has told us you knew each other."

"How is Cynthia?" Ames asked. Coming from someone else the question might have seemed perfunctory. Ames, however, seemed genuinely interested in Mrs. Denton's well-being.

"She's a fine person and she seems to be doing well," Josie replied, "but then I wouldn't really know." She paused and regarded Ames carefully, mindful of the strict time limits he had placed on their interview. "So what about Professor Denton; how well did you know him?"

Ames leaned back in his swivel chair and folded his hands in his lap, revealing a gold wedding band on his left ring finger. On one section of his desk an arrangement of old family photographs included a group shot of Ames, his wife, and what seemed like his two sons on a small fishing boat in some tropical locale. "We weren't exactly close friends," Ames began thoughtfully, "but Gilbert and I knew each other for quite some time. I first met him when he was in high school. His family had migrated to the valley from Oklahoma in the thirties, and he was hired by my family as a summer ranch hand."

"And you worked together?"

"I had just finished up my degree in engineering at Stanford, and my father thought it would be a good idea if I came home and got some calluses on my hands before I joined him here at Ames Engineering." Ames smiled slightly, as if recalling a fond memory. "So I went home and worked one last summer supervising a bunch of roughnecks building a new corral and stables. Gilbert was a member of my crew. And I don't mind saying he was one of my best workers."

"But how did a man like you come to develop an interest in a poor kid like Gilbert Denton?"

"Just because my family had money, Ms. Guzman," Ames answered testily, "doesn't mean we were snobs. When my grandfather arrived in Bakersfield, his pockets weren't exactly lined with gold. It took a lot of hard work for the Ames family to get where it is today."

"I'm sorry, I didn't mean to offend you," Josie said. It was the second time in less than five minutes that either she or Dennis had offered an apology. Men like Ames, who were used to getting their way, were adept at putting people on the defensive and at structuring discussions on their own terms. Such people always made for the most difficult interviews.

"Anyway," Ames continued, "Gilbert was the one ranch hand I could talk to. I got to know him and encouraged my dad to put in a good word for him with one of his friends on the board of regents of the University of California. I don't know how much it actually helped, but Gilbert won a scholarship to Berkeley."

"He must have felt indebted to your family."

"Oh, I don't know," Ames said modestly. "Gilbert was a smart kid, and he'd no doubt have succeeded on his own."

"Did you keep up with him after he became a professor?" Josie asked.

"Not really. He went on to write his books, and I moved down here to help my father run the business.

We'd exchange Christmas cards and occasionally run into each other when we were both back in Bakersfield, but it wasn't until about a year before that awful firebombing that we reconnected."

"How did that happen?"

"He phoned me at the office and told me about that book you mentioned."

"How did you feel about that?"

"I was tickled pink that the Ames clan figured so prominently in Gilbert's study." Ames chuckled to himself. "I invited him out to the ranch and let him rummage through our old photo albums and scrapbooks. He really seemed to get a kick out of that."

"Did you talk about politics and the environment?"

A slight scowl crossed Ames' face, the kind of expression, Josie assumed, he affected when disagreeable subjects came up at board meetings. "Politics and environmental issues were always a sore spot for us, even when we were young."

"Did you disagree about water projects like the Peripheral Canal?" Josie asked.

Josie thought Ames looked slightly surprised, and even a bit uncomfortable, at the mention of the canal. "We did indeed," he said. "I was a major supporter of the canal, and I tried to talk some sense into Gilbert on the issue. For a time there I thought I had succeeded in turning him around to my way of thinking, but I was wrong."

"Did you have some kind of falling out?" Josie pressed for more details.

Ames shook his head. "No. I just think that in the end Gilbert had a fatal flaw that tied him to those people who were out to save the whales and the forests from predatory businessmen like me."

"Why was that a fatal flaw?"

"Because it wound up getting him killed." Ames pressed his thick right forefinger on the intercom and summoned Agnes to his office.

"You're referring to the Saviors of the Earth?" Josie inquired.

"I'm referring to your client, Ms. Guzman, who was convicted of murdering Gilbert and his son—what is it now, twelve years ago?" As Ames looked at Josie and Dennis, his face hardened and his tone became accusatory. "I don't think I'll ever understand why the courts let these cases drag on forever."

Before Josie could mount a reply, Agnes reentered the office. She took up a position midway between the door and Josie, dutifully awaiting instructions.

"Agnes," Ames said, "I'd like you to give each of our guests a copy of our prospectus on their way out." Turning to Josie, he added, "Our company brochure should answer any questions you might have about the history of Ames Engineering. If not, and you still want to drop off a subpoena, I'll leave word with Agnes on how you can contact my attorneys. I keep a half dozen or so on retainer."

Both Ames and Josie knew that there would be no subpoenas. The old man had given her exactly twenty minutes of his time, answered all of her questions, and told her virtually nothing of value about the Ashbourne case.

As she and Dennis said their good-byes to Ames and Agnes, Josie felt almost foolish about having wasted both their time and her own. It was not until she and Dennis had returned to her Beemer in the building's underground parking lot that it hit her. With all the legal talent available to him, the only reason a man like Ames would take time out to speak to an investigator on a twelve-year-old murder wasn't because he was afraid of a little subpoena. It was to find out what Josie was after. She may have been the one asking the questions, but it was Ames who had really conducted the interview, controlling its content and direction from start to finish.

EIGHTEEN

After being toyed with by Ben Ames, Josie wanted nothing more than to go for a swim or a long jog and let her frustrations fade into the sunset. It took Dennis—good old debonair Dennis, who sat through the tête-à-tête with Ames like a dumbstruck altar boy—to remind her that the afternoon's agenda was only half completed. They had one more stop: the city of Pomona on the eastern edge of Los Angeles County, where, according to Carlos' old report, Bob Gardner ran an auto-repair shop out of his home.

"I don't think Peter would ever have forgiven you if you had knocked off early," Dennis teased as they sped along Interstate 10.

"I think Peter's problem is that he can't forgive himself," Josie replied. From their initial introduction over Sunday morning breakfast, she and Dennis had established an easy, chatty rapport, and she sensed an opportunity to pump him for personal information about Harrigan. For Josie, sharing her innermost concerns with a gay male, even one she had just met, was entirely in character. Living in San Francisco's Mission District, just a few blocks from the lavender mecca of Castro Street, she numbered several gay men among her better friends. She especially liked their company during periods like the present, when her love life was in a lull, finding them to be an invaluable source of solace, insight, and irony about men in general. They were so much easier to talk to than straight guys and in some ways even easier than many women.

"This is true," Dennis answered thoughtfully, "but then he's been through an awful lot."

"You really like him, don't you?"

"He's a good person. The best boss I've ever had." A smug little smile crept over Dennis' face. "And the best-looking one, too. That chiseled chin, those soft blue eyes."

"What's that supposed to mean?"

"You think I didn't notice the way Peter's face lit up when you strolled into the kitchen yesterday? I thought it was Christmas all over again. Your face, too, for that matter. I don't think it was the blueberry pancakes he was flipping that had the two of you so hot and bothered."

"It was that obvious?"

"Honey, even a blind drag queen would have noticed," he said in a swishy voice he would use only in the company of someone with whom he felt entirely comfortable. "I don't see what's holding the two of you back."

"Well, to begin with I hardly know him." Although her eyes were glued to the road, Josie's tone betrayed the depth of her interest.

Dennis gave her a you-must-be-kidding look, replete with open mouth and raised eyebrows. "What you see is pretty much what you get. From what I understand, he was something of a social activist in college but nothing too extreme. Mostly, he was a dedicated family man, devoted to his wife and kids, and his work." As he related Harrigan's story, Dennis became suddenly serious, diverting his eyes to the passenger window before continuing. "Peter was one of the luckiest guys you'd ever want to meet. He had everything he ever wanted, and in a matter of seconds he lost it all."

"I know," Josie responded in a voice filled with empathy. "I shouldn't have been so critical of him. But he seems to have rebuilt a life for himself."

"To a certain extent I guess that's true," Dennis agreed. "He has a few friends and he dates occasionally, but there's nobody special." His tone was reassuring, like a high school kid encouraging a shy friend to pursue a new romance.

"What about the rest of his family?"

"Peter doesn't talk much about his childhood, but I know that he was born in Boston and that his parents moved to California when he was in high school."

"Are his folks still alive?"

"They passed away before I came to work for him. He has a brother in Phoenix, but they don't seem to speak very often, at least not that I'm aware of."

"Sounds like he's become a real loner."

"Sounds like a good opportunity for someone to get in on the ground floor before someone else beats her to it. It's been a long time, and I think Peter's ready for a real relationship." As Dennis spoke, he pulled down the flap on the passenger-side visor to make a quick check in the mirror of his blond coiffure.

"It's perfect," Josie said.

"What's perfect? Your chances with Peter?"

"No," Josie said in a studied deadpan. "Your hair."

Dennis gave her another incredulous gaze as she pulled onto the freeway exit for Gardner's home.

No one would know it from its present smog-choked environs, but the city of Pomona derived its name from the Roman goddess of fruit. Back in the 1920s, when orange groves lined the land and W. K. Kellogg raised Arabian horses on his huge ranch, the name was a good fit. But by the mid 1990s the city had long since forgotten its pastoral history.

With a population well over a hundred thousand, Pomona was the home of the widely respected State Polytechnic University and the host of the annual Los Angeles County fair, held every September in the community's immense multipurpose Fairplex. But like many mid-sized American cities, the place had become a casualty of declining tax bases and racial unrest. With the growth in population and the closure of many of the defense and aerospace plants that had taken up residence in the town after World War II, Pomona was definitely a community in decline, plagued by a flight of businesses from the downtown section, random street crime, and black and Latino gangs that had turned the poorer neighborhoods into after-dark shooting galleries.

Bob Gardner lived in a racially mixed stretch of modest wood-frame homes east of the freeway. It was the kind of neighborhood where kids played baseball in the streets, the women hung laundry on backyard clotheslines, and tattooed men drank cans of Coors as they worked on old cars in the front yards of their ramshackle residences. In a more up-scale area the neighbors might have complained that Gardner had no less then six beat-up vehicles—two Honda Accords, a Toyota Celica, a Buick Skylark, and two small-bed Ford pickups—squeezed onto the weed-covered patch in front of his house. Here, his de facto parking lot was never an issue.

Josie parked her Beemer on the street and, with Dennis in tow, walked down the driveway that ran along the side of Gardner's home. The driveway led to a two-bay garage where BOB'S AUTO SERVICE offered cut-rate repairs at unbeatable prices. To accommodate his customers, Gardner had turned what had once been a large backyard into another parking lot, covering the turf with asphalt. At the moment there was a Dodge Tradesman van with a red and white sign on its side that read HUBCAP BOBBY'S and about eight other vehicles of both recent and classic vintage on the lot. Some of the cars had their hoods open, some had their front or rear ends jacked in the air, and others simply stood idle, ready to be picked up by their owners at the end of the day.

Josie and Dennis found Gardner underneath an old Studebaker Silver Hawk with a couple of cracked taillights and a slightly twisted front bumper. "We're looking for the owner," Josie said to the pair of long legs outfitted in grimy blue jeans that were sticking out from under the Studie.

"You found him," Gardner said. "I'll be with you as soon as I loosen this sucker."

A few grunts and heavy clangs of a crescent wrench

on steel later, Gardner rolled out from under the Studie. He stood up and wiped his hands on a grease-stained rag he retrieved from the back pocket of his jeans. "This old honey still has her original trans, if you can believe it," he said, squinting as his eyes adjusted to the glare of the afternoon sun. "It's in there tighter than a virgin's—"

He stopped short of completing the metaphor when he realized he was in mixed company. "If you're looking for Bob's Auto, you've come to the right place. I'm Bob," he said, cracking a friendly grin in anticipation of signing up a set of new customers. Standing fully erect, Gardner was about six foot two, rawboned and wiry, with a broad, weathered face, badly pockmarked skin, and stringy brown hair tied off in a shoulder-length ponytail. In addition to the dirty jeans, he wore an old black T-shirt, with a tear in the seam over the left shoulder and a faded logo in red handwritten script that boldly proclaimed, PSYCHIATRY KILLS.

"We're not here about cars," Josie told him.

A concerned and agitated expression crossed Gardner's face, turning the toothsome grin into an angry sneer. "If it's about that accident last week on the freeway exit," he said loudly, "I told the insurance company all I'm gonna say."

"We're not here about that, either," Josie assured him. "We want to ask you some questions about Harold Ashbourne."

Gardner hesitated, as if canvassing his memory bank. "I haven't heard that name in a goose's age," he said, sounding surprised but relieved that his recent freeway mishap hadn't occasioned Josie's visit.

"I thought that by this time the state would have put old Harold out of his misery."

"He's still very much with us," Josie said, "and we intend to keep it that way." She reached into her purse, pulled out a business card, and handed it to Gardner.

Gardner studied the card for a moment and then stuck it in one of his front pockets. "I spoke to an investigator from Frisco a few years back about the case and told him all I know, which isn't a hell of a lot."

"I'm his partner," Josie informed him, "and this is Dennis Witter. Mr. Witter's a paralegal who works for Peter Harrigan, the attorney representing Harold."

Gardner extended a grimy hand to Dennis, who shook it with the utmost reluctance, taking care to avoid any contact between his cherished threads and the oil stains that seemed to cover every square inch of Gardner's body.

"Well, it's about time I took a little break," Gardner said. "Besides, my daddy used to say a man would be a fool to turn away a pretty lady without hearing what she had to say. Why don't we step into the office?" He looked at Josie and gave her a leering little smile that made the crow's feet around his eyes crinkle and his nostrils flare. Even with a good wash and scrub, he had the kind of face that only a mother reptile could love.

If she hadn't been working on a death-penalty case, Josie would have taken a rain check for the next hundred-year flood rather than follow this odd specimen of late-twentieth-century manhood indoors.

But duty called and she resigned herself to spending the duration of her Pomona holiday in close quarters with Gardner. "Lead on," she said without enthusiasm, waiting for Gardner to show them the way.

Gardner took them up the back stairs and onto a small service porch, where he knelt down and removed his sneakers. "House rule, no shoes inside," he said, sounding like a docent instructing museum patrons to keep their hands off the Rembrandts.

Josie and Dennis exchanged dubious glances but followed Gardner's example, removing their footwear.

The back door opened onto a cramped little room that may have been free of boot prints but otherwise looked like Gardner had retained the services of Homer Simpson as his interior decorator. No more than six feet by ten, the room must have been originally designed as a laundry or pantry. Gardner had converted it into an office, covering the floor with a green indoor/outdoor carpet and the walls with tacky wood-veneer paneling. The walls featured an assortment of black-and-white classic car photos and a *Sports Illustrated* swimsuit calendar, displaying the bikini-clad charms of a super model romping through the surf somewhere in Jamaica or St. Thomas. Another lurid poster—a centerfold from an off-road magazine, showing a well-endowed biker chick in a black leather jacket, spike heels, and fishnets straddling an oversize Harley—was hung on the wall directly over the old wooden desk where Gardner did his paperwork on a surprisingly late-model personal computer. Apart from a broken-down blue vinyl sofa opposite the desk, the rest of the room was a disaster, with stacks of yellowing newspapers rising halfway to the ceiling and a dozen or more half-opened cartons of small auto parts crammed into the corners.

Gardner removed a big glass ashtray filled with a week's worth of cigarette butts from the sofa and invited his guests to be seated. "Excuse me for a moment while I log off the computer," he said, taking a seat at the desk. "I started a letter to my dad this morning before I got busy with that little Silver Hawk you found me under. One of these days I'm gonna wrote an autobiography, 'The World According to Bob.' " He chuckled at his own joke and seemed completely unaware that his laughter went unshared. "Actually, I just write a lot of letters to the old man. We've worked up quite a little correspondence over the years. I've kept all of his letters and made photocopies of all the ones I've sent him."

His current musings safely stored on the computer, Gardner lit up an unfiltered Camel cigarette and swung around on his desk chair to face his guests. "Sorry about the mess, but the maid hasn't been here in at least five years," he quipped. "I have her buried in the backyard along with Jimmy Hoffa." He laughed again, more heartily than before, and offered Josie and Dennis their choice of Winstons or Camels.

"No, thanks," Josie said, speaking for both herself and Dennis. "We don't smoke." Intended as a subtle hint for Gardner to douse the cigarette before she died of secondhand exposure, her plea went unheeded. The guy was not only annoying, she thought to herself, but dense.

"Everyone has his own brand of poison," Gardner

replied, blowing a plume of blue smoke in the air. "I guess this is mine. Now, what was it you wanted to ask me?"

Josie ran through the now well-worn checklist, explaining that Ashbourne's hearing was fast approaching and that the defense team had come to believe that someone associated with Saviors of the Earth, other than their client, was responsible for the Denton murders.

Had their conversation not been interrupted by three phone calls from Gardner's customers, the interview would have been completed in record time. "It's like I told the first investigator," Gardner said after getting off the phone with the owner of the Silver Hawk, "I was in San Diego, staying with my mother, when Denton's house was firebombed. I heard about it on the news."

"Would your mother be able to confirm that?" Josie asked.

"Not unless you're good with a ouija board," Gardner answered. "She passed away two years ago."

"What about your father? He's still alive."

"Lives in a rest home in Tucson, but he wouldn't know anything. He and Mom divorced when I was in high school. You're welcome to the address, and I can vouch for the fact that he pens a pretty hot letter."

"No, that won't be necessary," Josie answered. The last thing she needed was to hunt up the old fart who spawned the fruitcake in front of her.

As Josie paused to ponder her next line of questions, Dennis chimed in. "How did a guy like you," he asked, gazing at the low-brow surroundings, "get hooked up with a group like Saviors?"

"You mean, how did a redneck kid who grew up in a trailer park win friends among the nattering nabobs of negativism?"

"Something like that," Dennis replied, chuckling in spite of himself at Gardner's invocation of Spiro Agnew's description of America's left-wing intelligentsia.

"Have you ever been to an ACLU meeting and seen the way all the white professionals fall all over poor people and minorities?" Gardner answered Dennis' inquiry with a question of his own.

"I'm not sure I get your meaning," Dennis said.

"The people who ran Saviors were rich kids who were either in grad school or already had their Ph.D.'s They wanted someone from the working class to give themselves authenticity, to convince them that they weren't really intellectual snobs."

"You must have been a little younger than the others," Dennis observed.

"Young, impressionable, and filled with a lot of resentment, especially toward the military."

"You were in the service?" Josie asked, attempting to reassert control over the interview.

"The Marine Corps. After my discharge, I went to the Bay Area, got a job with AAMCO overhauling transmissions, and got admitted to Berkeley under the GI bill."

"Who recruited you to join the Saviors?" Josie asked.

"I was an undergraduate in one of Charlie West's classes on European Marxism. Charlie was a pretty good teacher, and he and I got to know each other.

He invited me to one of their meetings, and before long I was one of the gang. To prove how egalitarian they were, they made me part of the group's steering committee. You might say I was a token hire. It was my job to take minutes of all our weekly meetings."

"You wouldn't happen to have kept any of those minutes," Josie asked, waving a hand in front of her face to chase away the smoke from Gardner's second Camel.

Gardner shook his head as he took another deep drag. "They were kept for two weeks and then burned. We were very paranoid."

"Did you know about the friction between Denton, Debray, and West?" Josie asked.

"Sure, who didn't?"

"Did you ever hear either Debray or West threaten Denton's life?"

"I never heard anyone threaten Denton's life, never."

Although Gardner delivered his answer resolutely, there was something in his voice, a trace of evasion perhaps, that led Josie to suspect she hadn't asked the right question. "Did you ever hear anyone connected with Saviors threaten anyone *besides* Denton?"

Gardner abruptly ground out his cigarette in the overfilled glass ashtray and tapped the fingers of his right hand nervously on his thigh. "Now, that's a different question," he said with a sly grin, as though he appreciated Josie's interrogation skills.

"Does the question have an answer?"

Gardner thought for a moment, contemplating how he could best frame his response. "West always blamed his troubles with Denton on Debray. He thought Henry shot off his mouth too much and was going to get the two of them shitcanned from the department, not that he cared all that much about Debray. And, of course, Debray did get himself fired. Anyway, about a month before I left Berkeley, after me and Charlie got good and drunk at his place one night, he asked me how much I thought it would cost to hire someone to put a bullet through Debray's brain."

"Did you take him seriously?"

"Hard to say. Charlie was pretty looped at the time. But if you've ever met Professor West, you'd know that he's a very serious man."

"Is that why you left Berkeley, because of the infighting between West and Debray?"

"No, I just think I realized that the life of the mind wasn't meant for grease monkeys like me."

Josie and Dennis nodded at each other in agreement over Gardner's self-appraisal and the fact that the interview had run its course. They stood up to leave and followed their host back onto the porch, where they slipped back into their shoes and prepared to exit down the driveway. "Thank you for your time, Bob," Josie said, extending her hand.

Maybe it was the way she said his first name or maybe he was just starved for company, but Gardner politely ignored Josie's proffered hand shake. "Before you leave, there's something else I want to show you," he insisted. The enthusiasm in his voice indicated he was not about to take no for an answer.

Despite her desire to get back on the road, Josie followed Gardner to his garage and watched as he opened one of the two bay doors. As she stood in the sunlight on the threshold of the open door, it was difficult for her vision to adjust to the darkness of the interior. But when Bob switched on the overhead light, all was revealed. Hubcaps, row upon row, mounted from floor to ceiling on all three walls, the room was packed with chrome polished hubcaps gleaming in the reflected light.

Momentarily dumbstruck, Josie diverted her eyes from the hubcaps to Bob, who stood like a proud father beaming at the menagerie. "It's the largest private collection in the county," Gardner said. "I've got caps for everything from 1940 Fords to sixties Corvettes and seventies Impalas. I keep a detailed inventory on my computer of every one I buy and every one I sell. It's amazing what that little PC can do."

"Sounds impressive," Josie said, looking back at Dennis to make sure she had not lost all contact with reality.

"I run a booth at the swap meet every other Sunday over at the Fairplex," Gardner continued, "and once a month at the Rose Bowl in Pasadena. If you're ever in the neighborhood, you might want to stop by." He reached inside his shirt pocket and handed her a business card with an R. Crumb-style freehand drawing of an old American auto with its hood up and a mechanic with an oversize wrench performing surgery on the engine. "Since you gave me your card, I thought I'd return the favor."

"Thanks," Josie said weakly, accepting the card. "I'll make a note of the swap meets," she promised, hurrying back to Dennis' side. "But right now we've really got to run."

"It's been nice talking to you, Josie," Bob called out to them as they beat a speedy retreat down the driveway.

"Looks like Peter has some competition," Dennis teased as they walked. "Poor guy probably hasn't been laid in a decade."

Josie gave Dennis a sharp jab in the ribs with her elbow, causing him to grab his side in pain. "Ow, what was that for?" he cried.

"For letting your imagination out of the toilet."

"Hey, I'm not the one who left my business card with that nut. He probably thinks you like him."

Against her better judgment she cast a backward glance down the driveway. Gardner was still there, standing in front of the garage, holding Josie's card in one hand and waving good-bye with the other.

NINETEEN

Crossing the Golden Gate Bridge and heading north on Highway 101 was in some ways like entering another country. From the fog-shrouded headlands of Marin County on the bridge's north side to the rolling ranch land and wineries of Sonoma and Mendocino and the redwood forests beyond, the highway wound through a scenic wonderland that could turn even the most rock-ribbed Republican free marketeer into a save-the-sparrows fanatic. Along the entire stretch, there wasn't a single big city. No smog, no carjackers, no pimply-faced teenagers armed with the latest assault weapons threatening to cut your life-span in half. Just acre after acre of winding rivers and clear lakes, fertile valleys, and coastal mountains plunging to the sea.

Although Harrigan could easily have hopped on a Tuesday morning commuter flight out of San Francisco International, he decided to make the journey up Highway 101 to Sylvia Peterson's home in Eureka behind the wheel of his rented white Chevy Corsica. Like many of the choices he made, the decision to drive was partly nostalgic and partly pragmatic.

The pragmatic part was that the tiny Eureka airport was one of those fly-at-your-own risk fields without instrument flight control or jet service. The place was also prone to fogging over on a moment's notice. Harrigan hated the roller-coaster rides offered by the dinky turbo props that flew into such airports, and the last thing he wanted was to be marooned in some dingy diner waiting for the clouds to lift. In the end, he convinced himself that a long excursion on the road would be safer and possibly even quicker.

The nostalgic part was that the trip up 101 took him along the banks of the Russian River. Years ago, one hot August, when his older son, David, had just turned two and the thought of a second child was still light-years away, he and Stephanie had parked the toddler with his maternal grandmother while he and his still very young wife took off on a two-week self-guided tour of the river and its environs. He and Stephanie fished and swam and spent a sun-splashed afternoon canoeing their way past the all-male Bohemian Club, near the old resort town of Monte Rio, where the country's rich and famous retreated every summer in a ruling-class ritual of psychic and political renewal. When they weren't on or in the river they took time out to sample the state's best chardonnays at the local wineries, and they divided their nights between sleeping under the stars and bunking in at an assortment of rustic cabins and turn-of-the-century bed and breakfasts. After their trips to Mexico, it was about the best vacation Harrigan ever had.

Retracing the route he followed that distant summer brought back the expected memories, but to Harrigan's surprise, they aroused little, if any, sadness. For the first time since the accident on Angeles Crest, he was able to savor the good times he shared with Stephanie without the dreaded sensation that the best part of his life was behind him. It was an old cliché that time heals all wounds, but there was no denying the strange new sense of possibility he felt as he motored north.

There was also no denying the reason for the strange new feeling. In fact, he could sum up the reason in a single word: Josie.

She'd been on his mind since they'd met. And while the attraction at first was purely physical—she was, after all, enough to give a dead man an erection—it was by now much more than that. After his interview with Fred Wallace, Harrigan had waited for her phone call at the Hotel Mayfair like an expectant father, pacing the floor and impatiently calling the desk clerk every fifteen minutes to check on his messages. When she finally rang about eight o'clock, she was at her sister's place in Highland Park. The noise of TV sitcoms and shouting kids could be heard in the background, and Josie sounded tired and frustrated as she recounted the details of her encounters with Ben Ames and Bob Gardner. She felt her afternoon of scrambling had turned up no useful information. The disappointment in her voice was palpable, as if the strain of the Ashbourne case had finally gotten to her.

For the first time in their brief relationship, Harrigan found himself comforting Josie instead of being on the receiving end. He reminded her of what she had always told him—that every successful investigation consisted of a series of small steps that might seem unimportant by themselves. He told her that her interview with Gardner, as weird and gnarly as the guy seemed, actually had been very helpful, serving to cast further suspicion on Charles West as the "Judas" they'd been searching for. And while her talk with Ames may not have turned up a smoking gun or anything close to it, she had wasted only a few hours and had managed to close off an avenue of investigation that would have led nowhere and cost them days of precious time to pursue.

Within minutes of receiving Harrigan's pep talk, she was back to her wisecracking self, making jokes about Gardner's hubcaps and Dennis' too-perfect blond coiffure. "Adonis meets the thing from under the Studebaker," she laughed.

Her spirits restored, Josie agreed to meet Harrigan for dinner back in San Francisco Wednesday evening. Although ostensibly just another meeting on the Ashbourne case, neither of them really expected to transact much business at their reunion. Even if they were unprepared to say so over the phone, the invisible wall that had separated them as attorney and investigator was beginning to crumble. Since they would both be in transit for most of the next two days, they made plans to exchange messages about where and when to meet through the Hotel Mayfair's switchboard. In the meantime Josie had some other matters to take care of with that P.I. friend of hers in downtown L.A. while Harrigan tried his hand at putting the final nail in the coffin of Charles West's alibi for the Denton bombing.

After an early night at a roadside motel, Harrigan had no trouble locating Sylvia Peterson's home the following morning. The old yellow Victorian with a wrought iron fence was exactly where Fred Wallace had told him, on a bluff overlooking the coast on the south end of Eureka.

Harrigan phoned ahead and found Sylvia waiting for him on the front porch. She sat patiently on an unfinished hand-carved two-seat wooden bench while Harrigan parked his car and walked up the set of concrete stairs to meet her.

Sylvia Peterson was a handsome woman in her mid-forties, slim and physically fit, with thick black hair, cut just below the ears, large blue eyes, and a pair of thin red lips that seemed almost to disappear whenever she clenched her teeth in moments of intense concentration. She and Harrigan exchanged pleasantries and the usual idle banter about the quaintness of Eureka and the north coast. Taking a seat in a low-slung Adirondack chair across from Sylvia, Harrigan remarked on the size of the local harbor, and Sylvia informed him that both the fishing and timber industries, once the economic mainstays of the north coast, were actually in the second decade of an irreversible recession. "The biggest cash crop in Humboldt County today," she remarked with a trace of sarcasm, "is marijuana. The attorney general sends so many surveillance planes over the hills out here, it sometimes seems like Vietnam."

Judging from the number of long-haired middle-aged men, old VW buses and Day-Glo rainbow signs Harrigan had seen over stores in the vicinity, Eureka was clearly a refuge of the counterculture, albeit a far kinder and gentler one than Berkeley. "Well, I didn't come here to score," Harrigan quipped.

"No, you came here to talk about Harold Ashbourne," she said, the muscles of her face tightening ever so slightly. "At least that's what you said over the phone."

"I need to ask you a few things about the night of the firebombing." The directness of Harrigan's question not only signaled an end to the pleasantries, but served as a warning that he intended the interview to be very specific and pointed.

Sylvia pitched forward in her seat, preparing to deal with whatever questions Harrigan threw at her. "I think it's terrible what happened to Harold. He was such a sweet guy. But I told the police everything I knew."

"You mean about the Scrabble game?"

"That's right. Fred, my ex, and I were in our old apartment. Charlie West came over around ten with a couple bottles of chianti. We started to play around ten-thirty and didn't finish until at least one in the morning." Sylvia noticed the skeptical expression on Harrigan's face and added, "I even showed the police the scorecards of our game. They looked them over but gave them back. I guess they didn't need them."

"It's hard to figure the police sometimes," Harrigan said, momentarily backtracking. "They may have thought it would have been easy for you to dummy up the scorecards and that there was no way to tell if they were genuine."

"Well, there was no way I could have dummied up my phone records. I ordered a large pizza around eleven, to be delivered. The cops checked out the call."

She paused for a moment to assess how well her story was playing. "I also spoke to an investigator from the public defender's office, but he wasn't very interested in what I had to say, either."

Harrigan knew from his inspection of Ashbourne's trial file that the public defender's office had interviewed most of the ex-Saviors in person. The file was unclear, however, on what kind of contact, if any, had been made with Peterson. "Did Ashbourne's public defender send someone out here to speak with you?" Harrigan asked.

"No, he only called on the phone."

"When?"

"Sometime in 1983, after I moved up here. I told him pretty much what I told the police, about the Scrabble game and all. The entire conversation must have taken five minutes."

Although there was a time in Harrigan's life, back in high school, when he too had gotten interested in Scrabble, the image of Peterson, West, and Wallace wiling away the night over seven-letter word scores seemed too cute and easy. "Tell me," he asked, trying to disguise his incredulity, "how is it that a group of radicals out to remake the world would sit around drinking red wine and playing Scrabble? It seems a little out of character."

"Not really," Sylvia answered. "I've been a Scrabble and crossword junkie all my life." She gestured toward the copy of the *New York Times* Sunday crossword lying on the wooden bench next to her. "I was working on a new puzzle when you drove up. I even teach an adult extension course in crossword design at Humboldt State."

Harrigan gave her a searching look, and she continued, "That's the branch of the state university in Arcata, about ten miles north of here. I teach English lit." She gave him one of her thin-lipped smiles. "I'd be there this morning, but I have a kid inside with the flu."

"I don't suppose Fred gets up here much to see the kid."

"No, he doesn't, but then the child isn't his." Sylvia's back stiffened defensively as she spoke. "Fred and I were divorced twelve years ago. We rarely see each other."

"I must have gotten my information wrong," Harrigan replied, surprised by Peterson's disclosure.

"It's okay," Sylvia said with a fatalistic sigh. "Melinda's father is an English professor at the University of Michigan. I'm afraid he wasn't any more committed to a relationship than Fred."

There are always two sides to a failed marriage, Harrigan thought to himself. Maybe Fred Wallace wasn't the aggrieved spouse he had appeared to be back in San Francisco.

As Harrigan paused to consider his next question, the front door of the house opened and a young girl took a halting step onto the porch. Though pale and tired-looking, she was a pretty kid, with long, braided black hair and big blue eyes like her mother's. The rest of her face, however, from the long, straight nose to the high forehead and the rounded chin, bore no resemblance to Sylvia. It took Harrigan only a few seconds to recognize the child as the girl he had seen in Professor West's Berkeley office.

Harrigan waited as Sylvia excused herself to deal

with the girl. She was gone for no more than a minute, during which Harrigan could hear her scolding the girl about getting out of bed against doctor's orders. "How well do you know Charles West?" he asked when Sylvia returned.

The question seemed to catch her completely off guard. Her back stiffened again and those thin little lips all but vanished as a look of quiet panic flashed across her face. "We were good friends back in the old days," she answered vaguely. "We see each other maybe two or three times a year when I manage to get back to Berkeley. Apart from that," she said, shrugging her shoulders, "I'm not sure what I can say."

"You can start by telling me what your daughter was doing in West's office last week," Harrigan said, raising his voice the way he did while going in for the kill on a witness during cross-examination. "You can tell me why your daughter called West 'Dad.' There isn't any English teacher in Michigan, is there?"

Sylvia rose from the wooden bench like someone had pricked her with a knitting needle. "I'd appreciate it if you'd keep your voice down," she said icily. "I told Melinda the truth about Charlie only last summer, and she's taken it pretty hard."

"So what *is* the truth about Charlie?" Harrigan continued in a softer tone.

Sylvia sank back onto the bench and brought her knees to her chest, looking for an instant like an anxious adolescent. "I wish I could tell you it was some kind of youthful indiscretion," she said, color rising in her cheeks. "You know how casual sex was before AIDS became a household word. But it was more than that, and things became very confusing. At first I thought the baby was Fred's. He's listed as the father on her birth certificate, and for a long time he continued to think that he was."

"West was the cause of your divorce, wasn't he?"

"You've been talking to Fred, haven't you?" She waited for Harrigan's answer and took his silence as an affirmative. "Fred's never forgiven me or Charlie," she continued. "I can't help it if I fell in love with someone else."

"Is that why you lied to the police about West being with you on the night of the bombing?"

"Is that what Fred told you?" She jumped to her feet again, her voice quaking and her blue eyes wide with anger. "He seems to get more spiteful by the year."

"It doesn't matter what Fred told me. What matters is what you tell the federal court." Harrigan reached inside his sports coat and pulled out a neatly typed subpoena commanding Sylvia's appearance at the upcoming hearing in front of Judge Blake. "Lying to the police is bad enough," he added, handing the document to her. "Compounding the lie with perjury could earn you a hefty sabbatical in prison. The federal penalty for lying under oath is five years. That's a long time to be separated from your daughter. Think about it."

"It might surprise you, Mr. Harrigan, but I think about my daughter every day of my life," Sylvia assured him.

"I'm sure you do," Harrigan replied. It was the most genuine statement she had made during the entire interview. While it was clear that she still was not ready to budge from the phony alibi she'd given West, Harrigan could see the apprehension and uncertainty etched on her face. "My phone number's printed on the subpoena," he said, walking down the steps from the porch. "Call me."

The long drive back to the city gave Harrigan plenty of time to think about Sylvia Peterson. Like virtually all the other ex-Saviors, she was lying through her teeth. The only difference was that her lie—the bogus tale about the Scrabble game with Charles West—was very clear, specific, and central to the upcoming hearing in front of Judge Blake. Even if, for the moment, Peterson was still willing to front for West, Harrigan felt certain that she would crack as soon as she was placed under oath. There were some people for whom lying in court was as easy as writing up a grocery list, and there were others whose conscience, or fear, always got the better of them. The threat of a perjury prosecution already had Peterson looking nervous, and unless Harrigan was very much mistaken, the lady also had a conscience, which in the end would lead her to cut West loose.

With Peterson in the bag and ready to implicate West, Harrigan would have yet another basis for his IAC claim against Ashbourne's trial lawyer, Arnold Barnes. Whether because of booze, laziness, or a rush to accept his own client's guilt, Barnes had failed to conduct an in-person interview with one of the key members of the Saviors' steering committee. No trial attorney worth his malpractice premium would have been satisfied with a mere five-minute phone call to Peterson.

And then there was Fred Wallace. When Sylvia started to talk, he, too, could be expected to come around. Wallace hated West and had gone along with the alibi reluctantly, probably out of some misguided sense of loyalty to his ex-wife. His bar card and thriving law practice notwithstanding, once Wallace got started venting his feelings about West, he would make the professor look like a pipe-smoking, academic version of Charles Manson. West would be left with no plausible explanation of his whereabouts for the Denton murders other than the truth—that he was in the Berkeley Hills serving up the kind of cocktails that weren't meant for drinking.

But would West's downfall be enough to win a retrial for Harold Ashbourne? The firebombing, after all, had been the work of two perpetrators. Although Ashbourne and West were unlikely crime partners, the prosecution wouldn't hesitate to suggest that terrorism makes for strange bedfellows. They'd be only too willing to put West into the death chamber along with Ashbourne.

Of course, if Debray ever made good on his promise of providing Harold with an alibi, the case would look entirely different. The problem, as always, was that Debray hadn't made good, and Harrigan knew from his years of practice that the worst thing a lawyer can do is count on an unpredictable witness to deliver exonerating testimony. In the end, it would all come down to Judge Blake and whether or not he thought there were enough lingering doubts about Barnes' trial performance and Ashbourne's guilt to warrant a new trial. Any way you sliced it, Blake was Ashbourne's ace in the hole, an unrepentant liberal in an age when judges were nearly as eager as politicians to see the ultimate penalty enforced.

With Harrigan mulling over the details of the case, the long drive south passed quickly. He stopped for lunch in Mendocino and phoned the Hotel Mayfair, delighted to hear that Josie had left a message suggesting that they meet for drinks at six at the Vesuvio Café near the City Lights Bookstore in the city's North Beach section.

Back in his Corsica, Harrigan felt like a kid getting ready for a big date. The weather, too, took a turn for the better. Matching his upbeat mood, the clouds and fog that had clung to the north coast gave way to brilliant sunshine over the wine country and the Marin headlands. As he approached the San Francisco area, he tuned in the afternoon jazz program on KZSF.

It was five-thirty and still sunny and warm when Harrigan crossed the Golden Gate Bridge and queued up in the long rush-hour line to pay his three-buck toll before reentering the city. As he waited, the jazz hour was followed by news headlines: some promising signs in Bosnia; continuing turmoil in Latin America on the international front; economic crisis on the state and local level; and the sudden death of the oldest sitting judge on the Federal District Court for the Northern District of California.

Correspondent John Aragon came on the air, reporting that Stanley Blake, ill for many years, had died in his sleep of natural causes Tuesday night. News of the judge's death had been delayed until that afternoon at the request of his family. "Blake is survived by his wife of fifty-four years, his three sons, and two daughters," Aragon said. "A spokesperson for the district court announced that the judge's caseload, which had dwindled in recent years as his health declined, had been transferred to the newest member of the federal bench, the Honorable Thomas Taneda, formerly of the Los Angeles County Superior Court. Since Judge Taneda had no existing caseload of his own, he is expected to proceed with his predecessor's cases without postponements or delays."

Harrigan received the news of Judge Blake's demise like a man struggling to make sense of a world in which the laws of physics had suddenly been repealed. He remained motionless for a good sixty seconds until the blaring horns of the angry motorists behind him brought him cringing to his senses.

TWENTY

The report of Blake's death and Taneda's appointment to the Ashbourne case was a severe double setback. Had he received the news under similar circumstances a year ago, or even last month, Harrigan might have considered joining the nine hundred or so other lost souls who had disposed of their troubles by taking a quick plunge over the rails of the Golden Gate Bridge. Although he was safely beyond such desperate measures now, the idea of going toe to toe with Yojimbo was more than enough to dispatch his newfound sense of possibility into the cold gray waters of the bay. If Bill Pickering and his colleagues at the attorney general's office knew anything about the Honorable Tommy Taneda, they were probably wearing pointy party hats and blowing plastic noisemakers in their high-rise office suite.

As Harrigan left the Golden Gate behind him and inched his rental car into the city's crosstown rush-hour traffic, the image of Pickering high-fiving his secretaries and associates slowly faded. Harrigan's mood, however, only darkened. Only an hour ago he had actually entertained thoughts of gaining a new trial for Harold Ashbourne. Now, with Blake gone, the prospects for a fairy-tale ending to the case had given way to a defense attorney's worst nightmare. Taneda would not only bring his pro-death penalty instincts to the hearing, he'd be out to show the world, and especially those who might nominate him to still higher judicial offices, that he was the most hard-nosed minority jurist this side of Clarence Thomas. He would also, no doubt, relish the opportunity to repay Harrigan for forcing him to dismiss the drug prosecution against Eddie Garcia in his last stand as a superior court judge.

With visions of Taneda dancing in his head, Harrigan found his way to North Beach and left his Corsica in an indoor parking structure on Columbus Avenue. The Vesuvio Café was just two blocks away, directly across from the beat poet Lawrence Ferlinghetti's famed City Lights Bookstore, on a little alley the tourist-minded city council had renamed Jack Kerouac Alley. After spending the day behind the wheel it felt good to walk, and Harrigan set a brisk pace, driven forward by the idea of meeting Josie and getting thoroughly plotzed.

Even if he had deliberately set his mind to it, he could not have selected a better location for drowning his frustrations. Since it had first opened its doors in 1949, Vesuvio's had garnered a well-earned reputation as a landmark watering hole in the traditionally Italian North Beach section of the city. A haven in the 1950s for beat icons like Kerouac and touring literati like Dylan Thomas, the bilevel café was a little worse for wear, but its quirky decor had managed to survive the lure of high-tech makeovers. As in its salad days, Vesuvio's ground floor still sported the

same trademark stained-glass windows festooned
with exploding volcanoes, peace symbols, street
scenes, and handwritten verse. The same curious slogan—WE ARE ITCHING TO GET AWAY FROM PORTLAND, OR-
EGON—still hung over the front entrance, painted in
bold black letters against a gold-tinted strip of sheet
metal. And inside, the same kitschy works of art,
from the painting of Homo Beatnikus to the poster
of the typical beatnik family, still hung on the walls,
recalling the café's past.

Judging from the size of the crowd around the
downstairs bar, Harrigan wasn't the only patron on
a mission to find solace in Vesuvio's liquid tonics. In
addition to a handful of locals who had appropriated
the tables near the door for games of chess and cards,
the place was packed, primarily with well-dressed
business types and tourists intent on making the
most of the café's happy hour.

Harrigan ordered a double shot of Glenlivet and
spent the next ninety seconds in search of Josie,
bumping into an anonymous and increasingly boozy
succession of fellow customers. Satisfied that she had
not yet arrived, he climbed the stairs to the less con-
gested mezzanine. He found a small but deserted
Paris-style café table with two wooden saloon chairs
and took a seat, directly across from an alcove-like
booth occupied by a hand-holding young couple. A
sign above the alcove drolly announced that the
booth was RESERVED FOR LADY PSYCHIATRISTS. The
young couple seemed oblivious to the injunction and,
from the looks on their faces, to be years away from
any need for counseling.

Harrigan flagged down a waitress, ordered another

double, and stared out the window. Unaccustomed to imbibing on an empty stomach, he was well on his way to achieving the desired alcoholic haze after only a couple sips.

Unfortunately, the emerging stupor brought with it a rush of pointless self-recrimination not uncommon to those who drink too much and too fast. With the Ashbourne hearing approaching, he began to blame himself for the debacle he foresaw. If only he had insisted on an earlier hearing, he would have had the benefit of Judge Blake instead of having to watch helplessly as Yojimbo sent Harold Ashbourne packing to the afterlife. If only he had put a half nelson on Debray that afternoon in Berkeley, he might even be able to force Taneda to rule in his favor. A better lawyer would never have let his star witness disappear. Never mind that if he had demanded an earlier hearing, he would have had less evidence to present on Ashbourne's behalf than he had now, even without Debray. The third shot of scotch, though just a single, allowed for no such mitigating considerations. Besides, beating up on himself was one of the things Harrigan did best, and this evening he was in rare form.

Josie read the effects of alcohol and regret on Harrigan's face like an advertisement on a bus-stop bench.

"I haven't seen an expression like that since my cousin died of leukemia," she said as she slipped into the seat across from Harrigan. She held a tall, frosty glass of gin and tonic with a lime twist in her right hand and flashed a warm, concerned smile.

"I'm afraid someone *has* died," Harrigan said, stone-faced but far from sober. "The Honorable Stanley Blake has joined that great tribunal in the sky. His place is being taken by an old acquaintance of mine named Thomas Taneda. I'm surprised you haven't heard."

The smile left Josie's face. "I've been on the road all day listening to tapes." Although she had never heard of Taneda, she had a keen sense for disaster. She pushed her drink aside and reached across the table and did the same to the remains of Harrigan's scotch. The last thing they needed was to seek salvation in a bottle. "Exactly how bad is it?" she asked.

It took some sobering up, but after an hour filled with two cups of espresso, much hand wringing, and a long trip to the rest room, Harrigan managed both to clear the cobwebs and bring Josie up to speed on the perils and proclivities of their new judge. The process proved surprisingly therapeutic. Finding renewed strength in each other, they vowed to put on the best hearing possible and to carry the fight for Ashbourne's freedom to the Ninth Circuit Court of Appeals after Taneda gave them the expected horse whipping.

They also vowed to put some food in their stomachs. Since Vesuvio's served only liquid refreshments, this was a project that required a change of venue. Josie suggested that they drive back to the Mission and duck into the Café Tyre, the little bistro where they had eaten the night they met, and which featured Tanya the belly dancer on Wednesday evenings.

"If you're a good boy," Josie said teasingly, "I'll let you slip a dollar inside her harem pants."

"You'll let me? Doesn't Tanya get to decide for herself?" Harrigan laid down a pair of twenty-dollar bills and stood up to leave, his mood lifted by Josie's playful banter.

Outside, the sunshine of the afternoon had given way to the cool, damp air of a typical Bay Area night. A bank of fog had begun rolling in, obscuring the top of the Trans-America pyramid. Josie and Harrigan stopped for a moment to browse the window displays at City Lights, then headed directly up Columbus Avenue for the parking structure where, by chance, each of them had left their cars on the sub-basement level.

To most people, it would have gone unnoticed, but Josie immediately spotted the superficial scratch where the clear-coat red frame met the window of her BMW's driver side door. "Something's wrong," she shouted to Harrigan, who had opened the door of his Corsica about ten parking stalls away and was preparing to drive back to the Mission District.

With Harrigan hurrying to her side, Josie opened the Beemer's door and reached for the trunk release. Besides her spare tire and jack, the only thing left in the trunk was the earthquake-preparedness kit she had purchased from a car wash six months earlier. "Someone's taken my overnight bag and my briefcase," she shouted angrily.

She slammed down the trunk and did a slow burn around the Beemer, looking for more evidence of the break-in. Still steaming, but finding nothing suspicious, she returned to the driver's door and pointed accusingly at the small scratch below the window. "The bastard must have used a slim-jim," she said.

"I'm sorry," Harrigan said in a soothing tone. "After what happened at my house, I know just how you feel." Gazing at the violated vehicle, he added, "I wonder how he managed to disable your car alarm."

"I never use it in parking lots," Josie sighed. "I got tired of all the false alarms caused by people bumping into the car."

Harrigan walked toward Josie and gave her a consoling hug. She let her head rest on his shoulder for a few seconds, then slowly pulled away and ran a hand nervously across her forehead. "My tape recorder and a copy of my interview notes were in the briefcase."

"I'm sorry," Harrigan said again, fumbling for a way to dissipate Josie's sense of loss. "What happened is a pain in the ass, but it's not a catastrophe. You can write off the recorder and the briefcase as business losses, and I'm sure the thief is just going to throw the notes away. You have another copy and—"

"You don't understand," Josie said, interrupting Harrigan before he could complete his sentence. "Somebody followed me here. I went back to my office to make you a copy of the notes, and a white car picked me up on the way out. It stayed with me all the way to this parking lot. I wanted to tell you earlier, but I wasn't really sure if it was my imagination getting the better of me."

She took a step toward the Beemer, preparing to get inside, then turned to face Harrigan again. "I don't want to sound paranoid, but I can't help thinking that this incident and what happened at your house are connected. Someone could be following us."

"It's possible, but I doubt it," Harrigan said. "The sheriffs back home were sure the job on my house was a garden-variety break-in. Some new gang's been working its way up into the hills near my home and finally got around to me. And there must be hundreds of car burglaries every day in this town."

"But I was followed here," Josie insisted.

"What kind of car?" If she had been followed, the cops would want to know.

"I'm not sure. A Chevy or a Ford. It looked something like that Corsica you're driving, or maybe a Taurus or a Tempo. I didn't pay much attention until we hit Columbus Avenue."

"Sounds like a tourist in a rental car just taking in the sights. Did you get a look at the plates and the driver?"

Josie shook her head, annoyed at herself for not paying closer attention. "All I can say is that the driver was a white guy."

"Well, that helps narrow our list of suspects to a few million," Harrigan said with a wry smile.

"And you're on the top of that list, buddy," she chided, shaking her head, her anger and worry beginning to subside.

Her eyes stayed with Harrigan as she slipped into the driver's seat. "About dinner," she said, inserting the key into the ignition. "I probably should phone in a theft report to the police."

"I'll be happy to take a rain check," Harrigan offered, doing his best to disguise his disappointment.

"I'm sure Tanya and her undulating abdominals will be good for another night."

She hurried to correct him. "No, that's not what I had in mind, I was just thinking it might be quicker to stop for some takeout and make the call from my place."

"Sounds great." Harrigan nodded in approval. "Why don't you head home and I'll meet you there with some Chinese?"

In a town with more Chinese restaurants than you can shake a won ton at, grabbing a few egg rolls and some cartons of shrimp fried rice, chop suey, and beef with broccoli ought to have been easy. But by the time Harrigan found a parking spot and waited his turn in line, a good forty-five minutes had gone by. When he finally arrived on the steps of Josie's Queen Anne house with a bag of take-out cartons in his arms, it was past ten o'clock.

His stomach growling, Harrigan pressed the doorbell and waited. Although the porch light and the lights on both the first and second floors were on, Josie failed to respond. Harrigan pressed the bell again and once more elicited no answer. Thinking the bell might be broken, he began to knock on the front door, first softly and then with increasing force.

A series of disheartening thoughts began to race through Harrigan's mind. Had Josie gone out to the police station to file an incident report? Had some other emergency called her away? Had the white car followed her home?

The possibility that Josie was inside and *unable* to come to the door could not be ruled out. The idea sent Harrigan into a panic. He threw his shoulder hard against the front door, but the door was made of solid oak and showed no signs of giving way. Quickly Harrigan looked around the porch for something to use as a makeshift battering ram. He picked up an old wooden deck chair and prepared to slam it against the door when he heard one of the double-hung upstairs windows slide open.

"Peter, is that you?" Josie called. "Where the hell have you been?"

Harrigan took a step away from the door and put the chair down. From his immediate vantage point he was unable to see Josie's face, but her voice sounded clear and unperturbed, except perhaps for some minor consternation caused by his tardiness. "I've been ringing your doorbell," he answered, relieved both that Josie was safe and that she had not witnessed his less than stellar John Wayne imitation.

In less than ten seconds the front door opened. "I'm sorry," Josie said, beckoning Harrigan inside. "You were gone so long I thought I'd have time for a quick shower. I must not have heard the bell." She had on a blue terry cloth robe tied loosely around her waist and a red bath towel wrapped around her still wet hair. Even without her makeup she was a sight to behold.

Harrigan followed Josie into the dining room and was delighted to find the table set, complete with candles waiting to be lit and an unopened bottle of chardonnay chilling in an ice bucket. With a thick oriental rug under his feet and a tasteful display of Mexican-American art on the walls, Harrigan felt relaxed and ready for a good meal. "Let's eat," he said, rubbing his hands together with anticipation. He set the bag of takeout on the table and, turning away from Josie, began to unpack the cartons.

Later, it would be difficult to recall exactly how it happened. Her version would always differ in slight respects from his. But somewhere between lighting the candles and ladling the fried rice into a bowl, their bodies met. It was just a gentle brush at first, something they easily could have ignored but, without speaking, chose not to. As if on cue, the red towel dropped to the floor and the terry cloth robe swung partially open, exposing the smooth olive-toned contours of Josie's breasts. She had a small football-shaped birthmark just above the rim of her right cherry-brown nipple that seemed longing to be caressed and an inviting look on her face that seemed to say, "What are you waiting for?"

From that instant there was no turning back. Harrigan tore off his jacket, shirt, and tie and took her in his arms. He stroked her face and kissed her gently on the lips. She pulled him closer and drove her tongue into his mouth. He ran his hand along the inside of her parted thighs, letting it come to rest on her warm, wet center. She struggled to undo his belt and took his stiffened member in her hand.

Moaning with a desire neither had known in years, they fell to the oriental rug, consigning the Chinese supper on the table above them to the status of a post-coital snack.

TWENTY-ONE

It was a hell of a way to begin the stretch drive toward the hearing, and it left Harrigan's head spinning with unanswered questions. Were he and Josie falling in love, or were they just two middle-aged teenagers with runaway hormones? Would the passion that had overcome them endure, or would it dissipate when the stress and combat of the Ashbourne case that had brought them together was over? All Harrigan understood for sure was that his life had taken a radical U-turn, and he had absolutely no regrets about what had happened.

He had begun his Bay Area odyssey with a trip to Sproul Plaza for a showdown with Henri Debray, the man he'd been searching for since the day he was appointed to represent Harold Ashbourne. He had wound up watching Debray slip away but had somehow managed to bed his investigator. If anyone had predicted such an uncanny turn of events prior to his Berkeley trek, Harrigan would have suggested that they double their dosage of Haldol. Today he might ask them to read his palms or feel the bumps on his head. Then again, maybe it all was inevitable. In retrospect, the most difficult thing to figure was not that he and Josie had gotten together, but how they had held their desires in check at all.

The problem for Harrigan now was keeping his mind on his client and away from Josie's unending physical charms. Even if he and Josie were still on a last-name basis, that would have been no easy matter, not simply because of the charms but because the prospect of going forward with the case left Harrigan feeling a combination of anxiety and dread. With the case now residing in the merciful hands of Tommy Taneda, the last thing he wanted was to set foot back in federal court.

Instinctively his thoughts turned to requesting a continuance of the hearing. Postponements were the last resort of a desperate defense attorney, the next best thing to winning for those whose ultimate defeat was preordained. Any hope, however, of finding relief in the refuge of delay disintegrated the moment Harrigan returned to his Pasadena office Thursday afternoon. He found Dennis, a cup of non-fat *latte* in one hand and a one-page fax in the other, manning the reception desk and eagerly awaiting the boss' triumphal return. "This looks pretty important," Dennis announced, an expression of concern on his otherwise eternally optimistic face.

Issued on the official stationery of the United States District Court and signed by Taneda's clerk, the letter was addressed to Harrigan and Deputy Attorney General William Pickering with reference to the Ashbourne case. "Dear Counsel," the short note began stiffly, "Due to the unfortunate passing of the Hon. Stanley Blake, the above-entitled matter has been transferred for hearing to the courtroom of District

Court Judge Thomas M. Taneda. Judge Taneda will
expect both parties to be prepared to proceed with
the evidentiary hearing as scheduled at 10:00 A.M.,
Monday, October 16, 1995. Absent extraordinary
cause, no continuances will be granted. Any further
inquiries may be directed to the undersigned."

Harrigan carried the fax into his private office and
sank into his desk chair, mentally reeling from the
grim finality of the words that Taneda himself had
undoubtedly dictated. Outside of Mississippi or Ala-
bama, there probably wasn't another judge who
would preemptively deny a continuance request, especially in a case that had been assigned to him only
as a result of a colleague's death. Most federal judges,
even the most hard-nosed conservative s.o.b.'s drawn
from corporate law firms or prosecution agencies,
would have thrown a judicial shit fit for having a
death-penalty case dumped in their lap at the last
minute. Most would have responded by placing the
Ashbourne case on some distant back burner, behind
the misdemeanor and immigration files on their
dockets and their vacation plans for scaling the Him-
alayas with a gang of Sherpas.

But Tommy Taneda had no wife and kids, and as
long as Harrigan had been trying cases in Los
Angeles, he had never heard the judge utter the
words "bon voyage," except perhaps to a defendant
he had just sentenced to a multiple-year stretch in
state prison. If Taneda had instructed his clerk to fax
the "Dear Counsel" letter, it meant that the judge
expected to complete his review of the case record
and be up to speed for what he surely viewed as an
opportunity to prove to the world that there was at

least one jurist in California prepared to end the interminable hold-ups that prevented the death penalty from being implemented.

It also meant that Harrigan had no time to waste dreaming of Josie's lustrous dark hair and the warmth of her firm female flesh pressed against his. He set down the letter, took out a legal pad, and got down to work.

The succeeding days passed in a blur of midnight L.A.-to-San Francisco plane connections and early morning conferences in both cities. Caught up in the last-minute details of serving subpoenas, making arrangements with the state Department of Corrections for Harold Ashbourne's transportation to federal court, and prepping their expert witnesses, Harrigan and Josie managed to squeeze in a few nights together. They were just enough to keep a permanent bulge in Harrigan's fly, but as the case drew nearer the opportunities for romantic rendezvous dwindled and finally disappeared.

In the end, passion yielded to practically and the mounting demands of the case. Like a boxer sworn to avoid sex before a big bout, Harrigan opted for the lawyer's version of self-enforced monkhood. He reserved a one-bedroom "business person's" suite at the Mayfair for the duration of the hearing and steeled himself for the sleepless and solo nights that lay ahead. It was a sacrifice to separate from Josie, but a necessary one, he told himself, if he had any hope of sustaining his concentration.

After making arrangements with Dennis to forward his phone calls to the Mayfair, Harrigan spent most of the Saturday before the hearing packing and flying back to the Bay Area and most of Sunday at Josie's office debating the order of proof he would pursue in court. Although the scope of the proceeding would be limited to the IAC issues Harrigan had raised against Ashbourne's trial attorney, the order, or sequence, in which Harrigan proved his case was up to him. But like the future of his personal relationship with Josie, there was no easy answer as to how best to proceed or how things ultimately would turn out. The fact that he would have to start the hearing without Henri Debray was for the moment his paramount concern, and it left him tossing and turning in his hotel bed.

Still uncertain of his final game plan, Harrigan pushed open the heavy walnut-stained doors to Judge Taneda's seventeenth-floor courtroom at 9:45 A.M. The big room's austere marble and wood appointments seemed to reflect the fact that federal courts were like tiny fiefdoms, in which judges with lifetime tenure wielded nearly absolute power. Tommy Taneda had finally found his element.

He was still standing in the gallery when Bill Pickering tapped his shoulder from the rear and thrust an overly exuberant hand in his chest. Flashing a confident winner's smile, Pickering greeted him like some private school preppie out to greet a rival at the beginning of tennis match. "I hear you and our new judge go back a long way," Pickering said in his irritating nasal voice. He had a grin on his face so wide his dapper little mustache looked like it had been penciled in with eyeliner.

Before Harrigan could reply, John Goodnow, the AG's beefy no-neck investigator, joined them, followed in short order by Josie. Harrigan had to restrain himself from giving her the morning wakeup kiss he had been unable to deliver earlier. There were formal introductions all around, and as Harrigan made his way to the counsel table, the gallery began filling up with a noisy collection of reporters and civilian voyeurs out to experience the vicarious thrills of witnessing the final stages of a capital case. Harrigan caught a sidelong glimpse of J. Arnold Barnes, the attorney whose alleged incompetence had resulted in Ashbourne's death sentence, sitting like an overweight accused child molester in the first row of the gallery. For the briefest moment Harrigan felt a measure of empathy with the man whose reputation he was duty-bound to destroy.

A heavy silence set in as the court reporter and the clerk took their places. A moment later, the bailiff called the morning proceeding to order. "All rise. The United States District Court for the Central District of California is now in session, the Honorable Thomas M. Taneda presiding."

In another instant the rear door to chambers swung open, and Tommy Taneda emerged, five feet six inches of heuristic intensity clad in a loose-fitting black robe that made him look like Batman's little brother. Striding purposefully to the bench, Taneda took his seat on high and proudly surveyed the assemblage before him.

Calling the case to order, Taneda noted the appearance of counsel and let his gaze linger for a moment on Harrigan. "It's good to see you again, Mr. Harrigan." The judge managed a weak smile as he stroked his neatly trimmed goatee.

"It's an honor to be here, Judge," Harrigan responded respectfully, wary of Taneda's unusually cheerful disposition.

His capacity for pleasantries exhausted, Taneda diverted his eyes to the court file and the minutes of the last session with Judge Blake. "This is the time and place for the evidentiary hearing ordered by my predecessor," he intoned, his gaze now shifting between Harrigan and Pickering. "The presence of the petitioner, Mr. Ashbourne, has been ordered. I understand that the bus from that facility is expected shortly."

Taneda looked in the direction of his clerk, who nodded in agreement with the accuracy of the judge's remarks. "Before we commence," Taneda continued. "I want to assure both sides that I have read the record of the state court proceedings, including the transcripts of the petitioner's superior court trial and the preliminary proceedings conducted in this court before Judge Blake. In consideration of the issues framed by Judge Blake, which do not appear overly complex, I expect the hearing to proceed expeditiously and without undue interruption." He tapped the fingers of his small right hand on the bench. "Are there any matters to take up before we hear opening statements?"

Both Harrigan and Pickering rose from their seats simultaneously, vying for the right to be the first to address their concerns to the court. The two attorneys exchanged uneasy looks before Taneda announced that he would hear first from the attorney general's office.

"In our last appearance in front of Judge Blake," Pickering began, "we objected to the addition of an individual known as Henri Debray to the petitioner's list of witnesses for the hearing. Judge Blake gave us leave to take the witness' deposition and instructed Mr. Harrigan to alert us immediately if he had any contact with Debray. We have as yet to hear anything from either the witness or counsel."

"I'm familiar with the prior order," Taneda assured the prosecutor. "Are you requesting the court to preclude the witness from testifying?"

"I would strenuously object to any preclusion order," Harrigan interrupted, drawing a stern look of reproach from Taneda. "I would also request that my client be present for any argument on the issue."

"I have no intention to deprive your client of his opportunity to be present for the hearing, Mr. Harrigan. But this is a preliminary matter, not the hearing itself," Taneda admonished. "I should think an attorney of your experience would appreciate the difference."

As Taneda spoke, his eyes narrowed with controlled anger and a blush rose in his cheeks. Perhaps the strain of jumping into a death-penalty case in his first week on the federal bench was more than Taneda was able to handle.

Realizing he had virtually no case without Debray, Harrigan decided to keep up the pressure. If Taneda forced him to go forward before Ashbourne's arrival, he might be able to preserve his client's absence as a possible issue for appeal. "I apologize for the interruption, Your Honor, but I want our objection to going forward in the petitioner's absence noted for the record."

"I'm sure our very able court stenographer has already taken care of that," Taneda replied icily.

Before Taneda could utter another syllable of invective, the side door to the lockup swung open. Dressed in a blue prison jumpsuit and looking frail and frazzled from the morning's commute, Harold Ashbourne entered the courtroom under the escort of two unsmiling deputy U.S. marshals.

As the judge's gaze shifted from Harrigan to the newly arrived prisoner, his face broke into the closest thing to a broad smile Tommy Taneda might ever have displayed in open court. Speaking with renewed aplomb, Taneda noted Ashbourne's appearance and ordered the deputies to deposit him in the chair next to Harrigan.

"Mr. Ashbourne," Taneda continued after allowing the prisoner a moment to greet his attorney, "the attorney general has moved for an order to preclude you from calling one Henri Debray as a witness at this hearing. Your counsel was just about to enlighten all of us as to what contact, if any, he's had with the witness."

Harrigan felt the eyes of all assembled on him. "We've made every effort to locate the witness," he said, directing his comments as much to his worried client as to the court, "but we have no better idea than Mr. Pickering where Debray is today. I do, however, still believe that he will make good on his promise to appear for this proceeding and give his testimony. I ask the court to give us that opportunity."

"That's not good enough," Pickering snapped after Harrigan had finished. "The State will be severely prejudiced if a witness who has evaded court process and discovery is allowed to testify at this late date."

"Any prejudice the State suffers," Harrigan countered, "will be greatly outweighed by the prejudice to the petitioner. Harold Ashbourne has spent more than a decade on death row for a crime he did not commit. He should not be penalized for a witness' tardiness in coming forward. If Henri Debray does appear and is able to provide exculpatory testimony, a preclusion sanction would surely inject reversible error into the record in the event of an appeal."

Taneda leaned back in his chair, appearing to weigh Harrigan's warning while doing his best to maintain an outward calm. The term *reversible error* sent a shiver down his judicial legs. Although he was singularly unmoved by Ashbourne's claim of innocence—the federal and state prisons were, after all, full of ax murderers and psychopaths who claimed never to have seen a dead body—the idea of having the Ninth Circuit Court of Appeals overturn his first big federal case was surely an unsettling prospect.

"It seems to me," Taneda said, as if emerging from a contemplative fog, "the issue is premature and need be resolved only when, and if, the witness actually appears. If the witness fails to appear, the sanction request will be rendered moot. My ruling, therefore, will be deferred."

Hearing no objections to what was plainly a face-saving cop-out, Taneda announced his readiness for opening statements. "As the petitioner bears the burden of going forward, I'll hear from his counsel first."

Harrigan rose to his feet and with a legal pad clutched in his right hand walked to the wooden lectern in front of the counsel tables. He glanced at the notes he had scribbled on the pad only hours ago, then paused to collect his thoughts. Over the past four years he had imagined himself countless times at precisely this moment, confidently outlining the evidence that would right the terrible wrong that had been done to his client and which in the end would save Harold Ashbourne's life. Now, with Debray's whereabouts and intentions still unknown, he fumbled for a way to begin.

He thought back to the cardinal rule of opening statements he had learned as a law student and had lived by as a trial attorney. *Summarize the evidence you intend to offer, but never promise more in your opening than you know the evidence will prove.* If you do, you'll wind up losing your case before the last warm body leaves the witness stand. The rule was the same in jury trials as in hearings in which judges serve as the trier of fact, such as today's habeas proceeding.

Knowing that Taneda would make him pay dearly for raising claims he ultimately could not establish, Harrigan chose his words carefully, aiming for just the right combination of broad generalizations he knew could not come back to haunt him and enough specifics to prevent Taneda from reaching any premature conclusions before all the evidence was in.

"If it pleases the court," Harrigan began with a respectful nod toward the bench. "Thirteen years ago, a horrible crime took the lives of a most respected man, Professor Gilbert Denton, and his teenage son. Neither the professor nor his son did anything to provoke the crime. Both were asleep in their beds in their Berkeley Hills home when their lives were suddenly taken. Neither, surely, deserved to die."

Harrigan took a step away from the lectern and cast a sympathetic glance at Ashbourne, who sat with his head tilted downward and his hands gently folded on the counsel table. "And neither does Harold Ashbourne, the petitioner in this proceeding, deserve to die for the Denton murders."

Harrigan took another breath and, staring directly into Taneda's impassive eyes, offered a clear and balanced summary of the evidence that had led to Ashbourne's conviction—from the elderly eyewitness who identified Ashbourne at trial to the fingerprint found on the broken wine bottle in front of the professor's home and the pile of Saviors leaflets discovered in Ashbourne's apartment that branded Denton a traitor to the environmentalist cause. Rather than run away from the damning catalogue, Harrigan chose to confront it head on.

"I realize that the petitioner's jury found the evidence against him persuasive, and I completely understand why. Given what the jury heard, they had no other choice.

"We're here today, however, not because of what the jury heard but because of what they did not get to hear. On the issue of guilt and innocence, they never got to hear Harold Ashbourne tell them that he was nowhere near the murder scene on the night of the firebombing. They never got to hear Ashbourne tell them that he spent the evening at Sproul Plaza in Berkeley talking to Henri Debray. The jury never heard from Mr. Ashbourne because his lawyer insisted that he not take the stand.

"Nor did the jury ever get the opportunity to hear Henri Debray corroborate Mr. Ashbourne's whereabouts on the night of the murders. While Debray had left Berkeley by the time of the trial, Mr. Ashbourne's lawyer never bothered to look for him and never bothered to contact Debray's mother, who was still alive during Ashbourne's trial, still residing in New York, and who was for a time still in touch with her son. Such omissions, among others, show that the pretrial investigation of the petitioner's alibi defense was woefully inadequate.

"Hearing nothing of Mr. Ashbourne's alibi, the jury naturally returned a guilty verdict—albeit a flawed one—together with an equally flawed finding of special circumstances. And having returned that flawed guilty verdict, the jury never got to hear, during the penalty phase of the trial, the sad history of neglect the petitioner suffered as a child. In the absence of such mitigating evidence, the jury quite naturally returned a death verdict instead of exercising its discretion in favor of a life term.

"In this proceeding we will endeavor to present the missing evidence the jury never got to consider, and we will show that the reason that evidence was not presented was that Harold Ashbourne was denied his constitutional right to effective assistance of counsel."

Taneda, who had begun making notes of Harrigan's contentions, put down his pen and brought his bearded chin to rest on his right hand in the fashion of Rodin's Thinker. "I assume you'll be backing up your claim with appropriate expert testimony," he said. Though tinged with irritation, Taneda's question was a fair one. In order to establish his IAC claims, Harrigan was obliged to call expert witnesses to state their opinions about Barnes' alleged incompetence.

"Yes, Your Honor," Harrigan answered, still standing behind the lectern. "We'll be calling attorney Andrew Dryer on the guilt-phase IAC question and Dr. Russell Rosen of the California State University at San Francisco on the penalty phase. They, along with members of Mr. Ashbourne's former political group and the petitioner's parents, will enable us to show not only that Ashbourne was denied a fair trial but more important that he deserves a new one to present his side of the story."

Harrigan paused again and looked at the front row of the gallery for Josie. Her beaming face told him what he already knew—that the opening had gone better than he had any right to expect. Feeling himself on a roll, Harrigan considered disclosing his suspicions about Charles West, but pulled back at the last second, preferring to keep the potential blockbuster to himself until either it was confirmed or he became too desperate to care.

"Thank you, Counsel," Taneda said perfunctorily as Harrigan took his seat. "Mr. Pickering?"

The deputy prosecutor stood and straightened his tie. "With the court's permission, Your Honor, the State would like to defer its opening remarks until the conclusion of the petitioner's case. With the situation surrounding Henri Debray unresolved, we think that's only fair."

Whether Pickering was feeling the heat from Harrigan's unexpectedly strong opening, declaring a strategic retreat, or simply looking for an opportunity to regroup, there was little doubt that Taneda would come to the state's aid.

"Sounds like a reasonable request to me," Taneda replied without soliciting Harrigan's input. "We'll stand in recess until two o'clock, when the petitioner will be expected to call his first witness."

Taneda reached for his gavel to bring the session to a close but stopped in mid-motion as his eyes met Harrigan's. "The bailiff and the marshals shall also be instructed to make the prisoner available for consultation with his attorney in the lockup over the lunch break," he said in a conciliatory tone. He nodded in Harrigan's direction in a rare gesture of respect as he brought the gavel down.

TWENTY-TWO

In any trial, maintaining momentum in the presentation of evidence is nearly as important as the nature of the evidence itself. With Harrigan's strong opening statement, the momentum was in his favor. The problem was how to keep up the pressure before Debray's absence caused the pendulum to shift back to the state.

With this consideration in mind, the decision to call J. Arnold Barnes to the stand as the petitioner's first witness seemed to be the best available option. Apart from Ashbourne, Barnes alone could supply a complete overview of the state court trial. It was Barnes' ass, in a professional sense, that was on the line, and rather than allow Pickering to get the first crack at Barnes in the State's case, Harrigan favored a preemptive strike.

Although there was always a risk in beginning your case with an unfriendly witness, a brief conference with Ashbourne in the lockup convinced Harrigan that he had no other choice.

Still visibly agitated from his late arrival in court, Ashbourne had the look of man on the edge as the marshals admitted Harrigan into the court's holding cell at the start of the lunch recess. "I want to take the stand, Peter," he shouted, slapping his right palm hard against the wall of the cell. "I want to tell those bastards what it's like to have your life destroyed for something you didn't do." The dim overhead lights cast long shadows under Ashbourne's bespectacled eyes. As he spoke, he began to pace about the cell, his face twisting with an anger Harrigan had never seen.

"You'll get your chance," Harrigan said in a reassuring tone. The fact that Ashbourne wanted to testify was a positive sign, but in his present condition there was no way he'd hold up under cross-examination. "But first I want you to get used to being in court. I also want you to hear all the other witnesses before you're placed under oath to tell your side of the story. That's an important advantage."

Harrigan watched Ashbourne's rage give way to what he could only interpret as a mixture of resignation and remorse.

The pacing ceased and Ashbourne slumped onto the wooden bench that ran along the lockup wall. He let his head sink into his hands. Then he began to sob. "I know you're right," he said between breaths. "It's just been so damn long and I'm afraid, Peter. I'm afraid. What if we lose?"

The sobbing, too, was something Harrigan had never before seen in his client. It was both unnerving and odd to see a death-row con, even one as decidedly non-macho as Ashbourne, looking so weak and vulnerable. Yet Harrigan knew the display of emotion was no act. He'd be a basket case, too, he thought to himself, if he were in the same position.

Feeling a new sense of urgency, Harrigan knelt be-

side Ashbourne. He put his hand around the back of
Ashbourne's neck and pulled him forward until their
foreheads nearly touched. "I'm going to rip Barnes
another asshole for you on the stand," he said. "Bill
Pickering's going to think he's been in a nuclear war.
I promise."

Harrigan remained in the lockup discussing his
ideas for the case until Ashbourne regained his composure and the marshals brought his client a turkey
sandwich and soda. Then he made his way to the
courthouse cafeteria for a last-minute strategy session
with Josie.

He found her working her way through a chef salad,
bought one for himself, and got right down to business.
It didn't take long for him to convince Josie how
they should proceed. Whether or not Debray came
forward on his own volition, they would pursue a
two-pronged approach. They would force as many
concessions as possible from Barnes on direct examination and use their experts to underscore the deficiencies in Barnes' performance at both phases of the
original trial. At the same time they would build
their own affirmative case in support of Ashbourne's
alibi, implicating Charles West and an as yet unknown accomplice as the real perpetrators of the
firebombing.

They would also step up their efforts to find Debray, beginning with a search of the area's AIDS hos-
pices for the fugitive's old significant other, Kathleen
Simpson. To that end, Josie had already scheduled a
two o'clock meeting with one of her Castro Street
buddies who served on the board of BACDA, the
Bay Area Coalition to Defeat AIDS. With a little luck

they could even be in a position to win by the time Ashbourne was finally ready to testify.

If J. Arnold Barnes looked the part of a guilty kiddie molester cooling his heels in the gallery at the start of the morning's session, he looked like a man ready to lose his lunch when Harrigan called his name at roughly five minutes after two.

Barnes took a couple of deep cleansing breaths as he parked his ample frame on the blue upholstered seat below Taneda and received the oath, his face taut, his speech slow and deliberate. Never to be mistaken for a *GQ* fashion plate, he wore a department-store three-piece suit that was at least a decade out of style and showed the ill effects of having been let out twice to make room for an expanding midsection. With the remaining strands of his graying hair combed over his head to hide his male pattern baldness, Barnes looked nothing like the smooth trial lawyer Pickering had wanted him to appear.

Harrigan took Barnes through a standard series of foundational questions concerning his academic background and his rise to a senior deputy's position with the county public defender's office. Barnes explained that he received his law degree from Berkeley's Boalt Hall and until his retirement from the PD in 1988 to part-time private practice had logged nearly twenty-three years as a public defender.

"During your long tenure with the public defender, how many murder trials did you handle?" Harrigan asked.

"Over twenty, perhaps as many as thirty."

"And how many of those were death-penalty cases?"

"Six."

"Including the Ashbourne case?"

"Yes."

"And what were the results in each of those?"

Barnes looked plaintively in Pickering's direction and, finding no assistance, let his head dip slightly. "Death verdicts were returned in each."

"A clean sweep for the prosecution," Harrigan editorialized.

"That doesn't mean the witness was remiss in his duties," Taneda broke in, offering Barnes an escape hatch from the hole Harrigan was digging for him.

"Was Harold Ashbourne's case the last death-penalty matter you tried?" Harrigan asked.

Barnes paused again, hoping for another judicial bailout. Receiving none, he took a hard swallow and answered, "After the Ashbourne case I was reassigned to property and drug offenses."

"And that was because of your problem with alcoholism, was it not?" Harrigan exchanged a quick sidelong glance with Ashbourne, who sat at the counsel table thoroughly enjoying the torture inflicted upon his old attorney.

Harrigan's question caused Barnes to wince. "I was reassigned for stress-related reasons."

Harrigan hesitated, as if waiting for Barnes to elaborate, while he walked over to the counsel table and pulled a manila legal file from his briefcase. He removed a document from the file and held it up like a pitch man on a TV commercial. "I have in my hand a memorandum from your personnel file, Mr.

Barnes, which indicates that you were reassigned pending your completion of an alcohol-rehabilitation program."

"Is there a question pending?" Pickering asked in a feeble effort to shield the witness.

Rather than wait for a ruling from Taneda, Harrigan rushed to pose his next question. "You were reassigned because you needed to dry out, isn't that true?"

"It's true that I had a drinking problem," Barnes conceded. "But the problem had nothing to do with the way I handled the Ashbourne case."

"Didn't it?" Harrigan asked rhetorically, strolling back to the lectern with two volumes of the transcripts from the Ashbourne trial under one arm. "On December 8, 1982," he continued, opening one of the volumes to a page marked with a yellow Post-It sticker, "in the midst of a motion to suppress evidence found in a search of the petitioner's home, the trial court was forced to call a half-hour recess because it feared you had arrived for the session in what the judge referred to as 'a condition of inebriation.' Isn't that true?"

"Yes," Barnes answered nervously, visibly annoyed that Pickering wasn't doing more to protect him.

"And the same thing happened again a week later during a change-of-venue motion, did it not?"

"I was going through a divorce at the time," Barnes offered, "but I think you'll find that the rest of the trial went forward without any similar disruptions."

"Let's talk about the rest of the trial, then," Harrigan said, as if accepting an invitation to do so. "One of a defense attorney's primary duties, especially in a capital case, is to investigate all potential defenses, true?"

"Of course."

"And did you do that in the Ashbourne case?"

"Yes, I did," Barnes answered, shifting uneasily in his seat. "I had Mr. Ashbourne subjected to a mental-status evaluation by two court-appointed psychiatrists, and when I confirmed that he suffered from no gross impairments, I argued the case on reasonable doubt."

"And yet you kept Harold Ashbourne off the witness stand, preventing the jury from learning the truth."

"I did not think his testimony about spending the evening with his friend Henri Debray was credible," Barnes said breathlessly, his eyes studiously avoiding the counsel table where Ashbourne sat. "I thought the testimony would backfire and lead the jury to conclude that Ashbourne was lying."

"What exactly did you find incredible about Ashbourne's alibi?" Harrigan asked, ratcheting up the level of disdain in his voice. "Did you find him inarticulate?"

"No," Barnes shot back.

"In fact, your psychiatric reports confirmed that Harold Ashbourne was a person of high intelligence."

"That's correct," Barnes acknowledged.

"Did you find any aspect of his statement internally inconsistent?"

"No."

"Did you find any aspect of his statement insincere?"

"I found the entire idea of an alibi that relied on Ashbourne spending the night of the murders with a fugitive to be unavailing and counterproductive. The firebombing had been committed by two persons, and the police regarded Debray as the prime candidate for the second perpetrator." Barnes managed to find some inner reserve of courage, and articulated his position with surprising passion. Whether or not he believed his decision to keep Ashbourne off the stand was appropriate, he obviously had many years to rehearse the lines.

"Speaking of Debray," Harrigan countered, "was he ever charged in connection with the bombing?"

"No. As far as I know, there was never sufficient evidence to clearly link him with the crime," Barnes conceded.

"And what efforts did you make to locate this prime suspect?"

"None," Barnes replied confidently.

"You had the services of a full-time investigator assigned to your case, didn't you?"

"Yes."

"Did you ever consider sending him to New York to interview Debray's mother in an effort to locate him?"

"The police had put out an all-points bulletin for Debray and came up empty-handed," Barnes replied evasively. "I saw no reason to duplicate their efforts. Debray's mother refused to speak with the police. There was no reason to believe she would have reacted any differently to my investigator."

"So the answer to my question is no." Harrigan pressed for clarification.

"Sending someone to New York would have been a waste of time and resources."

Confident that his own expert would testify that the failure to interview Debray's mother could not be justified on fiscal grounds, Harrigan chose to move on to other subjects. "Harold Ashbourne was a member of the steering committee of the group known as Saviors of the Earth, wasn't he?"

"Yes."

"And the other members of the Saviors' steering committee, were they interviewed?"

"Of course." The tone of Barnes' answer conveyed a touch of irritation, as if he had been insulted by the insinuation that he would have overlooked such an elementary procedure as interviewing the remaining key Saviors. "Each and every one was contacted. And each and every one had an alibi for the murders."

"And you knew that because each and every one of them was interviewed in person." Harrigan cast a quick glance at Taneda to make sure the judge caught the emphasis he gave to the words "in person."

"That's right."

"And the interviews were conducted at your direction, I assume."

"Yes."

"And you reviewed the reports your investigator prepared on them."

Barnes hesitated a moment before answering. "Of course."

"You would agree that a failure to conduct detailed in-person interviews would have been a dereliction of your professional responsibilities?"

"There was no dereliction, Counsel," Barnes replied defensively.

Mindful that Sylvia Peterson had not been interviewed in person, Harrigan took a half step back from the lectern. Whether Barnes had forgotten about Peterson or had never bothered to check up on his trial investigator's work, Harrigan was confident that the error in failing to confront Peterson in the flesh, when eventually revealed, would leave Barnes looking either like a liar or a fool.

Deciding again to save the Peterson-West bombshell for later, Harrigan shifted the direction of his examination once more. "What about Ashbourne's parents? Did you interview them?"

"We spoke to his father at some length," Barnes answered thoughtfully. "His mother, however, was unavailable. As I recall, she was suffering from a rather severe bout of depression."

"And you found no hint of either child abuse or neglect in your investigation of Mr. Ashbourne's background, I take it."

"None whatsoever."

"Did you even consider directing your psychiatric experts to look for child neglect?"

Barnes cracked a slightly bemused smile, as if he was certain Harrigan had wandered into a blind alley. "Mr. Ashbourne came from a most reputable family, something that's very unusual in death-penalty cases. As far as I was concerned, there was nothing to consider in the areas you've raised. That's why I chose to present a picture of him in the penalty phase of the trial as a young man who had gone to school and had basically played by the rules of society until he came under the sway of the so-called Saviors."

Sensing Barnes' confidence growing, Harrigan paused to look around the courtroom. The temporary break in the action was designed as much to lull Barnes into believing Harrigan was becoming weary from the verbal sparring as to see if Josie had returned from her afternoon meeting. The tactic was played out to perfection. Finding Josie in a rear row of the gallery, Harrigan gave a barely perceptible nod in her direction, then abruptly returned his gaze to Barnes with a smile on his lips that said, "Get ready, fat boy, for the heavy artillery."

"Isn't it true, Mr. Barnes, that Harold Ashbourne complained to you during the trial about your drinking habits?" Harrigan inquired sharply.

"Yes, at one point he did," Barnes answered tentatively, visibly disappointed that his tenure on the hot seat was far from over and, even more disconcertingly, that the subject of his fondness for the bottle was being raised again.

"And isn't it also true that you and Mr. Ashbourne quarreled over his insistence on testifying and your equally adamant insistence that he allow you to try the case as you saw fit?"

"I think you're exaggerating the intensity of our disagreements," Barnes said, "but it's no secret that we argued, and there's nothing particularly unusual about that."

"Isn't it also a fact, Mr. Barnes, that Mr. Ashbourne

threatened to complain to the judge about the fact that you continued to drink throughout the trial?"

"I don't recall anything like that," Barnes insisted. "And as I said earlier, I stopped drinking by the time the jury was impaneled."

"Do you recall telling Mr. Ashbourne that if he complained about your drinking, you would withdraw from the case and that he'd be given a new lawyer who had never tried a murder?"

"Absolutely not," Barnes answered, his face suddenly flushed.

"Isn't it true that the real reason you kept Harold Ashbourne off the witness stand was that you feared he would expose you as a drunken, broken-down attorney in front of the jury, the press, and the public?"

Harrigan's question brought a bright smile to Ashbourne's face and a red-faced denial from Barnes. The denial coincided almost to the millisecond with Pickering's objection to the unprofessional "form" of Harrigan's accusation.

Taneda reached for his gavel to restore order. He reminded Harrigan that the attorneys who appeared before him were expected to conduct themselves at all times as gentlemen and officers of the court. Harrigan in turn offered a hollow apology and turned the witness over to Pickering. On his way back to the counsel table, Harrigan gave his client a discreet thumbs-up, as if to say that he had delivered on the promise he had made in the courthouse lockup.

Realizing that Barnes was damaged goods and, even more important, that the State had a friend in Taneda, Pickering kept his examination to a minimum. After eliciting some additional data about the early days of Barnes' legal career before drink and a failing marriage beat him down, Pickering had Barnes recount the rather extensive list of good character witnesses he had called on Ashbourne's behalf at the penalty phase of his trial—the high school teachers who said that Ashbourne was quiet and well behaved, the hometown minister who said that Harold was a good boy, even the old soccer coach who fondly recalled Ashbourne's once promising footwork.

Pickering then posed the question he knew Taneda had been waiting to hear. "Was your decision not to call Harold Ashbourne as a witness based on your desire to keep him from complaining about your drinking, or was it a tactical decision?" Like the magic word on the old Groucho Marx quiz show, *You Bet Your Life,* which caused a little birdie to drop from the ceiling, the term *tactical decision* had a talismanic significance in IAC cases. As long as the trial attorney's act or omission could be construed as a reasoned choice based on a consideration of proper trial tactics, the lawyer could not be found guilty of IAC. Under the rubric of trial tactics, some judges would excuse almost any course of conduct short of smearing excrement on the courtroom walls.

"Absolutely," Barnes answered. "As I said before, I thought the story about Debray was so incredible it would only cause the jury to retaliate against Mr. Ashbourne for lying. I was also afraid Mr. Ashbourne would use the witness stand as a platform for espousing his radical political views. That's why I kept him off the stand for both the guilt and penalty phases. And in the end the decision to keep him off was a mutual one."

Pickering thanked Barnes for his candor and passed the witness back to Harrigan, who asked one final question: "You would agree, would you not, that your so-called tactical decision to keep Ashbourne off the stand backfired completely?"

"I can't help it if the jury chose not to vote my way," Barnes replied.

"No, I'm sure you couldn't help it," Harrigan said.

Barnes was excused, and Taneda brought the afternoon session to a close.

Harrigan found Josie in the corridor outside the courtroom and took his leave of Pickering, who was busy giving his spin on the day's proceedings to a pair of newspaper scribes and KZSF's John Aragon.

"I hope they offer Pickering a permanent spot as a guest commentator," Harrigan remarked facetiously as he and Josie stepped inside the elevator en route to the underground parking lot. "It might give him something to do at night besides haunt the local law libraries."

"I don't know what you're complaining about," she said with a smile. "You seem to have had a pretty good afternoon."

Harrigan shrugged his shoulders in a noncommittal gesture as if to signify that he'd need more than a pretty good afternoon to convince Taneda to grant Ashbourne's habeas petition. "How did *your* day go?"

"So-so," Josie answered. They exited the elevator and began walking to her car. "My friend seems to think if Kathleen Simpson really does have full-blown AIDS, she is probably in a hospice. There are several in the area."

"Will he help us find her?"

"He has inside contacts with almost all of the facilities, but he can't tell me where she is. That information's confidential. That's the bad news."

"And the good?" Harrigan asked as they arrived at Josie's Beemer.

"If he finds her, he'll leave a message for her to call my office. Assuming she has the strength and the inclination, we may hear from her. If not, we'll have to find Debray without her."

Her report delivered, Josie fished her keys out of her purse and turned her thoughts to more sensuous matters. "I realize you've taken a vow of chastity," she said with a grin, "but how about some dinner? You look like you could use some more home cooking." She took a half step toward Harrigan, and before either of them had time to worry about being watched, their lips met and her right thigh was pressing suggestively against his loins.

Harrigan's answer to the dinner invitation was drowned out by the sound of the beeping car horn not more than five feet away from them. Startled, they separated and looked over to the white Ford Tempo that had stopped in the parking lot's exit lane.

"I saw that," John Goodnow shouted like a school-yard smart aleck. Goodnow slid his ample frame to the passenger side of the Tempo and rolled down the window for a better view. "Hey, don't mind me," he said loudly, "I see a lot of things." Sensing his presence was about as welcome as a two-way mirror in a rest room, Goodnow retreated almost as quickly as he had come on the scene, but not after promising to see both of his new pals "around campus."

As Josie watched the Tempo pull away, her smile faded. "He's the asshole who followed me to Vesuvio's, Peter," she said, her face ridged with anger and concern. "I'm certain of it."

TWENTY-THREE

Josie might have been sure about Goodnow's Ford Tempo, but Harrigan was far from convinced. On the way back to her place, he spotted no less than a half-dozen white compacts. Including his rented Chevy Corsica, that made seven, though none, admittedly, came equipped with an E license plate that marked the Tempo as a government vehicle and exempted it from the usual requirements of annual registration with the Department of Motor Vehicles.

Even if Goodnow had followed Josie to Vesuvio's, there was no reason to believe he had slim-jimmed the front door of her BMW. Not only was Goodnow too much of clod to succeed as a car thief in a crowded parking facility, but there simply was too much risk associated with ripping off the briefcase of your opponent's investigator at the outset of a federal-court death-penalty hearing. Unless, of course, Bill Pickering was less than the straight-arrow prosecutor he seemed. In that event there might be no telling what the State would do in order to maintain its competitive edge. Like industrial spies, a lot of litigators would give their right testicles for a surreptitious peek at the other side's papers.

Lacking any immediate answers, Harrigan put the issue on hold as he found a parking space outside Josie's house. First things first, he told himself, eagerly anticipating the softness of Josie's embrace. With their relationship no longer a professional secret, there was little reason to decline her invitation for a little horizontal recreation before filling their stomachs and returning to their quarters to prepare for tomorrow's labors.

Their lovemaking, though still physically inspired, seemed to lack the emotional connection of their earlier sessions, as though the pressures of the case somehow prevented them from doing anything more than getting their mutual rocks off and then going their separate ways. Never given to great flights of optimism, Harrigan couldn't help but wonder if something more than just the case had suddenly come between them. Perhaps, he tried to tell himself, their relationship was just going through one of those difficult growing periods, or experiencing an inevitable lull or a moment of redirection, after which it would be stronger than ever. The alternative—that their relationship would prove to be just another short-term wonder, like all the others Harrigan had known since the Angeles Crest tragedy—was another possibility but one that he refused to consider. Still, as they kissed good night around eleven o'clock, they both knew, without saying a word, that they had reached an important crossroads. Any further resolution of their future would have to wait until the hearing was over.

It was with some misgivings that Harrigan made Ashbourne's father his first witness on Tuesday

morning. The misgivings arose not because Ashbourne Sr. wouldn't make a credible witness, but because he was strictly a penalty-phase witness. His
testimony would be offered to highlight the miscues
J. Arnold Barnes had made during the sentencing
portion of Ashbourne Jr.'s trial—that Barnes had
failed to offer mitigating evidence of child neglect
that might have persuaded the jury to return a life
sentence instead of a death verdict. Even if the old
man had an Oscar-winning day baring his soul as a
lousy parent, his evidence would be unrelated to the
more significant contention that Barnes had also
fouled up the guilt phase of the trial.

All things being equal, Harrigan would have preferred to proceed in the same order as the original
trial, leaving the penalty issues for last. But with Debray, his key guilt-phase witness, still on the loose, he
had little choice but to reorganize the sequence in
which he presented his evidence. Although there was
nothing inherently wrong in doing so, he knew he
ran the risk that Taneda would view the tactic as
another device to buy time while he waited for Debray to appear. Worse still, Taneda might regard the
move as a concession that Ashbourne's guilt-phase
IAC claims against Barnes were insubstantial. Barring
the unforeseeable, Harrigan planned to follow Ashbourne Sr. with Dr. Rosen and, assuming she was up
to it, Ashbourne's mother.

For a man in his late seventies, Harold Ashbourne
II was remarkably well preserved. Tall, lean, and
with his gray head of hair thinning but for the most
part still intact, Ashbourne Sr. arrived in court with a

confident but understated bearing, attired in a sober charcoal black pinstripe suit befitting a successful retired investment banker. Apart from a pair of bifocals and the deep crow's feet at the corners of his eyes, he looked like a man ten years younger than his age.

Harrigan welcomed Ashbourne Sr. to the witness stand, had him declare his age—seventy-eight—for the record, and proceeded to elicit a capsule summary of the witness' own life history. Through an intelligently paced Q and A, the witness emerged as a man born to one of the Bay Area's old-line commercial families who, by dint of pedigree and good fortune, was stiff and overly formal by nature and long used to having other people shield him from many of life's unpleasant aspects. He had enjoyed the best private schools and summers in Switzerland as a boy, a guaranteed admission to Harvard, and a position waiting for him in the financial community upon graduation. He was also the beneficiary, or victim, depending on one's point of view, of a virtually prearranged union with Claudia Morehead, the debutante daughter of a successful furniture importer, whom he married in a society-page wedding at age twenty-five.

"And Harold Ashbourne III, the petitioner in this proceeding, is the only child that you and Claudia Morehead had?" Harrigan inquired, homing in on the issues at hand.

"Yes. We delayed having a family until we were both in our thirties, which was a little later in life than most couples of our generation. After that we tried for a time to have other children, but by then my wife was unable to . . ." The witness' voice trailed off, as if he was recalling a distant period of sadness or regret.

"And what kind of father would you say you were to Harold when he was a boy?"

It was a blunt question and quite abrupt after the amiable manner in which Harrigan had handled the initial phase of his examination. But it was also a fair inquiry, and Ashbourne Sr. pondered it carefully, his eyes drifting to his son, who sat nervously at the counsel table in his prison clothes, avoiding his father's gaze. "In some ways I would describe myself as an ideal father. We sent Harold to the Dennard Academy in Marin County, which I attended as a boy, and to the best summer camps. He had a new Corvette when he turned sixteen, a fully endowed trust fund, all the material things a young man could ask for."

"And in other ways?" Harrigan asked, interrupting the laundry list of luxuries that young Harold had savored.

"In other ways," the witness began slowly, "I suppose I wasn't a very good father at all." He looked at Harrigan as if expecting a follow-up question, then decided to continue on his own. "I was a man of business, with many responsibilities, Mr. Harrigan. Those responsibilities, I'm afraid, were my life."

"Did you and Harold have any special activities—father and son activities—you used to do together?"

The elder Ashbourne paused to canvass his recollection. "When Harold was a toddler, I sometimes read him bedtime stories. He was especially taken, as I remember, with tales about medieval knights and castles."

"And as he grew older?"

"Apart from seeing that Harold's needs were taken care of and having dinner on those evenings when I was free, we didn't spend a lot of time together."

"Did the two of you ever play catch, go swimming, fishing, bowling, or do other things that fathers and sons traditionally do?"

"I don't think I've ever played a game of catch with Harold in my life," Ashbourne Sr. answered, wiping away a tear that had suddenly formed in the corner of his eye. "I suppose I always assumed that if I tended to my work, Harold's future would take care of itself."

"And while you were putting all your energies into business, did your wife shoulder the primary responsibility of raising Harold?"

The witness brought his hand to his chin, grimaced slightly, and slowly shook his head. "Claudia suffered a severe case of postpartum depression following the birth. After that she was never the same. We hired a German couple to live in our guest cottage to help with our domestic affairs."

"And this couple acted as Harold's principal care givers?"

"Until Harold turned nine and was sent to boarding school at Dennard."

"After you sent Harold away to Dennard, how often did he return home?"

The old man hesitated, searching his memory again. "On average, I'd say about one weekend per month, plus major holidays. Summers were at overnight camp on the Oregon coast."

"Did you ever have any heart-to-heart talks with your son as he was growing up?"

"If you mean conversations about the birds and the bees, the answer is no," the witness responded, pausing to wipe his glasses with a pale blue monogrammed handkerchief.

"What about just talking to your son to see how he was developing as a young man, did you engage in those kinds of discussions?"

"I monitored his progress in school, made sure he was developing satisfactorily, and reprimanded him when he seemed to be flagging in his responsibilities. I always thought he was headed for a bright future."

"Would you say you were a harsh task master as a father?"

"At the time I didn't think so. I behaved much the same as my father did toward me. In retrospect," the old man sighed, "you see things much more clearly. I wasn't there for my son very much when he needed me."

"Did Harold ever complain that he wanted you to take a greater interest in him?"

The question struck a nerve and brought a new wave of moisture to the old man's eyes. "Harold was a very quiet child. He never gave us any trouble until he went away to college." Hesitating for an instant, he added, "There was one occasion, however, when he was twelve or thirteen when he did come to me."

"About what?"

"His school class had planned a spring camping trip to Yosemite, and Harold asked me to come along."

"What happoened?" Harrigan asked, moving from

the counsel table to the lectern. From the corner of his eye he could see his client shift uneasily in his seat.

"Initially I was very receptive to the idea. I went out and bought us new camping gear and was all set to go. I was really looking forward to the event. But then something came up. I had to make an emergency trip to Zurich for a meeting with a group of investors."

"And how did Harold react to the news?"

"I don't know," the elder answered ruefully. "I called from the airport and left word over the phone with the headmaster's office. I don't think Harold and I ever discussed the matter afterward."

"You mentioned some problems that arose after Harold entered college," Harrigan asked, moving the examination to more contemporary themes.

"Yes," the elder Ashbourne remarked, suddenly showing a stern side. "The first sign occurred even before college, with his grades. They were good enough for Berkeley, but not for Harvard."

"Did that disappoint you?"

"Very much so, and I let Harold know just how disappointed I was."

"And how did he react?"

"From that point on, Harold changed." The witness looked again at his son in another effort to establish eye contact, but the younger Ashbourne looked away. "It was as though I didn't know him, as though I never knew him."

"What happened after that?"

"He went off to Berkeley and started to grow his hair long, began to experiment with drugs. He was like a different person."

"Did you continue to support Harold?"

"Until his junior year, when he dropped out of college and decided to find salvation in India," the old man answered tensely. "I let him keep his trust fund, which by then contained more than a hundred thousand dollars, and basically lost touch with my son."

"When did you next see your son after he dropped out of college?"

"I didn't see Harold again until the penalty portion of his trial, when I came to court," the witness answered with a somber expression, his voice riddled with guilt. "I tried to see him in jail, but he refused to come out of his cell."

"And you refused to pay for your son's defense, isn't that true?"

Ashbourne Sr. took a deep breath before answering. "Yes, and it was the biggest mistake of my life, for which I will never forgive myself."

"And tell us, if you will, why you feel that way."

"If I had paid for Harold's defense and seen to it that he'd gotten the best lawyer available, my son might not be in the position he is today."

The witness' answer brought an objection from Pickering, who had remained mute and nearly motionless until that point. "Move to strike, Your Honor," the deputy AG said. "Calls for speculation."

"That's true," Taneda replied, also stirring to life. "But it's essentially harmless. I'll allow it for the limited purpose of explaining the witness' feelings."

"During the course of your son's trial," Harrigan continued, "were you interviewed by Harold's lawyer, J. Arnold Barnes?"

"Mr. Barnes came to my home and spoke to me about the schools Harold attended, the sports he played as a boy."

"And you testified about those matters at the penalty phase of the trial, did you not?"

"Yes."

"At any time before or during the trial did Mr. Barnes ask you, as I have today, about whether or not you had been a good father to your son?"

"No."

"At any time did Mr. Barnes send a psychologist or a social worker to interview you about your relationship with Harold, as I sent Dr. Russell Rosen to interview you?"

"No. Mr. Barnes told me he had decided on his approach to the penalty phase and that he was satisfied it was a good one. He was going to put on evidence to show the jury that Harold was a person of 'good character and upbringing,' as he put it. I remember him saying that no jury would return a death verdict against a person who came from such a good family."

Harrigan paused for a moment to check his notes. "Looking back on your role as a parent," he said, returning his gaze to the witness stand, "do you think that your son grew up in a good family environment?"

"No, I'm afraid I don't."

"Why didn't you tell Mr. Barnes about the matters you've testified about today?"

"Because he never asked, Mr. Harrigan. Harold's defense was in his hands and he never asked." Ashbourne Sr. delivered his answer with the clear and unequivocal tone of a corporate executive long accustomed to apportioning responsibility and assigning blame. To Harrigan's great relief, he sounded both self-assured and convincing.

"Just one further question," Harrigan advised the witness, seeing that he was beginning to tire. "After your son's conviction, did your relationship with him improve?"

"I would say only marginally," Ashbourne Sr. answered with a sigh. "I've tried to see him on occasion in prison, but he only rarely agrees to come out of his cell. And he continues to refuse any financial assistance from me for his appeals." The old man ran his right hand across his brow and squeezed the bridge of his nose. "I never realized how deep his hurt must have been."

After a brief conference with investigator Goodnow at the railing that separated the gallery from the interior of the courtroom, Pickering took the witness on a brief but confrontational cross-examination, seeking to take advantage of the same fatigue that had prompted Harrigan to end his direct. "No one prevented you from telling Mr. Barnes that your son was a neglected child, did they, Mr. Ashbourne?"

"Mr. Barnes was the lawyer on the case, sir," the witness replied testily. "It wasn't my place to second-guess his way of handling the case."

"But that's exactly what you're doing now, isn't it?"

Ashbourne Sr. hesitated, a man caught in a contradiction of his own making. "I'm telling the truth," he managed to say weakly.

Strictly speaking, the answer was nonresponsive

and subject to a motion to strike, but Pickering let it pass unchallenged. "You love your son, Mr. Ashbourne, don't you?" he asked in a softer tone.

"Yes," the witness answered warily.

"And you feel guilty about what you see as your role in bringing him to his current state."

"Yes."

"And one way to expiate that guilt would be to have this court rule that Mr. Barnes is responsible for Harold's fate. Isn't that true, sir?" With his Ronald Coleman mustache bobbing up and down as he spoke, Pickering looked like a menacing chpipmunk, but there was no denying that he had done an excellent job of exposing Ashbourne Sr.'s bias and undermining his credibility. The fact that it had taken Pickering less than half the time to score a direct hit than Harrigan had spent on his painstaking direct examination made the prosecutor's performance all the more impressive.

"I did not think my guilt was the issue here," the witness shot back, once again evading Pickering's inquiry.

"That's true, Mr. Ashbourne, you're not the one on trial here at all," Pickering said in a conciliatory manner. The smug half smile on Pickering's face as the elder Ashbourne descended from the stand spoke louder than any cross-examination that the momentum had begun to swing back in favor of the state.

TWENTY-FOUR

Josie found Harrigan in the courthouse cafeteria, sharing a quick bite with Dr. Rosen and trying desperately to put an optimistic gloss on the morning's proceedings. "It doesn't sound like things went badly at all," she heard Rosen remark as she joined them at their table. "Actually, if you had gotten the old man to say anything more volatile, he wouldn't have sounded sincere. Trust me, that family is just dripping with latent pathology, and Harold Ashbourne bears the scars from it."

Harrigan wiped the last traces of a sourdough and turkey sandwich from his chin and introduced Josie to the doctor. She took a seat and waited as Rosen, a man in his early fifties with a pleasant round face and a fringe of frizzy brown hair ringing a dome-shaped bald head, completed his reassurances before announcing that she had arrived with important news. Sensing that his status as a witness might compromise their conversation, Rosen politely excused himself and departed early for the courtroom.

"So what's so important that you had to chase away my expert?" Harrigan asked with mock annoyance. In truth, he wasn't at all bothered by her un-

scheduled appearance. After spending the entire
morning with Ashbourne Sr. and Pickering, Josie was
even more of a visual treat than usual. And despite
Dr. Rosen's encouragement, Harrigan had no desire
to resume the hearing any sooner than necessary.

"We've found Simpson," she replied with a smile
but sounding all business. "Or to be more precise,
she found me."

"Where is she?" Harrigan asked, his spirits bright-
ening with interest.

"In a hospice in the Haight run by the Better
Day Foundation."

"So we're in luck. Your friend must have some
pretty good connections."

"My friend had nothing to do with it," she said.
"He hadn't even called Better Day. Simpson left a
message on my answering machine entirely on her
own."

Harrigan gave Josie an astonished look.

"I spoke to the hospice administrator about an
hour ago. She said it would be okay if we dropped
by this evening. But she also told me Kathleen hasn't
got much time left. She has AIDS dementia, Peter.
I'm not sure we'll get much out of her."

The news was more than enough to puncture Harrigan's short-lived sense of buoyancy. "Maybe you
should go over there right now. She's probably heard
from Debray. How else could she have known about
you?" There was a measure of desperation in his
speech and a similar look in his eyes.

Josie shook her head gravely. "I've already thought
of that, but Kathleen gets her treatment every afternoon. She won't be able to see us until seven at the

earliest." She reached across the table and took Harrigan's hand in hers. "We're doing everything we can, Peter."

Harrigan gave her hand a gentle squeeze and regarded her closely. She was right, as usual, and for the briefest instant he allowed himself to imagine what life with Josie would be like without the burden of trying to save Harold Ashbourne's life. A succession of images danced through his mind. He saw the two of them jetting off to some exotic locale with lots of palm trees and sand. He saw the two of them staying together, building a home, maybe even starting a family. Could they do it? Did they want it badly enough to make it all happen? He wanted to stay with the images and see where they would take him, but there was no time. "I know we're doing everything we can," he said finally, releasing her hand. "It just never seems enough."

Apart from a couple of news-wire stringers plus Josie and Goodnow, who exchanged occasional mistrustful glances from first-row seats on opposite aisles of the spectator section, the gallery of Taneda's courtroom was empty. The remainder of the looky-lous who had packed the audience for the previous sessions were either taking late lunches or had moved on to the county courthouse to observe even more gruesome trials in progress. Housing and jobs might be in chronic short supply, but one thing you could always count on finding in the Bay Area, Los Angeles, or any other big city in late twentieth-century America, was a good murder trial or a rape, or even a high-priced medical malpractice case. To

those who got their kicks observing other human beings in crisis, the law provided the most consistent
entertainment in town.

While some attorneys might have mourned the loss
of spectator interest, Harrigan was actually relieved
to have the courtroom virtually to himself. With a
sparse gallery there would be less temptation for
Pickering to posture in the name of the State and for
Taneda to imitate the right hand of God. With any
luck, Taneda might even start paying attention to
the evidence.

As a witness, Dr. Rosen turned out to be every
bit as encouraging as he had promised over their
lunchtime sandwiches. An exceptionally poised
speaker, he was one of those interdisciplinary schol-
ars who had entered academia as much out of an
intrinsic interest in his areas of study as to obtain an
outlet for his liberal political views. He was fervently
anti-death penalty but was blessed with a rare ability
to articulate his views without rancor or dogma.

Responding to the usual foundational questions
about his education and career, Rosen testified that
he held both a doctorate in clinical psychology from
the University of Michigan and a law degree from
Yale. After five years as an itinerant assistant professor at various colleges in the Midwest and on the
West Coast, he landed a tenure-track position in the
psychology department at San Francisco State
University.

"I maintained a small private psychology practice
as well as a full-time academic load for my first three
years at State," Rosen explained. "After I obtained

tenure, I became an adjunct professor of law and psychology at the Hastings College of Law, run by the University of California, here in San Francisco. I'm also a fellow of both the Western and American Psychological Associations and a past chair of the latter's psychology and law division," he disclosed, rounding out his curriculum vitae.

"Over the years," Harrigan inquired as he strolled from the counsel table to the lectern, "have you developed any special areas of interest within your profession?"

"At first I was strictly a generalist," Rosen answered with studied modesty. "But beginning in the early 1980s, I became increasingly attracted to the debate over the efficacy of capital punishment and the role that mental health professionals play as expert witnesses in death-penalty trials."

"Was there anything specific that drew your interest to the death penalty?"

"I'd say the reasons for my interest were part personal, part professional, and part political," the witness answered, exchanging curious looks with Taneda, whose ears seemed to perk up at the mention of the P words. "As the father of two young children, I was, and remain, very concerned about crime and neighborhood safety, and I was interested in exploring the popular notion that our crime rate would drop if the death penalty was implemented more frequently."

"And the professional?"

"In 1982, in response to a request from a group of second-year law students, I began teaching an elective course on psychology and the death penalty. Our

mission was to look at the history of capital punishment in twentieth-century America with a view
toward examining, as I alluded to earlier, the changing role of mental health experts in capital cases."

"Have you ever testified before in a capital case?"

"Since 1983 I have served as a penalty-phase consultant in twelve capital trials in California, and more
recently, I served as legal co-counsel, concentrating
on penalty-phase evidence, in three other trials. As a
dual professional, you might say that I've learned to
wear two hats, one as a doctor and one as an
attorney."

Rosen went on to explain that unlike those experts
who limit their opinions to guilt-phase subjects such
as a defendant's sanity or mental state at the time
of the alleged offense, the work of a penalty-phase
consultant was to research the defendant's background and character. "By the time of the penalty
phase of a capital case," Rosen said, sounding increasingly professorial, "the defendant has already
been convicted of first-degree murder with special
circumstances. My job is to dig into the defendant's
personal history, to interview the defendant, his family and friends, and to inspect his medical, school,
military, and criminal records until I know him better
than he knows himself. Only then can a sympathetic
portrait of the defendant be presented to the jurors,
who will ultimately be asked to spare the defendant's life."

"And have your efforts met with success?"

Rosen paused to make certain of the accuracy of
his response. "Ten of the twelve trials in which I
acted as an expert witness, wearing my psycholo-

gist's hat," he said with an affable smile, "resulted in penalty-phase verdicts of life without parole rather than the death penalty. The three cases I worked on as legal counsel also resulted in life terms."

The answer brought another momentary but noticeable pause to Taneda's note taking. Of all the experts Harrigan might have hired to render an opinion on the Ashbourne case, Russell Rosen was uniquely qualified.

"Now, you also mentioned a political reason for your interest in the death penalty?" Harrigan asked.

"The witness is not going to give us a sermon against capital punishment is he, Mr. Harrigan?" Taneda interrupted, letting his pen fall to the writing surface in front of him. There was the slightest hint of the blue vein above his right temple, betraying an early stage of annoyance.

"Not at all, Your Honor," Harrigan assured the court. "However, since the bias of any witness is always at issue, I thought it prudent to address Dr. Rosen's point of view on direct examination rather than allow the state to bring it out on cross-examination." Harrigan saw Pickering turn his gaze toward the lectern and give a knowing nod, as if to signify that he appreciated the tactical maneuver.

With the court's fears at least partially assuaged, Harrigan resumed his examination. Rosen acknowledged that he had always been a foe of capital punishment and had been drawn to the field in part because of his firm belief that "state-sanctioned killings could never succeed in curbing the murder rate." Harrigan then turned his attention to Harold

Ashbourne. "At my request, Doctor, did you interview the petitioner?"

"Soon after my appointment in this case by the late Stanley Blake, I conducted a series of in-depth sessions with Mr. Ashbourne at San Quentin Prison. In addition to performing a mental-status exam and taking a detailed personal history, I administered a standard battery of tests, including the Minnesota Multiphasic Personality Inventory, or MMPI; Thematic Apperception Test; Rorschach Inkblot; Incomplete Sentences Blank; Wechsler Adult Intelligence Scale—Revised, and a Bender Gestalt. I also spent a good eight hours in conversation with Mr. Ashbourne's parents."

"And as a result of your efforts did you reach any conclusions regarding Mr. Ashbourne?"

Dr. Rosen paused to peruse the thick manila file he had taken with him to the witness stand before answering. "I found Mr. Ashbourne to be a well-groomed individual, appropriately oriented as to time and place, logical in thought and with well above average intelligence. I also found, however, that he exhibited traits associated with what the American Psychiatric Association's *Diagnostic and Statistical Manual of Mental Disorders*—the DSM-IV—characterizes as a Cluster C, Axis II, 301.6 dependent-personality disorder."

The DSM-IV was widely viewed as the bible for classifying psychological disorders, and as Rosen rattled off the relevant DSM section number, both Pickering and Taneda flipped through the pages of the pocket DSM manuals they had toted to court to follow the doctor's anticipated testimony.

"Can you explain what this disorder means, Doctor?" Harrigan asked in a neutral tone.

"In the broadest terms, those suffering from this disorder exhibit an extreme need for others to take care of them, usually commencing with the onset of adulthood." As Rosen spoke, Ashbourne began to fidget nervously in his seat, prompting the doctor to soften his tone. "The dependent personality has a great deal of trouble making everyday decisions on his own. He prefers others to take responsibility for his decisions and to provide him with constant reassurance and support. He is overly concerned, often to the point of an obsession, with fears of rejection and is frequently unable to assert his own will because of those fears. I found Mr. Ashbourne's involvement with the disorder to be in the moderate to severe range."

"What kinds of people generally suffer from this disorder?"

"From a social perspective, the disorder transcends gender, race and economic class," Rosen answered clinically. "But according to my research, it develops most frequently in women who are overly dependent on their spouses for financial and emotional support and in both sexes during the late teens and early twenties in young men and women who have lacked strong role models or parental authority figures in their formative years." Harrigan could see from the engrossed expressions on the faces of Pickering and Taneda that Rosen was making a strong impression. Although it remained highly unlikely that the doctor would succeed in winning them over, Rosen could not easily be dismissed as just another self-absorbed windbag who would say anything for an expert-witness fee. Sensing that Rosen, too, felt good about his testimony, Harrigan opted to give his witness as much uninterrupted time as Taneda would allow. "Could you tell us about the research that you personally have performed with regard to this disorder?"

"In addition to conducting a rather extensive survey of the literature, I have delivered two Psychiatric Association conference papers on the subject and published four articles dealing in whole or in part with the topic." Rosen took a breath and, with a cautious nod toward Ashbourne, added, "I've also diagnosed the condition in several of my patients, most recently in this case."

Harrigan took a step back from the lectern and, affecting an academic air, asked, "How do people develop this disorder? Are they born with it, or do they acquire it over time?"

"That's a good question," the witness answered with a wry smile. "The issue of nature versus nurture is one that traverses virtually all schools of psychology. My own view is that certain individuals have predispositions, which are brought out and reinforced by the circumstances of their lives."

"What was it about Harold Ashbourne's life that made him a dependent personality?"

"Emotionally, Harold Ashbourne grew up as a virtual orphan. His parents were at the same time very controlling and very distant. From the time he was an infant until he went off to college, day-to-day care was entrusted to others. I know it may sound trite, but I'm afraid that it's true—children need to be loved and, just as important, they need to *know* that they are loved in order to develop a healthy sense of self-esteem. Harold's parents may have given him new cars and fine clothes, and may actually have loved him, but when it came to one-on-one contact, especially with his father, Harold was every bit as neglected as a poverty-stricken child placed into foster care."

"In your opinion, Doctor, did the kind of neglect Harold experienced as a child affect his life as an adult?"

"There's no question about it," Rosen answered resolutely. "The decision he made to leave college in his junior year and seek spiritual fulfillment in India and his later entry into left-wing politics were all motivated by a desire to find the love, guidance, and direction he lacked as a child."

"And his friendship with Henri Debray, was that part of this process, too?"

"Mr. Debray was the father that Harold never had," Rosen responded, drawing a look of anger and surprise from Ashbourne. "Even after spending a decade on death row, he expressed nothing but the most fulsome praise and adulation for Henri Debray. And the fact that Debray may have deserted him left Harold feeling that he, rather than Debray, was to blame for the precipitous end of their association."

"Are you saying that Mr. Ashbourne was not attracted to the group Saviors of the Earth by his political beliefs?" Harrigan's inquiry drew another noticeable response from Ashbourne, whose back stiffened as the foundations of his ideological commitment were publicly called into question.

"No, I'm not saying that Mr. Ashbourne's political

beliefs were insincere," Rosen said in a modulated voice intended as much to soothe Ashbourne's feelings as it was to convey his professional opinions. "I am saying, however, that having found a home for his political beliefs, Harold Ashbourne embraced the group Saviors of the Earth as a kind of surrogate family and Debray, as head of that family, as a surrogate father. He derived not only a sense of purpose from those associations but his entire sense of self-worth."

"Doctor, do people who suffer from the dependent-personality disorder experience much emotional pain or torment because of the condition?"

"It varies with the individual," Rosen acknowledged. "In some cases the disorder can be mild and little more than a nuisance. But in others it can cause quite a bit of secondary anxiety and even depression, especially if the dependent personality has no authority figure in his life or the authority figure threatens or is compelled to leave. It's my opinion that Harold Ashbourne lived with a great deal of pain in his life, looking for such an authority figure."

Harrigan walked slowly back to the counsel table and began paging through a manila file he retrieved from his briefcase until he came to the pretrial reports filed by the two court-appointed doctors who had examined Harold Ashbourne before his trial. After confirming that Rosen had reviewed both the reports and the testimony from the penalty phase of Ashbourne's trial, Harrigan posed the question he had been building toward all afternoon. "Based on your review of the trial records, as well as your interviews with the petitioner and his parents, do you have an opinion as to whether the penalty phase of Mr. Ashbourne's trial was presented in a competent manner?"

"The penalty-phase defense, and the investigation behind it, was definitely deficient," Rosen answered resolutely.

"You are aware, are you not, that over a dozen witnesses, including Harold's father, were called at the penalty trial to affirm the petitioner's good character and his achievements as a secondary-school student?" Harrigan raised his voice as he spoke, as though he were challenging his own witness' credibility.

"I think that emphasizing the petitioner's good character was perfectly appropriate," Rosen conceded. "However, the failure to identify and present evidence on the personality disorder and history of child neglect from which Mr. Ashbourne so obviously suffers was inexcusable. Had the jury received a competent psychological profile, the petitioner's achievements would have seemed all the more impressive. And more significantly, the jury would have had a basis for according him a measure of sympathy instead of viewing him as a spoiled child who thought he was above the law. In my view, what the jury heard at the penalty phase left it with no other alternative but to return a death sentence."

"Weren't the psychologists who examined Mr. Ashbourne prior to trial at fault for not pointing out his dependent-personality disorder?" Harrigan's tone was still skeptical and challenging.

"From what I could tell from reviewing the file," Rosen answered, "the doctors performed only a cursory mental-status examination to determine his mental state at the time of the firebombing. They limited their inquiry because that was all they were asked to do. No, the fault here lies squarely with Ashbourne's trial lawyer. He was the one calling the shots. Had he asked for a more complete psychological work-up, I'm sure he would have gotten one."

Satisfied that he had gotten the most out of Dr. Rosen, Harrigan passed the witness on to Pickering for cross-examination.

From the State's perspective, Rosen presented both a problem and an opportunity. The problem arose from the fact that the good doctor had done a bang-up job expounding his views on the dependent-personality disorder, building what seemed at first like a minor personality glitch into a potentially significant illness. There was little doubt that J. Arnold Barnes had mishandled Ashbourne's penalty trial. Whether as the result of too many last calls at too many happy hours or too much reverence for the Ashbourne name, Barnes had ignored any hint of child neglect while investigating his client's background. Although Taneda might ultimately be umimpressed with the hardships that young Harold endured, there was little point in challenging Rosen on the existence of those hardships.

The opportunity, ironically, also arose from Dr. Rosen's sterling performance. It pertained, however, not to the penalty but the guilt phase of Ashbourne's trial, and the alibi defense that Barnes had also chosen to ignore.

"Doctor Rosen," Pickering began respectfully, "as a defense penalty-phase expert you're called upon to present evidence to the jury that could mitigate the gravity of the offense the defendant has committed, isn't that true?"

"Yes," Rosen answered warily, uncertain of the direction of Pickering's cross. "As I alluded to earlier, the goal is to persuade the jury that the mitigating factors about the defendant and his background outweigh the aggravating factors that might warrant the death penalty."

"And more specifically, one of the things you're often called upon to explain is the conditions, whether they be social or psychological, that may have led the defendant to commit his crime."

"My job, Counsel," Rosen replied defensively, "is to assist the defense in developing an approach to the penalty phase that will elicit the most sympathy for the defendant. That's no secret. In some cases, particularly where the defendant's guilt is undisputed, that may involve generating an explanation for the defendant's criminal behavior."

"And that's exactly what you've done here, isn't it, Doctor?" Another snide half smile slowly crossed Pickering's thin lips.

Pickering's question brought Harrigan out of his seat like an alarmed mother hen. "Counsel's question," he objected, "not only grossly misstates the doctor's testimony, but it calls for an opinion on the ultimate issue of the petitioner's guilt or innocence. As the court well knows, such opinions are inadmissible under both California law and the Federal Rules of Evidence."

Pickering's bold move and the objection it drew offered Taneda the opportunity he'd been waiting for to come to the State's aid. "Were this the guilt phase of an initial trial," Taneda replied, stroking his chin in a posture of thoughtful repose, "the objection would be well taken. But this is a proceeding on habeas corpus concerned with reviewing the constitutionality of the defendant's conviction in a prior trial. Strictly speaking, the defendant's guilt or innocence is not the issue here.

"The peitioner has alleged ineffective assistance of his trial counsel, J. Arnold Barnes. With regard to the penalty phase of the petitioner's trial, the claim, as I understand it, is that Mr. Barnes was ineffective for not calling an expert to testify along the lines that Doctor Rosen has here. It seems to me that Mr. Pickering's question relates to the wisdom of presenting such testimony. The fact that such testimony may also tend to reinforce a belief in the defendant's guilt does not render Mr. Pickering's question improper. The objection is overruled."

Elated at Taneda's careful exegesis, a beaming Pickering requested the court reporter to reread the fateful question.

"I haven't been asked to render an explanation for the petitioner's alleged criminal conduct," Rosen protested, still very much on the defensive, his face flushed with annoyance. "Nor have I formed an opinion on whether he actually participated in the firebombing of Professor Denton's home."

"But what you have told us, Doctor, is that Mr. Ashbourne is a dependent personality who came to look upon Henri Debray as a kind of second father?" Pickering's needling tone imparted a malicious quality to the question.

"That's true," Rosen said.

"And one of the character traits of the dependent personality," Pickering continued, "is that such persons will do almost anything to win or maintain acceptance and approval from the authority figures in their lives. So when Mr. Ashbourne's surrogate father was fired from the Berkeley political science department, wouldn't he have come to his father's aid?"

Faced with the prospect of seeing his credibility completely destroyed, Rosen had to concede Pickering's point.

"In fact, to remain in the good graces of his surrogate father, wouldn't Harold Ashbourne have done anything Henri Debray asked, including throwing a flaming wine bottle through the front window of Gilbert Denton's home?"

There was complete silence as Rosen paused to consider Pickering's latest broadside. Like an overconfident chess player facing an imminent checkmate, Rosen was desperately seeking a way to regroup. "Mr. Ashbourne had no prior history of violence," he said finally. "Nor did his test results indicate an antisocial-personality disorder or show significant signs of sociopathy. And while he was certainly a victim of profound neglect as a child, I know of no episodes of the kind of physical or sexual abuse in his childhood that one often finds in persons who later commit acts of homicidal rage. So to answer your question, Counsel, I don't think I've provided you with anything close to an explanation for the defendant's alleged criminal conduct."

Blindsided by Pickering's cross, Rosen's comeback was given off the cuff and without the scholarly references or self-assurance of his earlier testimony. Under the circumstances, however, it was effective. Though it might not have undone all the damage that Pickering had inflicted, it succeeded at least in removing the smug smile from the deputy AG's face. With both sides content to cut their losses, Rosen left the stand without further questioning.

The decision to close the afternoon with Harold Ashbourne's mother was dictated both by the need to maintain an appearance of continued confidence in the child-neglect issue and Harrigan's fear that Taneda might rush him into the guilt-phase aspects of the case if he had no other witness to fill up the last hour of court time. From this perspective, Claudia Ashbourne seemed the ideal witness. Harrigan intended to have her profess her love for Harold— something she had not been asked to do at the penalty phase of her son's trial, since she had not been called to testify—and to send her back across the bridge to her hillside chateau in Marin County.

As per their prior arrangements, Mrs. Ashbourne arrived at the courthouse at three o'clock sharp, in the company of a uniformed limo driver. She made her appearance looking satisfied, well bred, and refined. Dressed in an understated dark blue business suit, she was, like her husband, in surprisingly good trim for someone in her mid-seventies, with a thick crown of curly white hair and soft hazel eyes that crinkled into catlike slits when she smiled.

The sight of Claudia on the witness stand was the first glimpse that Harold had taken of his mother in over two years, and it sent him into a quiet panic. "I don't feel right about this," he whispered to Harrigan. "You shouldn't have called her." He hastily scribbled a note on a legal pad and passed it to Harrigan. "I don't want her to see me like this," it read in a shaky hand. "Get her off the stand ASAP."

Harrigan took the note and folded it into the breast pocket of his sports coat, then turned to face the desperate eyes of his client. Even if slightly exaggerated, Ashbourne's discomfort at seeing his mother was understandable. "I'll be brief," he said reassuringly as he stood to begin his direct examination.

Initially at least, Claudia Ashbourne appeared to have little of substance to say. Responding to Harrigan's concise questions, she declared her affection for Harold and stated, for good measure, that she would have said so at her son's trial if only she had been asked by J. Arnold Barnes, her longstanding bouts with depression notwithstanding.

Harrigan thanked Mrs. Ashbourne for her candor, but before he could utter the ritual phrase "Nothing further," the witness insisted on continuing her testimony. "There's something else I have to say," she announced in a quavering pitch. "I'm sorry, Harold, but it has to be done."

Ashbourne hunched forward and dropped his head in his hands, hiding from his mother's gaze as she began. "It has to do with the reason Harold was sent away to the Dennard Academy."

"Mother, don't!" Ashbourne sprang to his feet, yelling above Claudia's weak voice. His repeated cries pierced the somber atmosphere of the courtroom, prompting Taneda to reach for his gavel and, with a show of authority, to admonish the petitioner back into seat.

"The reason we sent Harold away," the witness continued at the court's direction, "was that he had been molested by the German couple we hired as caretakers."

"What kind of molestation?" Harrigan asked, trying vainly to disguise his utter surprise and to regain control over the direct examination.

"We found pictures—naked pictures of Harold—taken in the guest house by Gunter and Olga, some of them in very suggestive poses. It was sickening." As the old woman recalled the grim discovery, her body slumped into the witness chair, her formerly youthful face abruptly contorted into a mask of wrinkled pain. "Although we could detect no signs of physical abuse, we immediately dismissed the caretakers and decided it was best to send our son away. I've since come to believe that if we had handled the matter openly instead of trying to sweep it under the rug, Harold might not have grown up with the resentment he felt toward us. I blame myself for what has happened."

"And what happened to the caretakers?" Harrigan asked.

"We threatened to prefer charges unless they went back to Germany. I have no idea what became of them."

Completely unprepared for the revelations he had just heard, Harrigan was paralyzed with indecision. On the one hand, there was no denying that Mrs. Ashbourne had breathed new life into the theory of child neglect. Even a cold-blooded reptile like Taneda would have to view Harold Ashbourne's childhood in a new and more sympathetic light. But there was also an obvious downside. Harold's all-too human resentment at being a victim of sexual abuse, given time to incubate over the years, was just the kind of condition, as Dr. Rosen had suggested, that could serve to explain a turn to violence as an adult. Whether she thought she was helping her son or simply clearing her own conscience, Mrs. Ashbourne had presented Harrigan with a two-edged sword.

How, then, should he proceed? Given Mrs. Ashbourne's unpredictability, he decided to end the examination before the witness could drop any more hand grenades. There was only one last question he had to ask, and although he knew that the answer could be devastating, he also knew Pickering would jump on it if he remained silent.

"If Mr. Barnes had asked you to testify at your son's trial," Harrigan inquired, clearing the tension from his throat, "would you have disclosed the matter of the nude photographs, as you have today?"

Mrs. Ashbourne mulled the question over for a moment, then answered resolutely. "No, to be honest, I don't think I would have had the courage back then. I didn't even mention it to Dr. Rosen."

Harrigan thanked Mrs. Ashbourne for her honesty and sank back into his chair, his shoulders sagging with the realization that his client's own mother had seriously undermined the penalty-phase IAC case against J. Arnold Barnes. Even if Barnes had been strung out on grain alcohol during Harold Ashbourne's trial, Taneda would never fault him for failing to put on evidence that a witness more than a decade later acknowledged she would not have revealed.

Just as significant was the effect that Claudia Ashbourne's testimony had on her son. From the moment Taneda ordered him to resume his seat, Harold Ashbourne was like a man whose sense of identity had been severed at the knees. Unable to look at his mother as she left the witness stand, he also adamantly refused to discuss her disclosures with Harrigan, insisting instead to be taken directly back to San Quentin for the night. As he was escorted back inside the courthouse lockup, the two-edged sword his mother's testimony seemed to present earlier was looking more like a guillotine.

TWENTY-FIVE

There was little point in ruminating over the afternoon's debacle in court, but Harrigan couldn't help replaying it in his mind, first over a quick dinner with Josie at the Mayfair coffee shop and then on the drive to the Better Day Hospice. Although he had never really held much hope that Taneda would accept his IAC claims on the child-neglect issue, he hadn't expected the issue to collapse on him before the hearing was even half over. Yet that was exactly what had happened. In the ultimate nightmare scenario, the evidence he had offered to prove the incompetence of J. Arnold Barnes laid barely a glove on the boozy trial attorney but had wound up instead making Harold Ashbourne look more guilty than ever. Harrigan had underestimated Bill Pickering's skill as an adversary, and he also blamed himself for what was clearly his own less than stellar performance. The worst part was that for the first time since signing on as Ashbourne's lawyer, Harrigan was beginning to question his client's claim of innocence.

"What if we've been conned," Harrigan muttered half to himself as they entered the Haight District in

Josie's Beemer. "What if Ashbourne really is guilty?" The pain in his voice made it seem that the question was far more than a professional query. The words carried not only a quality of uncertainty but a sense of hurt and betrayal.

"I'm sure it won't be the first time a client's lied to you." Josie tried to sympathize while watching for oncoming traffic and a parking space.

"It's not like he didn't remember the German couple." Harrigan continued to seethe. "He's been writing a personal history for years now and never mentioned a thing about them. He lied to me, dammit. What if he's lying about the firebombing, too?"

"Then Barnes made the right call in keeping him and his alibi defense off the witness stand." Josie maneuvered the Beemer into a metered spot halfway down the block from the hospice. "Then we lick our wounds, pick up our paychecks, and go on to the next case. You can't blame yourself, Peter."

She gave him a tender look and saw that her words of reassurance had failed to ease his discomfort. "But I wouldn't give up yet," she added in a more optimistic tone. "What was it the fat lady sang? It ain't over till it's over."

Harrigan shook his head and chuckled, amused by her muddled references but heartened by her seemingly limitless capacity to rouse his flagging spirits. "Unless Yogi Berra's taken to wearing drag, I think you have the fat lady confused with a rather well-known baseball player," he corrected her.

"Whatever." She smiled coyly, affecting a wise-guy attitude. "Either way, it ain't over yet." She opened the driver's-side door and pointed in the direction of their next destination.

The Better Day Hospice was housed on a large corner lot two blocks from Haight Street. A two-story Italianate Victorian that had been converted into a four-unit apartment after World War II, the building's subdivisions had been torn down and the structure restored to something resembling its original floor plan in the late 1980s after the property was acquired by the Better Day Foundation, a nonprofit AIDS service group funded largely by donations from wealthy gay and lesbian activists.

A cheerful hand-painted sign over the front porch of the building depicted the organization's logo—a bright orange sun shining over the glistening blue waters of the San Francisco Bay—and a bronze plaque by the front doorbell carried an inscription that informed visitors that the hospice was a refuge for women stricken with the deadly AIDS virus.

The hospice administrator answered the door. A plain-looking woman in her late thirties with straight shoulder-length brown hair, she introduced herself as Shelly Thomas. "What you're about to see may be unsettling," she said matter-of-factly, "so please be prepared. We have ten women patients with us at the moment, and many are quite advanced."

Ms. Thomas led them across a large combination recreation and living room, where a half-dozen women sat on couches and overstuffed armchairs, some conversing quietly, others reading magazines or watching a rerun of *I Love Lucy* on a medium-size color TV. Though Harrigan had never been in an

AIDS hospice before, it was easy to discern the well-nourished visitors from the patients. Ranging in age from the mid-twenties to the late forties, the women of Better Day exhibited, without exception, the sickly pallor, weight loss and, above all, the look of haunted, bone-weary fatigue and defeat that mark the final onslaught of an incurable disease. And these were the healthier patients, who were still able to get out of bed for a couple of hours each day. For Harrigan and for Josie, too, seeing them was a wrenching experience that made the pressures of their own lives pale in comparison.

Kathleen Simpson was already in her fourth week at Better Day. She had spent the past five days confined to a hospital bed in a room at the rear of the first floor, too far advanced to join her fellow patients in the living room. "For the most part, she's still lucid," Thomas said. "She told me earlier she very much wants to speak with you."

They found Simpson awake, reading a recent issue of *Newsweek*. A half-finished *New York Times* crossword puzzle lay on the nightstand next to the telephone she had used to phone Josie's office. Apart from the hospital bed and a medical supply cart parked outside an adjacent bathroom, the room had the feel of home, with a set of large double-hung windows overlooking a backyard patio and an assortment of nicely framed pen-and-ink drawings of Bay Area street scenes hung on the walls.

Although gaunt and suffering from profound weight loss, Simpson looked pleased to see Harrigan and Josie and seemed to know who they were even before Thomas made her introductions and left to continue with her evening duties. Simpson smiled a weak hello and, with her right hand operating a remote control, raised the back of her bed.

"I'm glad you came," she said in a soft voice, looking at Harrigan.

He took Simpson's right hand in his. He felt a tremor move through his stomach and the back of his legs from the limp and nearly lifeless quality of her grip. For an instant he recalled experiencing the same sensation—the uncomfortable realization that he had come face to face with death—when as a child he made a final visit with his terminally ill grandmother. "It's good to meet you, Kathleen," he said, "and I'm very happy you wanted to talk with us."

"I know you," Simpson insisted, uninterested in an exchange of pleasantries. "I've written to you at your law office in Pasadena."

"When?" Harrigan inquired, his curiosity aroused both by her knowledge of where he practiced and her adamant tone.

Rather than answer Harrigan, Kathleen turned her eyes to Josie and pointed her right forefinger at the wall. "Do you like my drawings?" she asked. "I did them myself."

"They're lovely," Josie replied, strolling to the wall for a closer look. The sketches, which varied from poltical cartoon caricatures to near photo-realism, were richly rendered and showed an advanced mastery of perspective and light and shadow indicative of professional training. They were each signed with the initials "K.S." and bore various dates from the early seventies through the early nineties.

"I was an art student and a teacher of calligraphy,"

Simpson explained proudly, then suddenly turned her attention back to Harrigan. "Do you know there's a magic root from Africa that kills the AIDS virus? They are going to give it to me. Maybe he'll bring it."

"Who?" Harrigan asked, sensing to his dismay that Kathleen was lapsing out of lucidity.

"Him," she answered wearily, pointing at a small sketch of a bearded young man hanging above the dresser on the opposite wall.

"It's Debray, isn't it?" Josie asked, making an educated guess on the basis of the old descriptions contained in her investigation file.

"Has he been here?" Harrigan asked a bit too sharply.

"I've written to you," Simpson said again, appearing to ignore Harrigan's inquiry. "A long time ago. From Portland, pretending to be Henry. I said he was coming to save Harold, but he lied. He broke his promise."

"A letter?" Josie asked, turning to face Harrigan.

Staggered by Kathleen's disclosure, Harrigan ran his fingers through his hair. "Just before the accident on Angeles Crest, I got a letter that the lab initially authenticated as Debray's. It was a nearly perfect forgery." He leaned toward Kathleen and spoke softly. "And you called my office earlier this month, didn't you?"

"To warn you to be careful."

"Do you know who killed Professor Denton?" Harrigan asked.

Kathleen shook her head. "Only that they're after Henry, too."

Josie took a step closer to Kathleen and gently stroked her face. "Has Henry been to visit you?"

"He asked me to marry him," Kathleen replied, her brown eyes growing weary. "He said we would go to Africa and find the magic root."

"I think we've gotten about as much information as we can," Josie said to Harrigan. "She looks like she needs to sleep." Josie lowered the backrest, fluffed Kathleen's pillows, and motioned Harrigan to leave.

Kathleen shut her eyes and had appeared to drift off when she suddenly spoke again. "Henry said he would see you tonight at eleven at the Cowell Theater in Fort Mason." Finding a hidden reserve of energy, she managed to prop herself up on her right elbow. "He said for Mr. Harrigan to come alone. That's what he said." She seemed to laugh quietly to herself as she let her head fall to the pillow and closed her eyes, drifting away to the sanctuary of sleep.

On their way out of the hospice, Shelly Thomas confirmed that Kathleen had indeed had a visitor two days ago—"a dark-haired, bearded gentleman named Andy Baron, who said he was a friend from the old days. He stayed with her for about an hour but hasn't returned or called since."

Fort Mason was the kind of public space that could exist only in a freewheeling, liberal town like San Francisco. A former army port named after the fifth military governor of California, the site offered majestic views of the Bay from a sprawling complex of old shed-like warehouses constructed on piers along the eastern border of the city's marina. Since the early seventies, when the property was rescued from the hands of private developers and incorporated into the Golden Gate Recreational Area, the old fort had been the home of a staggering array of artistic and cultural organizations, small specialty museums, restaurants, and a youth hostel that gave the place the feel of a city within a city.

The Cowell Theater was one of the fort's newer additions. Together with a large entry hall used to showcase the works of local artists, it occupied the entire length of Pier Number Two. Harrigan left his rental car in the large parking lot off Bay and Franklin streets and made his way to the theater on foot, arriving at the front doors fifteen minutes ahead of schedule at 10:45. A set of posters pasted on a kiosk outside the entrance announced that a concert of Irish traditional music had been in progress since 8:30.

Except for the theater, the other establishments within the old fort had closed for the day. With the fog closing in and the air turning chilly, Harrigan fastened the top button of his shirt and flipped the lapels of his sports coat up around his neck. Then he waited.

A young couple, arm in arm, passed him, hurrying along in the chill night air. A group of boisterous teenagers shouted in the distance. A gray-haired old man in a black overcoat crossed the parking lot in front of the theater, about fifteen yards from Harrigan, softly singing a Nat King Cole melody. A pair of cats chased each other along the edge of the water. The sound of the waves crashing against the pier muted the sounds of their screeching and lent an ominous rhythm to Harrigan's thoughts. This was, he was all but certain, Ashbourne's last chance, and there was absolutely no guarantee that Kathleen Simpson had gotten Debray's message right or that Debray would finally make good on a pledge.

At eleven o'clock the concertgoers began to filter slowly from the building, a trickle of younger and more hardy souls at first, following by increasingly larger numbers of what must have been an audience of several hundred folk music fans. Harrigan walked determinedly toward the front entrance for a better view of the patrons, barely noticing the Nat Cole tune "Unforgettable" being crooned just behind him.

Turning around to find the source of the singing, Harrigan came face to face with the gray-haired old man he had seen just minutes earlier crossing the parking lot. "You came early," the little man said, smiling through his wrinkles.

As little as a month ago, Harrigan would have had great difficulty discerning the stage makeup and authentic-looking hairpiece the man wore. With all that he had been through, however, he recognized his visitor instantly as Debray.

"Let's stop the games, okay?" Harrigan's tone was sharp and angry. "I have a client with reservations for the little green room who needs your help."

"That's why I'm here," Debray protested. "Taking in the sights of Fort Mason isn't exactly high on my agenda." He brought his forefinger to his mouth, gesturing for Harrigan to modulate his tone as the concertgoers ambled past them.

"I need to know if you're going to testify," Harrigan said more softly but with undiminished urgency.

"Better than that, I'm going to bring Charles West with me." Debray's eyes opened wide. "He's prepared to acknowledge his part in the bombing. He didn't know the professor and his son were home."

"Who was his accomplice?" Harrigan asked abruptly.

"You'll have to hear that directly from West." Debray delivered his answer evasively, and he took a small backward step in anticipation of another irate outburst from Harrigan. "Just give me until tomorrow afternoon. West and I will come together. Trust me." He smiled and then, like a Hollywood agent scheduling a power lunch, added, "Say around two?"

Harrigan paused for an instant, pondering the odds of trusting a man who under any normal set of circumstances would have been a candidate for a right cross to that soft spot between the left orbital and the ear. He quickly realized, however, that he had no choice but to let Debray dictate his own terms of cooperation.

"Okay. But you're not leaving this time without telling me how to contact you."

Debray seemed to bristle at the demand, prompting Harrigan to add, "Trust is a mutual thing. I think you owe as much to Harold."

As Harrigan waited for an answer, Debray's eyes darted over Harrigan's shoulders. A heavy male voice shouted Harrigan's name from across the parking lot. Startled, Harrigan wheeled around in the direction of the noise. It took a moment for his mind to comprehend the elephantine figure of John Goodnow charging toward him.

Instinctively, Harrigan turned back to face Debray, intending to grab him by the scruff of the neck and prevent him from doing another of his patented disappearing acts. It was too late.

By the time Goodnow arrived huffing and puffing at Harrigan's side, Debray was gone. Harrigan fired a barrage of X-rated expletives at Goodnow, and lost a precious thirty seconds in the process. Goodnow was duly chastened, but the damage he had caused was irreversible. A quick search of the exhibition hall offered Harrigan and Goodnow a whirlwind opportunity to see the hall's current display of black-and-white photos depicting the lives of migrant laborers toiling in the fields of the Central Valley, but the search yielded no sign of a little gray-haired old man in a black overcoat.

TWENTY-SIX

Harrigan was still seething when he entered Taneda's courtroom on Wednesday morning. If the case law on the subject of interfering with a witness interview had been only slightly more stringent, he might have followed through on the idea he had nurtured overnight of moving for a sanction to prohibit Goodnow from wandering the streets unaccompanied after sunset by a responsible adult for the duration of the hearing. After last night and the incident at the parking lot near Vesuvio's, something had to be done. But there was no law that prevented a state investigator from following a lawyer from one public venue to another, and with Goodnow steadfastly denying that he had broken into Josie's Beemer, Harrigan knew that the most he could prove was that Goodnow was guilty of lumbering ineptitude.

Harrigan also knew that if he raised his complaints in a formal motion seeking sanctions for Goodnow's gaffe, Taneda would likely side with Pickering and find the motion to be an attempt to limit the State's access to Debray. Given Debray's late addition to the witness list, such a finding might well prompt Taneda to rule that the only way to protect the State's right to a fair hearing would be to preclude Debray from testifying altogether. The prospects of seeing his complaints boomerang against him called for muted discretion, at least in front of the court.

Pickering, however, was another story. Finding the bow-tied deputy prosecutor unpacking his briefcase at the counsel table, Harrigan approached stealthily from the rear. Forgoing any attempt at the usual early morning banter, he stated his position abruptly and with a degree of sarcasm that must have sounded more than a little rehearsed. "I want you to keep King Kong on a tighter leash before he causes any more destruction."

Looking more amused than threatened, Pickering turned to face Harrigan and arched his eyebrows. "If you mean Mr. Goodnow, he called me late last night. I might have thought that you two would be old pals by now, the way you carried on together out there at Fort Mason."

"He disrupted an interview that might very well have shed light on the truth in this case," Harrigan shot back, his tone growing bitter and aggressive. "Or aren't you really interested in the truth?"

"The People are always interested in the truth," Pickering replied smarmily as he rose from his seat, his razor-thin mustache twitching with feigned indignation. "And just to prove *how* interested we are, you can tell me what Debray said to you last night before Mr. Goodnow arrived. If Debray's going to be a witness, we have a right to know."

Pickering glanced at his wristwatch. "You can either tell me or tell His Honor. I'm sure Yojimbo—I understand that's what your cronies in the defense bar call him—would be happy to begin the morning with a recap of your nocturnal escapades."

With Taneda set to take the bench in five minutes, Harrigan had little time to weigh Pickering's threat. All things considered, Pickering held the advantage. "Debray told me that he'll be here this afternoon with Charles West. West is prepared to admit his role in the bombing."

"That he was Ashbourne's accomplice?" Pickering raised the corner of his mouth in a crooked half smile at the news.

"I never got that far, thanks to you-know-who." Harrigan looked toward the rear of the courtroom and gestured at Goodnow, who had just made his appearance through the portals of justice. "Just keep your gorilla away from Debray this afternoon. I don't want to give him any reason to bolt again."

"Let's see," Pickering mused caustically, pausing briefly to glance at the witness list he had placed on top of the counsel table before Harrigan had set upon him. "You're going to put on your guilt-phase IAC expert this morning, and in addition to West and Debray, you'll also be calling . . ."

"Sylvia Peterson and Fred Wallace," Harrigan answered impatiently as Goodnow, nodding his good mornings, took up his customary position in the first row of the gallery.

"Sounds like a regular reunion of the old gang. Are you sure you can squeeze them all in?"

"We'll go as far as we can and then come back for more tomorrow. I want you to promise you'll keep Goodnow away from Debray before we can put him under oath." Harrigan gave Pickering an even stare before resuming in a more accommodating tone. "Look, I don't know any more than you what Debray will say. If we don't finish with him this afternoon, we can have him remanded into custody as a material witness without either one of us having an opportunity to interview him alone."

It was Pickering's turn now to weigh the pros and cons of cooperation. A typical prosecutor, out to display another defendant's testicles in his trophy case, would have told Harrigan to stick his plea for cooperation where the sun doesn't shine. A typical prosecutor would have renewed his motion to exclude Debray from testifying or at least insisted on an adjournment for the purpose of taking his deposition. But somehwere beneath the cold bureaucratic exterior, Pickering still thought of himself as something of a crusader for justice, and for all his desire to win, he believed that Harrigan was risking just as much as he was by putting Debray on the witness stand without advance preparation. "Okay," he answered after making Harrigan sweat for another good half minute. "You've got a deal."

After a slight delay caused by the late arrival of the morning bus from San Quentin, Harrigan called his guilt-phase IAC expert, Andrew Dryer, to the stand. Like Dr. Rosen, Dryer came to court readymade with unassailable credentials—a law degree from Harvard; a ten-year stint with the San Francisco County DA, the last three spent as supervisor of the major crimes division; and a partnership, now nearing the end of its second decade, in one of the county's leading business and white-collar defense firms.

With over twenty murder trials under his belt, roughly two-thirds as a prosecutor and the rest from the other side of the lectern, Dryer was perhaps the ideal expert witness, skilled in virtually every facet of federal and state trial procedures.

Impeccably attired in a blue Armani and with nary an out-of-place hair on his carefully coiffed snow-white pompadour, Dryer took his seat beneath Taneda's watchful gaze, a manila file containing the notes he had prepared on the case resting in his lap. To those accustomed to the gruff style of the hard-nosed trial lawyer, Dryer was something of an anomaly, presenting the image of a softspoken elder statesman, a sort of Alastair Cooke of the Bar, eager to impart his wisdom to the combatants before him while personally remaining at a safe distance above the fray.

Harrigan took his witness through the usual introductory questions, covering the many highlights of Dryer's education and legal career. In response to a pointed question that drew a brief look of envy or awe from Taneda, Dryer frankly acknowledged that for the past five years he had been charging upward of $300 per hour in "fee-generating cases" as a law firm partner. "In this case, however," he continued, "I've elected to testify on a pro bono basis, waiving the usual stipend awarded by the court. I've had a career filled with success and good fortune, and I think it only right that I donate a portion of my time on behalf of those who would be unable to afford my services."

With the preliminaries over, Harrigan plunged into the heart of Dryer's work on the case. "At my request,

Mr. Dryer, have you reviewed the transcripts of the trial in the case of *People* versus *Ashbourne* and the pleadings on file in this habeas corpus proceeding?" The witness answered affirmatively, and Harrigan continued. "And have you conducted that review for the purpose of rendering an opinion on whether the petitioner, Harold Ashbourne, received effective assistance of counsel at the guilt-phase of his state court trial?"

"My view," Dryer began, "is that the petitioner's counsel did not perform adequately in several interrelated respects, including the failure to search for the petitioner's alibi witness, Henri Debray; the refusal to call the petitioner as a witness at the trial; and, of course, counsel's rather dismaying lack of sobriety at key points in the proceeding." Judging from his tone, it seemed as if Dryer took no pleasure in finding fault with the performance of a colleague, even one as remote as J. Arnold Barnes, whom he had never met.

Harrigan proceeded to establish Dryer's familiarity with the central role that Debray played in Ashbourne's alibi, then asked, "In a criminal trial, is it ever acceptable for a trial layer simply to decline to search for a key alibi witness?"

"Assuming that the trial lawyer has sufficient resources, the accused is mentally competent, and the alibi is not inherently incredible," Dryer responded professorially, "such a search would be among the advocate's foremost duties."

"We'll come back to the credibility of the alibi in a moment," Harrigan advised. "But first tell us, if you will, how a reasonably competent trial attorney might attempt to locate a witness who has gone into hiding."

"Trial lawyers, working in conjunction with investigators," Dryer intoned modestly, "are often called on to locate reluctant witnesses. Even with a witness who has elected not to be found, it is important to remember that people do not simply disappear. Efforts can, and indeed must, be made to find them."

"But in this case," Harrigan countered, taking up the role of devil's advocate as he had with Dr. Rosen, "the reluctant witness, Henri Debray, was not only intent on disappearing into the radical underground but, from all accounts, was an exceptionally resourceful individual. How can you find fault with the petitioner's counsel for failing to find him?"

"The fault that I find," Dryer said, hastening to correct Harrigan, "is not so much that counsel failed to locate Debray, but that he chose not to try and in the process violated the first rule of any successful missing-persons search."

"And what is that?" Harrigan prompted.

"Begin before the trail gets cold. Depending on the case, there are a variety of techniques that can be employed: motor vehicle department checks, medical records inquiries, credit reports, skip traces. In this case, however, with a mercurial personality like Debray, the best way to proceed would have been by interviewing Debray's friends, associates and, above all, his surviving family members."

Dryer gave his answer with the ease of one used to handling tough questioning. Pausing only to catch his breath, he added, "The petitioner's counsel knew that Henri Debray wasn't really some fanciful French café intellectual but was born in Brooklyn, New York, as Henry Dershaw. At the time of the firebombing and his disappearance, Mr. Dershaw's mother was still alive and, if I recall correctly, living in the same Crown Heights apartment where Henry was raised. Yet she was never contacted by the defense. As a result, the best chance to locate Debray and confirm the petitioner's alibi was defaulted without ever pursuing it."

"Are you aware, Mr. Dryer, that Mrs. Dershaw refused to speak with representatives of the prosecution prior to the trial?"

"In our adversarial system of justice, the defense can never rely on the prosecution to conduct its interviews for them." Dryer took a moment to clear his throat, a self-conscious gesture designed to add a certain scholarly touch to his developing exegesis. "Even with a willing witness who has no reason to shade her comments in favor of one side or the other, there can be no substitute for the defense's own in-person interviews. And in the case of a witness like Mr. Dershaw's mother, who might be fearful of the prosecution's motives for wanting to locate her son, the necessity of direct contact is all the more imperative. Just because she refused to speak with a State investigator doesn't mean that she would not have spoken with someone from the defense team. Her son may have told her that Mr. Ashbourne was innocent—"

"But you have no way of knowing, Mr. Dryer," Taneda said, breaking into the colloquy between Harrigan and the witness, "whether Mrs. Dershaw would have spoken with the defense, whether she in fact knew where her son was, or whether her son told her anything about the petitioner's involvement in the crimes at issue."

"That's true, Your Honor," Dryer answered respectfully, "but Debray has executed a declaration stating that he spent the first six months of his exile in upstate New York, living in a cabin owned by his mother, and—"

Pickering jumped to his feet and hurriedly joined the emerging free-for-all. "I would remind the court," he said loudly, "that Debray's declaration is inadmissible hearsay."

"I was simply going to add before I was interrupted, Your Honor," Dryer said testily, "that the only person alive today who could answer Your Honor's questions is Henry Dershaw himself."

"When and if he testifies, you mean," Taneda commented, arching an eyebrow and directing his gaze at Harrigan.

"We expect to see Mr. Debray this afternoon," Harrigan informed the court. Then in a cautious tone, "I alerted Mr. Pickering this morning."

A few uneasy seconds ticked away as Taneda considered Harrigan's disclosure. "Then I suggest you get on with your examination of Mr. Dryer," he said finally.

Harrigan thanked Taneda and turned his attention back to the witness. "On the subject of witness interviews, is it ever, in your view, permissible to substitute an interview over the phone for an in-person contact?"

The question—for which Harrigan not only had Debray's mother in mind but also Sylvia Peterson—

drew a quizzical look from Pickering, but the deputy AG raised no objection.

"A phone call, no matter how long, can never substitute for a direct contact when the investigation of a potential defense is at stake," Dryer answered. "There's no way I know of to assess credibility through the ear piece of a plastic receiver."

Believing that Dryer had covered all the necessary bases to show the deficiencies of Barnes' pretrial investigation, Harrigan decided, as he had earlier, to forgo any direct reference to the perfunctory telephone interview the defense had conducted with Sylvia Peterson until Peterson took the stand herself. Shifting the focus of his inquiry, he asked, "You've also told us, Mr. Dryer, that you fault Mr. Barnes for declining to call Mr. Ashbourne to testify in his own defense. Can you explain the basis of that opinion?"

Dryer cocked his head to one side, preparing to deliver another mini-lecture on the dos and don'ts of criminal practice. "Mr. Barnes put on what is known in the trade as a 'reasonable doubt' case. He had his client plead not guilty, he challenged the prosecution to prove its case and, by implication, he told the jury that Mr. Ashbourne had no role in the firebombing. Yet he put on no case of his own."

Dryer took another dramatic pause and looked in the direction of Ashbourne, who sat in his freshly laundered prison uniform, listening intently to every word. "If the prosecution's evidence of guilt is substantial—and I would have to agree that it was in this case—the jury ordinarily will want to hear from the defendant himself."

Dryer let his eyes shift between Harrigan and Pickering, as if he were lecturing a pair of younger associates. "Jurors are ordinary people, and I say that with no intent to disparage them. The Fifth Amendment may require that they be instructed not to draw adverse inferences from the defendant's decision to remain silent, but psychologically they will want to hear the defendant deny his involvement in the crime. In this case, with such an articulate defendant, it was particularly important for Mr. Ashbourne to take the stand. Without hearing from him, what other option was available to the jury but to return a conviction?"

"But what about the petitioner's claim that he spent the evening of the firebombing in the company of a man who not only fled the scene but had a longstanding feud with the murder victim?" Harrigan pressed on. "Wouldn't a jury concerned with discovering the truth have dismissed such an alibi as self-serving?"

Dryer took a breath, then delivered another unflappable answer. "All alibis, Mr. Harrigan, are by their nature self-serving. And as for the jury's mission to determine the truth, my point is simple. The only version of the truth they heard at the petitioner's trial was the version presented by the State. Harold Ashbourne might just as well have stayed on his jail cot and let the twelve good citizens in the box send him their verdict by mail."

"And Mr. Barnes' problem with alcoholism, how does that figure into the opinions you've stated here today?"

Dryer crossed his arms over his midsection and

shook his head in a demonstration of thinly veiled disgust. "Those problems, in my view, not only magnified all the others that we've mentioned but they may have caused them. How any attorney can claim that he made a reasoned tactical decision to keep his client off the stand when he had come to court without his sea legs is beyond me. From my perspective, Mr. Barnes was very fortunate to escape from the Ashbourne trial without a referral to the state bar."

Knowing that he could not have articulated the case against Barnes with any more certainty or verve, Harrigan announced that he had no further questions and strolled confidently back to the counsel table, turning to give Ashbourne an encouraging wink as he slid into his seat.

Despite his best efforts on cross, Pickering was unable to shake Dryer from his opinions. The morning session drew to a close with the image of J. Arnold Barnes' incompetence indelibly inscribed in the court stenographer's notes and the blue vein above Taneda's temple thickening by the quarter hour.

TWENTY-SEVEN

Long accustomed to riding the ups and downs of the courtroom roller coaster, Harrigan refused to take any comfort from the morning's triumphs. Although Dryer's performance had been stellar, Harrigan knew that everything that had transpired until now had merely been a form of litigious foreplay. The heart of the case—the underlying proof that Ashbourne actually had an alibi and wasn't the pampered flame thrower the justice system had branded him—still had to be proved. In the absence of such proof, any mistakes J. Arnold Barnes might have made would be what the law books called "harmless error," and the execution squad at San Quentin would no doubt keep a nylon death diaper nice and dry for Harold Ashbourne's final day on earth.

Declining interview requests from a pair of local reporters and the omnipresent radio point man, John Aragon, Harrigan took a solitary lunch in the courthouse cafeteria. As he ate, his gaze shifted impatiently between the morning edition of the *Chronicle* and the cafeteria entrance, where any second he hoped to see Josie returning from her trek to San Francisco International and the financial district, with the afternoon's leadoff witnesses, Sylvia Peterson and Fred Wallace, in tow.

Although he knew he could have better spent the lunch hour ironing out the kinks for the direct examinations that lay ahead, he found his interest drawn to the "think piece" at the top of page three. Under a bold headline—"New Agreement on Water Use Threatened"—an article by the paper's environmental writer told of a proposal by a coalition of agribusiness interests to buy the federally owned and operated Central Valley Water Project, the older of the state's two main aqueduct systems, inaugurated in the 1930s. The more recent State Water Project, the article explained, had been inaugurated in the 1960s.

"Last December," the story read, "the governor ended years of political controversy when he announced the approval of a new water-allocation formula to protect the fragile ecosystems of the Sacramento Delta and at the same time ensure acceptable deliveries of water to central and southern California. Many experts now fear that the water-allocation accord could unravel if the federally owned system is sold to reduce Washington's budget deficit. Although sale of the federal project has been tabled for this fiscal year, the proposal will likely be reconsidered in the future."

While the details of the plan to sell off the Central Valley Project were of little interest to Harrigan, the quotes from Robert Jenkins three-quarters of the way through the long article stood out as if they were directed specifically at Harrigan himself. "If Congress ever ratifies the proposal to sell the CVP, the water wars of the past, like the Peripheral Canal referendum of 1982, will seem like minor skirmishes. I don't think the people of California want to refight the old battles. I think they want to leave them in the past and move on to an era of truly sound environmental policy."

Harrigan dwelled on Jenkins' observations about the Peripheral Canal as he finished the last of his tuna melt. It was the Peripheral Canal that had served as the pretext for Debray's raging feud with Professor Denton and which, at least on the surface, had figured so prominently in Denton's murder. Now the canal was, as Jenkins put it, a battle of the past and it was time to move on.

Sooner or later, the Ashbourne case would also be a battle of the past. Harrigan would have to move on with his life, and Ashbourne, one way or another, would have to come to terms with his. Having lived with the case since before the death of his wife and kids, Harrigan felt both exhilaration and terror at the thought of bringing the matter to a conclusion. Would he feel that an intolerable burden had been lifted from his shoulders, or would he experience the kind of emotional letdown soldiers returning from war often encounter? It was an interesting question but one that was also premature. Whether you believed in it or saw it as the last vestige of socially acceptable barbarism, capital punishment offered the purest form of legal warfare in a country that seemed to be addicted to such combat. In the middle of battle, it was both dangerous and unwise to think about anything but winning.

He took another quick look at the environmental story, then carefully tore it from the rest of the paper and, ignoring the stares of those around him, ripped it into small pieces.

Rather than take Sylvia Peterson to the cafeteria, Josie escorted her directly to Taneda's courtroom. Although she knew that her failure to meet up with Harrigan downstairs might spark some momentary anxiety, there was little point in trying to arrange a last-minute prep session over coffee or tea. From the moment Peterson stepped off the twin-engine commuter plane from Eureka, it was clear that she had come to court only because she had been served with a subpoena. "I don't want to make your job any harder than it already is," she practically hissed at Josie on their way into town from the airport, "but I want to testify and get back to my daughter as soon as possible." As far as the content of her testimony was concerned, Peterson insisted on remaining silent until she was sworn in.

At five minutes to one, Josie and Peterson were the first civilians to be admitted for the afternoon session. They quickly found a couple of empty seats in the first row of the gallery and, without uttering another word, waited for Harrigan.

"If looks could kill," Harrigan thought to himself as his eyes met Sylvia's five minutes later. He had seen the same kind of expresssion before on the faces of witnesses hauled into court against their will. It was a look filled with equal parts of fear, anger, and dark anticipation, a look that came only to those who felt alone and trapped.

Harrigan made a weak effort to say hello to Peterson, then turned his gaze toward Josie, who rose from her seat for a quick conference on the other side of the spectator railing. "She's not a very happy camper," Josie said, keeping her voice low as they reached the counsel tables.

"If I were in her shoes, I'm not even sure I would have shown up," Harrigan replied, opening his briefcase to retrieve a yellow legal pad.

"That's another thing," Josie said quickly, a sudden urgency in her voice. "Fred Wallace is missing."

Harrigan gave her a blank stare as he struggled to comprehend her disclosure. "Maybe he just wants to get here on his own. Have you checked with his office?"

"I've spoken to the secretaries both at his downtown office and in L.A. No one's heard from him in over twenty-four hours. He missed an important deposition in a products-liability action yesterday."

"What does Peterson know about it?"

"You'll have to ask her that yourself. The only thing she's told me is that she has a return flight to Eureka at six."

If Peterson knew where Wallace was, she wasn't about to admit it, even under oath. Outfitted in a modest but businesslike two-piece brown woolen suit, with her thick black hair clipped economically below the ears, the most she would acknowledge was speaking with Wallace two days ago. "He called to tell me he'd see me in court," she said. "As for where he is today, I have no idea."

"Did you talk with him about the testimony you expected to give today?" Harrigan inquired as he took up his position at the lectern.

Peterson smiled wanly to herself and shook her head. "He didn't ask and I didn't tell," she said tersely, clenching her teeth between breaths. "I may be his ex-wife, but I'm not his mother."

"But you are the mother of Professor Charles West's child, aren't you?" Harrigan's question was the legal equivalent of a hard slap in the face, acid in tone and intimate in content. Designed to get the witness' attention and bring an early end to her bad-girl attitude, the question caused Peterson to squirm uneasily on the stand as she braced herself for more fireworks.

The question also elicited a spirited relevance objection from Pickering and a swift and stern admonition from Taneda. "I trust this line of inquiry is going somewhere, Mr. Harrigan. The court will not tolerate attacks of a personal nature on the witness."

Only slightly deterred by Taneda's grim visage, Harrigan resumed the offensive. "What about Charles West? He's also been subpoenaed to appear this afternoon. Have you spoken with him?"

Peterson shook her head again. "I haven't spoken to Professor West in at least a couple of weeks, and, no, our conversation had nothing to do with Harold Ashbourne or the Denton bombing. We talked only about our daughter's progress in school." She took her first direct look at Ashbourne. Her expression, though still hard-edged, betrayed a hint of sympathy and sorrow.

Ashbourne returned her gaze. From their conference in the lockup, he knew of Harrigan's suspicions about West. His heart pounded at the mention of West's name.

"Both West, Wallace, and you were at one time members of the steering committee of the group known as Saviors of the Earth, true?" Harrigan asked.

"I was the only woman accorded that honor." Her answer resonated with renewed sarcasm, the one emotion which seemed never to desert her.

"And during the course of your association with Saviors, did the group take a position on the cross-delta water project known as the Peripheral Canal?"

A lazy smile spread across Peterson's face, and for a moment it almost seemed that she might break into laughter. "You might say the canal became for us what the crucifixion was for the early Christians."

"It sounds as though you no longer believe in the principles the Saviors stood for," Harrigan commented, attempting to use a little sarcasm of his own to break down the witness' defensiveness.

"The principles were fine," Peterson answered coolly. "The men who ran the group were something else."

"You mean West and Henry Dershaw, also known as Henri Debray?"

"They turned the Saviors into their own little empire," Peterson replied, displaying a new willingness to open up. "I realize that sort of thing happens a lot in small left-wing splinter groups, but we had a unique perspective on environmental issues that made us more important than our numbers. The rest of us should never have allowed Charlie and Henri"—she pronounced Debray's name with an exaggerated French accent—"to use us in their tenure battles with Professor Denton."

"I thought the animosity toward Professor Denton arose because of his stand on the canal."

"The canal was just an excuse," Peterson answered crisply. "Charlie and Henri were devoting too much time to their radical games and neglecting their teaching responsibilities. The professor terminated Henri and threatened to do the same to Charlie." She took a deep breath, then added, "From that point on, Denton became the antichrist."

"And each and every Savior became a suspect in his murder," Harrigan interjected.

Sylvia's complexion paled slightly. "I gave the police an alibi for myself, West, and Fred Wallace, and I can assure you that I had nothing to do with the bombing."

"But you lied about West."

She hesitated, then answered, "Yes."

"Why?"

"Because I was pregnant with his child, and I was in love with him," Peterson said weakly, her voice trailing off as she revisited a part of her past she had dearly hoped to leave behind.

"Were you ever interviewed during Harold Ashbourne's trial by an investigator working for the public defender's office?"

"After I moved to Eureka, I received a phone call from a man who identified himself as an investigator with the Alameda County Public Defender."

"And you told the investigator roughly the same thing you said to the police?"

"Yes."

"At any point did the investigator ask to speak with you in person?"

"No, he never called me back."

Recalling Andrew Dryer's testimony on the importance of interviewing all witnesses in person, Harrigan knew that he had scored a strategic hit in his IAC claim against J. Arnold Barnes. "Did you actually see Charles West at all on the night of the Denton fire-bombing?" he asked, pressing the attack.

"I saw him the next morning. We had breakfast at a place on Telegraph."

"And did he ask you to alibi for him, or did you volunteer to do that on your own?" Harrigan's voice rose as he steered his direct examination to its expected climax.

"The request came from him. I never asked where he was the night before. I only know he wasn't with me."

Harrigan hesitated for an instant as he considered the prospects of eliciting further admissions from Peterson. Hoping to conclude on a high note and believing that he had accomplished as much as he could with Peterson, he turned the witness over to Pickering. The abrupt announcement that he had no further questions seemed to catch both the deputy AG and Peterson by surprise.

Pickering rose from his seat and nervously cleared his throat. "You know, do you not, Ms. Peterson, that you could be charged with obstruction of justice for lying to the police about Charles West? Or are you lying now?"

Peterson let her eyes fall to her lap and spoke in a muffled voice. "I've lived with the lie I told the police for over a decade. It's haunted me like a bad dream. If finally telling the truth could possibly help Harold, I'm prepared to do it."

"And yet you lied to Harold's investigator when he spoke with you during the trial, didn't you?"

"We only spoke for five minutes over the phone," Peterson answered, her voice assuming the flat tone of someone whose life has taken a sudden nosedive.

"Would it have made any difference if the investigator had gone to Eureka and spoken to you in the flesh?"

Peterson considered the question for a few heavy seconds before answering. "Yes, I think it would have."

"You would have told the investigator what you've testified to on direct examination today?" Suddenly Pickering realized that he was on the verge of losing a critical issue in the IAC case against J. Arnold Barnes, and his voice began to crack with emotion.

"No," Peterson answered guardedly. "I think I might have told him the whole truth."

"I would remind you, Ms. Peterson, that you've taken an oath to tell the whole truth this afternoon," said Judge Taneda, his eyes narrowing with annoyance and the redoubtable blue vein rising above his temple.

"The truth, Your Honor," Peterson answered, "is that neither Fred nor Charlie was with me when Professor Denton and his son were killed."

The look of distress on Pickering's face was matched only by the looks of satisfaction on Harrigan's and Ashbourne's. Two men had been seen running from the Denton crime scene. Now, more than twelve years later, two men who had been shielded by a phony alibi were suddenly reborn as prime suspects. Peterson's disclosure was for Ashbourne the closest thing to a genuine ray of hope since his jury had straggled into court that gray afternoon long ago to pronounce him guilty of double murder.

Struggling to disguise his mounting sense of panic, Pickering resumed his cross-examination. "And tell us, if you will, what happened to Mr. Wallace on the night of the bombing."

Peterson wrung her hands together, feeling the weight of the entire courtroom on her. "Our marriage was unraveling at the time, largely because of Charles," she said with palpable discomfort at having to disclose the intimate details of her life. "We had another nasty argument, and he stormed out of our apartment."

"And when did he return?"

"About eleven-thirty." She managed another ironic smile. "He said he had gone to the movies, to see *The Verdict.* The next day I told him I'd give him an alibi if he went along with the one I cooked up for Charles."

"Do you know where Mr. Wallace was before he arrived home that night?" Pickering asked, looking as though he had regained a semblance of composure.

"No."

"He never told you that he participated in the bombing?"

"No."

"So as you sit here today, you have no personal knowledge who killed the professor and his son."

"That's true," Peterson admitted, suddenly appearing weary from the ordeal of answering questions.

"Just one or two further questions," Pickering said as he flipped through the pages of a thick manila legal file. "To your knowledge, were West and Wallace interviewed in person by the investigator from the public defender's office?"

"Yes, I believe they were."

"And they are both very convincing individuals, aren't they?"

The question prompted an objection from Harrigan, who complained loudly that the inquiry called for speculation as to how others might regard West and Wallace. To Harrigan's mild surprise, Taneda sustained the protest, but there was no denying that Pickering had made a partial recovery in muting Peterson's earlier revelations. On balance, while Peterson had clearly helped in the IAC case against Barnes, the ultimate issue remained unresolved. As Josie escorted Peterson from the courtroom at two-thirty, both lawyers knew that the outcome of the case would turn not on whether the alibis of other ex-Saviors had fallen but on whether Harold Ashbourne could prove that he had an alibi of his own.

The look of disappointment and dismay on Josie's face as she returned to the gallery was all that Harrigan required to know that Debray had failed on his promise to appear. Not only that, but West and Wallace remained AWOL as well. After a fifteen-minute recess spent working the public pay phones in a futile attempt to locate West and Wallace, Harrigan faced the grim prospect of begging Taneda for a continuance. Before he could mouth the words, however, help came from an entirely unexpected quarter—the judge himself.

"The court takes a dim view of witnesses who disregard subpoenas commanding their appearance," Taneda announced as he called the court back into session. "During the recess I was informed that the U.S. Marshal's Office would be able to serve bench warrants on both Charles West and Frederick Wallace as soon as this evening. I'm also concerned, of course, about Henry Dershaw. But as I understand it, he's not under subpoena and therefore has not violated any court order."

Taneda paused and gave Harrigan a look, which for the judge might have passed as a sign of empathy. Either that or Taneda was just pissed at the brazen disregard the subpoenaed witnesses had shown for the court's authority. In any case, the result worked to Ashbourne's benefit. "The warrants for West and Wallace will issue forthwith," Taneda concluded, reaching for his gavel. "This proceeding will stand adjourned until nine a.m. tomorrow morning."

Fearing that Taneda's bench warrants, however motivated, might prove ineffectual, Harrigan spent the next hour in the courthouse lockup preparing Ashbourne to take the stand on his own behalf as Thursday's lead witness. In view of the fit Ashbourne had thrown on the first day of the hearing, Harrigan expected his client to be eager finally to get his turn to take the oath. He found Ashbourne instead fixated on Debray's latest disappearance and either unwilling or unable to focus on his own testimony.

"I never thought it would come down to me," Ashbourne kept repeating from his seat on the lockup bench. "I can't believe he didn't come." He folded his arms across his chest, dipped his head, and closed his eyes in a posture of defeat. "It's over, isn't it, Peter?"

Struggling to control his exasperation, Harrigan took a seat next to Ashbourne. He felt the case slipping away with Ashbourne's despair. "It's only over if you decide to give up," he said, groping for the right combination of encouragement and realism. "Right now I want you to forget about Debray and concentrate on all the things you've told me over the years about yourself and what happened the night of the bombing."

"What the hell can I say that could possibly make any difference?" Ashbourne shot back. "Without Debray they'll think I'm just another con lying to save his own ass. Besides, I'm not even sure I can remember all the things I've told you. The way I feel, I'll probably lose my breakfast before I answer your first question."

"Then the bailiffs will have to clean up your mess, and we'll continue," Harrigan said, hoping that a touch of humor might help to restore Ashbourne's resolve. "Everyone gets a little stage fright when they make their first statement in court. It happens to me in every case I try. But the butterflies will go away, believe me."

"I don't know," Ashbourne muttered underneath his breath.

"Don't worry about making any speeches. Just listen to my questions and tell the truth."

"The truth?" Ashbourne asked vacantly.

"The truth," Harrigan repeated. "There's no need to embellish or fabricate. Besides, the truth is easier to remember, and in this case it's on our side." He put a reassuring hand on Ashbourne's shoulder before leaving the lockup.

After a quick shower and a change into more casual clothes, Harrigan joined Josie for dinner at the Café Tyre. While Harrigan had been playing the role of Knute Rockne with Ashbourne, Josie had driven back to Fred Wallace's town house near Golden Gate Park. The report she delivered was anything but promising. She had found the town house dark. Worse, the neighbors hadn't seen Fred for the past thirty-six hours.

Lacking a better alternative, they settled into a corner table and tried to let the café's soft string music soothe their jangled nerves as they placed their orders and tried to take their minds off the case. The food was as delectable as ever, and after only a few bites Josie felt her appetite return and the tension in her back ease. Harrigan, however, remained tightly wound, barely able to pick at his food.

"You can't get tomorrow off your mind, can you?" Josie asked as the waitress carted away Harrigan's half-eaten entree.

"Actually, it's tonight that I can't get off my mind," Harrigan answered.

"Well, I think we'd better plan on going ahead without Wallace. Whatever the reason, he's bolted, and I'm sure he's packing enough cash to hide out for the rest of the hearing."

"Then that leaves West."

"And you want to go to West's place in Half Moon Bay to make sure the marshals serve him with the bench warrant." She nodded her head and cracked a crooked half smile, confident that she had read his thoughts accurately.

"How long would it take to get there?" Harrigan asked, wiping his mouth and rising to his feet to pay the bill.

"About forty-five minutes if we take the Beemer instead of that pile of spare parts you're driving."

Once known as Spanish Town, Half Moon Bay was settled by Italian and Portuguese farmers who made their living growing artichokes and Brussels sprouts. By the 1980s, however, the community had become something of a fashionable retreat for well-heeled professionals seeking refuge from the city, who had transformed it into one of the Bay Area's trendier suburbs. The old harbor, once the exclusive preserve of fishing boats, now was also home to all manner of pleasure craft, and many of the area's Victorian mansions were converted into pricy getaway weekend bed and breakfast inns.

Despite his avowed commitment to egalitarian politics, Professor Charles West had managed to overcome his scruples to purchase a three-bedroom California redwood-style home with upper and lower decks affording views of the Pacific. Built on a hill, the home offered West peace and seclusion. Except tonight.

If the convoy of black-and-white police vehicles in the street outside West's home wasn't enough to signal that something terrible had happened, the van from the county coroner's office was an unmistakable red flag. Josie found a parking spot down the block, and with her investigator's badge opened wide, she and Harrigan pushed their way through the throng of confused neighborhood residents.

At the foot of West's driveway stood an ashen-faced John Goodnow. He waved them past the band of yellow police tape at the foot of the property and promptly gave them the bad news. "I think you're going to be at least one witness short tomorrow. Charles West is dead."

"When? How?" Josie and Harrigan asked simultaneously.

"The medical examiner says sometime late last night or early this morning. A bullet in the chest, another to the side of the head. Looks like a .38-caliber." Goodnow shook his head and shrugged his massive shoulders. "I'm sorry. I really am."

Harrigan took a hard swallow as the coroner's crew began to wheel the body, shrouded in a vinyl morgue bag and strapped to a gurney, down the drive. "Any suspects?" he asked.

"The place was really torn up inside. The local cops peg it as a hot-prowl burglary, or maybe one of those follow-home jobs. One of the neighbors knocked on the front door and became concerned when no one answered. The police were already here when I arrived."

Goodnow gave Harrigan a searching look, as though he sensed that Harrigan regarded his presence at West's home as yet another breach of propriety. "I followed the marshals out here to make sure the subpoena was served—just like you, I assume."

Harrigan could only nod at Goodnow's explanation. He and Josie stayed at the scene just long enough to see the gurney loaded onto the van. As the earthly remains of Charles West disappeared inside, they felt that a piece of themselves had died along with the man who, after Debray, may well have been their last hope.

TWENTY-EIGHT

Still reeling from West's murder, Harrigan could sense the worst-case scenario taking shape the moment he entered the courtroom Thursday morning. The cops had put out APB's for Wallace and Debray, and there was Pickering, the People's tribune, sitting at the counsel table, engaged in quiet conversation with a well-dressed middle-aged professional. Harrigan recognized the suit as Walter Krinsky, the State's expert on IAC. With the case dwindling down to Ashbourne's last-ditch appearance on the stand, the deputy AG had taken the precaution of calling his expert in early for what he no doubt concluded would be the final day of testimony. Like the seasoned advocate that he was, Pickering was always thinking ahead.

Pickering politely reintroduced Krinsky to Harrigan, and at nine o'clock sharp the State's expert took his leave, pledging to remain "on call" at his downtown office. Moments later, Ashbourne was led out of the lockup and Taneda took the bench, appearing calm but even more grim-faced than usual. After a brief scan of the courtroom, which seemed slightly more crowded than usual with a ragtag assortment of reporters and spectators, Taneda called the case to order. "The marshal's office has reported to me on the death of Charles West. While I'm certain that this tragedy presents a setback for the petitioner, I want to advise the parties that I intend to move on with the hearing." He paused as his eyes fell on Harrigan. "The petitioner may proceed."

Harrigan leaned over toward Ashbourne. "Just relax and tell the truth and you'll do fine," he whispered. Then he stood and, in a voice booming with false confidence, called his client to the stand.

Although dressed in his prison blues, with his hair parted neatly on the side of his head and his thick horn-rimmed glasses perched atop his delicate aquiline nose, Ashbourne looked more like a worried CPA than a menacing double murderer as he pledged to "tell the truth, the whole truth, and nothing but the truth."

Harrigan walked to the lectern and glanced at the list of questions he had jotted down late last night on the legal pad now resting in front of him. "Mr. Ashbourne," he began in a solemn tone, "did you participate in the 1982 firebombing of Professor Gilbert Denton's home in the Berkeley Hills?"

"No, I did not," Ashbourne answered resolutely, shifting his bony posterior around in the upholstered swivel chair to find a more comfortable position.

"I'm going to come back to the night of the firebombing in a moment or two," Harrigan advised. "But first I want to ask you about the testimony your mother gave earlier in this proceeding." He knew that the subject of his mother's testimony would make Ashbourne anxious and perhaps even take him by surprise. But it was an issue that had to be confronted, and Harrigan thought it best to do so quickly and early.

"I don't want to talk about it." Ashbourne's face flushed with irritation.

"I just want you to tell the court if your mother testified accurately about the photographs the German caretakers took of you when you were a little boy," Harrigan counseled patiently.

Ashbourne clenched his teeth and then dropped his eyes to his chest in a now familiar pose of resignation. He had been many things in his life—a spoiled rich kid, a neglected child, a hippie, a seeker of truth, a political dupe and, most recently, a resident of death row—and he had somehow come to terms with, and even found a residue of honor in, all his various incarnations. But one thing he had never admitted, one thing he would have hidden from the world forever, was that his family's domestic help had made him the object of their kinky sexual games. Now, as his own lawyer waited for an answer, he appeared utterly alone and trapped by his past.

After a thirty-second delay that seemed to last half the morning, Ashbourne mustered the courage to reply. "Yes, it's true." He spoke hoarsely at first, and then the dam inside him suddenly burst. "But there was never any touching. They never asked me to touch their genitals, and they never touched mine. I want you to know that."

He grimaced and tried to keep calm. "Olga and Gunter, those were their names, used to have me take my clothes off and pose first with her and then with him, and then by myself. Sometimes they'd rent costumes—Greek and Roman togas, Renaissance wardrobes—but the nudes were their favorites. I thought it was all a game until my mother found some photos in Gunter's room. Then I was sent away to Dennard, and Gunter and Olga, I guess, agreed to go back to Germany so they and my parents could avoid a scandal."

"And you never told this to your trial attorney?"

Ashbourne dropped his eyes again. "I never told anyone until today."

"But you did tell your trial attorney that you weren't involved in the firebombing?" Harrigan asked, returning to the alibi that Ashbourne's jury had never gotten to hear.

With the issue of the porno pictures behind him, Ashbourne heaved a sigh of relief and at last seemed to relax. "Many times," he answered.

"Tell us, if you will, exactly what you told Mr. Barnes about what you did on the night the professor and his son were killed."

"I went to see Henri—Henry Dershaw, perhaps I should say—about nine o'clock at the fountain in Sproul Plaza. He had asked me to meet him there earlier that afternoon. He said he had something very important to tell me about the Saviors."

"And did you meet him?"

"He came along about ten minutes late—he had a habit of showing up late for meetings. I suppose it made him feel important to keep other people waiting."

"What were you and he wearing at the time?"

Harrigan asked, seeking to show the extent of Ashbourne's recollection.

"I had on a flannel shirt and jeans. It was a pretty warm night."

"And Debray?"

"An old denim jacket cut off at the waist, with one of the buttons he liked to wear from the May '68 events."

"The what?" Taneda, eyebrows arched, inquired for clarification.

"The revolutionary left-wing uprising that occurred in Paris, France, in May 1968," Ashbourne explained, sounding the part of a diligent history student. "Debray was in Paris at the time as some kind of exchange student, and he participated in the uprising. The button he had on was imprinted with one of the slogans from the Left Bank: 'Power to the Imagination,' if I remember right. Debray was very proud of it."

"And what did you and Debray do?"

"We talked and we walked." Harrigan gestured with a nod of the head for Ashbourne to continue, and the petitioner added, "We started out in the plaza and took a long walk through campus, past the Bancroft Library, up University Drive by the Greek Theater, then down Gayley Road, and finally to People's Park, which was where we separated and I went home."

"And what did you talk about?"

Ashbourne halted as if he was seeking the right words or trying to wring the sadness from his mind. "The end of the Saviors," he replied haltingly. "It was why he wanted to talk, to tell me that he had decided to make things official. Debray and I were very close, and he knew I'd take it hard if I heard it from someone else. We shared a house together until the spring of 1981."

"Did he tell you why he was disbanding the Saviors?"

Ashbourne frowned at the question and shook his head. "He said we had fulfilled our mission and outlived our usefulness."

"Did you believe him?"

"I wanted to, but everyone knew the real reason was that his tenure battle with Professor Denton had failed and the group was splitting apart at the seams from personality conflicts between him and West."

"Did you participate in producing any of the leaflets distributed by the Saviors that labeled Denton an envionmental traitor because he refused to condemn the Peripheral Canal?"

"We all did. When it came to standing up to the ruling class, the professor was a real wimp," Ashbourne answered without a trace of remorse. "But I didn't help to kill him."

"Did you know that others had planned to bomb his house?"

"I was as shocked as everyone else when I read about the fire the next morning."

"Where did you last see Debray?"

"Under one of the trees at the far end of People's Park. That's where we finished our walk and went our separate ways. He promised to call the next day, but I never heard from him again."

"Did you ever tell your trial attorney that you wanted to take the stand in your own defense and tell the jury the things you've testified about this morning?"

"Too many times to count." Ashbourne gave his response with a visible sneer.

"Did Mr. Barnes ever agree to put you on the stand?"

"At first it seemed like he had an open mind, but after he started drinking, he made up his mind to keep me off."

"You were personally aware of the drinking?"

"Are you kidding?" An incredulous smile stretched across Ashbourne's lips. "Even the deputies and the defendants next to us in the interview room at the jail could smell the liquor on his breath."

"Did there come a time when you threatened to tell the trial judge about Mr. Barnes' drinking?"

"About midway through the guilt phase of my case, I complained to Barnes about the way he was sloshed all the time," Ashbourne answered carefully. "I told him I would report him to the judge unless he let me tell my story to the jury."

"How did Mr. Barnes react?"

"That was when he threatened me."

"How?"

Pickering rose to utter a hearsay objection. The protest, however, was overruled, after Harrigan pointed out that any verbal threat Barnes had made to his client would qualify as an exception to the hearsay rule as an admission against the trial attorney's "professional interest."

Given the green light by Taneda's ruling, Ashbourne measured his response carefully. "He told me that if I complained, he would withdraw as my counsel and see that he was replaced by someone fresh out of law school."

"How did that make you feel?"

"It scared the living cra—" Ashbourne caught himself at the last second, correcting his language with an apologetic nod. "It scared the daylights out of me, and I went along with his plan to try the case on reasonable doubt."

Harrigan took another look at his notepad. So far, so good, he thought to himself. For a man whose corroborating witnesses were either dead or fugitives from justice, Ashbourne had done an excellent job of speaking out in his own behalf. There was just one more *i* to dot before turning the witness over to Pickering. "What time was it when Debray left you the night of the firebombing?" Harrigan asked.

It was a vitally important question, and Ashbourne had to know from yesterday's prep session that it was coming. Still, he hesitated as though he'd been caught off guard. "Approximately eleven o'clock," he answered in a voice that suddenly sounded weak and wavering, his eyes locked on Harrigan.

The word "approximately" hung in the air. In everyday discourse the term was both commonplace and acceptable. People used it all the time to describe their arrivals and departures from dinner dates, parties and work. When it came to alibis, however, the term could be the kiss of death. Harrigan, Pickering, and most of all Taneda knew that the firebombing had taken place at eleven o'clock. "Approximately" just wouldn't cut it.

Hoping that Ashbourne was just being overly cautious with his language, Harrigan sought to head off the problem before Pickering turned it into an overt disaster. "Were you wearing a watch at the time?"

"I didn't own a watch," Ashbourne answered.

The sheepish expression on his face suddenly reminded Harrigan of the way his boys had looked when they dropped chocolate Popsicles on the living room rug and denied all culpability despite the dark stains on their T-shirts and hands. Whenever he saw that look, he knew the kids were trying to hide something. He knew that Ashbourne was trying to hide something too, about the time when he and Debray parted. If only he had ended his Q and A without bringing up the question of time, he might have avoided the problem. Having raised the issue, however, he had to continue. "Were you paying close attention to the time?" he asked anxiously.

"Not really."

"Is that why you've testified that you parted with Debray at 'approximately' eleven o'clock?" Trying to fight through the adrenaline coursing through his system like an electric current, Harrigan made a valiant effort to sound confident and hopeful.

Ashbourne brought his right hand to his chin and gave it a few thoughtful strokes, then dipped his eyes to the floor once more. "I'm sorry," he mumbled through his hand. "I have to tell the truth. All these years, I think I just assumed that it must have been eleven o'clock when Debray and I split because that's when the police said the bombing occurred." He lifted his head and stared at Harrigan as if seeking forgiveness. "To be honest, I can't say for sure when Debray left me. It may have been eleven, but it may have been earlier. I've never been very good at keeping track of the time."

More stunned than angry, Harrigan stared back at his client as the full weight of "the truth" settled over him. In the litigation business there was a term for the phenomenon of having your own witness perform a one-hundred-eighty-degree about-face in his testimony. It was called "rolling over." Harold Ashbourne was by no means the first witness to "roll over" on Harrigan, but none of his clients had ever come this close to committing suicide on the stand. "Did you kill Professor Denton?" Harrigan asked finally, unable to conceal the desperation he felt.

"No," Ashbourne answered. Having unburdened himself of the secret he had been carrying, he sounded astonishingly firm and self-assured. "After leaving Debray, I went straight home, just like I told Mr. Barnes during my trial. I had no role in the firebombing of the professor's home."

Seeking to avoid any further surprises, Harrigan announced he had no further questions and like a shell-shocked soldier found his way back to the counsel table.

Pickering's cross-examination—in fact, the rest of the day's proceedings—went by in a blur that Harrigan might have completely forgotten if the court reporter had not made a verbatim record of the testimony. Although he stuck to his claim of innocence, Ashbourne dug himself more deeply into a quagmire of inconsistencies as Pickering brought out the fact that it would have taken no more than fifteen minutes to drive from the university campus to the Denton home. Worse still, Ashbourne also acknowledged that he had no alibi witnesses who had seen him after he left Debray on the night of the bombing.

Sensing a kill, Pickering took a quick stroll from the lectern to the counsel table, where he leafed through his litigation case and pulled out a three-page document entitled "Declaration of Harold Ashbourne." With Taneda's permission, he calmly approached Ashbourne and placed the document in front of the witness. "You remember signing this declaration some three years ago?"

Ashbourne answered in the affirmative.

"And in the declaration, which was filed by your attorney with this court, you laid out your claim about being with Debray until eleven o'clock on the night of the bombing, didn't you?"

Ashbourne backed away from Pickering like a person seeking to avoid a bee sting, but he said nothing. For the moment he appeared incapable of mouthing a reply.

"You didn't use the term 'approximately' back then, did you?" Pickering continued his attack, adjusting the corner of his bow tie as he spoke.

"No, I didn't," Ashbourne conceded, finding his voice at last.

"You lied in that declaration, and you're lying now about your involvement in the firebombing."

"All I can say is that I've told the truth today," Ashbourne stammered in reply. "I went straight home after leaving Debray. I never killed anyone in my life."

"Then how do you explain the fact that your fingerprint was found on one of the incendiary devices uncovered at the Denton home?" His confidence soaring, Pickering's mustache nearly twitched with excitement as he asked the final and seemingly fatal question.

"I have no idea," Ashbourne answered softly. "I have no idea."

After Ashbourne's dramatic rendition of a dying man's last words, Walter Krinsky was the only witness called by the State, and his appearance, commencing after the noon break, was brief and virtually unnecessary. With his testimony immeasurably bolstered by Ashbourne's admissions, the State's IAC expert opined that J. Arnold Barnes not only had made the right tactical call in keeping Ashbourne off the stand, but that he would have been absolutely incompetent to have placed him before the jury.

There was little Harrigan could do in his cross-examination of Krinsky other than extract the now familiar concessions that Barnes' drinking was a definite "no-no," and that Barnes should have sent an investigator to New York to look for Debray and one to Eureka to speak with Sylvia Peterson in the flesh. In any other case such miscues would have cried out for a finding of IAC against Barnes, but in view of Ashbourne's revelations, none of that seemed to matter anymore. Nothing Harrigan said in his closing statement about Barnes' oversights or the mysterious death of Charles West and the disappearance of Fred Wallace elicited anything more from Taneda than a contemptuous curl of the lips.

By four o'clock the hearing was over, and Taneda adjourned the session, promising to prepare his written decision "by the close of business next week."

Moments later, the marshals came to take Harold Ashbourne to the lockup and the bus back to San Quentin. Yielding to their command, Ashbourne turned to face Harrigan for the last time. They stood no more than a foot apart, locked in a silent stare filled with loss and regret. Harrigan searched his mind for words of encouragement. He thought about mumbling a few pieties about keeping the case going through a new round of appeals, but looking at the broken and bent figure of his client, he wondered if Ashbourne could find the emotional fortitude to sustain himself while the appeals wound down to their inevitable unhappy conclusion. There were suicides on death row every year, and Ashbourne, from past experience, was a prime candidate.

While Harrigan ruminated, it was Ashbourne who broke the quiet. "I'm sorry, Peter," he said in a virtual whisper. "I know I wasn't straight with you." Then he gestured toward the witness stand with a slight nod of his head. "But I told the truth up there, just like you asked. If nothing else, I want you to believe what I said today."

"I do," Harrigan answered instinctively, uncertain, in fact, whether he did or not.

TWENTY-NINE

Harrigan pushed his way through a swarm of reporters who were more intent than ever on garnering a soul-searching final interview from the attorney for the losing side. "No comment," he snapped at one print jockey who asked how he felt to have his own client sabotage the hearing. "Why don't you run that one by Mr. Pickering?" he admonished another, who inquired how long he thought it would take until Ashbourne's execution date was set. To his rear, Harrigan could hear Pickering speaking in a particularly solemn tone about how justice had been served. "Capital punishment is a somber subject, to be sure, but it's also the will of the people," the deputy AG warbled triumphantly. "We're very pleased with the way things went in the hearing."

At the moment, finding Josie was the only thing on Harrigan's mind. In the midst of the afternoon's spiral, he had turned his head from the counsel table to seek her out no less than three times. On the first two occasions he saw her seated in the gallery, returning his weary gaze with a look of stoic encouragement. The third time, however, she was gone. Maybe he had simply missed her, or maybe she had only stepped away for a minute to get a drink or answer nature's call. Or maybe the final unraveling of the case had just proven too much for her and she had already left for home.

Before Harrigan could complete his inventory of the possibilities, he found her pacing the seventeenth-floor corridor. She must have heard his footsteps because she turned to face him even before he called her name. Almost simultaneously, without speaking a word, they dropped their briefcases and fell into each other's arms. It was a sensitive embrace, filled with familiar textures and fragrances, warm and comforting but not the least bit sexual. Physically and emotionally spent from the intensity of their failed efforts, they remained locked together for a good half minute, Josie doing her best to fight off the urge to sob and Harrigan calling on those inner resources men have invoked since the cave days to hide their pain in public. Slowly, they drew apart and walked to the elevator that would take them to the building's indoor parking lot.

Except for John Goodnow, who squeezed his bulky frame into the lift just as the doors were closing, they had the elevator to themselves. Goodnow smiled sheepishly at them. "It must really be tough dealing with what happened today," he said clumsily but nonetheless sounding sincere.

Taking their silence as a sign of approval to continue, he added, "Well, at least you have each other." He smiled again, even more awkwardly. "Heck, all I've got to look forward to is a hot shower and another death-penalty case with Pickering." Laughing at his own obvious foibles, he extended his hand for a pair of farewell shakes before stepping off the elevator at the parking structure's first level. "Good luck to you two."

"Maybe he's not such a bad guy," Harrigan commented as they reached their cars on the bottom tier. "Just a big oaf doing his job, even if it means sending my client to his eternal reward."

"I think *you're* right about the oaf part," Josie said, suddenly sidling up to him with a coy grin on her face. "And I think *he's* right about one thing, too." She took Harrigan's quizzical look for an invitation to complete her thought. "That we have each other." She moved toward him, planted her lips on his, and with catlike dexterity inserted her tongue in his mouth. Unlike the therapeutic hug they had shared on the seventeenth floor, this one sent a sexual stirring through his loins. Had they been anywhere but in the middle of an underground parking lot, they might have carried things to the next level of excitement and made up for all those nights spent alone during the hearing. Given the circumstances, they settled for a discreet round of neck nibbles and tongue wrestling before coming up for air.

"I don't want you to fly back to L.A.," she whispered in his ear.

Harrigan considered for a moment whether it was right for a lawyer who had just lost the biggest case of his career to be cheek to cheek with his investigator and dreaming of doing the nasty. The thought, however, had no staying power, and another look at Josie's luminous saucer eyes chased it away. "You have a better idea?" he asked, cupping his hands around her bottom and pulling her closer.

"Don't I always?" She kissed him lightly on the tip of his nose and gently broke free from his grasp. "I'll pick you up at your hotel in an hour. Make sure you're packed and ready to leave."

There are things people do for love or lust that they ordinarily would regard as frivolous, crazy, or just too damn exhausting. Driving to Big Sur on a dark October evening, with a threat of coastal fog in the weather forecast, was one of them. But with Josie announcing that she had managed to make a reservation at the Triton Inn, Harrigan eagerly accepted her plan.

After dropping off Harrigan's rental car at the airport, they headed south on Highway 101. When they reached Monterey, they took the turnoff for Route 1, the Pacific Coast Highway. It was already nine o'clock and overcast, and they could hear the crashing of the surf as they navigated through the sharp curves along the coastal road. By the time they rolled into the parking lot at the Triton, it was after ten and the fog had moved in with a purpose. For the first time in memory, Harrigan felt completely absorbed in the present. Not even the afternoon's debacle intruded.

The Triton Inn was a sprawling hand-crafted hostelry constructed with parquet floors, beamed ceilings, and paneled walls of rich unfinished cedar. Subdivided into separate four- and six-unit guest quarters, the lushly landscaped complex rose high into the hills overlooking the rocky, erosion-scarred outcroppings that plunged into the beaches of the Pacific Ocean below. Harrigan had made the breathtaking drive through Big Sur, as the area between Monterey to the north and William Randolph Hearst's castle at San Simeon to the south was known, a half dozen times before, but he had always driven straight through or stayed the night at a campground with Stephanie and the boys. He had noticed the Triton only from the highway, but had received accounts of its sumptuous Japanese hot tubs and heated clothing-optional pools from friends and clients, who, less encumbered by children than he, rated it a must-see attraction. From what he could tell at first glance, the descriptions he'd heard barely did the place justice. Even at night and shrouded in the mist, the inn was the closest facsimile to heaven on earth he had glimpsed outside of his favorite hideaway near Puerto Vallarta.

After a quick snack, he and Josie found their way to their room, built a fire, and picked up where they had left off in the courthouse parking lot. Even by their standards, the sex was scintillating. The fire sent their silhouettes dancing across the room as they shifted positions, exploring each other with hands and mouths, murmuring and moaning loud enough to shake the overhead light fixture and make the next-door neighbors sit up and take notice. He penetrated her again and again, in the missionary style and from the rear, her hips arching toward him as he pulled her closer and she cried out his name. Then she was on top with her hands pushing against his shoulders, grinding rhythmically, rapid and hard, slow and smooth, until finally sated, they collapsed together in a serene sleep.

It wasn't until breakfast that the issue of what to

do with the rest of his life crept back into Harrigan's consciousness. If he could have kept his face nuzzled against Josie's cheeks forever, the issue would have been a no-brainer. Not being a medieval potentate, however, he felt reality tugging at his shirtsleeves as he watched the waves hitting the rocks from the Triton's terraced café.

"I guess one of these days we'll have to figure out where all this is going," he said with a gentle smile as she joined him at the table and took the first sip of her morning coffee.

"I thought we might be able to wait for that until we got back to L.A." She returned the smile and reached for his hand. "There's no need to rush."

Harrigan had begun to formulate a kind of safe and noncommittal reply when his eye caught a little man with black curly hair settling his breakfast bill at the cashier's station. The two men fixed each other in a momentary stare before the man sauntered off and Harrigan returned to his omelette. In another instant Harrigan flew out of his seat, shouting Debray's name as he raced through the lobby and into the parking lot.

This time there was no escape. Harrigan caught up to him just as Debray was closing the driver's-side door on his black Nissan Sentra rental car. Given his advantages of size and strength, Harrigan had no trouble pulling the diminutive fugitive from his vehicle and standing him up the side of the car in a police-style shakedown.

"What the fuck are you doing here?" Harrigan barked, holding Debray roughly by the lapels of his corduroy sports coat. Debray's spindly frame shook in Harrigan's grasp.

"I followed you here from the hotel," Debray said, displaying neither the intimidation that a man of his stature might feel under similar circumstances nor the pomposity that Harrigan had found so grating in their prior encounters.

"Why didn't you show up for the hearing?" Harrigan demanded.

Catching sight of Josie hurrying to join them, Debray hesitated. "After Charlie was shot, I figured there was no point. My appearance wouldn't have helped Harold, and it wouldn't have done me any good either."

"Why follow us here?" Josie asked.

"I wanted to see that you were okay." He grinned. "I was even going to apologize before you came after me. You know, you really have a nasty temper."

"Cut the crap," Harrigan snapped back, balling his right hand into a fist.

"Like you, I'm on my way to L.A." Debray's face twisted as Harrigan tightened his grip on his jacket. "I told you that Charlie was ready to admit his part in the bombing. That's why he was killed."

"I still don't understand what that has to do with L.A.," Harrigan said.

"I figured that if the other party responsible for Denton's death can't be brought to justice in court, I might as well handle things myself."

"What other party?" Harrigan demanded again.

"Bob Gardner." Debray looked at Harrigan and Josie in turn, as though to convey his disappointment at their ineptitude in overlooking the Pomona mechanic's potential as a killer. "Now, if you'll just let me get on the road," he added, nodding toward the steering column of his vehicle.

"I don't think you're going anywhere." Josie broke into the conversation. "At least not without a chaperon." Reaching into her handbag, she deftly revealed just enough of a small-caliber handgun to cause the blue steel barrel of the weapon to glint in the morning sunlight. The serious look on her face reinforced the impression that she indeed was practiced in wielding a weapon. "Get your bags and leave the keys to your car under the front seat. You can call the rental company later and tell them where to pick it up."

Debray offered no resistance or words of protest. If anything, he appeared relieved by the prospect of having company for the long drive south. "I never argue with a thirty-eight," he said, and dutifully opened the Sentra's trunk, revealing a single oversize olive green army surplus duffel bag.

As Josie escorted Debray to the back seat of the Beemer, Harrigan took a quick inventory of the contents of the duffel bag before loading it into the Beemer's trunk. "There must be enough makeup and wigs in there to keep a Beverly Hills salon supplied for a year," he said as he settled into the passenger seat.

"A boy has to keep up his appearance," Debray quipped from the backseat, as though warming to the opportunity to entertain and amuse his captors. Far from being an unwilling hostage, Debray quickly assumed the role of unofficial tour guide, expostulating on the historical lore of Big Sur and the local landmarks they drove past. The Henry Miller Library just south of the Triton; the Esalen Institute, birthplace of the 1960s human potential movement farther along Highway One; the garish Hearst Castle at the area's distal tip in San Simeon. All were placed in their proper geopolitical perspective in the cosmos according to Henri Debray.

Finally, even Debray seemed to tire of the sound of his voice, and as they pulled off the coast route and back onto U.S. 101 below San Luis Obispo, Harrigan turned the conversation back to the Ashbourne case. He recapped Ashbourne's withering performance on the witness stand, and in a grave voice that indicated he wanted a response unembellished with quotes from Marx or Shakespeare, he demanded, "I want you to tell me what really happened the night of the bombing."

Debray gazed idly out the window at the scenery and the traffic, as if unnerved by Harrigan's suddenly hostile tone. "It was pretty much as Harold testified, at least from his standpoint. We split up at People's Park around ten-thirty. I gave him some b.s. about having to see Kathleen."

"And where did you really go?" Harrigan demanded.

"I went back to my apartment, packed my bags, and took a bus out of town."

"Why?"

"To save my scrawny little Brooklyn ass." Debray took a deep breath for what portended to be a detailed accounting. "Charlie and Bob wanted me to join in their game. They said they'd pick a time when the professor was down in Kern County so no one would get hurt. I hated Denton as much as they did, but I couldn't see firebombing his house. It was too much like the Symbionese Liberation Army. I tried to talk them out of it right up to the afernoon of bombing. They threatened to kill me if I ever went public with what I knew."

"And then you went to New York?"

Debray nodded. "Just like I said in the declaration I gave you. My mother agreed to let me spend some time in the family cabin up in the Adirondacks. But Ma was an old political activist, and she started to pressure me to help out my fallen comrade. She even threatened to turn me over to Harold's lawyer if the lawyer ever called her."

"And you were too much of a scared little piece of shit to contact the lawyer yourself," Harrigan said with a sneer.

"Actually," Debray replied defensively, "I wasn't sure I could provide Harold with an alibi, given what I knew about the timing of the bombing."

"So why did you lie in your declaration about being with Harold up until eleven o'clock?"

"I figured it was now-or-never time for Prince Hal, and that with any kind of a break, Charlie West would either come forward and tell the real truth or I'd show up at the hearing, lay out the alibi, and no one would ever be able to disprove it." He hesitated for an instant, as if recalling some long-lost and highly ironic detail. "I might have known that Harold would break down and tell the truth. He was always a banker's son at heart."

"How did you manage to support yourself all

those years?" Josie interjected. "You must have changed your identity almost as often as your socks."

"About as regularly as some people see the dentist," Debray corrected her. "It's not really difficult when you think about it. People die all the time, even little kids. In each new town I'd research old newspaper obits and pick out children born about the same year as me but who died young. You'd be surprised how many birth certificates you can get that way. From there it's just a short hop to getting a Social Security number and a driver's license. And if that avenue wasn't available, there were always people in every big city who made a living out of selling fake papers. Hell," he added, reaching into his back pocket and pulling out a credit card from his wallet. "Steve Roberts here even has a gold Master Card with a ten-thousand-dollar line of credit."

"Why should I believe you about West and Gardner?" Harrigan asked, bringing an abrupt end to Debray's lecture on the ways of a fugitive.

"Well, if you're looking for corroboration, I'm afraid Charlie isn't available any longer." Debray flashed a smartaleck grin at Harrigan. "Bob Gardner, on the other hand—"

"Has the word *psycho* written all over him," Josie interrupted. Turning to Harrigan, she added, "I think he's telling the truth, Peter."

The truth—now, that was a concept that had gotten kicked around pretty good the last few days, Harrigan thought to himself, his eyes still trained on Debray. "We'll see," he said. "Otherwise you can do the rest of your explaining to the cops back at Half Moon Bay."

THIRTY

It was one thing to interdict Debray's one-man crusade to exact vengeance on Bob Garner. It was another to abscond with him back to L.A. while he was wanted for questioning up north. Harrigan knew all too well that unless their venture yielded huge dividends, he and Josie could wind up paying for their sojourn with the loss of their professional licenses or facing obstruction of justice charges or worse. But since they had taken Debray and assumed the legal risks that came with him, the question of what to do with him until they could formulate an appropriate method of dealing with Gardner took on paramount importance.

Harrigan mulled the matter over as the afternoon wore on and they drove past Santa Barbara and Ventura and finally across the L.A. County line. There were, unfortunately, no easy answers. Harrigan could turn Debray over to the attorney general's office and save his own ass, but there was little likelihood that the AG or any other law enforcement agency would mount a serious investigation of Gardner. The AG would probably file Debray's claims about Gardner with the stories of extraterrestrial wiretapping they received from mentally disturbed citizens every other day. In the meantime they'd step up the pressure to schedule Ashbourne's execution as soon as legally possible.

The more Harrigan played out the options in his mind, the more certain he became that they would have to act alone if they stood any chance of building a provable case against Gardner. That meant deciding on a plan and keeping Debray safely concealed until they could set it into motion. Whatever the plan turned out to be, he knew that for his sake and for Josie's, it had to be one worthy of the risks they were taking.

As they neared the outskirts of downtown, the idea hit Harrigan like a splash of cold water. "Take the Interstate Five cutoff," he said abruptly, "and then the exit for César Chavez Avenue."

"Have you thought of something, or are you just hankering for a cold margarita?" Josie asked.

"I know someone who owes me a big favor," he answered, glancing at his watch. It was three-thirty. If Eddie Garcia was keeping normal business hours, his tuck and roll shop would still be open.

Known as Brooklyn Avenue in the days when East L.A. was home to the largest concentration of American Jews outside New York, the thoroughfare that served as the main artery of the city's Hispanic barrio had been renamed after the late president of the United Farm Workers Union, César Chavez. The name change reflected a shift in demographics that had been taking shape since the 1960s, especially in the Boyle Heights district closest to downtown. The avenue's kosher butchers had been replaced by *car-nicerías*, its Jewish bakeries by *panaderías*, and as the community became ever more dependent on the automobile, body, upholstery, and repair shops became as numerous as the old corner drugstore.

Garcia's Nip n' Tuck, as "El Gato's" place of business was known, occupied a prominent position on the corner of a block of tiny discount clothing shops and mom-and-pop taco stands. Although situated in the middle of what the cops considered high-crime territory, the block was virtually free of the gang graffiti and tags that defaced public and private property in most parts of the city. By contemporary Los Angeles standards, the area had a surprisingly safe and easy feel to it.

Set apart from both the sidewalk and its neighbors by a tall chain-link fence, Eddie's establishment consisted of a large blacktopped parking area for convenient customer parking and a three-port cinder-block garage, where the proprietor and his crew of employees, dressed in gray coveralls and black hairnets, spent their time beautifying old Chevys, Buicks, and Lincolns with everything from tasteless faux leopard-skin upholstery to extremely pricy hand-tooled glove leather. For a complete interior makeover, Eddie offered his clientele their choice of a complementary dashboard or rearview mirror ornament. Plastic Jesuses for the religious; oversized fuzzy dice for the traditional *barrio* motif; scale-model Raiders helmets for the sports fan. There was also a small converted two-bedroom house in the back of the lot that did double duty as a business office and an occasional crash pad for friends and workers who either got too high or too lucky with one of the female customers to go home to the wife and kids.

Josie found a parking space on the street, and under the watchful eyes of Eddie's Friday work crew, she and Harrigan escorted Debray across the parking lot. Despite the fact that she was in the company of two men, the sight of Josie in her form-fitting jeans and cutoff leather jacket elicited a chorus of *orales*, *mamacitas*, and exaggerated sighs of passion from the employees. To a man, they hopped out of the cars they were working on and scrambled for position to inquire after the needs of their newest clients.

Before any one of the workers could mouth a complete introduction, a booming voice sounded from the direction of the small rear house. "Let's show some respect for the lady, homes."

Harrigan saw Eddie advancing toward them. Dressed in a pair of khaki chinos, a button-down blue silk shirt, and a gray blazer, and still as thin and wiry as Harrigan recalled, Eddie had the look of a guy preparing for a Friday night on the town. "Mr. Harrigan," he said, smiling and extending his hand, "what brings you to this side of the river?"

"I need a favor, Eddie," Harrigan said, returning the smile but getting straight to the point. "Our friend here needs a place to bunk in for a day or two." He nodded toward Debray.

"No problem," Eddie answered, his sharp, dark eyes beaming with pleasure at the opportunity to repay his *abogado* for saving his *nalgas* from the dreaded three-strikes law. "The back house is empty, and if you want, I can have Frankie and Chuy stay with him." He gestured toward his work crew, which had only just begun to take their eyes off Josie and return to their respective rehab jobs. "*Mi casa es su casa*, just like I told you."

"I may also need a little muscle," Harrigan added. "Nothing heavy, just for show, if you know what I mean."

"No problem," Eddie said without hesitation.

Harrigan arranged for Frankie, a big kid of twenty-five with a diminutive gold nose ring in his left nostril, to fetch Debray's duffel bag from the trunk of Josie's Beemer. Then he turned to face Debray. "We'll be back for you as soon as we can. In the meantime, Eddie's *casa*, as he says, should be comfortable enough."

Harrigan thanked Eddie again and, with Josie by his side, strolled back to the Beemer. In the background he could hear Frankie chatting amiably, "Hey, you look like one hungry dude. You like *carnitas*?"

"I consider it a culinary delight."

"Does that mean you like it?" Frankie asked for clarification, taking in Debray's skinny frame. " 'Cause if you're a vegetarian like one of them Hare Rama guys or something, we can always order out for Chinese or cheese pizza."

By the time Harrigan and Josie climbed back inside the Beemer, Frankie had his well-muscled arm draped over Debray's shoulder and the two men were making a beeline like fast friends for the front door of the rear house. Debray will either have them talking bout the Chiapas uprising by ten o'clock, Harrigan mused to himself, or they'll have him working on a low rider and ready to cruise Whittier Boulevard.

"Is this your idea of a Boys Town reunion, or do you actually have some kind of plan in mind?" Josie asked with a look a mild bewilderment as they sped away down César Chavez Avenue and headed back to the freeway.

Rather than answer, Harrigan met Josie's inquiry with a question of his own. "Do you remember our Judas, the person Ashbourne said had infiltrated the Saviors?"

"I thought we decided he was Charles West."

"Or Bob Gardner." Harrigan smiled teasingly and began to gaze purposefully out the window as though he were looking for something.

"So you've decided to believe Debray?"

"Do you still have Gardner's business card?" he asked, once again ignoring her question.

"I think so," she said, reaching into her purse.

Without further explanation Harrigan directed her to pull into a Mobil station near the entrance to the freeway. Taking Gardner's card from her, he hurried off to the pay phone at the back end of the lot.

"Bob's Auto," the husky voice on the other end said after picking up on the fifth ring. "This is Bob."

"Listen, Bob," Harrigan said, doing a slightly hammy but passable imitation of a working stiff. "I've been looking all over the San Gabriel Valley for a set of caps for my '70 Impala. A friend told me to give you a holler."

"I'm sure we have something in stock," Bob said,

"but I'm just about to close and I'm not open tomorrow."

"What aobut the Fairplex? I heard you operate a booth Sundays at the swap meet."

"Afraid not," Bob answered quickly. "This Sunday I'm at the meet in the Rose Bowl parking lot. If you can make it to Pasadena, just look for the van with the sign 'Hubcap Bobby's.' The meet opens at six, and I'm out of there by three."

Harrigan could hear Bob take a deep drag from one of his unfiltered Camels before clicking off.

Josie thought "the plan," when Harrigan laid it out to her over dinner, was a long shot at best. Lacking an alternative, however, she reluctantly agreed to go along and by bedtime had become a dedicated convert.

While Harrigan spent Saturday morning scoping out the Rose Bowl, Josie made an impromptu visit to her P.I. friend in L.A. They met back at Eddie's Nip 'N Tuck at two, Harrigan with a better sense of the lay of the land and Josie with a new ultra-zoom lens camcorder and a custom-made audio mini-cassette recorder that looked like a gadget lifted out of 007's underground laboratory.

"The video camera's nice but pretty standard," she explained, depositing the camera on the kitchen table of the Nip 'N Tuck's rear house as Harrigan, Eddie, Debray, Frankie, and Chuy looked on. "But this little doodad's kind of special," she added, holding a silver-plated ballpoint pen in one hand and grabbing an ordinary mini-cassette tape recorder from her handbag with her other hand.

"Looks like a regular old pen, doesn't it?" she asked, clicking the instrument into writing position. "It works just like any other." She drew a stick figure and the name BOB on a piece of scrap paper as their eyes followed her hand.

"I don't get it," Eddie said, gazing at Josie's artwork.

"Every time you click the pen on," Josie explained, "a little battery inside it operates just like a TV remote and turns on the recorder. Every time you retract the pen, the recorder shuts off." She demonstrated the principle with a quick playback of Eddie's comment, adding, "The recorder's powerful enough to pick up voices from as far away as ten yards. My P.I. buddy specializes in domestic surveillance cases, but I figured Debray could get the hang of it pretty quickly."

Debray, for his part, had apparently come out on the losing end of the culture clash with his overnight hosts. Rather than converting Eddie's boys to a higher level of political consciousness, Debray seemed to be the one transformed. Gone was the curly black wig and the clothes he had been wearing in Big Sur, replaced by a dirty T-shirt and a set of baggy coveralls, just like the ones Frankie and Chuy seemed to have been born in. If it hadn't been for his pale complexion and his natural red hair (which, to Harrigan's amusement, turned out to be thin and wispy, with a Friar Tuck bald patch at the crown), Henri might well have passed as one of the local *vatos*.

Debray's visual metamorphosis provided Harrigan with the final inspiration needed to set his plan in motion. With the aid of one of Eddie's old Pendleton shirts, a generous quantity of heavy makeup, some hairspray, and a hairnet to flatten out the curly black-haired wig, the transformation became complete. Even Debray's mother, God rest her soul, would have mistaken him for a *cholo*.

"You're now Lalo Martinez." Harrigan smiled broadly at the new man in front of him. "You're from Pacoima, and you've come to the Rose Bowl looking for specialty items, particularly hubcaps, for a pair of 1950s Studebakers you've restored. Frankie and Chuy will be window-shopping at a nearby booth, just in case you get it into your head to bolt. Think you can handle the role?"

Debray gave Harrigan a bemused smile as he adjusted his hairnet in a handheld mirror. "It'll be the performance of a lifetime, *ese*." He puffed up his chest and swung his right arm behind his back, macho style, as he spoke.

The look was good, Harrigan thought to himself, but the barrio slang and body language still needed some polish. "Brush up on your accent tonight, and Gardner will think you're Frankie's cousin."

Following Harrigan's script, the ragtag band arrived at the swap meet with clockwork precision, traveling west from Harrigan's home on the 210 freeway along the foothills of the San Gabriel Mountains in three separate vehicles: Eddie, Frankie, Chuy, and Debray in a beatup old Ford; Josie in the Beemer, with her hair tied back underneath a Dodger cap; and Harrigan, toting the camcorder, in his Audi. They found parking spaces in the main public lot

close to the perimeter road ringing the Rose Bowl
and set off on separate paths for Gardner's booth.

Although it was barely nine o'clock, the meet was
already jam-packed with bargain hunters of every
description. There were Vietnamese families from the
San Gabriel Valley, upscale yuppies from San Ma-
rino, newlyweds from Glendale, even mean-looking,
tattooed bikers who had ridden their hogs in from
Long Beach. Like an occupying army, they covered
the huge main parking lot and the grassy area closer
to the stadium. The swap meet's vendors were located on the other side of the grass, across another
access road. They had set up their booths and stalls
behind a makeshift chain-link fence in a smaller
parking lot, which was subdivided into separate
areas or "gates." There they hawked everything from
hand-thrown clay pots to used lawn furniture and
vintage comics.

Despite the crowd, it took Josie less than ten minutes to spot the HUBCAP BOBBY'S logo painted on the
side of Gardner's van near the entrance to Gate No. 1.
Gardner's stall, filled with rows of brightly polished hubcaps piled on three long wooden folding
tables, was about twenty feet away, next to a booth
selling used video games. On spotting the van, Josie
gave a hand signal to Eddie, who sent a similar sign
in Harrigan's direction. The rest was now up to
Debray.

While Josie, Debray, Eddie, and the boys paid their
five-dollar admission fees and slipped inside the
vending area, Harrigan took up a surveillance post
between two pickup trucks on the grass, a good forty
yards from Gardner's stall but with a good angle on

Gardner and Debray. He turned on the camcorder, looking, in his jeans and brown leather bomber jacket, like a tourist trying out a new toy. The camcorder's powerful zoom lens practically enabled Harrigan to see the blue lines on the little notepad Debray had taken from the pocket of his Pendleton to jot down prices from the racks of classic hubcaps in Gardner's stall. As long as Debray had the pen clicked on, Harrigan knew that Gardner's comments were being recorded. The video he was shooting would serve as a backup, confirming the time, place, and date of whatever Gardner said.

From all appearances, Debray was indeed giving the performance of a lifetime. Like any merchant trying to make a sale, Gardner approached his latest customer with unsuspecting enthusiasm. He grabbed a couple of original Studebaker Hawk caps and held them in the light for Debray's inspection. Debray in turn placed the pen behind his ear and ran his hands over the smooth finish of the hubcaps, mouthing what seemed to be words of appreciation.

The two men repeated the same ritual with another set of hubcaps and appeared to have consummated a sale. But as Gardner reached for a box to pack up the merchandise, the muscles in his face grew taut and the color seemed to drain from his cheeks.

This was the moment, Harrigan thought, when Debray, as per the plan, revealed his identity and calmly opened up the subject of the Denton bombing. The idea wasn't to get Gardner to blurt out a full-blown confession—a man who had lived all those years with the knowledge that he had committed a double murder wasn't likely to be the confessing type—but to get him so hot, bothered, and confused by the sudden turn of events that he uttered just enough to show that he knew things about the bombing that only a hands-on perpetrator would know. It was a technique reminiscent of the way cops sometimes planted jailhouse informants in the cells next to murder suspects to elicit incriminating details about their crimes. Sometimes it worked wonders, and sometimes the tactic fell flat on its face. Harrigan's hope was that with Debray and the audio tape, he'd have enough newly discovered evidence to file a motion to reopen Ashbourne's habeas hearing.

The longer Debray kept Gardner talking, the better the chances of success. Pleased by what he saw, Harrigan turned the camcorder off for a moment and moved a few yards closer to the hubcap stall. He switched the unit back on just as the pen fell out of Debray's ear. In one awkward and ungainly motion, Debray stooped to retrieve the pen as the minirecorder tumbled out of the inside vest pocket of his open jacket.

Seeing the recorder, Gardner reacted swiftly and violently. A devastating right cross to the chin sent Debray dropping to the blacktop like a rag doll. Seconds later, Josie, Eddie, Frankie, and Chuy converged on the hubcap stall, along with a motley assortment of curious patrons and an overweight security guard, who dropped his can of Diet Pepsi and began to order everyone to "settle down."

Harrigan, too, began to rush toward the booth, but his stride was broken by the rising shouts of a woman over the gathering crowd. "Get down, he's armed!" the woman screamed.

Stopping in his tracks, Harrigan hopped onto the hood of a late-model Oldsmobile for a better view. At Gardner's booth a free-for-all had broken loose between Eddie and the boys and a few of the Long Beach bikers Harrigan had seen earlier. The security guard was trying with little success to break up the melee.

From the booth, Harrigan's eyes darted to the Hubcap Bobby's sign. With a large handgun pointed directly at Josie's back, Gardner had succeeded in clearing a path to his van, easily discouraging any would-be pursuers along the way. He forced Josie inside and slid into the driver's seat next to her. Then he brought the handle of the gun down viciously on her left temple.

Josie slumped into the passenger seat as Gardner started up the vehicle and slammed it into the chain-link fence in front of him. Its headlights shattered from the impact, the van screeched onto the parking lot.

With Eddie and the boys pinned down by the commotion inside the vending area, only Harrigan was free to give chase, but with only one good leg and the camcorder tucked under his arm like a football it was no contest. By the time Harrigan reached his Audi, Gardner was already on the perimeter road and heading for a turnoff that would eventually take him to the freeway.

Acting out of instinct and desperation, Harrigan gunned the engine and slalomed his way out of the parking lot and onto the road. His horn blaring and his eyes set hard on the van, he gained a little ground but not enough to make a difference. Then, for some unknown reason, whether because of a mechanical problem or perhaps to shove Josie into the back of the van, Gardner slowed down just long enough to allow Harrigan to remain in hot pursuit.

From the Rose Bowl, Gardner tore through the quiet, tree-lined neighborhood above the stadium and set a course for the 210 freeway. The sound of his approaching van sent a group of Spandex-clad bicyclists scurrying to the sidewalks for cover. A gang of grade-school kids tossing a football in the street dropped their pigskin and ran indoors.

Instead of heading east on the freeway in the direction of Pomona, as Harrigan expected, Gardner went west. Then, with the Audi still on his heels, he gunned the van onto the exit for the Angeles Crest Highway.

It was a clear autumn afternoon, and the narrow, winding road ascending into the San Gabriels was crowded with sightseeing motorists in search of the breathtaking panoramas of the city that the highway offered. Gardner displayed a rare combination of driving skill and utter disregard for the safety of others, blasting his horn, flashing his lights, narrowly avoiding a head-on collision with a Toyota pickup heading down the mountain, and sideswiping a brand-new Buick Regal that failed to pull over quickly enough on a short straightaway to let his van overtake it. Although it shimmied from the strain of accelerating past the three-and four-thousand-feet elevation marks, the van remained ahead of the pursuing Audi, disappearing momentarily from Harrigan's view and then suddenly reemerging as it tucked into and out of the highway's hairpin curves.

For Harrigan, negotiating the switchbacks re-opened all the old wounds. Even though he lived at the base of the San Gabriels, he had not set foot on Angeles Crest since the accident all those years ago. The idea of returning was one of the unspoken demons he had learned to live with by shutting it from his mind. And yet here he was, following a madman who not only had destroyed Harold Ashbourne's life but now threatened to destroy Josie's as well. Gripping the wheel tightly, he fought to keep his concentration, but his head began to buzz with memories of the accident. He could almost see Stephanie's terror-stricken face in the seat beside him. Her screams and those of his sons rang in his ears, desperately urging him to save them.

Harrigan struggled to shake off their images. Josie was in Bob's van, he reminded himself, crying her name aloud. Unlike his family, she was still alive, still a part of his life, if not its very center. He would not let Gardner take her from him. He slapped his foot again on the accelerator.

Although the van packed a newly overhauled V-8 engine, the Audi seemed to have a narrow edge in performance and power. Harrigan whizzed past a VW bug driven by an aging hippie in a tie-dye T-shirt, who flipped him a peace sign. He flew past an expensive Landcruiser driven by a young woman with Christian Dior shades and a set of manicured red nails, who flipped him the bird for narrowly cutting her off.

Even though Harrigan was by no means Gardner's equal behind the wheel, he managed to close within two car lengths as the two vehicles climbed to forty-five hundred feet. For the first time since the chase began, Harrigan could see Gardner's face, wide-eyed and intense, in the van's side mirror.

For a split second Gardner seemed to smile, as though he sensed Harrigan's distress and was enjoying the experience. Then, dropping the van into overdrive, he began to pull away, nearly forcing a carload of teenagers in a big Chevy Nova off the road as he swung the van sharply through another switchback.

Gardner's reckless maneuver caused the Nova to swerve onto the rocky shoulder of the road. The Nova's driver, a young Chicano with a 49ers cap worn backward, reacted quickly, steering his vehicle sharply away from the skid and back into the center of the highway, blocking Harrigan's path. Unwilling to place the Nova in further peril, Harrigan hit his brakes hard, his pulse pounding and his body bracing for impact. The air was filled with the sound of screeching tires and the acrid scent of burning rubber as the Audi decelerated rapidly, narrowly avoiding a rear-end collision that could have sent either vehicle tumbling off the side of the mountain. Both Harrigan and the teenagers escaped without injury, but Gardner's van had disappeared.

Harrigan drove on for a few agonizing seconds, and even succeeded in passing the Nova, but losing sight of Gardner brought the old demons flashing back, more menacing than ever. The voices of Stephanie and the kids began again to explode inside him. Once more, he saw their anguished eyes and felt their bodies collide and fracture as he lost control of his Honda. He felt the terrible responsibility of causing their deaths. Worse still, he felt the responsibility of causing the harm that had come to Josie. *His* Josie. Although she had willingly joined in his plan to tape Gardner, the idea was his and his alone, just as the idea of driving his family to these same mountains seven years ago had been.

Thinking the chase was over, Harrigan brought the Audi to a stop at a narrow turnoff overlooking a steep, tree-lined ravine. It wasn't far from here, perhaps a half mile up the grade, that the accident occurred. His hands shaking, his face drenched in sweat, he fought his way back into the present. He took a deep breath and tried to collect his thoughts. The past, like his family, was dead. Saving Josie was all that mattered.

There was a fork in the highway ahead that would give Gardner the choice of either proceeding to the observatory on Mount Wilson or driving deeper into the San Gabriels to Big Pines and Palmdale. Harrigan knew that if he made the wrong choice and went in the opposite direction from the van, he might never find Josie alive. As he considered the options, his thoughts were broken by the concussive sounds of a helicopter. He opened his door and craned his head skyward, spotting a sheriff's rescue chopper. Someone from the swap meet must have phoned for help. His spirits lifting, he shifted the Audi into drive and swung onto the highway, intending to follow the flight of the helicopter as it climbed above him.

And then it happened. In a flash. In a second of insanity, as terrifying and unreal as the original accident. The sight of the van bearing down on him, veering sharply into his lane from the switchback above the turnoff, coming at him full bore, left Harrigan with no time to think. Acting on pure adrenaline, he crushed the accelerator to the floor, sending the Audi spinning against the rocks on the opposite side of the highway. The van continued toward him, missing the swerving Audi by a mere six inches.

Harrigan could hear, but did not see, the van skidding into the turnoff. He listened, with his head tucked in his hands and his sense of the future slipping away, as the van careened over the flimsy guardrail and belly-flopped onto the ravine, exploding as it plunged to the bottom in an orange and black ball of smoke and flame.

THIRTY-ONE

"Run that by me one more time, if you will, Mr. Harrigan," Judge Taneda said from his lofty courtroom perch. His Honor's tone was exasperated, and the blue vein over his temple had never been bigger.

Harrigan took a step away from the lectern and cast a backward glance at Josie in the spectator section. Though healing nicely, the bruise on her forehead from the handle of Gardner's gun was still visible. The scrapes on her hands and forearms were also healing. Harrigan thought for a moment of how close she had come to dying on Angeles Crest. She had regained consciousness on the floor of Gardner's van just as the sheriff's helicopter began to circle above them. Hearing the chopper, Gardner knew his getaway had failed. Josie managed to jump to freedom as Gardner made his U-turn for a final kamikaze-like run at Harrigan's Audi. Harrigan had told her that she needn't attend the hearing, but she insisted on coming. As their eyes met in court, she nodded her head slowly and gave him an encouraging half smile.

Harrigan returned the smile, then turned his attention back to the motion to reopen the habeas corpus hearing he had filed only ten days after receiving Taneda's decision denying Ashbourne's writ petition. The motion to reopen, technically entitled a "motion for a new trial," had been prepared in a five-alarm hurry to meet the statutory deadlines set by the Federal Rules of Civil Procedure. It was, admittedly, not the best-written work that Harrigan had crafted in his career. There was no doubt, however, that it was hands-down the most compelling. It had to be.

Taneda had issued what was for him a scholarly and balanced decision. To Harrigan's great surprise, the judge ruled that J. Arnold Barnes had indeed rendered substandard service to the petitioner. Barnes' failure to look for Debray, his failure to send an investigator to interview Peterson, and above all, his drinking could not be written off as tactical judgments made in the heat of trying a capital case. What was lacking in the petitioner's case, however, was prejudice. "Even if Barnes had performed in the manner expected of an experienced trial attorney," Taneda wrote, "the outcome of both the guilt and penalty phases of the petitioner's state court trial would undoubtedly have been the same. The evidence presented at the hearing on habeas corpus is insufficient to alter this conclusion."

Harrigan cleared his throat, preparing for a long morning. Since there would be no testimony, Ashbourne remained in his cell at San Quentin, awaiting Taneda's ruling on the motion. Harrigan knew that the motion's outcome depended entirely on him.

"The exhibits attached to our motion constitute newly discovered evidence requiring that Your Honor's decision be withdrawn," he began confidently.

"Those exhibits include a new and lengthy declaration from Henry Dershaw, a.k.a. Henri Debray, who is now in custody awaiting his own trial for the murders of Gilbert Denton and his son; a transcript of a tape-recorded conversation between Debray and Robert Gardner; and inventories from the California Department of Justice concerning searches of the homes of both Gardner and Benjamin Ames.

"Both Debray's declaration and the tape recording confirm that Harold Ashbourne had no role in either the preparation or the execution of the 1982 firebombing."

Listening intently, Taneda had the look of a man whose sense of reality had been deconstructed down to the toenails. "And the crime actually was carried out by—"

"Charles West, Gardner, and Debray." Harrigan spared the judge the effort of completing his query. "After leaving Ashbourne at People's Park, Debray joined West and Gardner, and the three of them drove to Professor Denton's home in the Berkeley Hills. Once there, West and Gardner hurled two incendiary devices through the windows of the home while Debray remained behind the steering wheel of their getaway vehicle. The investigating agencies assigned to the case at the time of the petitioner's state court trial confirmed that those devices were makeshift Molotov cocktails packed with oil and gasoline in wine bottles. According to Debray, the bottles were left over from a prior social function attended by the petitioner, during which he innocently left his fingerprints on one of the bottles."

"And the motive behind the bombing?" Taneda asked weakly.

"Mr. Debray," Harrigan answered, savoring every stress wrinkle on Taneda's tortured brow, "is prepared to testify as to that as well. Both Debray and West had longstanding grievances against the professor relating to their employment in the political science department. Both West and Debray were also, as the court knows, founders of the radical environmentalist group Saviors of the Earth and sworn opponents of the proposed Peripheral Canal project."

Harrigan launched into a brief disquisition on the history of the canal project and was even prepared to augment the dog-and-pony show with a large color relief map of the Sacramento Delta, but Taneda waved off both the display and the lecture with a broad sweep of his robed right arm. "The idea of bombing Denton's home," Harrigan continued, putting the map away, "arose only about a week before the crime was actually committed, when the professor discovered that West and Debray had drawn up plans to bomb the Edmonston Pumping Station in Kern County if the canal project was ratified by the voters in the June 1982 referendum. Debray maintains that they were never really serious about the plot, but Denton refused to listen. The professor threatened to turn them over to the police."

"And Mr. Debray has come forward now to clear his conscience?" Taneda asked sarcastically.

"Not entirely," Harrigan replied solemnly. "He's come forward because he has AIDS and realizes he can't survive in the underground much longer. His plan was to prevail on West to come forward with him and somehow pin the majority of blame for the bombing on Gardner. As we've seen, I'm afraid, the idea was poorly conceived and doomed from the start."

"Mr. Gardner, I take it, supplied the technical know-how for the firebombing," Taneda said.

"Yes, Your Honor, utilizing the training he received during his military service. But his motive for participating in the firebombing had nothing to do with his opposition to the Peripheral Canal. Robert Gardner was the illegitimate son of Benjamin Ames."

Harrigan stopped to let the full weight of this disclosure of Gardner's lineage sink in before proceeding. "Gardner joined the plot against Denton in order to protect his father's name, to discredit the environmental movement, and turn the referendum in favor of those who, like Ames, had a financial stake in seeing the canal approved and built."

"Has that been confirmed, Mr. Pickering?" Taneda asked testily, hoping against hope that the State might save him from the ignominy of having to overturn his decision.

Pickering stood, addressing the court in a prosecutorial deadpan. "The DOJ, in conjunction with participating local law enforcement, has conducted searches of the homes of Robert Gardner in Pomona and the Ames Ranch near Bakersfield. Among other items"—he paused to leaf through a thick legal file—"we found a series of letters between Gardner and Ames, covering the period from roughly the late 1970s to one written by Gardner to Ames less than two months ago. Taken as a whole, they confirm that Mr. Gardner was the product of a union between

Ames and a local teenager, with whom Ames had a brief affair one summer when Professor Denton worked as a hired hand on the family ranch. They also leave no doubt as to the roles played by West, Debray, and Gardner in the firebombing."

"And am I to understand that the State has voluntarily shared these letters with the petitioner?" Taneda's voice grew more exasperated. Although a long line of United States Supreme Court decisions dating back to the landmark 1963 case of *Brady* v. *Maryland* required the State to turn over any exculpatory evidence, even if discovered in the post-conviction phases of a case, Taneda had grown accustomed to prosecutors who hid the ball, played games with discovery, and generally made the defense squirm and beg for *Brady* material. He could never admit it, but it seemed to cause him physical pain to see that Pickering had honored the letter of the State's obligations without putting up so much as a whimper of protest.

"That's correct, Your Honor," Pickering said smartly. "It's the law."

"Copies of selected portions of those letters are attached to my motion," Harrigan chimed in with a timely reminder that served only to deepen the hue of the judge's telltale blood vessel.

With Taneda all ears and vein, Harrigan carefully outlined the remainder of the new evidence. "Embittered by the fact that Ames took no interest in him, Gardner at first sought to get back at his father by joining Saviors, a group that stood for everything Ben Ames hated. Eventually, however, he sought a reconciliation and the financial support that came with it. And while Ames initially balked, he jumped at the chance to let Gardner be his eyes and ears inside the environmental movement at Berkeley after he learned of Denton's book project."

Harrigan took a minute to outline the scope of the professor's last book for Taneda's benefit, explaining that Denton had planned to feature the Ames family in his study of landholding patterns in the Central Valley. Returning to the subject of the professor's demise, he continued, "Even Ames' wife didn't know that he had fathered an illegitimate child, and he lived in great fear that Denton, in whom he had confided the fact of his dalliance during that distant summer, would eventually discover Gardner's identity and go public with his knowledge.

"It's not clear whether Denton discovered Gardner's identity on his own or whether Gardner, thinking that the discovery already had been made, unwittingly disclosed his paternity himself. In one of his letters to Ames, from January 1982, Gardner reports on a meeting with the professor. Ostensibly set up as a routine office visit between an undergraduate and the department head, Gardner disclosed his paternity and begged the professor not to reveal his identity to his friends in the Saviors group."

Harrigan ran his right forefinger through the text of Gardner's letter until he found the desired passage, which he quoted verbatim: " 'I told Professor Denton that I had made my own way in life without any help from my father and that any disclosure of the accident of my connection to the Ames family would cause me great embarrassment and shame. I even worked up a few tears to make the performance convincing.' "

"And the professor's response?" Taneda asked.

"According to the letter, Denton said he had no plans to disclose Bob's paternity. We know, however, that a month or two later, the professor chided Debray for not realizing that his group had been infiltrated by an unnamed individual with close ties to the pro-canal forces. It's also apparent from the tone of Gardner's later letters that neither he nor Ames trusted the professor to keep quiet."

"Are you saying that Benjamin Ames ordered his son to kill Professor Denton?"

"No, Your Honor," Harrigan answered with a shake of the head. "He only wanted Gardner to keep him informed about Denton's progress, using his connections with Professor West, who was assigned to help Denton with his research. And neither West nor Debray knew that Gardner was spying for Ames until the drive back into Berkeley after the bombing, when Gardner told them who he was. According to Debray, Gardner took perverse delight in the stunned reaction of his cohorts, elated that he had outsmarted the college boys and confident that they would do nothing to reveal his secret. Just for good measure, he threatened to kill them both if they did."

A brief silence ensued, broken by Pickering. "After Mr. Ames learned of the murders and his son's role in them, he responded not by informing the authorities but by sending Gardner monthly money orders, which enabled the son to set up a car-repair business in Pomona."

Taneda began to flip through the pages of Harrigan's motion, arching his eyebrows as he read. "I see that the murder weapon from the West shooting has been recovered, along with two round-trip plane tickets from Ontario Ariport to San Francisco."

"The murder weapon was discovered at the crash scene on Angeles Crest Highway, where Gardner died last month," Harrigan interrupted. "The plane tickets were found at Gardner's home, along with a rental car receipt for a white Ford Tempo." Harrigan turned again to seek out Josie, and gave her a knowing nod. "The second set of tickets showed that Gardner flew to the Bay Area on the day of West's murder."

"Does Ben Ames know that Gardner killed Charles West?" Taneda asked.

"We have no confirmation of that," Pickering answered dryly. "On the advice of his lawyer, Mr. Ames has declined to answer any questions. However, in light of his knowledge of the Denton murders and his subsequent payments to Mr. Gardner, he has been charged as an accessory after the fact to those killings."

Taneda rubbed a hand across his face and cast a weary gaze at Harrigan, who took the silent gesture as a cue for him to sum up his legal position as the moving party.

"We commenced this hearing," Harrigan began, "with the claim that Harold Ashbourne was denied his constitutional right to effective assistance of counsel at his state court trial. We've cited numerous deficiencies in the performance of J. Arnold Barnes—most significantly, his failure to conduct a competent investigation into Ashbourne's alibi defense and his decision to keep Mr. Ashbourne off the witness stand. Your Honor has agreed that Barnes' trial work was indeed substandard, but you have found no prejudice resulting from his mistakes. The evidence outlined to you today shows that prejudice. It establishes the essential truth of Harold Ashbourne's alibi which his state court jury never heard."

Having laid out the facts, Harrigan paused before completing his prayer for relief. Knowing that Taneda would receive whatever he said like a dagger in the heart, he chose his words carefully, purging his speech of the usual hyperbole lawyers holding the upper hand employ to dunk their adversaries' noses in the toilet. "I ask, therefore, that you either reopen the evidentiary hearing so that live testimony may be received to confirm our position or, in the alternative, that you issue the writ, ordering that Mr. Ashbourne be given a new trial in state court or that he be released forthwith from custody if the People elect not to retry him."

Taneda pivoted in his swivel chair as he shifted his eyes from Harrigan to the deputy AG. "Mr. Pickering?" he inquired in a tired voice.

"We submit the matter," Pickering responded, a corner of his jaunty mustache upturned, reflecting the irony of his position. "I would only add, Your Honor, that the state of California has no interest in executing the innocent." Pickering had at least six other death-penalty cases to look after, and it was no sweat off his buns if he ran up a white flag on this one.

While technically falling short of an official declaration of surrender, the AG, in voicing no opposition to Harrigan's motion, left Taneda with little choice. Here he was, the most junior judge on the federal bench. He had just issued a decision in his first death-penalty case, dispatching the matter with such efficiency and élan that many of the most stuffed-shirt senior judges had dropped into his chambers to convey their personal kudos. Now he was faced with the humiliating prospect of overturning his own ruling. He'd be the object of jokes and whispers in the judges' washroom for months to come.

Like a trapeze artist suddenly stricken with an acute case of acrophobia, Taneda took a deep nervous breath and gazed wide-eyed at the copy of his prior decision lodged in the case file in front of him. Date-stamped and embossed with the official court seal, the decision seemed to stare back at him, mocking his black robes and the lofty professional position he had attained, daring him to speak. "The earlier decision of this court denying the petition for writ of habeas corpus is hereby withdrawn and nullified," he intoned finally, nearly swallowing his words. "The petition for the writ is hereby granted. Copies of my order shall be served on counsel and all interested parties forthwith."

It would take another two months of bitter legal wrangling for Harold Ashbourne to secure his release from San Quentin. Following the return of the case to state court, the Alameda County District Attorney's Office, the original prosecuting agency, was in no mood to let Ashbourne waltz out of custody without paying some kind of penological price. Although they lacked a shred of credible evidence, the DA's office huffed and puffed about charging Ashbourne as a conspirator in the planning of the Denton murders. The office also did its level worst to pressure the U.S. attorney to bring federal perjury charges against Ashbourne for allegedly lying in his prehearing declaration about being with Debray until eleven o'clock on the night of the bombing.

It was a chintzy and vindictive position for the DA to take, but after spending a quarter of his life on death row, Ashbourne refused to blink. Finally, with the feds refusing to bite on the perjury angle and its conspiracy case crumbling before it could get off the ground, the DA relented, and one damp overcast morning Ashbourne walked out of court a free man with Harrigan at his side. Like a real American, he told the reporters who gathered around him on the courthouse steps that he was contemplating a civil suit for false imprisonment against both the county and the state. If he managed to draw the right kind of jury, he added in a rare display of braggadocio, he might eventually emerge from the lawsuit lottery as a self-made millionaire.

Harrigan, too, received a certain measure of freedom about a week after Ashbourne's release when the local cops uncovered a computer disk under a loose floorboard in the old office of Bob Gardner's home. The disk was seized, analyzed, and eventually forwarded to Bill Pickering, who had a copy sent to Harrigan as a personal courtesy.

The disk turned out to contain the most complete chronology yet discovered of the bizarre exploits of Robert Gardner. Although not all of the entries could be confirmed, there was one that nearly brought Harrigan to his knees: Under cover of darkness in May 1988, after reading Harrigan's comments in the *L.A.*

Times about being on the verge of a breakthrough that would prove Harold Ashbourne's alibi, Gardner drove to the Harrigan home three nights running. On the first two he simply watched, waited, and pondered the odds that the breakthrough might be genuine and that his days of anonymity might be numbered. Gardner had no way of knowing that all Harrigan had received was a bogus letter from Kathleen Simpson and that Debray was still far afield and on the lam. On the third night of his surveillance, Gardner turned his increasingly paranoid thoughts into action.

Finding Harrigan's Honda parked in the driveway, Gardner calmly inserted an ordinary hypodermic filled with acetone into the rubber brake hoses behind the passenger side front and rear wheels. In a matter of days, he knew, the acetone would degrade the hoses to the point of failure. In the aftermath of an accident, no one would be able to tell if the mishap was caused by wear and tear, operator error, or a manufacturer's defect. Best of all, with any luck Ashbourne's lawyer would either be dead or sufficiently disabled to derail any serious effort he might make at overturning Ashbourne's conviction and exposing Gardner's role in the murders. The more recent burglaries of Harrigan's home and Josie's car, also chronicled on the disk, sprang from the same deadly combination of extreme paranoia and the desire for self-preservation.

After his initial rage abated, Harrigan finally found peace. There was nothing he could do to reverse the past. Gardner would always remain the demon who had taken his wife and kids, but he at last could absolve himself of the responsibility he had always carried for their deaths. Now perhaps he could finally lay all of their ghosts to rest.

And then there was Josie. In another three months, if all went as planned, he would put his Altadena home on the market, turn over his Los Angeles practice (Dennis included) to Mark Clemons, and hang out a new shingle in the Mission District near her office. In the meantime they would spend a good two weeks snorkeling and knocking back margaritas at Harrigan's old beachside hangout south of Puerto Vallarta. He had visions of the two of them rolling in the surf, making love in the sand, like Burt Lancaster and Deborah Kerr. Harrigan knew there would be ghosts there, too, but they would be gentle ones and they'd be happy to see him resuming his life.

As they boarded the plane for P.V. at LAX, everyone from the old Saviors group, except Fred Wallace, was accounted for, from Debray to Kathleen Simpson, who had succumbed to AIDS. Facing a federal indictment for tax fraud, Wallace's problems with the IRS had blossomed from the "office audit" he had faced at the time of his impromptu conference with Harrigan at the Hotel Mayfair into a criminal matter that threatened to earn him a prison term serving hard time as a love slave to some serial killer. Rather than brave such an unsavory prospect, he was still at large, no doubt bankrolled by the small fortune he had made from years of ambulance chasing and underreporting his profits. Rumor had it that Debray had offered to donate his duffel bag full of wigs to secure Wallace's tenure in the underground.

"It's a Saviors tradition, I suppose, to have at least

one fugitive among the alums," Harrigan quipped as he and Josie took their seats on the AeroMexico jet.

"The way I see it," she corrected him, "there's just one less asshole practicing law in this state." She gave him a soft kiss on the cheek, buckled her seat belt, and made sure he did the same.